THE LIGHT OF EVENFALL

J.E. ELLIOTT

By J.E. Elliott

World Guide

The Divine

Yath Ha — the gods, the Creators, Olru and E'ral; the two beings who wrote the world into existence; two separate entities often referred to as one individual

Kaetha — the helpers of Yath Ha; lesser deities that helped infuse the New Life with the means to survive

Divine Attendants — group of kaetha who led the war against Anöwe

Lhaeream the Knowing — Divine Attendant; the wisest kaeth and direct counsellor to Yath Ha; taught the New Life judgement, loyalty, and how to dream, and helped create the language Nraessa taught them

Mynil the Adventuring — Divine Attendant; most gentle kaeth who spent all her time exploring Fawllhä and the creatures Yath Ha created; sly nature put her in charge of the kaetha's strategies against Anöwe; taught the New Life adventure and curiosity, as well as sympathy and pity

Vulyn the Balanced — Divine Attendant; kaeth renowned for his unbiased decisions, counsel, and thought; taught the New Life thoughtfulness, intelligence, serenity, and lastly, taught them poetry and song; took responsibility for dead souls after New Life was turned mortal, ruling over Ashnagz

Nraessa the Bright — Divine Attendant; kaeth most loved by the New Life; taught the New Life compassion, courage, and faithfulness, as well as helped create and taught them the language they would speak

Anöwe the Fallen — once thought to be the most talented kaeth in Lyhrëon, allowing his arrogance to blossom; taught the New Life might, greed, and disobedience, using Vulyn's gift to his own advantage

Places

Alieus — an ancient empire long past; the picture of wealth and prosperity stretching across the western continent until a mystery caused it to fall

Aresan — small farming village in western Nokomic

Armiria — world inhabited by mostly humans and shifters; divided into two land masses, the east and west continent

Ashnagz — where mortals gather after death, before traveling to their final resting place; organized by the kaeth Vulyn

Eroz — world inhabited by mostly demons, fae, and dragons; divided into two land masses, Milganos in the north, and Hraesah in the south

Fawllhä — the original world Yath Ha created at the beginning of time before it was severed

Hraesah — land of the demons in Eroz

Lennael Mountains — a vast mountain range that divides Nokomic's western border from the Unclaimed Lands; its treacherous peaks and harsh weather make for sturdy protection

Lyhrëon — realm of the Divine

Milganos — land of the Fae in Eroz

Nokomic — a once great kingdom that fell into turmoil and disrepair after a mysterious army terrorized its peace seventy years before Rin and Zarus meet

Pits of Ashnagz — the depths of Ashnagz where individuals who commit heinous acts are sent until Yath Ha decides their fate; living or dead, souls sent to the Pits lie and wait for their sentence

Unclaimed Lands — while establishing borders five-hundred and forty-one years before Rin and Zarus meet, no kingdom of the western continent claimed these regions to rule; no major cities reside here, and very few villages were built since they were not protected by any governing body; these regions were either too inaccessible or two uninhabitable

Xandra — the new capital of Nokomic

Zelenia — the original capital of Nokomic which fell to Eretimis's might, causing the kingdom to fall into disrepair

Things

Breaking of Fawllhä — when the original world Yath Ha created was mysteriously severed into pieces, leading to the creation of the different races

Crimson War — a five hundred-year long war sparked among the mortal races, severing all trust and relations with one another and causing the travel between worlds to be outlawed; long forgotten by humans, but still acts as a warning to the other races

Ghren/ghran — male/female human-esque form of shifters

Narikaah — part demon, part dragon

New Life — the beings Yath Ha originally created at the beginning of time; once timeless, these beings were punished with mortality after falling under Anöwe's influence during the War of the Divine

The New Light — the group of Nokomai who waged war against the Resurrection in hopes to bring peace back to Nokomic

The Resurrection — the lawless organization that came to power after the fall of Zelenia; ruled through groups of criminal guilds, making Nokomic a dangerous place for half a century

Vulyn's Guiding Hand — a saying referring to the onset of death and meeting the ruler of the afterlife

War of the Divine — a war between Anöwe and the Divine soon after Yath Ha created existence; led to the New Life becoming mortals after Anöwe was defeated and the Divine no longer walking in the mortal realm

Worlds Alliance — a once great alliance held between each mortal race when bonds between the races were strong; fell to ruin during the Crimson War

For Ethan, I'd rescue you from any frozen fortress

Western Armiria

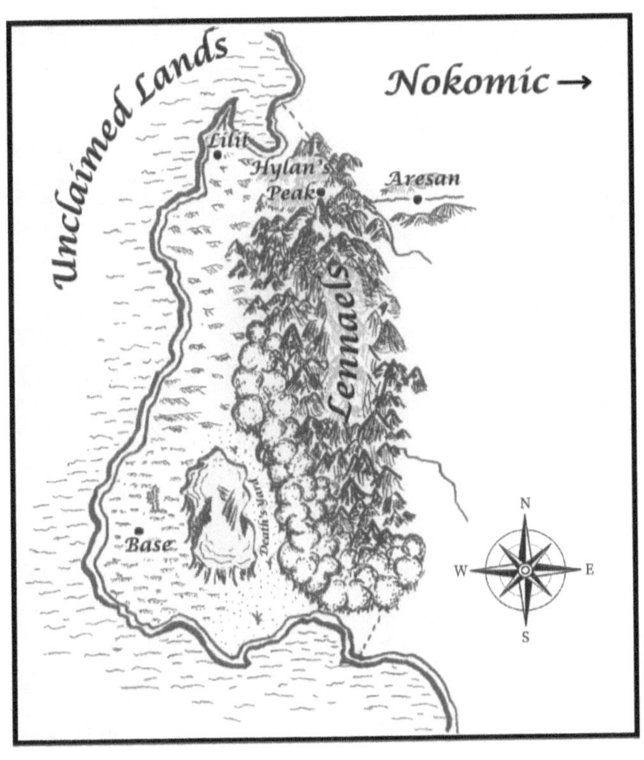

Unclaimed Lands
Nokomic →
Lilit
Hylan's Peak
Aresan
Lennaels
Death's Warren
Base
N
W
E
S

Part One

Visions

J.E. Elliott

Chapter One

R in Nowell braced her hands in the warm grass. Her head throbbed. Her knee ached beneath the crimson welling from her skin. A gray cast of clouds filtered out the sunlight, yet the arid air offered no relief. Had it been a day in the fields, she would have dropped everything to jump into the lake before her. Today, the water mocked her.

Luna knelt beside her on the lakeshore. "These things take time, Erin," she soothed. Not even the prince catching his breath behind them could hear her mother's hushed words.

Rin gritted her teeth. She kept her stare on the soft ripples in the water and refused to look at her mother's lilac eyes.

"I did it just as you said."

Luna nodded, but her mother's empathy did little as she hovered her slender hand above Rin's knee. "Magic isn't mastered in one night. Take the rest of the day off. We can start again tomorrow."

Rin finally looked at her mother. "No," she bit down on her frustrations, "I want to try again. If I could do it in the desert, I can do it now."

"Very well," her mother sighed. Rin's wounded knee suddenly prickled. She watched the energy thrum off her mother's hand like heat rising off metal. A moment later, the gash on Rin's knee was no longer present. A white scar replaced it. "Start from the beginning again and find the light from the desert."

***

The morning light cascaded into the Pit, warming the bed where Rin pretended to sleep. The others were up and about already, their voices trailing in through the cracks of the home. Sleeping in the bedroom meant she could slumber longer than the dawn-loving heretics downstairs. But the extra stretch of shut-eye was nothing to brag about. Her eyes slid open, loosing a groan as the dimness of the Pit greeted her. That's what she started calling the clearing deep within the Highlands; with only one opening for light at the very top, it was little more than a pit hidden within the rock. It certainly wasn't a comparison to the hellish Pits of Ashnagz, not in the slightest. The thought hadn't even crossed Rin's mind...

Go back to sleep and never wake up again.

Running laps around the perimeter of the Pit each morning wasn't the best motivator to get out of bed. Especially when it was her turn in the actual bed. No, Luna had them both hating mornings. She knew that for certain when she saw Genesis still huddled beneath his blanket in the chair across the room.

"Why did we ever agree to this training?" she grunted.

"I've heard plenty of stories about masochists," Genesis's raw voice croaked, "Never thought I'd end up being one."

"Masochism entails that you get pleasure from this."

"Well, it is nice to run freely after so many years." The blanket shifted, exposing his growing scowl at the light's touch. "Even if I end up vomiting afterwards."

Rin swung her legs off the edge of the feathered mattress. "That certainly humbles my whiny arse, but why does it have to be first thing when we wake up? Couldn't it be at a decent time of the day?" She stretched, flexing the muscles refusing to wake with her.

"You wouldn't have lasted a day in the barracks." Genesis fixed himself in a similar position.

She cast him a wry grin. "I think I'd have been a fine addition to whatever barracks were around in your day, Grandpa. They obviously had low standards, else they wouldn't have allowed you inside."

"Oh, however will I recover from this whelp's vicious attack?" Genesis threw his hands over his heart in a feign of offense. He nimbly dodged the pillow Rin threw.

To think she had been doing this for an entire month. A whole month since she walked into her mother's house, and she had yet to throw herself to the bottom of the lake.

Chapter Two

Cursing another restless night, Rin wobbled down the stairs of the cottage, combing her messy hair with her fingers. The chilled floor bit at her bare feet. Downstairs, the hearth sizzled, which only meant Feyne had already delivered today's breakfast. It was always a surprise what rodent he brought to the dining table that day, although lately it tended toward rabbit.

"I'm telling you, if you cook it incorrectly, your insides will be mangled just like mine."

"It's an egg—it takes no effort to prepare. How much of a moron do you take me for?"

"Is that a trick question?"

Rin made it to the bottom of the steps without retreating to the bed like she desired. Feyne hovered over the fireplace, spatula in hand, and Tatsuo lounged on the couch as Luna had instructed him to do every few hours. The dragon had been up and moving for weeks after he had passed out and nearly bled out that first night. Thanks to her mother, his wound was cleaner than the pavement before the temples of Xandra. But Luna was unyielding. Tatsuo still had a lot of recovering to do, and her hard work wouldn't be '*muddled up by sheer recklessness*'. *Narikaah* or not, walking after three days or not.

The duo couldn't have been awake for long.

Rin yawned. "Where's Ma?"

"Morning, Ms Magician," Tatsuo chimed, glancing over the arm of the sofa.

Feyne pointed his spatula toward the door without looking up from his eggs. "Just missed her. She's by the lake."

Rin nodded, moving closer to Feyne and looking over his shoulder. "Smells delicious. What is it?"

"Same as it always is," Tatsuo huffed, running through the fray of his fiery braid with his finger. "Eggs with a lovely side of hare. Where have you been for the last month?"

The shifter glared at the lounging dragon, a spark of taunt in his stare. "That's a lot of talk coming from someone who hasn't caught breakfast once."

"I told you already," Tatsuo objected, "Luna might very well break my legs if I tried."

"Sounds like a bunch of excuses to me."

"*My abdomen* just *healed*."

"Welcome to the real world, kiddo."

"I'm older than you!"

And thus Rin exited the house as their bickering stuffed the room so tightly that the air itself choked. She was glad they were talking again, even if they bickered like dogs and dragons. Since she spent most of her days training and nights studying, she didn't have a ton of time with Feyne or Tatsuo. When they eventually broke through their frigid distrust, it was a relief. Feyne had only recently started walking on two legs as a *ghren*. Losing Base weighed heavily on his shoulders, his eyes still haunted, but talking was something.

The door closed behind, and the silence of the Pit overtook the world. A breeze danced through her hair, blowing from the tunnel they had arrived through all those weeks ago. Across the lake, she found her mother. Honey colored hair and a lilac stare straight out of her memory. Rin had known for years that it was her father who bequeathed her the ginger locks and green eyes, but it seemed Rin received her father's shorter stature as well. Her mother wasn't towering, though the woman stood inches above her. Where her mother was thin and slender, Rin wore curves. In fact, she would never have been able to tell they were related if not for their round noses.

Rin wrapped her arms around herself and cursed for having worn only her undershirt outside. Brisk in the mornings, baking in the afternoons. The stone walls of the Pit kept out the blistering sun for most of the day, paradise compared to the roof of the plateau, but the heat slipped through each afternoon when the sun peeked over the window of rock hundreds of feet above.

"A bit chilly to go bare, isn't it?" Luna's voice trailed in the wind as Rin approached from behind.

"Not my best idea," Rin shrugged, "but it's not nearly as bad as Hilyan's Peak. I don't think I'll ever find anywhere as frigid as that place." She smiled, but Luna never enjoyed her humor. Rin's jokes only deepened her mother's dread.

"What is it?" Rin sighed, sliding her gaze to the woman's reflection in the pool below.

Luna's stare met her daughter's reflection. It had relaxed considerably over the last month as tensions eased, but today there sat a specific discomfort. Something akin to what a mother who ran off from her family twelve years ago would make if she wanted to say something she didn't think she had the place to say.

Rin took a deep breath. One of many in the past weeks. Her lips thinned into a straight line. "Just say it."

"I," her mother began, too quietly before finding her voice, "I've been thinking. The Lennaels don't have the most innocent history."

"Nor does Nokomic."

Her mother flashed the retort an unamused glance. "Have you ever heard of the story of the Hilyan Outpost?" Rin shook her head. "It was built atop the highest reaches of the Lennaels; meant to watch the Unclaimed Lands for suspicious behavior."

"So it's exactly like the rest of Nokomic's outposts." Rin shifted her weight on her bare feet. The grass nipped at her skin.

Luna nodded. "This was a unique location, though. The harsh environment called for the outpost to be constructed differently than the rest scattered across the range. It was barely livable up there, as I'm sure you remember."

It seemed the wind blew a little colder at the thought of the mountains. "Hard to forget. How did they work around the weather?"

"Instead of towns like the rest of the posts, the Hilyan Outpost was built as one grand estate. A fortress of sorts, stocked with food supplies, stalls for livestock, greenhouses, and room for the few families who went. All safely sheltered from the cold outside. The residents sustained themselves since there were no quick means up and down the mountain. It worked for the better part of three hundred years after the wars when the Unclaimed Lands were monitored. But," her voice bit bitterly, "that post stopped reporting to authorities two hundred years ago."

A feathery hum built in Rin's head, barely even there, but relentless against the silence that accompanied it.

Her mother continued, well aware of that tension. "The time frame lines up perfectly."

Rin snapped. "Do you truly think so little of the person that saved my life?" Zarus saved her. *Saved* her. Did that mean nothing to her mother?

"Demon."

Rin involuntarily wrinkled her nose. "What?"

"A demon saved you." She cast Rin a shaded glance. "Trust me, there is nothing compassionate about that male."

The bitter words left Rin scowling. "And what about Tatsuo? He's part demon, but I never see you spitting out his name."

"Tatsuo hasn't worked for Eretimis," her mother countered. Her voice was cool, like the breeze before a storm ever appeared.

"No," Rin bit back, "all he tried to do was murder me in a fit of wrongful revenge."

"Erin." Her mother sighed, but she grabbed her temper before it escaped. "Zarus Lowwenth is an infamous legend, and not a story that you ever want to be a part of. He carried out Eretimis's will for hundreds of years on magic users all over Armiria. So why, after two hundred years of hiding in the Hilyan Outpost, did he decide to help you? You don't understand how unbelievably out of character that was."

Rin scoffed. "And you do?" Gods, that hum rang and rang and rang. "I told you whatever history Zarus had with Eretimis, it ended—badly—and there is no going back from that. Whether you help me or not, I am rescuing Zarus Lowwenth from that fortress. End of discussion."

Rin stomped toward the house without giving Luna another chance to reply. She grimaced after yelling so loudly, but that's how it had been ever since she had arrived at her mother's home a month ago. Zarus had a less than trustworthy track record, which had been further explained by her long-lost mother, but why did it matter? He was her friend, and she wasn't turning a blind eye to that. What about Genesis? They still knew next to nothing about him, yet her mother agreed to train him to use his magic, just like her.

Smoke blew from Rin's ears by the time she slammed the cottage door behind her. She passed Feyne, Tatsuo, and Genesis without a word as she went to fetch her clothes.

By morning, Rin was itching to run.

Chapter Three

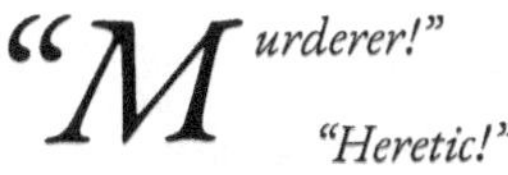

"*M*urderer!"

"*Heretic!*"

"*Tie the heathen down!*"

Smoke smothered Zarus's throat, stung his lungs. It blotted out the pale luminescence of the moon and cast a grey shadow onto the dirt below.

"*Bind his arms!*"

"*Gag his tongue!*"

"*Find us a whip!*"

The stone road cut into his knees. Mud covered the blood on his skin. He couldn't get his feet beneath him; every attempt sent another blow to his body. They made a show of his struggle. Doors crept open. Curious eyes peered into the mob to see what stirred the quiet village so violently in the dead of night.

Heat. That's all there was. Heat, rich and dense; heat, invasive and assaulting. Wrapping around his head, scorching his mind. The season favored neither day nor night, simmering the world around in a waxing sweat. Not an ounce of comfort, not a gust of coolness. That ice... where had it gone?

The center of town loomed near. They threw him into the middle of the square. The uneven stone cut his flesh after his head smacked down. More heat. More shouts.

"Break his legs!"

"Crush his bones!"

"Burn the monster to ash!"

Vicious and hateful. They screamed, begged, pleaded for his beating. For his pain, his torture. All for what?

Zarus's vision blurred as white hot pain cleaved into his head. His swollen eyes eventually opened. The crowd circled him. Their torches lit, weapons raised. Faces he knew. Faces that knew him for his sixteen years.

A shadow slipped by. Everything muted against the siren blaring in his mind. Was someone speaking? A voice. He knew that voice. That corrosive voice. What were they saying? He couldn't make out anything over the hum in his head. What lies were being told to his village?

"This monster deserves no pity, no love. He deceived us all, made us trust him so he could rip us apart! A monster, a heretic! Blood to be shed and rid of!"

A hand suddenly yanked him upward by his hair. He yelped, but no one seemed to hear. His voice wouldn't make it through the lies. Whoever held him let go. The pavement welcomed him again.

No one stepped forward, no one objected to the claims. Their masks removed, the truth blinding his eyes. Zarus parted his lips, but nothing crept past the blood welling in his mouth. He searched. Faces he had trusted, walked with day after day all his life, smiled at and laughed with. And one more. A new one. Behind everyone, tucked back in shadow, those dark, depthless eyes lingered. Watching him.

Zarus shifted his focus back to the one above him addressing the mob, and he cowered at the sight. Two men came forth from the crowd and held his arms. His shirt was torn from his back. The speaker rounded behind him, whipping the air into pieces.

The first whip was a warning. His sweat turned to ice. His mind numbed.

He opened his mouth, swollen lips throbbing and bleeding. His mind was weak and tired, but he had to defend himself when he stumbled alone.

"It wasn't me."

No one listened. He braced himself, knowing the worst would come. But it didn't.

The scene faded; a whirlwind twisted free of form. Cold, wet nothing licking up his skin, drowning all within its grasp. Shifting and morphing until a spark shattered the dark. Burning and bright, the obtrusive sun glared into his eyes. The wind threatened his balance. Zarus found his eyes, and they found rocky mountains, a ravine, a battle. raging. The blade at his side wasn't enough against the army that raced toward him. One hand smothered in ice, the other in the black mist he'd only recently delved into. Further they pushed, harder he fought. He conjured all the ice and shadow he could muster until he was surrounded.

No matter how many Zarus cut down, there was always a replacement. He damned the world when another battle caught his eye. Another soul fending off the horde, but pushed to the edge of the cliff. Their white hair caught the updraft of the gorge. They glanced his way. Sorrow, grief? Solemnity. Their lips moved, saying something that the battle distorted. Zarus's thoughts froze. The other's foot slipped beyond the reach of the cliff.

A maelstrom of ice and darkness formed in the wake of Zarus's despair.

The scene blackened as soon as it appeared. Zarus's eyes grew heavy, his mind clouded by exhaustion and fatigue. He lay on the ground. When had he fallen? There was something else. A voice in the distance. No malice within. But whose?

Zarus forced his eyes open to a new scene. He laid beneath the open sky, consciousness warming his senses. When he looked aside, eyes as blue as the crystal glaciers of the north watched him.

"Hey, wake up. They'll find you out here. We need to get somewhere safe."

***

The shadows on the other side of the curtain came and went. They never stayed long, or maybe they did. Left between the veils of consciousness, Zarus never knew how much time had passed before the Wraith Twins returned.

The air was thick enough to choke on, the stone floor frigid enough to scar. They had left him collapsed on the ground, void of consciousness. Each time the Wraiths walked through that curtain and into the prison behind the throne, they brought with them malevolent smirks and savage eyes. Thirsting for pain and suffering, and he their depthless spring.

Bound to his prison by Eretimis's seal and the promise of Rin's torture in the dungeons should he not comply. Zarus failed her. Any escape he made would abandon her in Eretimis's grasp.

The curtain parted. Zarus didn't bat an eye; he breathed, soaking up the remnant of solace before the Wraith Twins emerged. Hungered, they wasted no time before they placed their skeletal hands on his temples.

A chorus of agony thrummed through the war room.

It echoed over and over until it pierced through Zarus's mind and dominated his will. Tension tied down his body. His thoughts melted against the hands of those savage Wraiths. His screams writhed against his throat. He couldn't— there wasn't—

The Wraith Twins bled dry every ounce of thought and will and power in him until there was nothing left.

A jolt reverberated through his head, his heart, his very soul.

Raia and Tesyl dropped their hands from his temples. He crashed to the ground.

Dry, heaved breaths threatened to shatter his throat. The green flames emitting from the center brazier offered no warmth. Time after time, it felt like the Twins were trying to steal his spirit and deliver it on a silver platter to the Dark Tyrant. They probably were. Zarus gritted his teeth. His trembling arms barely lifted him off the stone before he fell again. He met the Twins' stare from his peripherals.

Tesyl circled around him, nudging his shoulder with her boot. He barely even felt it. "It seems he hasn't fallen into the abyss just yet, sister."

Raia bent over, her curtain of dark curls swaying shadows over his face. "We took twice as much as we did last time... yet his eyes are still full of such hate." Curiosity turned to malevolence in the sour twist of her smile. "I guess that means we haven't taken enough."

Where was it? The ice always ready at his reach, the darkness waiting for his command. Ground up, drained out. Nothing. Zarus reached and reached as the Wraith Twins walked closer, their smiles the greed of fire and flame. He found no magic. It abandoned him, just like his thoughts. Yet his head wasn't empty, not completely. Those pesky whispers of Divine inspiration echoed in the vast chasm of his mind, breaching what little privacy he had left while awake. Always so loud in the room behind the throne. Zarus couldn't do a damn thing to shut them out. At least the looming agony would drown out the voices.

Raia and Tesyl grabbed his arms and pulled him face to face with them. Zarus closed his eyes, hoping darkness would quickly claim him.

Chapter Four

"I see you have your father's way with words," the woman teased. Rin couldn't return it. A joke about the man who raised her alone was not the way to start this. However, Luna clearly didn't know how to proceed, either.

"I have a lot of my father in me," Rin mumbled, looking her mother over.

A cautious smile laced her mother's lips, elegant lines curving at the edges. "Aye, clear as day, I see him." The joy in her eyes did not last. "I don't understand, Erin, even if you set out to find me, you would have gone to Lilit. How could you possibly end up here?"

Rin exhaled a deep breath and opened her eyes. Nearly a month later, the sadness in her mother's tone when she saw Rin for the first time in twelve years still stung her heart. She wasn't sure how the reunion with her mother would go, but she never expected the dread in Luna's expression. Even after explaining how she found her way to the cottage hidden in the highlands, her mother's confusion didn't fade. In fact, to her surprise, saying Zarus's name only seemed to drive that fear home. And when Rin mentioned how Eretimis was after her? Her mother broke down in tears. Everything fell into place. The reason her mother fled twelve years ago. The way she healed Tatsuo's wounds without ever laying a hand on him. A white mage... It all made sense.

"I'd offer a coin for your thoughts, but I haven't any on me at the moment," Genesis chimed, breaking Rin's thought as she slowed to a walk. They both needed a break.

"You can owe me the next one you come across," she breathed out, although not nearly as violently as Genesis. The man could barely stand upright as he struggled for air. Three weeks they had been running around the fields of the Pit, and despite his hollow cheeks filling in, the days of sitting in a dungeon for seventy years still burned bright during his runs.

A deathly weight lingered around the field and caverns of the Pit, the same sensation as the first day. The type of air that flows through a graveyard. She wiped the sweat from her brow. The afternoon heat arrived early. "I'm going to rescue him."

Genesis nodded. "I believe you, and believe me when I tell you I'm going to help with that fantastical endeavor. But, um, Rin..." He finally stood straight. "By the names of Olru and E'ral, how do you plan on doing that?"

She huffed a sigh. Her stare lost focus as she thought about the impossible task. "I'll have you open one of your portals so I can go through and snatch him, Your Highness."

Genesis knew it was a jest, but he still frowned. "It doesn't work that way. I can only summon things, not send them."

Rin mirrored Genesis's frown. "I know, I know. I'm working on the plan." She paced back and forth, running her hand through her hair. After a few moments, she surrendered to exhaustion and fell onto the grass. "But she doesn't have to fight me so hard on it." It couldn't have been three hours since they had been jogging about the perimeter of the Pit. Rin lost count of what lap they were on.

'Run until you feel your lungs crushing, then go one lap more.'

Thanks for the advice, Mom. Over the course of three weeks, they could push themselves further every few days, but Rin's lungs were about to pop. Working with her father in the fields her whole life was the only reason she hadn't passed out.

Genesis considered her words, his dark hair stale with sweat. "You're talking about an impossible task, going to the most dangerous place in the world. I think your mother has a right to try persuading you out of it."

Rin frowned. "Then why were you so willing to join my suicide mission?"

"Because it's not my business to tell you what you can and cannot do, Erin," he sighed.

She glared. "It's Rin." They had all adopted the habit of calling her by her full name since her mother used it so frequently.

"You say *ya'saea*, I say *ya'shea*," he shrugged his spout of Caenlin. "Either way, I can't tell you what to do. But I owe it to Zarus to help you. Your mother, on the other hand, has not gotten to know the whimsical depth of Zarus Lowwenth in the flesh."

"I fear if most met the demon, they'd sooner crush his pretty cheekbones than save him from torture." Another breeze ran past them, smelling of sweat and dust.

"Plus..." Genesis added, "it's smart to be hesitant with anyone who has a past with Eretimis."

Rin arched a curious brow. "Even you?"

He weighed his response, mindlessly rubbing the cloth concealing his arm. Genesis had disclosed that he was the Dark Tyrant's prisoner for the last seventy years, but Luna was the one to discover that he was the lost prince of Nokomic who went missing during the fall of Zelenia. The only things that gave it away were his name and the fact he possessed magic.

"Even me," he finally admitted. "I wouldn't have blamed any of you for leaving me in the desert." He rubbed the back of his damp neck. "I was fortunate to find you, more so to be allowed to accompany you. When your mother offered to teach me to use my magic, I was touched more than I can say. Kindness has been rare in the last few decades, and it's something I don't expect to get used to, nor is it something I'll consume without thought..." He trailed off, looking up at the small piece of sky above. "*But for now*," Genesis continued, a devious grin spanning his face. "I'm going to beat you to the other side of this clearing..."

Rin saw the challenge appear in his radiant eyes. She was on her feet in a matter of breaths. She gave him her prettiest smile and took off sprinting. "Eat my dust, Masquarem!"

Rin hadn't heard Genesis talk about saving Zarus once since he agreed to help her weeks ago. He made the chances of a rescue more attainable, but then another unspoken factor still put a pin in the plan. The hum gnawing at the back of her head never let her forget it.

Chapter Five

"What fuels magic in humans?"

Rin and Genesis exchanged uncertain glances. The afternoon heat crept upon them all. It buzzed like a hornet's nest throughout the cottage, and Rin was trying so desperately to swat the swarm away from her mind. It didn't help that they had spent all morning sparring. After Rin voiced at dinner last night how she was interested in being taught to defend herself from demons and the dangers of Nokomic, she woke up to a surprise. Apparently, Luna was well-versed in many styles of combat. Today, they learned to spar with a staff rather than run, but it left Rin dozing the rest of the day.

Her mother's lesson hummed in one ear and slipped out the other. It was no mystery that she didn't inherit her father's knack for studies.

Luna didn't bat an eye at their collective cluelessness. She flipped around the ancient book on the table for her students to gaze at as she explained. "Humans are fueled by the heart." Rin lazily glanced at the withered page of the book, if only to keep her eyes from fluttering shut. A silhouette of the human body was illustrated on the center of the parchment, a pale blue aura encapsulating where their heart should have been. Old texts scrawled across the page, words as foreign as Caenlin to her. Writing that likely was Caenlin.

"Whether it be magic, decision-making, friendships, or stories; the heart is the driving force for humanity. Some people learn to ignore it, but its call is always there. Magic runs through our veins with our blood. We feel it coursing throughout our bodies, thrumming with our pulse." Carefully, Luna raised her hand; the distorted energy of her magic rose from her fingertips like heat off metal. She reached across the table and touched a slight scratch on Rin's forearm. The distortion sent prickles along her skin as the scrape healed instantly.

"I've noticed my magic runs with my pulse," Genesis said, straightening in his chair. "When it beats faster, my magic comes to me easily. But it's harder to control."

Rin furrowed her brows. A ball of uncertainty weighed in her stomach.

"Aye," Luna hummed, the fine lines of her face creasing in a smile, "the strength of a novice often varies with how the heart reacts. It's why our magic is the most reliable, but also the most dangerous." Luna tapped her finger against her cheek. "Think of an aqueduct. The water flows through it, the structure tells it where to go. When there's more water flowing, there's more stress on the parts holding the aqueduct together, and sometimes it can't handle it and overflows. Or worse yet, it breaks."

The words sent a chill through the air. Rin remembered all too clearly how she nearly crumbled beneath the weight of her magic. But something still didn't sit right...

Her mother continued, "Our magic is powerful enough to break the parts holding it together. That's why I make you run every morning. That's why you're working to get stronger. So that your body and heart can bear the weight of your magic without killing you."

Rin wiped the sleep from her eyes, wishing to be outside by the lake rather than stuffed into the stale air of the cottage. "Is that why you have us practicing those forms every day?" All this talk of hearts and veins and pulses... it didn't make sense. It didn't match how she felt that night when her magic ravaged her. When Errogan called her a white mage.

Luna nodded. "The forms help center yourself, calm your heart, and draw your fuel. They get the blood flowing, and using your arms or legs helps guide the magic to your will. I extracted the motions from a fighting style I learned many years ago." Luna never looked at the book on the table as she talked. These were all things she could grab from memory. Rin couldn't help but marvel. Her mother was at ease for once. Passion always brought out the best in people.

"You said that our magic is the most reliable," Rin started. "Does that mean other beings have different sources of magic?"

Tension spread through her mother's demeanor, but Luna leaned against the stone hearth behind her without stuttering. "Every race has a different fuel. Humans direct magic from their hearts; dragons have an inheritance straight from the Divine; shifters need no source to shift forms; fae are directly connected to their world, their very lives a living magic that's part of Eroz now."

Rin bit the inside of her cheek. "And the demons?"

Whatever bitter substance rested in Luna's words spread to the rest of her body. And with it, Rin could have sworn the air decayed. "The demons source their magic from their minds."

Genesis grunted. "How is the mind less reliable than the heart?"

"Think about it this way: have you ever tried to think straight with a headache? Or solve a problem with little sleep?" Her mother folded her hands together. "The mind—though depthless—is easily hindered. Humans are left physically exhausted after exerting too much magic at once. Demons are left in mental exhaust."

That unnatural sensation still rested thick in the air.

"What's the difference between mages and casters?" Rin asked, wanting to veer away from the topic of demons.

It was Genesis that answered. "Mages produce magic without spells, while casters can only use it through spells," he yawned, not even glancing at the book. Apparently, he read ahead. "Mage magic is unique to the user."

Rin leaned into the table. "Can mages not use spells?"

"Mages can cast." Luna stood straight, pulling her hair over her shoulder. "In fact, mages were the ones to teach casters the first spells."

The last rays of sunlight slipped out of the Pit one by one. Rin couldn't hold back her yawn. "How did that work?"

Her mother wandered away from the table to light candles as she explained. "A long time ago, there was only one world made by the gods, Yath Ha. It was called Fawllhä. But long after the kaeth Anöwe corrupted it, a calamity erupted that split the world apart. Yath Ha saw that the mortals scattered in these broken worlds would not survive on their own. The Creators blessed them with a gift of their choosing to help rebuild the new worlds. However, not all of them wanted the same thing, and they broke into groups of like-minded wishing."

"Those groups would eventually evolve into the races we know today," Genesis murmured as he listened.

Luna continued. "I don't know what each race asked for specifically. My old mentor was fuzzy on the details. However, I know only a select few mortals that would become humans were blessed with magic and chosen to guide the rest to prosperity. These humans saw the usefulness of their magic and sought to share it with more people. They searched for the source of magic over the centuries and eventually discovered how to draw from that power."

"Didn't you just say our hearts source our power?" Rin asked. An ache seized her head.

Luna shook her head. "Our hearts act as a fuel tank—storage for the source we naturally collect. Our magic, and all magic alike, is sourced from the power living in our worlds after Yath Ha created it. Once the worlds were bridged, the races studied each other's magic. Only two discovered how to use different forms. The humans saw how the fae exchanged power from Eroz to fuel their lives, so early mages learned how to draw more power from Armiria in the form of verbal spells and taught it to the non-magic folk of the time; the casters. However, the magic casters gathered after years of studying spells was not as powerful as the fae's or our original magic."

"So then why can't all humans use magic if the mages taught others who didn't receive the gift?" Genesis asked.

"No one knows exactly why, since magic is so rare nowadays," Luna hummed, sitting back down once the cottage was alight with the glow of candles. "It would be impossible to trace."

The candles lulled the conversation to an end just as the front door swung open. Tatsuo and Feyne waltzed into the house, reeking of sweat and dirt, one jest or another on their lips. They had been sparring for as long as she had been studying. Luna began collecting herself to prepare supper, but Rin still had one question.

"The demons were the other race to learn another magic, weren't they?"

Luna caught her gaze, something unpleasant brewing within, but thankfully it didn't shut her mother down. "Yes, they also learned how to cast spells."

"From the fae?"

Her mother's head shook. Something Rin pinned as smugness rested in her expression. "From us humans, actually. The fae's exchange of magic was too difficult for them to learn directly, so they had to take the humans' watered down approach. If you want to get technical, you could say human spells are stronger."

The idea of casters and mages was still so foreign. To think humans mastered the art of another magic before anyone else... "Mages are extraordinary," she muttered under her breath. It was only after the words parted her lips that she realized she was one too.

"Mages are springs of power, dear. It's a blessing and a curse." A shadow cast over her mother's face. Rin stole a glance from Genesis. The same ghost haunted him.

That's why Eretimis hunts us.

Chapter Six

"Okay, now dive in. I said *in*. In. Dammit, Rin, dive in before I push you in."

The heat from the afternoon rested on the walls of the Pit. The water swayed softly against the lake's bank. A world completely at peace. Or it would have been, had Genesis not been cawing orders at her like a senile crow.

Rin spun around on her heels. He stood in front of her in his own fit of irritation.

"*What does that even mean?*" she snapped. "I can't follow your orders if I don't understand what in Yath Ha's good name they mean!"

"*It means,*" Genesis stressed, "that you told us your magic felt like an ocean. So imagine it as a wave cresting toward you, then *dive into it.*"

"Genesis, if there was an ocean in front of me, I would drown you in it." Rin sighed, sitting on the warm grass at the bank's edge. "I don't understand. I summoned it so easily that night. What changed?"

Luna approached from where she had been watching, planting herself between Rin and Genesis. "You were in a life or death situation, Erin. Your body thinks differently during those times. It just reacts; knowing what it must do before we know. You need to access that power outside of a stressed reaction."

"And how do you suppose I do that?" She scrunched the grass in her fingers. "What about a demonstration?"

Luna's eyes hardened, but ignored the challenge. "Right now, you should listen to Genesis's advice—you asked for it. All of our magic comes to us in different ways. Knowing which way yours comes to you is an advantage."

Rin sighed. Her mother was right. Genesis *was* the one to summon his magic in the last month. She climbed back to her feet and faced the rippling water. Resuming the meditative stance her mother taught her, Rin inhaled deep and slowly blew it out through pursed lips.

"Good," Luna nodded, pacing back and forth behind her, "now imagine what it felt like last time, that wave crashing into you."

Rin immediately frowned, peering over her shoulder at her instructor. "It crashed into me and nearly crushed me."

"Which is why you need to dive into it," Genesis chimed from her side, taking up his own stance.

Before Rin could comment on the matter of diving again, Luna spoke. "You can't control the ocean, dear. You can only navigate the water." Her mother's hands aligned Rin's elbows and straightened her back. "Now close your eyes and imagine that ocean before you."

Okay, an ocean. Picture an ocean.

Rin had never seen an ocean. Nor did she know exactly how the waves coursed and crashed into one another. However, when her eyes closed, Rin saw it clear as day. The magic moved in a fit of tides, cresting and breaking onto the magnus stretch of the surface.

She couldn't have been more terrified.

Rin bit the side of her cheek. Pain grounded her amidst the waves twice her height. The grass below her feet turned to water, and her head dipped below without so much as a scream. The ocean rocked, robbing the air from her lungs and submerging her in a magic so wild, Rin couldn't find her bearings.

She swam and swam, but couldn't find the surface. Her lungs stung, her vision blurred, and nothing compared to the pounding of her head. She was stuck, defenseless. Only when Rin submitted to the terror—when she wrapped her arms around herself and waited for her lungs to burst—did she find release.

***

The fire in the hearth raged idly compared to her thoughts. Rin hadn't said a word the entire evening. Her mind was probably her least favorite place in the entire Pit—maybe even the Unclaimed Lands—but it was the only place where no one tried to talk about earlier.

Finding Genesis hovered above her when she opened her eyes was a surprise. Although the shock quickly palliated when she noticed his hands, and the violet aura they radiated. Luna and Genesis informed her that as soon as her eyes closed, she began panicking and swatting her arms about until she screamed and fell unconscious. Rin hadn't spoken since, remaining silent throughout dinner. She was grateful Genesis tried to distract everyone from talking about the afternoon, even if it brought unwanted questions to him. Questions such as how Zelenia actually fell, since there were no proven accounts that survived the last seventy years. Questions that guided everyone in front of the fire after supper, waiting patiently for the prince to tell his tale.

Genesis loosed a huff and stretched his legs on the handmade couch. Silence both soothed and agitated him until he found the right words.

"You all know I'm a user and I've spent the last seventy years in a dungeon. But I didn't know I was a mage until I was an adult, unlike most of them," he shot Rin a wry glance. "Like you. I only discovered my power because of Zelenia's invasion."

The lighthearted atmosphere evaporated. Luna had already explained that after the fall of Zelenia and the death of its king, the entire kingdom of Nokomic fell into an oily turmoil. The once great nation writhed beneath a civil war; corruption ran the land in the shape of an organization called *The Resurrection*. Once the central hub for peace and diplomacy on the continent, Nokomic deteriorated into the north's most dangerous territory. Of course, it wasn't all hopeless. Too long, but not too late, another group stood against the blight of the Resurrection. The New Light. Led by the brave Elyot Iver, the idealist waged war on the Resurrection and pledged to rid Nokomic of its stain. After eleven years, it was the sole reason the roads of Nokomic were walkable again.

"Believe it or not, there was a time when Nokomic sat in an age of peace," Genesis said a bit proudly. A smile warmed his tanning features. "Radiant as the sunset over Balahk's Reach and twice as rich."

"Peace held for four hundred and thirty years," Luna murmured from the table. She busied her hands with wood and a carver.

Rin swallowed an uneasy breath. She wished to have been alive for the peaceful times.

Genesis nodded. "I was in the king's counsel one day when a messenger delivered news of an unknown force destroying villages in the northeast of the kingdom."

He jumped to his feet, pacing as he recalled. "Times were easy. People settled their own problems; it was the perfect era to learn to rule a kingdom. I couldn't believe that someone suddenly assaulted Nokomic. Our allies held strong bonds with us. To make matters more difficult, the assailants were in and out of their scenes in the matter of a night." He scoffed. Perhaps thinking of the demon tyrant who tied it together in retrospect. "We even considered whether the people of the eastern continent had crept to the coasts of the Unclaimed Lands, but there hadn't been word from our outposts."

Rin softly asked, "What did your father do about it?"

He dragged his bright eyes to her. "My father did what anyone in his position would do and spent many long hours consulting with the king."

"Wait," Tatsuo interrupted, sitting up from the couch ever so slightly before Luna cleared her throat—a stern warning to lie back down. "I thought you said your father was the king?"

Genesis shook his head. "I said I was the prince, but King Aymon was not my father. I was the chosen heir to Nokomic, son of General Albus, the king's brother."

Feyne raised a curious brow. "Chosen?"

"Adopted, actually," Genesis shrugged. "The Queen was unable to bear children, so providing heirs fell to King Aymon's brother, Albus. Albus's firstborn was lost at childbirth and took his wife shortly after. Mourning, he decided to adopt me, which ended up healing two sick with one dose."

Rin scratched her head. Well, that certainly got lost in the ribbon of history. Then again, the ribbons of history were torn to shreds in the last few decades.

Genesis spoke to no one in particular. "The attacks were a mystery that kept us in the dark for months. Villages were wiped off the map. Our people began whispering about the king's competency." He sucked in a breath and wiped his face of old exhaustion. "My father made it his mission to hunt down whoever was wreaking havoc and drag them to justice. He built watch lines in the north, posted soldiers, but nothing helped. We were at a loss. The only person in the entire kingdom that seemed to know who invaded our land was the castle's librarian; the stout fellow dug up dusty old scrolls talking of creatures and monsters. Claimed these monsters were causing the chaos. We all thought he was mad." A heavy sigh left his lips. "I wish we had listened. Before summer's turn, an army of ten thousand marched toward Zelenia's gates. Urgent messages only deliver if the messengers are alive."

Genesis's voice cut harshly. "We organized an evacuation of the city with the little time we had. The citizens were told to flee through the southern gate into the Lennaels, and alert everyone along the way. But Zelenia is—" he caught himself, "was a large city."

"The evacuation saved most of the people living in Zelenia, Genesis," Feyne assured from his chair. "When word reached across the sea, that was the first thing I heard. That order that saved thousands of lives."

Genesis nodded. "We didn't have time to wonder how they appeared out of nowhere. The army was arriving from the north and would hit that gate first. They could only head west since the eastern gate led to a narrow bridge over a lake."

Tatsuo's head inclined. "Did you plan on countering them from the east?"

"East and south. We hoped to come around on their backside." Genesis fell back to his spot on the sofa near Tatsuo's feet. "Even against ten thousand, Zelenia was packed full of soldiers. We even had a handful of users in our midst. There was no war, everyone was home in the capitol—it made no sense for the demons to strike at Nokomic's strongest hub when it was so well guarded."

"Not if it wasn't a tactical shot," Feyne offered.

"Didn't have long to think that one over either," Genesis shrugged. "The bastards knocked the northern gate down. The Walls of Zelenia were a true marvel that stood for thousands of years, and in the blink of an eye, they crumbled. Thousands of years of protection gone in minutes."

Desolation stirred in Genesis's eyes. "My father had already left to lead the strike from the east, but my uncle and I were still in the throne room giving orders. Plans had changed, and I didn't know where my father was.

"Uncle and I were supposed to lead the southern front, but because of the breakthrough, we divided our forces. I led the south with the captain of the royal guard. King Aymon was charging head-on against the army to hold them back. I warned him of the dangers—we didn't know what we faced after the gate fell—but he persisted. He was a stubborn man." A half smile met his lips. "We set to leave when someone gave a warning. The city bled of all color, and the world tumbled out beneath my feet."

Luna's low voice chilled the room. "The castle fell after the gate. There are a lot of accounts of what struck it, most avoiding the word 'magic'. But any user you'd ask would say shadow magic. The shadows of everyone and everything disappeared from Zelenia; wrung dry like faded cloth." She saw Rin's curiosity. "Think of all the shadows in the city packed into one mass. A concentrated ball of energy, ready to release Flames with the smallest impact."

Rin bit her lip. "They hit the castle with an explosion?"

"One that turned the entire west wing to debris," Genesis said. "The explosion obliterated the throne room. I woke up in the pile of ruin and somehow found my way to the surface. When I found my bearings, I found a battle."

Genesis stared at nothing for a long moment, eyes unblinking. "The first time I saw Eretimis, he towered over the ruin. I thought one of Vulyn's Hands walked the battleground, waiting to guide lost souls. But I knew that wasn't true when I saw Errogan at the bastard's side taking life, not guiding it to the After."

Rin's gut squirmed at the thought of the white-haired demon.

"The Tyrant and his minion moved in a way that was not human. If you had to look twice, you were already slain. The search for my people didn't take long, but the search for the living was trickier. Crushed or gutted, that army showed no mercy as they flooded the streets. The smell... I didn't think it was possible to smell so much blood, so much waste."

Rin watched his face pale. His voice grew distant. "Genesis," she said carefully, "you don't have to tell us anymore—"

"I want to share," he interrupted. "I need to share this."

"I found my father standing against Eretimis." A weak grin tugged on his face, but Genesis could barely hold it. "General or not, that man would never run from anything. But dammit... I wish he had. I ran to help my father, but the Moonlit Bastard intercepted me."

Feyne stiffened. Rin knew he watched her, but she avoided the shifter's eyes. She let Errogan escape in the desert.

Genesis continued. "It felt like I had no strength when I fought Errogan. He'd strike, but not to kill me. He'd let me advance, then step out of my attack as though I bored him." A hard *tsk* caught his tongue. "He toyed with me while my father fought for his life, but he was as outmatched as I was. Finally, Errogan opened his mouth and called to his master."

"'*Finish him already!*'"

Genesis impersonated Errogan's voice, but it was more than that. Rin's heart clenched. The tone, the expression, the demeanor...

He shook his head, scoffing. "And you know what Eretimis said? *'Experiments require research, Errogan.'*"

He had the Dark Tyrant's oily voice down as well. Genesis had a knack for imitations, but a *thunk* in the back of the cottage seized Rin's attention. The tranquility of the home decayed. Rin looked toward her mother, wan and frozen. After a long moment, Luna's expression eased. She inhaled deeply, holding the air for nearly too long. The decay faded like it had never appeared as the prince went on.

"To think the destruction of my home was for some experiment... I charged toward Errogan, but he countered. He sent his blade through my leg and threw me to the ground. My father's step fumbled at the sight. Eretimis stole the shadows beneath his feet and sent them through my father's heart."

Rin heard the wind whistle through the tangible silence.

Genesis spat. "This internal cry in my heart forced me up, and I used it to send my blade into Errogan's gut. I ran to my father's side and dropped to my knees. The wound... it was—" He cut himself off. "His eyes lost focus before his voice. I don't remember those moments clearly. My heart ran so fast it felt like it would burst. But it didn't, and I did not join my father in the After." His voice was taut as a bowstring.

An oily understanding seeped through the room.

"The battle ended, and not one human remained. I accepted my death with squared shoulders. I couldn't save my people or my father. But life dealt me a bitter hand."

By winning the title of sole survivor, Genesis became Eretimis's first human test subject, which led to the discovery of his magic. Eretimis then started hunting down magic users. Join the Dark Tyrant, or die. That's what Luna thought it had been. Turns out the choice was to join Eretimis or be dragged back to his fortress and experimented on. Either way, they were never heard of again, save occasionally by Genesis in the fortress.

"Half demon. Half human." Rin repeated as the prince re-wrapped the bandage around his left arm. Discolored, scarred, and cracked; even Luna's eyes widened when he showed the aftermath of Eretimis's serum.

"How... how is that even *possible*?" Tatsuo asked, ignoring Luna's sharp eye and sitting upright. "You should be dead."

Genesis only brushed on the tortuous experiments that prodded his magic enough to show itself. It was enough to instill sickness in everyone.

"Because he's a user," Luna sighed, rising to her feet. She ambled toward the blazing hearth, sitting in the center of the sofa between the prince and *narikaah*. "Only magic could sustain life through a process so... harrowing."

Genesis leaned forward with his hands steepled against his lips. "Those experiments were the only reason I learned I was a user. I was under enough stress that my body buckled beneath it and fought back."

Rin hesitated, but asked, "Which power did you discover first?" She promptly earned confusion from her mother and two of her friends. "You can't tell me I'm the only one who's noticed? The man's hands are practically a different color every time I look at him."

Genesis stared at her blankly, but a pleasant surprise shined through. "You're nosier than a dog, you know that?"

Pride spread through Rin's smile. "Perhaps you should master the art of discretion, Masquarem. You summon things, and what else?"

Luna cut in as Genesis opened his mouth. "Erin, you shouldn't pry."

A glare nearly reached Rin's features. *Of course* you'd *say that.*

"No, Ms. Nowell, it's alright," Genesis assured, although his stare never left Rin's. "I actually discovered this one before I learned I could summon. For starters, I would like to state that I only use it when necessary." The prince went on after a heavy sigh. "I can influence emotions."

Silence seized hold of the cottage. Even the crackle of the fire seemed to pause.

"Is that why I gave you the last of the soup yesterday?" Tatsuo asked abruptly.

"Innocent until proven guilty?" Genesis offered.

The dragon stuck his nose up. "Nuh-uh, not this time."

"No one seemed to care when Rin nearly fried everyone in the desert..."

"That was an accident!"

"Look!" Genesis shouted. "I said I only used it when needed, right? Which has only happened a handful of times, *and even then*, I can barely hold a grip on any of you." He looked every one of them in the eye with a sternness Rin wasn't sure he deserved. After inquiring about the magic of the not-quite-young, yet not-quite-old prince, much came to light.

1. Genesis Masquarem could influence the emotions of those unfortunate individuals he had physical contact with.

2. The effect of this ability amplified if the one subjected to it had a weak will, or were easily influenced.

3. Those who were not expecting the magic usually fell victim to it, strong-willed or not.

4. Genesis had used this magic on all four of them *at least* once.

"What do the colors mean?" Rin asked. Magic, as new to her as it had been, had become something of boredom over the last month. She had delved so far into the study of its technique that the whimsy faded. Her attention could only focus so long on *The Short History of Yath Ha's Gifts,* or *Exiled in the Heart: A Novice's Handbook for Navigating Magic,* or even *The Last Accounts of the Sorcerer of Aelius.* But this? This was new.

Genesis yawned. "Different colors for different emotions. Rin, I think everyone should get to sleep—"

"How many shades are there? And what emotions do they correlate with? And how—"

Rin jumped out of her skin as a heatless flame appeared then disappeared on her shoulder. She whipped her stare to Tatsuo. "I think we pried enough answers out of him for today. You're listing as it is."

As if it had been hiding all evening, exhaustion rammed into Rin.

Luna yawned, pulling herself to her feet and straightening out her dress. "It's late. Everyone should start slowing down for the night."

The thought of running through the dewy field at the break of dawn had Rin's eyes fluttering shut. So when Luna helped Tatsuo up the stairs, Rin voiced no protests.

Feyne lit up the room as he shifted. The wolf prowled out the door to the grass where he preferred to sleep. Her mother and Tatsuo were already out of sight, the conversation of breakfast trailing behind them. Rin was too fatigued to realize that not everyone had left.

"Were your suspicions correct?"

She jumped again, earning a laugh. Genesis lounged on the sofa.

Rin loosed a grin. "I guessed you had some sort of mind control today when you woke me up by the lake."

"Violet tones bring relaxation," the prince said as he stretched. "I persuaded your mind to ease from whatever dropped you cold." She considered this while he broke into a smile. "What would you do without me, Nowell?"

She scoffed. "Where would you be without *me*, Masquarem?"

"Dead, just like you."

"Glad we're on the same page."

The ceiling creaked, drowning out the wind outside. Even the fire's dance had tired. Genesis's radiant blue eyes shone through the dimness of the room. Their magic trademark. Rin dropped her gaze, attempting to rub the sleep from her own.

"I'm glad you're out of the fortress. Even if you've become one of the biggest pains in my life."

Genesis placed both hands over his heart. "That's the sweetest thing you've ever said to me." His mischief disappeared when he spun around and headed for the stairs.

"Whatever you say, Your Highness."

"Nighty night, Erin."

Rin chucked the pillow in her hands at his head. Perhaps it was the exhaustion, or maybe he felt kind tonight, but the pillow hit.

Genesis disappeared upstairs. Rin crashed onto her makeshift bed and nuzzled into the blanket draped over the sofa. A remnant of her grin remained, but it wasn't enough to keep her fear at bay.

Genesis learned his magic in a dungeon by himself. Her? She couldn't even summon a drop without knocking herself out.

Chapter Seven

I t was an effort to stay upright, let alone conscious. Zarus couldn't tell whether the ground was damp or covered in a sickly chill. The stone brazier at the room's heart blazed wildly, its green flames the only light in the whole chamber.

Strength, child. He thinks he has won, but he knows not. We hide your true—

Zarus cut the divine voice off. Its persistence was wearing through his remaining temper. Louder than ever before in the chamber behind the throne. It was uninvited, yet chatted away every chance it could. He gritted his teeth and gently touched his forehead, brushing away the blood and grime that covered his skin. Finally cured of the poisonous serum, yet nothing to show for it. Zarus could have scoffed. He doubted the Wraiths above knew he was awake. After all, he held on longer this time.

"So this is how the Shadow of Evenfall ends? To be honest, I was expecting a bit more..."

"Weren't we all, Tesyl, dear. Once a name to be feared, now look at him... what a waste."

"Of time or power?" Zarus barely croaked out the words. He shifted his burning eyes to the twins; nothing but a haze of silhouettes.

"The legend still moves. Perhaps we didn't delve our nails deep enough," the eldest purred. Her smile spanned into a wild flare.

"Don't be foolish, Raia," Tesyl's ghostly voice hissed. The younger twin took a step closer to the light, apathy carving her features. "His power will fuel us for months to come. There's nothing left in him but breath and bone." Her straight lips curled, sadistic amusement guiding her words. "Perhaps even less than that."

Another voice spoke from the entrance, one made of darkness and nothing. "It has been over a month and he still possesses the strength to speak. That is something to be marveled at, sisters."

The hair on Zarus's neck raised. He glanced at the open curtain and the Dark Tyrant standing within.

"A pleasure as always, *uhlandyi*." Eretimis offered him a nod.

"I don't think you know what constitutes pleasure," Zarus groaned. His eyes burned. How was he still awake? He was empty and drained, as if there was nothing left in him but indifference. He had blacked out every other time the twins came to steal his power, albeit slower and slower with each, so what made today so different as to burden him with consciousness?

"I have robbed you of everything and yet you still feel the need to make such trivial remarks," Eretimis said with a breathy sigh, one that could have been taken as a laugh.

"Not everything," Zarus heaved. His head felt lighter. He slipped his eyes open, catching the bastard's gaze. "You've been gracious enough to leave my tongue in place. I have a feeling the remarks will end when you finally decide you've had enough of it."

Now those were dangerous waters to tread on, for Zarus still enjoyed his speech. Pushing his luck with Eretimis's temper wasn't in his best interest. But did it matter? Luckily, the Tyrant let it slip.

"You do not understand what it means to still be breathing. It is a shame how far you have fallen, boy. That mountain dulled your mind." The Dark Tyrant stepped into the chamber. He stopped on the other side of the brazier, the pale light twisting his features.

Zarus somehow found the breath for a retort. "There's a fine line between ignorance and indifference, Eretimis. I thought you'd be wise enough to discover that much."

A *tsk* met Zarus's ears, through the emptiness wading about his head. He summoned forth his praised strength and pulled himself upright.

Eretimis's haughty stare was waiting for him when he opened his eyes. "Always the student, never the teacher. Tell me, have you the faintest idea of what I am doing?"

Every word hammered a nail deeper into his temper. Zarus spoke through bared teeth as his vision swayed.

"Other than draining me of my magic, time and time again?" He looked to the Tyrant on the other side of the flames. A growl nearly slipped his throat, but Zarus caught it in time.

"Time and time again indicates you're looking for something, or waiting. The only time you've used force is when I've tried to fight back..." His thoughts swirled like leaves stuck in the wind. He caught them, but only after a bit of chasing.

"Based on today, I can only guess the Wraiths wait until I pass out to stop stealing my magic, because today is the only day I've stayed awake." If only he had lost consciousness. He pinched the bridge of his nose, holding tight to the flow of this trivial examination. "And each time it takes longer and longer to black out. If I didn't know any better, Eretimis, I'd say you're testing something."

Zarus let his hand fall to the floor. "Why are you so interested in the bank of my magic?"

The Dark Tyrant remained silent, still. He could have been mistaken for a piece of the brazier, if not for the malevolent smile spanning his face. "This is why you were always my favorite, *uhlandyi*."

Zarus's teeth finally bared at that name. "I'm not your student anymore."

"Forever a student, so long as you learn from me."

The Dark Tyrant twisted around with the poise of a phantom and pulled the curtain away as if his dark magic didn't seal it. "I will let you in on a secret, boy, for old time's sake." Zarus raised his brow, only then realizing everyone else had left the room. "The twins did not stop today because they thought you fell unconscious."

"Then why did they stop absorbing my magic?"

That dark smile deepened. "There was nothing left to drain."

Chapter Eight

"Do I get to know where you're taking me this time?"

Silence.

"Can I at least have a moment to catch my breath? Those hags *just* drained me of all my magic. That should constitute *some* form of—"

"*Blood 'n Flames, Zarus*, if you don't shut it, I'm going to rip out your tongue!"

Zarus almost smiled after Errogan yelled and threw him into the hall. "And here I thought that's what had happened to you."

Errogan snarled, but nothing more. He pushed Zarus into a stride. That had been the first thing he uttered since Eretimis instructed the white-haired prick to relocate Zarus. He stole a glance of his old friend while they walked through the masonry of the fortress. Beyond Errogan's scowl, a mending gash ran down twice the length of his temple. The kiss of bruising discolored his face. The wounds weren't fresh, but they weren't old either.

The duo passed a narrow window overlooking the gloom forever gathered above the frozen wasteland. The distant clash of blades in the armories trailed their way. Zarus grimaced with every step he took, whether at the nauseating throb of his head or the desire to speak. He finally yielded to the latter as he was directed around a corner. "That cut will heal faster if you use one of the healer's salves—"

Before he finished speaking, a fist collided with his cheek.

Zarus caught Errogan's wrist as his vision flared white and yanked him off balance. The demon stumbled, his face tumbling right onto the edge of Zarus's elbow. Though only his magic was stolen, Zarus's body still hadn't adjusted to the emptiness in his head. Errogan caught him by the neck and slammed him against the wall.

He tried to pry Errogan's grip free, but it held firm. He tried to find his voice, but it choked out. Zarus finally met Errogan's abhorrent stare. A bilious sensation twisted his gut when he looked at the demon's wounds from such a close distance.

Vision didn't grace him for long, nor did breath. Zarus's head swam, his hands clawing at those holding his throat. Blood drew from Errogan's skin, but he did not stir. He stared damnation into Zarus's soul. Teeth bared and ready to kill.

"I should have let you bleed out in that field."

Zarus stopped struggling. His hands fell to his sides, nothing but white light filling his eyes. A cool embrace fell onto him, and for a while he didn't know what happened. When he finally came to, he found himself gasping for breath, lurched over on his knees. He cupped his throat, and the ache of bruises sang in return. His head swayed, but Zarus cast his stare up.

Errogan towered over him, the loathing he showed moments ago having chilled to disdain—a knife in Zarus's gut. But someone else was there as well. He looked at the female as his eyes focused. She was average height for a demon. Her dark hair wove a braid that reached her mid back, and a sneer twisted on her brown lips.

"What seems to have happened here?" Her dark eyes looked from Errogan to Zarus. She crossed her arms and squared her broad shoulders.

Errogan's disdain surprisingly rolled away from Zarus. "Nothing that concerns you, Nessriq. Why are you here?"

Nessriq?

Nessriq shrugged, her expression following suit. "His Dark Majesty suggested I accompany you to transport the prisoner. He said I would benefit from learning about the infamous Shadow." Her gaze flicked to Zarus still on his knees. "I didn't know your orders implied killing the prisoner."

"They didn't," Errogan barked shortly. It was then that Zarus found the strength to climb to his feet. "And I don't need your supervision. Get out of here."

"My supervision?" Nessriq seemed amused by the very idea. "Don't work yourself up, Errogan. I'm only here to learn. It's not like you've done anything so monumentally foolish recently as to require my supervision." Her smile carved deeper, and if his head didn't sway so violently, Zarus might have been curious enough to ask. But it did, and he remained silent until Errogan snapped at the demon again then pushed him forward. He didn't remember the rest of the walk to the far reaches of the fortress. There was only the sheer weight of the hatred he saw in Errogan's crystal eyes. As the door slammed behind him, Zarus stood within the remnants of his old quarters again with only one thought.

What happened between us?

Chapter Nine

The aura danced around Genesis's hands on the bank of the lake. He delicately drew back from the magic. When the dark essence ebbed, his hand was not empty. Rin couldn't bring a smile to her face.

She looked down at her own callused hands and wanted nothing more than to slam them into the walls of the Pit.

Hours. She had been out there for hours. Rin spent nearly half of the night lying in the armchair before the fire, listening to the snores of her friends. Lessons had been more focused on using their magic, and while Genesis was thriving, Rin hadn't summoned a fleck of light or healing.

She hadn't wanted to wake the others, so she'd gone outside, laid in the fields, and watched the stars through the gap at the top of the Pit. Yet after an entire night of trying to find her magic, Rin was still convinced it was all in her head.

Now, standing beside Genesis as he summoned everything Luna asked, she couldn't have felt more useless.

Rin submerged her hands in the lake. The wading ripples relieved her dreadful heart, cleared her mind. It was a moment of solitude that she needed, but someone approached from behind and sat beside her.

It came as a surprise when the voice was much deeper than her mother's. "You look like shit."

Rin looked at the shifter. "I feel it too."

Feyne studied her. "Still nothing?"

She dropped her gaze.

"I've never been able to learn this way. I'm listening to all these theories of magic use, all these written accounts of what to do and how to do it, but I'm not seeing it up close."

There was a fine line between overstepping boundaries and what was okay to say. Rin had been walking that line ever since she met her mother, and anything that had to do with Luna's magic fell so far over. The best demonstration she could get was Genesis staying up late trying to help her. However, the head-start of teaching himself in the dungeons had worn thin after a week; he was as new to this as she.

Feyne fell silent. She didn't blame him; there wasn't much to say. She felt a nudge on her shoulder and glanced at the shifter's bruised fist.

"I really don't get what you're fretting so much about, Nowell," he shrugged, tucking his arms behind his head and closing his eyes against the sun.

Her forehead scrunched with the furrow of her brow. Feyne opened one eye. "You look like a fish when you do that."

Rin took a moment to rub her temples. "Explain."

At least Feyne found a laugh. "Rin, you are single-handedly the most driven person I know. You'll overcome this. Give yourself some credit." He smiled at her, a smile that had been all too rare lately.

She pulled her hands out of the water. "What makes you say that?"

"Well," he said, scratching the back of his head, "you left your home to search for someone you hadn't seen for twelve years, and actually found her."

She frowned. "Most people would call that foolish."

"I call it guts." He stretched out, laying back in the grass. "Few people have enough guts to accomplish that. And fewer would have enough to keep pushing for results like you do every day." He flicked an eye open at her once more. "Take a deep breath."

Rin choked on her breath. She rubbed her eyes, only then remembering her wet hands. "It's an impossible task."

Feyne considered this, staring up at the sky. "So is wandering onto a mountain and making friends with a demon. It's the impossible tasks that make life livable."

***

"Why don't you show me with your own magic?"

The question sat thick as wax in the space between them. Rin had never once seen her mother's magic. She'd seen her healing as a white mage, but not her personal power. Luna had always shut the conversation down before it even started. Rin had waited to ask in private. Everyone else was outside, and only Rin and Luna stood over the hearth.

She needed a different approach to learning and held firm in her resolve. The moment stretched on for what seemed like forever.

"No."

Rin blinked. "Are you sure? Learning through theory hasn't helped me at all. I think it would be better to see it, and you're—"

"I said no, Erin," her mother snapped. Enough that Rin flinched. Luna's hands stopped kneading the dough on the table. Her movements became stiff, as if a spider crept along her skin. "You'll find another way."

Rin hesitated after watching the tension grow in her mother, but she couldn't let the conversation end like that. She *needed* help. Keeping things as they were was a waste of everyone's time!

"Mother, please." Rin swallowed hard, closing her eyes in order to subdue the hum. "I can't do this alone."

Suddenly, something cracked. Luna threw the dough onto the counter, her hands slamming atop it. Nothing of her mother's soft voice remained. "I said no, Erin! I will not show you my magic! Stop asking and practice how I told you to achieve it for yourself!"

Rin stared, eyes wide. She knew her face paled as a ghostly tremble wrapped around her hands.

"Alright," Rin whispered, afraid her voice might shatter if she said more.

At some point, her legs carried her out the door. The world around rushed. Rin thought she heard a voice call her name from behind, one that was as broken as hers. She kept walking.

Chapter Ten

Aggravating as it was, the complaints of passing guards outside his door were the only way Zarus could tell how much time had passed.

It seemed Eretimis didn't feel the need to keep him in the dark anymore. No spells were cast on the walls to block everything out. He heard everyone passing outside his door, felt their presence, even identified their scents. The door, however, did have a lock on it. One crafted by Hraesah's master smiths that Zarus didn't possess the energy to pick until today.

The Dark Tyrant didn't lie when he said Raia and Tesyl drained him of his magic. Bled dry and squeezed to get out the last few drops. For days, Zarus struggled to stay upright, much less figure out a plan. He couldn't summon forth a sliver of magic—shadows nor ice—days after. When any ounce of his magic made its way back to him, it was in drops that deprived him of all his energy to use. It took the better part of forty days for his magic to return in full, and even then it was lacking. Calling ice cost him, teasing the frays of shadows took up more focus than he would have liked. As if in draining his magic, the Wraith Twins permanently kept part of it for themselves. Zarus knew that wasn't the case because no one had come to mock him over it. Whatever lid covered the wells of his magic was only known to him. He intended to keep it that way. For now, he sat before the door, working a thin piece of metal he pulled from the bed frame into the lock. Every Hraesan demon crafted their locks as a maze to navigate, but an escape would be easy. With no presence to track him, the demons infesting these halls wouldn't know which way he went until they caught his scent. It was searching the entire fortress for Rin that would be impossible.

A rhythm of footsteps sounded down the staircase spiraling to his door. Escape would have to wait. Whoever was out there, Zarus would rather them not find him staring at the lock like it would suddenly start doing tricks. He moved to the nearest chair. Book in hand and back to his company, Zarus's eyes skimmed over the words he had read centuries ago. The doorknob clicked.

"A knock of consideration would be nice from time to time," he muttered as he slid his eyes to the demon at the door.

Errogan scowled faster than the breath left his lungs. "You realize you're a prisoner, correct?"

"Am I?" Zarus closed the book with a *thump*. "I sometimes forget with such a pleasant room and three meals a day."

A bitter *tsk* sounded sharp as a blade. "If it were up to me, you'd be licking water off the dungeon floors to survive."

"Lovely chat as always, E. What do you want?"

"To know if you're still empty," Errogan sighed, walking into the room.

"How do you plan to do that?"

"Easy," Errogan chimed. Without so much as another utterance, the demon sent his fist barreling toward the side of Zarus's head.

The book fell to the ground. Zarus lifted his hand, a shield of ice forming on the floor between them. Errogan's fist collided with the ice. Shattering like brittle bone, the magic shield crumbled to the ground.

Zarus was already on his feet, putting space between the two of them before Errogan could advance. Surprisingly, he didn't.

"Not going to fight back?" Errogan sneered. Zarus readied for another hit, but none came. "Come to think of it, you've done nothing but roll over for the better part of the last month. Why so submissive all of a sudden?"

Zarus waited, but Errogan didn't budge. Whatever he was here for, it was not to attack him.

He eased his posture, letting his arms fall to his sides. "I don't see a point."

Those crystal eyes narrowed, searching. "Bullshit." Zarus raised an unamused brow, but Errogan continued. "I've told you before, you've always been a shit liar."

"No, you simply think too highly of yourself." Zarus's retort earned him a scoff, and nothing more. Whatever had soured the demon's mood the last time they were in each other's company, it had since passed. So had the bruises.

"Denial shines light, old friend. Say what you will, but I see it all over your face. You're afraid to act out of line. Fearing for someone's life, are we?"

Zarus's expression fell flat.

"You'll get the fight you're looking for if you're not careful, Errogan." Frost nipped at the tips of his fingers. A glacial gale swept over the room.

Errogan's laugh wrapped around his head. "Chill out, Evenfall. You've already given me what I came for."

Zarus stared a moment longer before something clicked. "You saw for yourself that my magic returned. So why are you still here?"

Errogan sighed, losing interest in the conversation. He removed a dagger from its sheath at his hip and kept his hands busy with it.

"Believe me, I'd spend my time doing just about anything else if someone didn't insist it was important to check on you."

Oh, save me from the pleasure of your insults. Zarus's eyes nearly rolled out of his skull. "Right, because that's all you do around here nowadays; chores."

Quicker than he expected, Errogan's temper flashed.

"If the other option is bending over as you've become so accustomed to, I'd much rather keep myself busy with work."

The dagger spun round and round his fingers. Some things never changed, except it used to be Zarus's knife.

Is that why Eretimis is having Nessriq spy on you? Zarus considered this as he shifted his weight, but he chose not to ask. Part of him still expected to be lunged at.

"So that's what we've become? Slave and dog. Eretimis was right: we've fallen far from our pedestals."

"*We* have done no such thing. *You* have," the white-haired demon bit down too quickly, too sharply. "When will you stop grouping me with your pitiful self?"

"When you convince me that we're no longer the same."

Errogan scoffed so hard, the words seemed to choke him.

"Don't flatter yourself, Lowwenth." He slid the dagger back into place on his belt. "Maybe we were similar once, but that was long ago." The amusement fell from his tone, replaced by contempt.

"You've fallen beneath me, Zarus, and there's no going back from that. We may share more than you could understand, but we are *never* the same."

Zarus narrowed his eyes. "What might we share if you're leagues above me, Reaper?"

It was an unfruitful shot in the dark. Errogan's sneer carved deeper. Silence would be his answer.

There's no end to his arrogance, is there? Zarus inhaled deep, calming his growing vexation. Without more to say, he raised an empty palm. The black aura of shadow formed in his grasp; the misty tendrils rising like smoke.

"There's your proof; will you leave me to sit in peace now?"

"You know it's never that easy."

Another sigh. Zarus shifted his stare to the door. There was no one else outside. It seemed Errogan truly believed he wouldn't fight back. That or Eretimis didn't think Errogan needed supervision this time.

"Fine," he finally bit, "let's get this over with. Throne room, I presume?" Errogan nodded, turning toward the door to lead the way.

Zarus might have kept a tight leash on his temper for Rin's sake, but Errogan was showing restraint in simply not kicking him while he was down. Of course, Errogan's version of mercy would be denied if Zarus ever brought it up, but he still made a mental note of it while he passed under the doorway.

Chapter Eleven

The shadows tugged toward the center of the throne room. All directed toward the throne and the Tyrant sitting upon it. An image frozen in time—well, not frozen. If ice framed it, Zarus would have drained himself into shattering it. Perhaps *branded* was the proper term. That brand pressed further into his mind as he walked to the dais steps. Not another soul in the room.

"What do you want?"

As always, bluntness didn't faze the Tyrant. There he sat, head resting in hand, on the obsidian throne.

"You never cease to amaze me, boy. Lesser demons died after the Twins took a third of what they stole from you. Yet already your magic is back and thriving. Is there an end to your spring of power?"

Zarus was in no mood for idle chatter. Errogan wore his patience thin, and he didn't think he could last an entire conversation with Eretimis without snapping. He met that hollow gaze and bared down.

"*What do you want?*"

Eretimis's unreadable expression cracked into a smile. Neither of them wanted to drag this out.

The Dark Tyrant spoke, the subtle pique in his voice sparking Zarus's alarm. "I admit, the way you kept this one hidden from me... it is worthy of credit."

Confusion flushed over in waves, but Zarus kept it far from his expression. Neutrality, apathy. Those were his allies.

"After all this time, through all the chasing," the Tyrant continued, straightening where he sat. "It still amazes me that Errogan took so long to figure it out..." Eretimis let out a cruel chuckle.

Zarus braced himself, more lost than he would ever let on. His mind raced to figure out what the bastard alluded to.

"So, I have to ask, did you know Rin Nowell was a white mage from the very beginning, or did you happen upon it along the way?"

Despite Zarus's effort, his heart leapt off a cliff.

"What—" He caught his confusion, biting sharply on the urge to finish the thought and sucked in a deep breath. "How did you come across it?"

Damned if he knew a thing of what the demon was talking about, but ignorance didn't suit him well. Zarus had been aware there was something unique about Rin from the start. He suspected she possessed a form of magic. However, a white mage? Is that what the ancient feel to her presence was?

Eretimis's studious stare sent Zarus's nerves on edge. Despite what Errogan boasted, Eretimis was the only one who could truly read through some of his facades. So he was pleasantly surprised when the tyrant took his bait.

"The same way you discover the magic of any being. Add a little stress."

Zarus's stomach twisted. Disdain morphed his expression into a snarl.

"Leave the girl alone, Eretimis." It was all he could manage through his raging thoughts. The shadows grew beneath him, darker than natural around his boots. Like the mist of a dream.

The Dark Tyrant huffed a humored sigh, leaning in toward the show Zarus was feeding him. "Even you cannot say you are not curious how far power like that can bend before it snaps, *uhlandyi*."

His nails dug into his palms, drawing blood the harder he clenched his fists. *Calm down. This will make things worse for her.*

Suddenly the veil of emotion dissipated, replaced with clarity. Zarus loosened his grip on the shadow magic lingering about him. He was being tested again, and he was playing into it like a fool. With Rin in Eretimis's possession... there was no limit to what they would force him to do. Lodged sorely between a mad tyrant and the blood of an innocent.

"I'd say you have me right where you want me, Tyrant o'mine." Zarus stood before the marble steps, looking up to the throne with an oily disgust swelling in his chest. "What do you plan to do with me?"

Eretimis leaned back into the throne, greyish fingers rapping away on the round of the arm. His voice was flat, the meeting coming to its end.

"I have narrowed it down, but have not chosen which option I favor just yet." Hollow eyes pierced into Zarus's skull, a phantom breeze catching the Tyrant's raven locks. "Perhaps I will subject you to each of them now that you are bowing down to me."

A scoff spat out of Zarus's throat. He raised his chin against the demon. "You'll have to cut me to my knees before I bow to you."

Amusement danced within the Tyrant's eyes.

"Is that the case?"

Something icy rippled through Zarus's core. Eretimis suddenly held his hand open to the left of the throne. On cue, a pair of guards marched through the entrances at the chamber's sides, the demon on the left drawing out her sword and placing it into her liege's palm. The guards remained on both sides, but the Dark Tyrant rose. He swayed with the shadows as he descended the steps. Zarus held his ground, kept his shoulders back. He didn't falter against that gaze. Not even when Eretimis stopped in front of him.

Eretimis held the blade vertically at his chest, one edge facing him, the other facing Zarus.

The sword hovered there, the flame's light glinting off the steel.

"Bow."

Zarus looked Eretimis in the eye. "Best start cutting."

The room stilled. The shadows swarmed from their corners, and the world around was left in monotony at the theft. Zarus stood as a statue; chin raised with an unbreakable stare. He saw the shift of the blade before he saw the shift of the demon. A whirlwind, mist and shadow converging in the blink of an eye. Warmth spilled from his cheek.

Sword in hand, Eretimis stood without a breath out of place. The grey blood on the sword's edge was the only indication he moved.

"I said *bow*."

Blood slid down Zarus's cheek. The scent of iron filled his nostrils. An instinct deep in the chasm of his mind told him to lash out, but he overpowered that side of himself long ago. He kept still, accepting the pain.

"Warnings won't do you any good."

"No, I suppose they will not. However, it is good to see that shell still holds up." Without another utterance, the light reflected once more, this time stabbing deep into Zarus's shoulder.

"Bow."

Anguish pierced into his muscle. Cold mixed with a blaze. Zarus did not step down. His arm strained, a stifle of tension that grew more persistent, but he held it down. Lifting his right hand, he grabbed the steel jutting out from his flesh, and drove it further in until the tip cut through the back of his shoulder. Grinding his teeth together, he barked, "Did I stutter?"

The steel drew back from his shoulder, pulling his body with it. Zarus's cheek numbed, his shoulder throbbing. A maelstrom of agony pulled him in, and he couldn't break free. Yet there he stood. His trembling hand pressed into the wound on his shoulder, blood and sweat lacing his body.

Eretimis grabbed the fresh wound with a suffocating grip and pulled him closer. Down drove the blade's steel into Zarus's upper leg. Slowly, steadily, the Tyrant sank the sword into the muscle. Twisting and turning, Zarus couldn't help his cry until Eretimis finally lowered the sword. Zarus nearly doubled over. His vision flared white.

He bit down on a snarl, gritting his teeth and flicked his watering eyes to the demon towering above him. "*I'm not finished y-yet,*" he grounded.

Eretimis mused at the sight, but his patience wore thin. "I can stand here for the rest of the day and remove your legs if I so desired, boy." He leaned in, just enough to cast a shadow over Zarus. "But you are of no use to me without them."

Zarus barked a laugh. "It looks like we've come to a standstill then." His shoulder numbed, his cheek burned, his leg felt like it was dissolving from the inside out, but Zarus never lowered himself to that floor.

"If that is the route you wish to take, I can arrange it. But," something akin to joy glistened in the Tyrant's eyes, if such a thing existed within him, "perhaps you would like to consider the well-being of that girl before you end your life." His voice fell low. "It would be distressing for her sake if you held dear to your pride."

Zarus's face ashened. "You—" he growled the word like an insult, "You—"

"Would not dare?" Eretimis looked at his victory and relaxed his smirk. "We both know it is a waste to ask, Zarus." He held out the sword at his side, the guard instantly appearing to retrieve it. Hands folded behind his back, the shadows of the room took back their place, and color returned to the frozen fortress. The phantom breeze picked up, freying the outline of the Dark Tyrant's silhouette into the shadows as he stood across from Zarus. "Bow before me."

Do not listen to his lies, young one—

Zarus cut the call short. There had been far too many conversations today. "*You bastard.*" His words cut through gritted teeth.

Eretimis waited.

Zarus Lowwenth slowly lowered to his knees, bowing facedown in his own blood.

Chapter Twelve

An explosion of steam simmered high from the middle of the lake.

Rin gritted her teeth, shouting from the dirt on the ground. "I said train with me, not try to kill me!" Sweat beaded down her body. She glanced at the violent bed of water.

"Were you *trying* to incinerate me?"

Tatsuo held his hands apologetically. A low whistle escaped his lips when he looked at the steam rising off the lake. "I didn't think it would be that strong."

Rin closed her eyes before they rolled to the back of her head. One calm exhale later, and she looked up at her friend. "It's good to see you working at full strength again," she smiled meekly, "but please don't burn me alive."

"That's as fair a request as ever," Tatsuo chuckled as the wind caught his braid. One stretch to the sky, and the dragon was twirling his spear from hand to hand, never once grazing the grass below. "Sorry, Erin, I'm still getting used to working at full capability again."

Her eyes narrowed. "It's Rin," she muttered before loosing a sigh and resting her hands in the grass. "I still can't believe this entire clearing is in the middle of the highlands," she mused. The Pit always turned into a field of beauty just after midday. The flowers glowed, the grass thrived, and the lake glimmered like a cave of gems beneath the sun.

"I certainly haven't seen anything like it before," Tatsuo agreed, taking in the stark walls towering around them. "Then again, there have been a lot of rare finds lately." He offered her a sympathetic look, and Rin couldn't help her huff.

She scrunched her knees to her chest. "What happened in the desert was a fluke."

"Then why are you going through all this trouble?" He slowly took a seat along the lakeshore, leaned in close, took one sniff, then waved the air away from his nostrils. "It leaves you smelling worse than Fuzz Face after he hunts."

Rin looked up and flicked the *narikaah's* nose. "If I smell so much worse, why don't you go back to Fuzz Face's company?" She leaned her arms back into the grass and closed her eyes.

"Have you met him? I'll take all the getaways I can muster."

Rin smirked. "Oh, so my mother knows about this excursion?"

It was at the mention of Luna that Tatsuo's expression fell. "I, uh... I mentioned I was stepping out." He scratched the back of his head with his talons, a shrug escaping his shoulders. "It doesn't seem to matter that I'm pretty much healed at this point. I thought she was about to break my legs when Feyne and I came back from sparring the other day."

Rin smiled. "Best to hobble back before she notices."

"I will soon enough for her to catch me, but..." his voice trailed, and she found his reptilian eyes falling on her. "I won't lecture you on the harmful ways of recklessness, Rin," he sighed, "but... don't get yourself killed in order to get results for something that can wait."

She pulled back her tangled hair. The ginger strands had been uncut for too long. "I understand I just started, but this training is a complete waste of time. Not for Gen, he seems to really be benefitting from Ma's instruction. But me? I feel like I'm playing pretend. Whatever happened in the desert, whatever I did... It was a onetime deal. I feel nothing I did that night, not while training. The most I get is a hum in my head when I'm holding back my temper. A memory that I'm losing the feeling of day after day." She wrapped her arms around her legs and buried her face in her knees.

Tatsuo sighed. "Rin, you really don't believe that, do you? You heard Luna and Feyne *and* Genesis tell you about white mages—what they're capable of. I mean, you brought me back from my deathbed. You're nothing short of untapped potential. And you brought Errogan to his knees."

Rin scowled at all the sense he was making. "Then why haven't I been able to cast any ounce of that potential?"

The *narikaah* shook his head. "Genesis has had seventy years to practice. With or without a teacher, that's enough time for anyone to explore their magic. Give it some time."

Rin rested her face on her knees. "I guess you're probably right. It's only been a month. I'm being ridiculous."

Tatsuo nodded matter-of-factly. "Exactly. Now," the dragon chimed, "I'm going to sneak back into the house before your terrifying mother ties me to it. Wish me luck, Nowell. Sorry for nearly torching you."

She couldn't help a grin. "Don't fret it... so long as you don't hit me." She straightened out and shrugged. "This is what I get for working overtime."

Tatsuo's eyebrows arched as he stood. "So I'm not going mad. It is your day off?"

"Aye, it is. I wanted to get in a bit more practice to make sure I remember it all."

"What's there to remember?"

"Well," Rin said as she knelt beside the lake and stirred the water with a finger, "Ma explained yesterday that since the heart fuels a human's magic, we can use our heartbeat as a sort of transmitter." She scooped up a handful of water and brought it to her lips. "The faster our heart pumps, the faster we'll be able to conduct the magic."

Tatsuo frowned, doubt hanging above those yellow-green eyes. "That sounds unreliable."

"Vastly," Rin assured. "But it's a start." Her shoulders rose in a disheartened shrug. "I haven't been able to summon anything, not even a flick of light. I'm trying anything at this point."

Tatsuo furrowed his brows in disbelief. "So when you said *don't hold back*, what you really meant was *fill me to the brim with fear and hope that stirs something?*"

Rin found the clouds soaring high above to be far more interesting than her friend's insinuation. "I don't know what you're talking about."

Concern weighed heavy in the *narikaah's* eyes. "Please don't hurt yourself, Rin."

Again, her gaze trailed away. "You're the one who almost torched me," she quietly reminded.

Finally, Tatsuo laughed. "Yes, yes, I did. But you jumped out of the way, so quit whining about it."

A wide grin spread across Rin's face as she hopped to her feet and followed Tatsuo toward the house. Afternoon studies commenced soon. What were they reading today, *Accounts and Queries of the Infamous?* The same leather-bound tome as yesterday. The same dry takes on the less than fortunate magic users who died at Eretimis's hand.

"You're right," she huffed. "I need to be patient with myself—"

The words severed from her tongue. A fatigue outweighing the afternoon heat and decay of the air suddenly smothered Rin's thoughts. She barely heard Tatsuo's panic as she hit the ground.

***

Her eyes were cast of lead. But that was all. No shiver ran through her spine, or grass bristled against her skin, or crashing of magic waves to indicate where she was. There was nothing.

She tried to stir her vision, but to as much avail as a mute bird's song. She didn't know whether her eyes were closed or open. It was nothing new, but a minor problem arose. The only tools at her disposal were her own thoughts. No matter how hard she tried to move her arms, stretch her legs, or blink her eyes, nothing stirred. It seemed the portal she had fallen into, faerie circle that trapped her, or any other happenstance explaining her situation, left her body behind. She couldn't even feel her own beating heart. Not in the numbing sense she had experienced recently through pain and exertion. It was simply as if she never had a body to begin with.

An ordinary human would have gone mad if they'd experienced half the shock as Rin. But she found herself curious instead. And a tad inconvenienced. She bit onto the side of her cheek, or would have if she had one to bite, and used her sole tool until she came up with something. A plea to Yath Ha, asking for a hint of what to do next. The gods thought it worth their time to listen for once.

The shadows around warped into haze, and haze warped into sight. Not her usual sight, not the vision from her eyes. This was the sight of an observer, a ghost. A looking glass formed before her, taking shape as though a current waded through the picture. Normally she would have approached to examine the picture suspended in darkness, but she also normally had legs. So Rin huffed another mental sigh as the picture slowly settled into clarity.

She gazed through the looking glass and found not the Pit where she had just been, but sunlight cutting through a canopy of trees. Strong and billowing in the winds, spanning high against the cloudless sky. Trees, wild and dense; a green thicket she had seen countless times.

A sob would have caught in her throat if such a thing were possible. There it was. *Her home.* The matted dirt road, chipped fences holding acres of tended lands, and smoke pluming out the chimneys far in the distance. If she were in control of the view, Rin would have turned around and looked for the river stretching far from the Lennaels behind. The people walking about, the animals perusing their fields... it was the same as it always had been. Aresan sat bustling in midday work, and all she could do was stare in bewilderment through a window, unable to grasp it.

"Why are you showing me this? Who are you?" she cried, shocked to hear her own voice cascade through the air; it ruptured like water crashing at the bottom of the falls. She received no answer, only a stir in the current.

In the blink of an eye, the scene faded. Or rather twisted. Corrupted. Cerulean skies faded black, not with the veil of night but the void of smoke. Smothered and choked by the greed of flames, spreading quickly through the tall grasses of farmland and paneled houses. That piercing hum bit into Rin's mind.

The sight was enough to find her body. Rin's throat stung with bile as her village burned. Blistering and festering with nothing to stop it. The river was close, but not close enough to keep the flames at bay. They were too high, too wild. She looked around Aresan, at the bodies scorched and the living frenzied into hysteria. Her heart found its place inside her chest, thundering her breath away. Yet nothing was as loud as the hum.

She couldn't do a damn thing, unable to reach the people who raised her, grew up with her. She could barely think past the panic, the horror, the sickness. A chill slithered up her spine, snaking around her neck until it choked out everything but the blaring of her mind.

Like glass shattering, Rin saw the current of the looking glass crack with a surge of her magic. It hit her core, moving out along her limbs. A flash of searing light wiped the burning away. She watched as that damning scene dissipated, turned to dust and then nothing. The void of shadow wrapped around her. She remained lost in the darkness. The image branded her mind, a visceral sickness Rin would never forget.

Chapter Thirteen

T he sun set, and a shadow had long since settled over the walls stretching high into the sky. Rin sat before the blazing hearth yet again. The fires of Aresan burned into her mind. The vision was still clear as the distant night sky. Yet, when she tried to explain how she woke up on the lakeshore with tears streaming down her cheeks, she could not force herself to speak.

"Erin…" her mother calmly pressed from her chair, "please, *please*, tell us what's going on." This was the first time Rin heard her mother plead. "We can't help if you keep it from us."

A warm hand suddenly slipped over her fist. "We're here for you," Tatsuo offered. He smiled, but she could see his concern through it.

How on Armiria would she even begin? She laid her eyes on the paths of her home that afternoon—those burning, ashen paths. Rin swallowed hard, an effort against her parched tongue.

A bold voice arose from the back of the room, where the fire's touch wasn't so warm. "It's not only your magic, is it?"

She looked to Genesis. Her face paled, and a sickly churn built in her core. Slowly, she nodded.

Feyne spoke from where he sat. "We've dealt with worse, Erin, we'll figure this one out too." It was an involuntary glare that escaped her. She bit down on the urge to tell the shifter not to call her that, but only caught her glower when she saw the grin spanning his face. Against her better judgment, a sigh of a laugh slipped her lips, but a laugh nonetheless.

As it usually goes when a bottle cracks open, everything spills out. The plethora of unusual dreams she'd had lately, and the voice that entwined her thoughts for over a month.

"Why didn't you tell anyone?" Genesis asked.

Rin shrugged. "I thought it was from the stress until now." Recalling the events was no easy feat. What truly unnerved her was when Feyne's warm complexion drained. His eyes focused on the flames incinerating the wood in the hearth.

Feyne's voice was little more than a whisper. "The gods themselves tried to warn us..." Rin raised question, but his ghostly voice continued. "The dream, the one before Base burned down..." his hardened eyes turned to meet her, "I had a similar one."

"That's why you were so frantic before we left..." Rin whispered. The image of that night burst in her mind.

"I thought the nightmare was only my worry of leaving... but when you told me about yours, I knew it meant something." His golden eyes closed. "I should have listened to them."

You're telling me... Rin thought. "Feyne, there was no way you could have known something like that was going to happen—"

"But it did." And there it was. The pain that had been bustling right below the surface all these weeks. His voice bit hard, his eyes strained tighter. He leaned forward into his knees. "It *did* happen, and the gods themselves tried to warn me! And I didn't listen." Sorrow streamed down his face, no more than a plea now. "I should have listened, Rin."

A trembling silence stilled the room. His eyes were still closed, elbows still leaning into his knees, but he whispered. "I had suspicion," he began, hand resting on his forehead. "Someone in Base had been leaking information to Eretimis."

Rin's stomach twisted.

"What made you think this?" Luna's voice was sharper than an asp's bite.

The shifter was silent. He sat upright, wiping his face. "Four months ago, Scarlette found a demon watching one entrance while she was on patrol." A weak grin slipped past his forced solemnity. "Human, demon, shifter, fae—no one slipped past Scarlette's bow. She stripped his weapons, bound him, blindfolded him, then dragged the demon down into one of the remote corners of the bunker for questioning. It was the dead of night. No one else was awake. She walked away from him to fetch me; not even five minutes had passed. When we both returned, the demon's bindings were loose on the floor and a knife was in his hands. His throat was cut open."

Genesis shifted in his seat. "Why would she leave him alone? Even if it was to get you, there's still the possibility he would escape."

Feyne snapped. "Don't talk about matters you know nothing of."

Genesis held his tongue. He glanced at Rin. "Base was a maze," she explained. "Even if he freed himself from the ties, he never would have found his way out without running into someone."

"There wasn't a blade in that room," Feyne added. "Scar never would have left one on him. The only way he got one was if someone placed it there while she ran to get me." He took a deep, exhausted breath. "It looked like a suicide, everyone else believed it to be, but there's no way it could have been. He was bound, weaponless. Someone cut that throat—one of us."

"And you didn't think to raise this concern to anyone?" Tatsuo asked.

Feyne nodded. "I shared it with Scarlette. I trusted her with my life and knew it wasn't her. Telling anyone else was too risky until we investigated it."

"Did you at least discover who the traitor was, or did you decide to bring my daughter to an infiltrated organization, anyway?"

"Mother!" Rin chided. Her hard eyes pierced into Feyne, but he did not falter beneath them.

"We never figured it out. I rushed Rin to Base so she could tell Scar and I everything she knew about Eretimis and hope we could use it to find our traitor. And now, there's little I can do about it."

Rin fell silent, biting the inside of her cheek. "The other members of Base? The ones spread about the continent."

"That's the little," Feyne huffed, but something of a snarl flickered in his expression. "I'm going to find them and figure out who caused this."

She couldn't quell the hesitation in her voice. "Where will you start?"

"An ally of mine is in Xandra."

A pang of sadness twinged through Rin's chest. Feyne was leaving, albeit to hunt for the person who sold him out.

"Maybe you should go with him, Rin."

She blinked once. Twice. She looked at Tatsuo. "Excuse me, but what business do I have in *Xandra*?" The city ridden with crime and brewing in violence.

"Well," the dragon yawned, "if you really think these are visions sent by the gods, then maybe you should go to Olru and E'ral's temple and ask about it."

The words trudged through her mind, thick and heavy. "Is that what you really think these are? Messages from Yath Ha?" She glanced around the room.

Genesis shrugged. "They could be anything, from the gods to hallucinations from all the sleep you've been missing lately." He leaned into his steepled hands. "Given the circumstances, I'd say it's best to bet Olru and E'ral would like a word with you."

"There's nothing else it could be," Feyne stated.

Perhaps it wasn't the worst idea... if the gods were trying to communicate with her, then why wouldn't she seek them out in the Temple of the Divine? Rin turned to the only one who hadn't answered. "Mother?"

Her lilac eyes stared wide. "How foolish can you children be?"

Tatsuo furrowed his brow. "You realize you're the second youngest in this room, right?"

"Please tell me exactly how we are being foolish?" Genesis scoffed. "The Temple of the Divine has deep roots leading to Yath Ha. It's the logical place to expect an answer."

Luna caught his glare and looked right back as if he were a rowdy teenager. "You're telling Erin to travel across the kingdom already crawling with demons—further north, mind you—while Eretimis is searching far and wide for her, simply on the hunch she might get answers from gods who have been silent for centuries."

"No one is telling her to do anything, Luna," Feyne mediated. "Tatsuo suggested."

Luna's narrow stare dug into Feyne. She was still outraged that the shifter risked bringing Rin to Base. "And does that change the integrity of the asinine idea?"

Tatsuo, to Rin's surprise, spoke calmly. "We would be at her side the entire way, Ms. Nowell. She would be safe—"

"What? So she would make it half a day before Eretimis's hunters find her and drag her to his fortress? How long were you able to hold back Eretimis's hunters at Base!"

Luna's firm resolve was tested as Tatsuo tried to reason, Genesis offered sharp contrasts, and Feyne's temper snapped. Shouts roared, fighting over the idea that Rin might leave for the kingdom's new capital to speak to the gods that haven't responded to anyone in years. An argument about Rin's life that no one gave Rin herself a chance to comment on. And steadily, it crept upon the cottage. That deathly feel to the air; decay and rot. As gradually as water starting to boil. No one noticed it except Rin, too busy in their shouts. It sat heavy, thick as cobwebs in her lungs. Her head dulled. Her heart pounded. Until something inside her stirred.

"*Enough*!" Rin's voice thundered, and when she glanced around, she found all eyes settled on her.

"Would you stop talking about me like I'm not here, and maybe—just *maybe*—ask what *I* think about this plan?" She cast them all an unfaltering stare, one that silenced everyone. At last, Rin let loose a hefty sigh, pulling her hair out of her eyes. "What makes any of you think you have the right to make this decision for me?"

Her mother's voice still had an edge to it. "Erin, I'm only trying to—"

"To what?" Rin bit back. "Tell me what I can and cannot do? Make me stay here in this plateau with you for the rest of my life?"

She saw the shift in her mother's expression, the upright nerve of her daughter speaking back to her, but Luna caught her ire. She proceeded in a softer tone. "It's safe here, Erin. No one's discovered me here—"

"Feyne did. You told me he met you because he found demons searching the highlands—searching for *you*." Her mother opened her mouth to protest, but Rin didn't let her. "You don't think I'm planning on staying here forever, do you? I have a life outside this hole, a father who is probably worried to *death* that I didn't return home over a month ago, and a friend I have to save from a psychopath's fortress! People I need to *avenge*!"

That last word acted as a knife in her mother's side. "Do not talk to me about vengeance, Erin Nowell. Do you think I haven't had friends dragged to that fortress? That I haven't *watched* them slaughtered in cold blood, unable to do a damned thing about it?" Luna's eyes narrowed, the fine lines of her face directing fire. "Why do you think I hide alone?"

Rin barely resisted the urge to laugh. Twelve years of confusion, twelve years of mourning. The fire blared behind, heating her back and casting dastardly shadows before her. "That's just it! That's exactly what you do here: hide. You sit down here and live your life in fear and do nothing about it; I understand that, I've lived the better part of my life that way!" Heat traveled along her limbs. Her mother's eyes widened. The healer parted her lips, but Rin did not stop, not with the thrum of pressure and heat straining her body.

"I'm sick of living that way! I'm done hiding, and I'm finished being a *coward*!" All it took was one moment. One little second of a loose temper. The magic shattered her mind and flooded into the cottage.

A light, blinding and white, exploded in the center of the house. A shockwave of energy flowed from her body in all directions. The fire surged with the pressure. Everyone tumbled back, but unlike the last time, the flicker of light faded the moment she sucked in a gasp. Blinded by light one moment, and dark the next. The fire burned out. By the time she caught her breath, Rin found the room a mess. The others weren't much better. Her mother least of all.

Wet gasps welled and drained from her lungs against the prevalent decay, but Rin found her voice through her teeth. "I am finished with that life because it's not a life worth living. I'm going to the temple in

Xandra. I'll ask Yath Ha what they are showing me directly, and then I'm heading north."

Tears lined her mother's eyes. "Erin, please... you will find nothing but death there. That demon is not worth killing yourself over!"

Rin stared at her mother. It was a face she carved into her memory as a child, one she swore never to forget, but now? When she looked at it now, she saw a stranger.

"You told me the first night I was here that you changed your name to Luna to hide in a life of isolation." She swallowed nothing but dryness. Exhaled slowly as sorrow twinged her throat, but she only narrowed her eyes. "I look at you, and I see nothing of Cissrey Nowell. The woman who told me to hold my chin high against any hardship—to square my shoulders and take conflict head on. She's gone. You're just a ghost of who she used to be."

Chapter Fourteen

B rooding clouds gathered in the high azure of Death's Yard. Rin looked into the grey stain, but she had no luck piercing through the veil.

How lucky we should be. Our third day out, and already we've beaten chance and hit rain in the wasteland.

Rin didn't know what she expected, but it certainly wasn't rain. According to Feyne, the last time it rained was months before in the spring. The chill was to be expected, in fact, Rin welcomed the winter with open arms. But rain? *That's one season too early,* she thought, as the first droplet fell from the heavens and hit her nose.

***

"Are you sure about this?" the shifter asked as he prowled across the field.

The moonlight shimmered on the lake, casting the world in a monotonous shade. Something in between dream and reality. Rin gazed upon it from the Pit's cave they'd stumbled through all those weeks ago. A brisk nod was her only response.

"Rin, you haven't even come close to gaining control over your magic yet... perhaps it wouldn't be the worst thing to stay here a little longer and figure things out."

"That woman used to make the world quake with only a glance." She flicked a sidelong look toward Feyne, to the bruise already forming along his jaw. To think she threw them all back without lifting a finger... She looked ahead.

"There's nothing I can learn here. I want to, I truly do, but all I'll gain in this pit is the knowledge my mother is gone."

A moment of silence; the draft from behind picking up her hair in the pause.

"You don't know that. There's still a lot to be found in that woman."

She considered this.

"Perhaps, but I know my efforts will be wasted here. They're better placed elsewhere, at least for now, while she figures herself out."

"I might have to agree with you there." A waxy quiet clogged her ears until Feyne sighed. "Look, I know what I was saying in there..." She cast him another glance. "You're right; I shouldn't have decided for you. I was caught up in myself. There are other options we can consider, other paths. Aresan is closer than Xandra. If you truly wanted, we could take you there instead. You could explain things to your father and explore your magic in a more suited environment." He frowned ever so slightly.

"Xandra is cleaner than it was eleven years ago, but it's by no means the safest place, nor the most discreet place to practice magic... The temple will be there in a few months, a few years even. There's no reason to rush across the kingdom right now, especially when you're a target of interest."

Rin mulled over this option, but she already made her decision.

"I won't risk bringing death upon my father." She let out a loud sigh, unfolding her arms despite the coolness of the night. "That voice—the gods or whoever it is—the messages they send. They're urgent." She shook her head, tracing her gaze to the opening at the top of the four walls, to the sliver of moon visible.

"I don't think I can afford to sit by and wait it out. A part of me fears only suffering will come from that. I can't imagine what my mother has gone through in the last twelve years, but I can't give her what she needs right now. Not while I have so many others relying on me. Xandra is my best bet for finding answers. I need to go to the Temple of the Divine and ask Olru and E'ral what they're trying to warn me of."

"I understand." Feyne said, although the exasperated roll of his eye was quick to follow. "I suppose Mr. Cryptic and Lizard Breath will want to accompany us as well."

Despite herself, a smile escaped. "Like it or not, you're stuck with us all for a while longer, Fuzz Face."

She expected a snarky quip in return, but he merely grinned. Perhaps he didn't want to go alone either. Rin inhaled a deep breath, crisp as the frost she still had nightmares about. But the decay remained. Her expression fell grim.

"Do you feel it too? The death in the air."

***

Sopping wet and wishing the sun would shine through the gloom, Rin adjusted the blanket her mother insisted she take over her shoulder. Luna and Rin had barely spoken since the outbursts three days ago.

Rin wished to apologize, but her mother was different the morning they left. Hollow, cold. Not toward Rin, but the world around.

"Rin, watch out—!"

Into the ditch she stepped.

Rin picked her foot out of the muddy divot in the earth. At least her boot stretched up most of her calf. She turned to the dragon beside her and smiled at him through the rain.

"Thanks."

Her hair plastered to her forehead, her clothes drenched down to the fiber. Rin wasn't too bothered by the sludge of mud already washing away. Having only grazed into Death's Yard this morning, Feyne said they would likely take three days to reach the forest below the Lennaels, but the rain was slowing them down.

The forest—the destined place of paths separated, friends introduced, and nightmares met. It seemed only the other day that the shifter swept Rin off her feet, swinging her away from certain demise. What would have happened if Errogan took her to the fortress? Would they have found her magic like they did with Genesis, or would it have hidden itself from them much as it did from her? She supposed it was pointless asking. Well, perhaps not entirely. That all depended on whether the gods broke an era of silence once she stood in the halls of the Divine. They were her last hope.

The patter of rain on the stream nearby rang endlessly, soothing minds weary from the day's trek. No one admitted it, but they had grown used to the comforts of a roof, of a bed. Tatsuo was still healing, but no matter how hard she tried, Rin couldn't summon forth one drop of her magic to further the body's natural process.

'Our abilities allow us to stitch together what has been torn asunder, but bodies are fickle. Sometimes they want to be stubborn and cling onto what's natural to them.'

Death. At least, that's what Rin assumed Luna had meant when she'd asked her mother why Tatsuo wouldn't heal completely.

The rain pattered. Rin didn't think it would ever stop.

Part Two

Tidings

J.E. Elliott

Chapter Fifteen

Thud. The wall rumbled. *Thud.* Once, twice, thrice. Zarus banged his forehead against the mantle of the hearth without pause.

Two worlds, five races, a plethora of languages, and he still had the sour luck to be assigned the chattiest guards in the entirety of Eretimis's forces. Perhaps that's why they were stationed outside his room; all the way in the far reaches of the fortress, away from everyone who had a say.

"Okay, but what about Far'Shei?"

"From the training hall?"

"Yes."

"She'd flog your ass before you ever laid a hand on her."

"You know, that doesn't sound so bad…"

Three hours. Three hours since the last shift change, and Zarus had been counting down the minutes until the next.

I admit I haven't been the most respectful of you damn deities, but this? Cruel.

Zarus rubbed his temples. Either the gods or Eretimis were laughing hysterically right then, and he had the secure opinion that both of them could go to the lower levels of Ashnagz and stick a thumb somewhere better left unsaid.

For Rin's sake, he had been rather well-behaved these last few weeks. He hadn't glowered at the maids who came into his quarters twice a day, interrupting his meditations to spy. He hadn't let his tongue slip when the Twins thought he could spend some more time in the war room behind the throne, where that damn voice insisted on whispering nonsense in his mind. Hadn't even said a word since that last conversation with Eretimis. To anyone. If a loose temper meant Rin's torture, then he would hold his temper. But this? This was a match igniting what little temper he had left.

"Okay, I think I'd start with Hiran from—"

Zarus's lips twitched. He stormed across the room, hand lifting to pound on the door and demand some *semblance* of silence. But he didn't get the chance.

"Eh, the rest are better off lit by a quiver of burning arrows," the other guard said, exhausted of the topic herself. "Anyway, have you heard any news of that human in the fortress?"

Wonderful. Gossip—a slap in the face to go with it. The curses were already forming on his tongue.

"Not other than they've been here for some time now, a few months, right?"

"Something like that. Kind of foolish to have 'em here if you ask me."

"Why's that?"

Zarus's teeth ground together. Rin Nowell was a prisoner, what more reason was there to keep her here? *Damn foolish stains of life on—*

"Well, why would his liege suddenly recruit a petty human to join our ranks?"

Zarus blinked.

"Don't get me wrong," the demon went on from the other side of the door, "I understand he was the main reason that shifter's resistance is no longer around to bite us in the ass, but was a *human* really necessary for that?"

He had to have misheard. A *human* working for Eretimis?

"I heard he's not even a user, just some nobody out of thin air. Although he's organizing something in Xandra. Trying to gather allies, I suppose. That's why His Majesty summoned Hraesah's general too."

Zarus was glad to be hidden behind a door. He wiped the dumbfounded shock from his face and walked to the window looking over the dead land. A human working for Eretimis, one the bastard willingly took in. And what of a resistance?

He sucked in a heavy breath, resting his forearm against the wall. The brittle dark oaks in the distance rattled in the surging winds. Eretimis was grasping for straws, or a more sour thought, he had gained even more influence over the two worlds. The former didn't stand with the Dark Tyrant's reputation too well. Zarus rapped his knuckles against the stone wall.

Only one way to find out, I suppose...

***

The knife cut deep, but not as deep as he was expecting. That was Zarus's first clue that something was wrong.

Errogan looked ashen, wan, a ghostly penumbra to his eyes with bags hanging beneath. Silence wrapped his tongue, and a weight slouched his shoulders. It could have been written off as a few lousy nights of sleep, but the cut into Zarus's forearm? That's where it became clear. For it was not the slice of his arm, but the fact *Erro-*

gan was the one collecting a vial of a *prisoner's* blood. Not one of the lower guards—not even this human supposedly working for the demons—but Errogan. Eretimis's right hand. Zarus had noticed the strain before, noticed the tension wrapping Errogan when he walked into the throne room during a few of Zarus's summons. But this—this unnatural silence clinging to the demon's lips—was a new level of unsettling. What turned this demon away from the Tyrant's favor so suddenly?

"Why don't you leave?" Zarus finally asked. Errogan flicked his gaze to him as he capped the glass vial, no snide remark or taunt quick in his throat. Just nothing.

Zarus didn't think he would get a reply today, but by some miracle, Errogan said in a hush foreign to him, "It's not that easy."

"Not that I've found," Zarus scoffed, perhaps trying a little too hard to lighten the mood for once in his life. "All it took was thinking you had died tragically. I found that the front door was the best door to slam." He shrugged, pressing down on the fresh cut on his forearm. Barely even a knick.

Eretimis was a bastard, maybe even the strongest bastard out there, but a bastard nonetheless. Zarus knew it right away, figured it out the moment he met the demon all those years ago when humanity first betrayed him. Zarus was only ever a pawn, a player made to be used. Errogan was different. He didn't see the Tyrant for what he was, the manipulation he wielded like a knife. Or perhaps he did, he simply idolized him anyway. Loyal to his last drop of blood. But maybe that wasn't enough. Pawns were still pawns, and maybe Errogan had finally learned.

Errogan said nothing. He stared at the crimson rolling around the vial. "You've always been terrible at optimism," he sighed. "Foolishness seems to be your forte, though."

"Dumbassery was always your strong suit," Zarus smiled at the white-haired demon. It was one step out of line. Remembrance of his resentment clicked into place like gears of a trapdoor, and down he fell.

"Shove your pity down below, Zarus," Errogan snapped. His hand clenched around the vial as it dropped to his side. "Unlike you, I'm here because I'm strong enough to stand my ground. All you've ever done is run."

Zarus considered this. "Perhaps you're right. Perhaps I've become rather good at getting away from situations I don't favor, such as a mad bastard trying to use me as his puppet. More than once, at that." He dropped his hand from the clotted gash. "At least I don't pout around, insulted by trivial tasks that are a waste of my skill."

A humorless laugh escaped Errogan's lungs. "Not anymore, old friend."

"Be that as it may," Zarus said, pacing toward the window's frigid draft. Ice danced on the tips of his fingers, stretching up to his wrist as he walked. "You seem as trapped as I do."

He heard the shift in Errogan's stance. His mouth opened to protest, but Zarus waved off the denial, a tail of frost trailing behind the motion. "And I know, I know, *we're not the same,*" he imitated the demon. "You've said it enough to send me to Hraesah's asylum."

The tranquil prick of speechlessness ensued. Long enough that Zarus glanced over his shoulder. He found crystal eyes cemented on the wooden floor, a mountain of thoughts piling higher and higher. Zarus didn't suppose he'd get any more from that conversation, so he went onto other things.

"Why are you robbing me of my blood this time?"

Errogan shuttered out of his daze. "Testing. Eretimis wants to see if it'll respond well to something."

The thought of being subjected to another serum sent Zarus's blood boiling. He didn't bother trying to hide the sickening notion. But no mockery followed.

"Be grateful he didn't decide to test organ tissue," Errogan warned. Something akin to exasperation simmered in his sigh rather than the usual vicious delight. He was exhausted, that much was clear enough. With nothing more to say, Errogan stuck the vial of blood into his pocket, then turned and headed for the door.

"You better hope that human's life was worth it, Zarus," his old friend muttered from beneath the doorway. "Dark things are coming, things you've signed up for. Nothing short of a miracle is going to get you out of it."

Zarus faced the demon. The words were loud and clear in the otherwise silent room. "What's his goal in all of this? What could he possibly be searching for?"

Something he had been wondering for a while. He shook his head; the search for Rin, draining of his magic, *centuries* spent pillaging and burning temples and shrines and villages throughout the world. All for what? What went beyond havoc? What was the purpose?

Perhaps it was the exhaustion dulling his intuition, or perhaps it was the same reason he had barely snapped at Zarus at all, but Errogan glanced over his shoulder to meet his old friend's vulnerable stare. "Do you remember that temple we found over four centuries ago? Damn place was tucked in the middle of nowhere, only that magic user inside to defend it."

Zarus huffed his humor. "I remember you making us jump off the cliff to get away from the human's attack, and wanting to kick Eretimis's teeth in for not telling us a caster was inside." The temple where they were sent to dig up information about magic users on Armiria. The temple where Errogan found the silver sword and dagger. The temple they didn't know was a temple until they got inside, and saw the stories told through illustrations on the walls.

The shadow in Errogan's eye subsided, replaced with a sly spark. "I made a trip back there recently, you know. The history of us mortals on the walls was fascinating. Wouldn't you agree?"

Zarus held his stare a moment. Errogan faced forward, but before he could shut the door, Zarus remembered one last thing.

"I hear there's a human in your ranks now," he said, careful not to sound too curious. "There was a time when I thought Eretimis would rather give up his reign in Eroz than side with those of Armiria."

Errogan tensed. The muscles in his neck grew taut, his shoulders holding a bit too square. "So did I," he growled, slamming the door hard enough for the wood to groan.

Chapter Sixteen

F ilth and grime covered the roads. The establishments looked branded by the flames of Vulyn's smite, and most of the people could have sent children wailing—their stench most of all. Shouts and curses echoed through the streets, among pleading vagrants and slurring drunkards and everything in between.

The tales of Xandra's infamy had been watered down so greatly Rin was practically treading through the runoff ever since they arrived.

The trek through southwestern Nokomic had been a tedious one. The greenery of the forest was a lovely sight, but the whimsy hadn't lasted long. Stuffed with brush and shrouded in mist, the thick wood concealed all. Sounds of shifting branches kept Rin awake most nights. However, the earthy stench of the soil and soft forest bed took her back to Aresan enough to warm her memory. All until that horrid vision of her home burning came to mind.

Feyne made the executive decision to ban all campfires at night once they left the forest for fear of attracting Eretimis's hunters. They traveled off road and stopped here and there in small villages. Although the villagers were kind enough to exchange supplies for work, none of them trusted the odd group of travelers passing through. The work kept them stagnant for a day and a half, but the supplies they gathered lasted them for the next week. Working for resources every few days kept them moving through the countryside. Some gave them money, some clean water, some refused them all together. And after each laborious day, Rin kicked back and watched the sky under the moon's pale light until she dozed off before dawn when the others rose.

Unlike the fallen city of Zelenia, a legendary wall did not guard Xandra. The city appeared gradually. Rin assumed they were getting close as farms appeared along the road in closer proximity to one another over the last day. Houses were distant and spaced at first, but the closer they drew in, the more cramped the living quarters became—dirt roads turning to cobblestone in no time. The farmlands along the roads were primarily empty. Harvesting season had come to an end, and winter was around the corner.

"It certainly has an aroma strong enough to keep us covered, eh?" Tatsuo mused as they walked through a narrow alleyway.

"Aye," Rin agreed.

After a month and a half of snaking their way through the wilds of Nokomic, they had next to no money left from their barters. Yet Feyne had been dragging them to and from taverns all day since their arrival. He led them through stingy roads and between buildings to avoid unwanted eyes. Not only those of demons anymore, either. The Resurrection, though pushed back by the New Light, still roamed the city. The organization's attention was not one to be sought after. Even Rin understood that.

It was Genesis who broke the city's unsilent silence, wearily watching the windows overhead. "Shouldn't we head to the temple? Xandra is big, but not as large as Zelenia. We could walk there before night draws too late."

Rin shook her head. "We should find a place to sleep first and figure out which areas of the city are safe to walk through."

Tatsuo half-glanced over his shoulder at her. "I think we'd be able to fend for our lives, Red." He twirled his fingers in the air the way he did when flames danced on their tips.

"As do I," Feyne added, "but fights bring attention, attention brings rumors, and rumors bring demons." He strode past the alley's edge and stopped where it opened onto the main street. The chill in the air kept most Xandrans indoors, but a few clusters of people littered the doors of taverns and businesses. None of them paid mind to the colorful party gathered in the shadows. "Learning a few rumors before we announce our presence may benefit us." He cast Tatsuo a wry glance, clapping the *narikaah* on the back.

Tatsuo's expression fell flat. "Is it hard to be this much of a pain? I would assume the displeasure of knowing you rubs off on yourself as well."

Rin let out an exasperated sigh, pinching the bridge of her nose. "Lhaerem's sake, would you two quit it and get on with the makeup kiss already?"

"I'd rather make advances on the fellow pissing on that brick wall over there," Tatsuo scoffed, gesturing to the drunk of topic—who was promptly interrupted by a round woman poking her head out of the building, whipping out a broomstick and slamming it into the back of the man's head. The nasty fellow didn't even have his pants up before he scrambled away.

Rin couldn't help but lose herself in a twisted reverie. She was finally in the big city, and it was just as her father described.

"I don't know; running about bare-ass like a headless chicken... he seems like your type," Feyne suggested. "You might lose your only chance at true love, Tat."

Feyne cast Tatsuo a lazy grin, Tatsuo opened his mouth to counter, and Rin was being robbed of her last remaining brain cell when Genesis spoke.

"So, how do you plan to get ahead of these rumors?" he asked Feyne, stepping between him and Tatsuo.

Throughout the entire month and a half they spent trekking through Nokomic, Feyne never explained what he intended to do in the city. He hadn't said anything else on the matter since that night in the cottage.

"My ally might help us with that."

Still not a friend. Rin couldn't help but frown at the idea of seeking guidance from someone Feyne didn't completely trust. "Where can we find this *ally*?"

"Depends on the day."

Rin's nose twitched with annoyance. They had been walking all day and night, not stopping to rest since the sun before yesterday. Now Feyne intended to search around Xandra until they found whoever it was that could help them. She held the groan tight in her throat. "Where do we start?"

Feyne smiled, and although she wanted to punch it right off his face, the expression eased her heart a bit. She still trusted him, and if he said this mystery person could help them, then she would believe him.

"This fine establishment right here," he said, gesturing in one wide sweep of the arm to the building that Tatsuo's bare-ass soulmate just relieved himself on.

Rin's heart sank a little, Tatsuo arched his brow in disbelief, and Genesis held his attention on the clouds growing overhead.

This is going to be a long day. Pinching the bridge of her nose, Rin suddenly felt it. That prod at her mind. She turned back, looking down the desolate alleyway, and found nothing but puddles and locked doors. A shift of the wind? It could have been the case, but her frown deepened. The hum in the back of her head put her on edge.

Single file, they walked through the narrow doorway of the tavern. Rin's eyes took a moment to adjust to the dim depths of the establishment. The room was small, dank, and smelled of rotting meat and stew. Thick smoke lined the air, and Rin's lungs spasmed upon the first inhale of the sweet fumes. Her head swayed with the chorus of conversation and tune of song. It may have been the middle of the afternoon, but more than enough people swarmed the warm hall; sitting or standing, talking or cheering. It was lively enough to lift some of the dread from her heart.

Feyne closed the door behind them. "You go find a table," he said, though his eyes lingered elsewhere. "I'll be over in a minute."

Without another word, the shifter prowled through the crowds near the bar until he met a group of men sitting in the back of the tavern. They looked less than eager to be greeted, but none tried to attack Feyne. They allowed him a seat and a conversation that was drowned by the sea of people.

Rin was the first to move. Her thoughts grew murky, her vision hard to keep up with. She found the only open table near a window and promptly cracked it open. A breeze of frigid fresh air bade off the warm heat of the tavern's smog. Before she even realized it, Tatsuo and Genesis were sitting down on the edges of the bench. Neither of them looked half as bad as she felt. She rested her head against the back of the bench.

She wondered what Zarus was doing at that moment. He had been imprisoned for almost three months. Her nose scrunched at the idea that she was about to go into the Temple of the Divine and ask Olru and E'ral what to do. The two gods who hadn't responded to any mortal in centuries that suddenly spoke in her head. And her father—oh, how she longed to see her father. But she wouldn't drag any of these dangers home.

Rin opened her eyes to find Genesis sitting back down. When had he left? The mug in his hand sparked her interest.

"Water," Genesis said, taking his hand and wrapping her own around the cup. "It should help clear your head a little." Rin stared down at the liquid with searching eyes. "Don't worry, I made sure it was clean."

"To whom did you promise a date to ensure that?" Tatsuo teased.

Genesis shrugged. "You must admit, I'm quite stunning when I'm not starved and covered in seventy years worth of dungeon." He then returned to Rin. "Eat this too. It's been a while since you had anything." He dropped a piece of stale bread into her other hand.

She gladly accepted. Honestly, the sight of food dampened her eyes. They ran out of their supply two nights ago, and everyone seemed too keen on finally getting into the city to stop and hunt. Rin regretted it since breakfast time yesterday. She devoured it in moments, wiping the crumbs from her face by the time Feyne waltzed to their table. He frowned.

"She's not here," he sighed.

She. At least that's something about their mystery ally. "Did you expect her to be here?" Rin asked, sipping the water. Her head already felt better.

The shifter shrugged, taking a seat and pushing Tatsuo aside. "It was a long shot, but those gentlemen over there gave me some information to assist our search." Rin glanced to find the group Feyne left belching and spitting onto the floor.

Genesis lifted his brow. "And what did these gentlemen say?"

"She's found at the taverns south of here this time of day. And that we should be careful on the streets. There have been a number of disappearances lately."

Tatsuo shoved Feyne out of his personal space. "Are we allowed to know anything about this lady, or are you keeping your usual shroud of vagueness?"

Feyne contemplated this for a moment. He was tired and preferred to speak only when necessary lately. With a soft exhale, the shifter dubbed it worth his time.

"Kah'Vi," he said. "She's an acquaintance who deals in secrets. We've known each other for years, relaying information if we ever run across one another. She typically hangs around Xandra, but sometimes ventures elsewhere around the continent. I'm glad she's been seen recently."

"What sort of information?" Rin asked.

"She keeps me updated on what the demons are doing these days."

A round of suspicious glances exchanged around the table. Feyne held up his hands innocently. "Trust me, she's not one to rat us out to Eretimis."

"Is she a human?" Tatsuo asked.

"No."

"Shifter?"

Feyne shook his head again. "Not a demon either."

Rin sighed out her exasperation, rubbing her temples. "If she's not human, shifter, or demon, then what is she?"

Feyne wiped some of the exhaustion out of his eyes. "Vi is a fae."

"Excuse me?" Tatsuo blurted. "You're trusting a *fae* not to turn her back on you?"

"What's the big deal?" Genesis asked.

Feyne shrugged.

The dragon rolled his eyes. "Haven't you ever heard stories about the fae? Aren't you worried about accidentally selling your soul?"

Feyne yawned. "No, but I understand how you might be fooled out of yours."

Rin failed to contain her yawn. "Tatsuo, do you have something against the fae?"

Of course, Rin had heard stories of the fae folk. They were human tales, yes, and most likely limited by human knowledge, but she was well aware of their tricky nature. Stories of people walking into fae territory by accident for a five minute stroll and walking out ten years later. Buried in nature and carefree. And dangerous to mingle with. However, Rin had also heard similar tales about demons.

Tatsuo flicked his hand out passively. "Not typically, but I don't like the idea of placing our safety in their hands at this particular moment." He shifted his disapproving stare to Feyne. "That's why he didn't tell us anything about her."

Feyne nodded. "Clearly there's prejudice. I figured I'd tackle that boar when I got to it."

Rin parted her lips to speak, but it was Genesis who started first. "With due reason, I would think." He exchanged a solemn stare with Tatsuo, then returned to Feyne. "The fae are nothing short of infamous in human myths; we had quite a few in Zelenia growing up. While I agree generalizations aren't becoming, I *do* think that we need to be cautious of whom we trust given our circumstances." He paused for a moment, slipping into thought. "Are the fae in allegiance with Eretimis?"

Feyne hesitated, his doubt translating to Rin's face as well. "To my knowledge, Eretimis only has allegiance from his fellow demons, and he has not yet swayed the fae's favor on Eroz. Demons and fae—they don't get along too well."

Rin crinkled her nose. *Did the demons get along with anyone?*

Tatsuo's concerns were well placed, but that didn't change their situation. She stared at nothing in particular as she spoke.

"Something tells me that the days of exchanging work for supplies are over. We have no money. We can't stay on the streets, and we can't go around asking strangers we don't trust for charity. I think luck would be more in our favor to trust Kah'Vi because Feyne says we can trust her."

Genesis yawned, stretching his back as well as he could on the wooden bench. "I assume the bit about fae dealing in trades didn't get lost in translation. What do we have to offer for her help?"

A chuckle escaped Feyne's throat. "Well, it depends." He smiled at them all, hands folding atop the table as he leaned into it. "Similar to Hot Flakes, here," a fine nod toward Tatsuo, "Vi is a bit of a wild card as opposed to her kind's typical nature. While I agree that some fae are bastards who won't think twice about stabbing you in the back if a better deal comes along, not all are like that. Vi is both. If she likes you, she most likely won't turn on you. If she finds you as an annoyance, then better watch your back." He shrugged. "So far, I haven't been an annoyance."

"Is she deaf?"

Feyne ignored Tatsuo. "Think of her as a rogue. She may or may not ask for something in return. It depends on who you are."

Rin pondered for a moment. "What's her motivation in giving you information?"

"Amusement."

She frowned. "Come again?"

"She sees the war with Eretimis as an inconvenience, and doesn't concern herself with it often. The demons make life more difficult for her in her travels, so she keeps tabs on them. She gives me those tabs when we run into each other because she knows I usually give Eretimis's demons a hard time. She's rather neutral."

"And you don't think that neutrality can be bought?" Rin was less certain by the second.

"I'm positive. Unbiased as she may be, she and I are still relatively close."

There wasn't an ounce of doubt in his expression. Feyne trusted this fae. Rin closed her eyes and took a deep breath. "Alright, I'm on board."

Genesis nodded, a silent compliance, but Tatsuo was hellbent on sleeping in the streets before seeking the help of someone who may or may not sell them out. As the hour drew on, and it was ultimately three against one, the *narikaah* relented. Before long, they filed back into the brisk city, searching for their saving grace before the sun descended the grey sky.

Chapter Seventeen

The rest of the day was as fruitful as it had been at the first tavern. Feyne received nothing but the same. '*Won't be finding her here this time o'day, lad.*' '*She'd be dead on the streets if I found her.*' '*If I knew, I'd be hightailing it there myself.*' All of which drove Rin's curiosity about this fae.

The day stretched on, crepuscular rays piercing through the monotonous sky. As evening fell, the chill in the air bit into them. The streets of Xandra became wealthier the further east they headed, and wealthier meant cleaner. The same type of disreputable establishments hid behind inconspicuous corners—corners she wondered why Feyne knew to search behind—but there was a different air to them. An air only the rich could afford. It was still late to be roaming the streets, no matter where they were.

"Are you sure he said he'd be back?" Tatsuo asked, unbothered by the chill as per usual.

"I don't see why he wouldn't come back," Rin frowned, searching the lantern-lit streets for any sign of Genesis.

He had waited until the lanterns along the streets were aglow, but Genesis finally had enough of the endeavor. He muttered something about meeting up at the center of town in an hour, then walked off without a chance for protest. According to the enormous clock tower a few streets away, it was an hour and three quarters later.

"Where else would he be?" A twinge of concern welled in Rin's gut. He hadn't even told them where he ran off.

Feyne yawned next to her, sitting close to keep both of them from freezing. "We can't wait around all night long." His eyes scanned the roads as well. "If he doesn't show by the end of the hour, we need to move on and find him tomorrow."

The thought of leaving Genesis worried her. *What on Armiria was he thinking by running off alone?* "Where are we going to go? As far as I'm concerned, Kah'Vi is a myth and you've been dragging us around on a goose chase all afternoon."

Tatsuo's brow furrowed. "Why would you chase a goose? It'd fly away before you could catch it."

Rin's expression sagged, unable to find the words to explain the unimportant. She shook her head, drawing her attention back to the shifter.

"Give him a bit more time," she said, even though she knew they couldn't. Aside from the cold, she couldn't stop looking over her shoulder all evening as if expecting to find someone staring back.

"Rin, we're already out here later than I'd like it to be." The wolf stole a glance of the clock for himself. "Xandra's safer than it used to be, but it's no Lyhrëon. We caught a few eyes in the last tavern. I don't want anyone coming out here and—"

"Planning on ditching me?"

Rin's heart skipped a beat. She whipped around, nearly smacking Genesis in the face. "What are you doing sneaking around like that?"

Genesis shrugged, taking a seat next to her on the bench. "Since Feyne spent our entire afternoon chasing this fae with nothing to show for it," the grievance was far from subtle, "I decided it would be best to search for supplies."

"What supplies?" Feyne asked.

Genesis reached into the pocket of his worn jacket. He pulled out two silver pieces and one copper, although his pocket weighed down with more.

"How in all the realms of Ashnagz did you sneak up on me with that much coin clattering in your pocket?" Rin marveled, though she kept her voice to a hush.

Genesis grinned. "I have my hidden talents, Nowell. You may eventually leave the street, but that extra sense you hone in it doesn't leave you."

"What street?" Tatsuo scoffed. "You were raised in a palace."

Genesis scrunched his nose. "No, I was brought to live in a palace when I was ten. I grew up on the streets of Zelenia before that." They each sent the prince a suspecting look. "Adopted, remember? Father picked me out of an orphanage. I learned how to beg from the rich far before that."

Rin stared. She supposed she never asked about his life before it became royal. "And these people, they just gave you the money?"

Genesis suddenly dipped his chin shyly, his radiant blue eyes flicking up to face her. To top off the act, he offered her the slightest grin. Her eyes rolled by the time he ran a hand through the loose strands of his hair. "They were some of the most generous women I've ever met. Some of the friendliest men too."

Rin pushed Genesis away. "You're insufferable," she laughed. Tatsuo feigned regurgitating onto the cobblestone, to which Genesis offered him an obscene gesture. "So, how much did your patrons give to you?"

Genesis dropped the beggar's stare. "Enough to find us somewhere to stay tonight."

Rin huffed a sigh of relief.

"We're going to have to find Feyne's friend by tomorrow night, or come up with another plan. I hit all the corners I could, probably a little too greedily. They won't be as friendly next time."

When Genesis turned to look at the clock tower, she saw the fresh bruise forming along his jaw. Not everyone was generous. She refrained from reaching out to touch the wounds, knowing her feeble attempts would fail to heal it.

So much for not drawing attention.

Feyne showed everyone to an inn he trusted not long after. Rin was very pleased to see that the business was mostly innocent, and if anything less than pleasant was going on, it was behind closed doors and well out of her concern. After the shades were shut, the door bolted closed, and the entire room checked for peeking eyes, it was lights out faster than a Meliboran boar charging off a cliff to avoid being hunted—a saying she couldn't convince Tatsuo as forming from true events.

With only enough money for two beds, Rin snagged Tatsuo as her bunkmate—she quite liked the ensured warmth of being beside the dragon. Genesis took the second bed, while Feyne stayed awake and watched the room for the first few hours. Yet once the deep breaths of sleep picked up, the image of Genesis's beaten jaw lingered in Rin's mind. Tatsuo's abdomen was still tender as well, she could tell by the way he walked and needed to take rests more often than the others. Of course he'd deny it if she ever asked, as Genesis denied the pain of his face when he laid down on the wrong side. She couldn't stand the lies of omission.

The shadows on the ceiling were her only source of entertainment for hours to come, long enough that she volunteered for the next watch. She decided on one thing while alone. She needed to find a space to practice.

Chapter Eighteen

T he pale light of dawn soaked the tips of Xandra, fending off the morning wind. An aeolian melody rang through Rin's ears as sweat dripped down her back and brow. She dove further into her mind, or at least attempted to.

She had stayed up all night, visions of her friend's injuries and flames dancing in the desert keeping her company. She didn't wake anyone else to keep watch. They needed rest, and that was evident enough since none of them stirred when she walked out of their room. She made sure to bolt the window and lock the door. The only suspicious person she found was a drunk passed out on the sidewalk across from the inn, but he hadn't stirred since she made her way into the abandoned courtyard behind the building. In fact, the isolation of the overgrown yard covered in dirt and surrounded by walls of vines was a blessing. It was a blind spot in the city, where the windowless walls were high enough to shield out curious eyes, and the ivy shrouded gate offered privacy to spare. It was exactly what she was looking for, even with the weight of her scimitar on her hip.

Rin held the prickling air in her lungs. She couldn't break her focus, couldn't let that murmur of magic slip through her grasp. A murmur she had finally stirred within herself after hours spent motionless and near breathless. Standing with eyes closed in the meditative form her mother taught her, Rin didn't dare move. She was within reach of the one thing she so desperately wanted, yet was utterly unable to take it.

She didn't know how she found the string of power within herself. Ever since her mother's instruction, she searched and searched within her heart for her magic. And no matter where she looked, her heart was void of it.

She nearly gave up and returned to the inn. But then a crow flew overhead, large and black as the abyss; an unexpected encounter that made Rin jump. It was then that she found it. The location of the hum. She could have screamed with joy, but the jubilance was hushed by a sour realization.

The hum sounded in her mind, not her heart as her mother instructed.

It was intoxicating to find herself so near the power. However, that's all she was: near. She discovered where it lay dormant inside herself, but she could not reach out and claim it. Like sneaking past a sleeping bear. And she knew, just *knew*, that if she tried to grab it, it would flee. Or worse, maul her. So Rin stood still. Her form breathlessly in check and mind clear so as not to scare off the power resonating a short reach away.

Nothing, *nothing* would take this moment away from her until she discovered how to grab that power—

The clatter of steel and shattered glass ruptured Rin's thoughts. Her eyes shot open, and the hum vanished. A collection of curses gathered on Rin's tongue.

Rin gritted her teeth, a swell of anger boiling in her chest. She stomped to the gate of the overgrown yard, but her frustration quickly turned to vigilance when she heard raised voices. Quietly, she snuck into the slumbering city. The mist of dusk sat heavy in the air, muffling the voices until she rounded the corner and found three individuals at the dead end of an alley.

Rin peered around the corner. Two men had backed a young woman against the brick wall. Cans of rubbish lay upturned around them. The man on the right was taller, more muscled, and held a black crowbar in his massive fist. The other man, the one on the left, was out of place. Too clean cut for this neighborhood, too well dressed. Tailored clothes stiff over his body, dark hair slicked back a little too far.

Clearly these were not friendly men, and clearly this woman was in some sort of danger, but she looked as though she was being told the time of day. The woman stood there, unamused. Rin inched as close as she could without stepping into the alley, enough to hear the conversation taking place.

"You may have every other person in this city fooled, but you should have thought twice about crossing me," the man on the left said in a low tone. "No one steals from my office without consequence." His deep voice filled the alley a little too well.

The woman's eyes flicked to the cobblestone below, looking around her feet and to her sides. Her lips pursed. It lit a match to the man's temper.

"What the hell are you doing?" he demanded.

"Looking," the woman murmured.

Something in the woman's appearance was unexpected. Perhaps the way the rising sun hit her dark face, like obsidian reflecting light. And something about the way her cool grey eyes offset the morning mist. She stood above the man in charge, though not as tall as the other.

"*Looking for what?*" he ground out. His lackey picked up on the man's irritation, adjusting the crowbar in his hand.

"Looking for the shits I give about what you have to say," she sighed, chewing on her bottom lip. Her eyes swept back to the man on the left. "Damn things must've fallen out of my pocket while you were droning on, De'Rina."

Rin snapped down on her snicker. The man did not find it so amusing.

De'Rina slammed his fist into the woman's jaw. Her head snapped to the side, body flung with it. She crashed into the brick wall behind, both arms catching against it.

"Cheap shot," she hissed, rubbing her jaw.

"Cheap shot for a cheap whore," De'Rina mused.

"Oh, save me the woes," the woman spat. Her voice was rich as she stood. "What did you expect from a lady who actually took an interest in your sleazy self for a change? Better yet, what did you expect letting her into your house? Honestly, Jonathan, you shouldn't trust a pretty face so easily. Any woman who thinks a trafficker is worth spending time with is up to something." The woman was practically asking for another strike, but she squared her shoulders.

De'Rina collected himself. "Before my friend here makes sure I don't find your nose sniffing around what's better left in the dark again, at least explain to me why you wasted your life so pitifully, Vi. You had so much potential."

The girl sized the man on the right up and down. She seemed unfazed, though her eyes lingered half a second too long on the metal bar.

"I take offense when anyone tries to sell me for their personal gain, but when they advertise who they work for in the process, I guess I can't help it. I'm the type of gal that holds a grudge." Contempt slathered her words, the grin replaced with disgust.

Jonathan De'Rina mulled it over. He eventually shrugged. "A shame, really, I could have used a light hand like yours around."

A deep, bitter laugh. "You can still have it," she smiled wide, white teeth flashing as she offered him an obscene gesture. It was then that Rin noticed two things: the girl was looking at her with that smile, and Rin had, at some point, stepped into the alley. Her hand was steady on her scimitar's hilt.

She hadn't even realized she moved, and now it was too late to retreat.

The woman eyed her hand—an invitation for Rin to draw the blade. Although when the her attention was on Rin, she missed the man on the right raise the crowbar. She caught the motion just in time, turning a headshot into a strike on the shoulder, but it was the woman's haunting scream that froze Rin's step.

An ear-piercing shriek ruptured from the woman's throat as she doubled over. Rin stared wide-eyed. A crowbar into the shoulder was bad, but it was a blunt object. She saw the smoke and the blistering red skin. It hadn't been intentional, for both men jumped back at the sight of the woman's bared teeth and tearing eyes. She dug her devastating glare into the man with the bar when he lifted it again. Their shock died down, and the woman screamed too loud.

Rin saw the chance and took it without a common-sense-worthy thought. She unsheathed her blade and charged at the man with the crowbar. The pommel of her sword fit nicely in the crease of his spine. His yowls echoed against the alley walls. He lurched to one knee, the metal bar clattering on the ground as Rin hit him on the back of the head.

The woman didn't hesitate either. She tackled Jonathan De'Rina onto the damp cobblestone. His head *thunked* on the pavement. Wrath burned in her grey eyes. She tore at his skin with her nails, clawing his face and neck and anything else she could find. The woman took his arm as he struggled out of the daze and forced his elbow over her knee with a sickening snap.

Rin winced.

The woman went from smug to feral in a matter of moments. De'Rina's screams eventually subsided to groans and moans. Eventually to silence. The quiet of a city barely awake overcame the alley, and Rin was left in a frenzy of adrenaline as she stood over the two men with the stranger.

Breathless, the woman stood, leaving De'Rina a bloody mess with an unnaturally angled arm. Rin couldn't help but stare at her shoulder. The woman eventually noticed.

"Vi," she said, her voice trembling. Despite the wound on her right shoulder, she held out her hand to shake.

Rin stared at it a moment, blinking a few times. *What the Flames just happened?* Her heart calmed. She took the hand and shook. "Rin." They both stood looking over the mess. "I'd reckon he won't be too happy when he wakes up."

"Agreed," Vi stated bluntly. "But first..." She walked to the side of De'Rina's unconscious body. Rin didn't know what to expect next, but nearly choked when the woman lifted her foot and stomped hard onto De'Rina's crotch. Vi casually made her way out of the alley, not another word to Rin as she walked.

Rin stared wide eyed, but she ran to catch up with Vi. Walking in step with the woman who stood much taller than she, Rin noticed her angular jaw. Her bones curved the skin on her body too elegantly. Unnatural; something about her was unnatural.

"So, uh, want to share what happened?" Rin pressed as they rounded the corner side by side.

The woman glanced to her side, blinking as if unaware Rin had followed her. She shrugged. "Six months ago, I was in Damrok, and poor Jonathan back there had an employee who thought he could make some money off me. Didn't end well for that fellow either." She smiled, stretching out her long arms into the air.

"Since I'm known to hold a grudge, I decided I would help The New Light's effort in incriminating the De'Rina name. I snuck into his office to find precisely which documents would do the job a few months ago. Damrok doesn't exactly appreciate foreigners enslaving their people, so when I handed them the sales records that took place in their territory, they were more than happy to put out a hunt for him."

Rin tilted her head. "Is that why he was in Xandra?"

Vi shook her head, a curious glance at Rin. Her coiled black locks swayed in the breeze. "No, De'Rina has been here for years, enjoying the chaos of Nokomic as much as any other sleazebag. You haven't heard of him?" They turned up the street to Rin's inn.

Rin shook her head. "New to the city."

Vi continued with the story. "Damrok wouldn't risk crossing into Nokomic to avoid offending The Resurrection, but the fearless New Light leader, Elyot Iver, was more than happy to help deliver him to Damrok's officials. The New Light officially started searching for him yesterday. De'Rina's troubles started when he let me into his estate, so I guess he connected the dots as to who pushed him into shit creek."

"He was so sure he'd be caught?"

Vi stopped her stride abruptly, Rin almost walked off without her. "De'Rina's slave selling was well known throughout the continent, but with everything else on their hands, The New Light couldn't tackle it right away. Being part of the Four Dealers—"

"The four what?" Rin interrupted, and she saw the flare of temper ignite in the woman's eyes. Fortunately, it subsided.

Vi's tone held an edge. "The Four Dealers are the heads of the Resurrection. Think of the Resurrection as guilds. The Four Dealers are the strongest and have the most influence over the other guilds. The top dogs. Though they're a cluster of bastards, they're not loyal to each other. Hitting one won't directly hit the others. More so, it would only hit their professions.

"Iver was balls deep trying to fight off the more prominent members of the Dealers, but De'Rina was still on his radar. So, when a chance to get rid of him arose, the New Light put all their power into finding him. They raided his mansion last night, but I guess De'Rina made it out before they got there." She pursed her lips, glancing through the buildings to where she left the man mauled. "He certainly won't be walking anytime soon..."

Rin's gaze trailed as well. "The New Light really is taking hold of things lately..."

"Indeed," Vi's resonant voice sighed. "Makes me wonder how long until The Resurrection is only a name in history texts." Silence thickened the air in their pause.

"Anyway, hold tight to that blade, Rin." Vi nodded to the scimitar. "Not everyone is thrilled the streets are being cleaned." And without even a *thank you*, she started walking in the opposite direction.

"Wait!" Rin shouted louder than she should have. "What about your shoulder? Aren't fae burns supposed to be nasty?"

Vi tripped mid-step. She flicked a stormy gaze Rin's way. "Aren't we the observant one?" Her teeth flashed a sly smile.

Rin ignored the alarm that smile instilled. "Your name is Kah'Vi, right?" She closed the gap between them. "I'm a friend of Feyne. We've been looking all over for you."

She arched a bewildered brow. "Feyne *looking* for me? He must be desperate to all Flames."

Rin pursed her lips. "I'll wrap your wound if you come talk with us." Deals and bargains, that's what she remembered from all the tales of the fae. That, and iron's sting. Rin's help was paid with Vi's story since she hadn't commented on any debt before she tried leaving. A conversation for a clean wound. Simple enough.

Vi thought it over for a moment, looked Rin up and down with studious eyes, then shrugged her good shoulder. "Why not? Nothing better to do with my day yet."

After giving the fae her jacket to hide the wound, Rin spent the rest of the walk to her room wondering if she had already unwittingly given Kah'Vi her soul.

Chapter Nineteen

The scorching sun was an empty threat behind the locked trapdoor. Zarus's eyes quickly adjusted to the darkness of the temple depths. They successfully snuck in, and having already been chased off by the human caster once, neither Zarus nor Errogan wished to idle.

Through long halls and dark quarters built of white stone, between looming pillars and spiraling stairs cast with gems, the temple stretched on, an unexpected labyrinth. Zarus led the search, unaware which way he was going. The domed ceilings echoed their footsteps despite their efforts to silence them. Errogan's patience had nearly run out when Zarus led them both under an archway, crafted masterfully by hands of a past age. A massive hall opened where the falling sun leaked through opaque windows.

The floor turned to white marble, unmarked by time. Sconces sat on the walls, the flames shining upon the breathtaking mosaics forged of dyed glass that covered each wall from floor to ceiling. The sun cast down through the glass, flooding a rainbow on the ground.

"Well," Zarus muttered, "I wasn't expecting that."

Errogan pushed him out of the way, taking in what the room offered. "Flames, who has time to build this shit?"

"People with stories to tell," Zarus carefully made way for the closest piece of art on his right. "People who don't want to forget, but also want

to keep it hidden from lingering eyes within their maze of a temple." He leaned closer, studying the glass depictions like it held a hidden prize somewhere between the slew of colors. A story lacking words. That was all he needed to find, and Errogan knew it too. Silence tied his tongue.

The first illustration showed a map. Or simply a landscape? Fields and mountains and rivers and shores. In the center, there sat a circle of white. Simple enough. The next mosaic told more of a tale. "There was a conflict of some sort."

Errogan raised an unimpressed brow. "Really? What possibly could have given it away?" He gestured his thumb to the orange and red and yellow glass in front of him; fire and flame consuming a world two mosaics from the first one.

Zarus rolled his eyes. "Look here," he said, pointing to the second mosaic. "This shows a battle. An entire army against one person."

He shifted his gaze to the center, where a mortal form holding a white circle above their head stood atop a world surrounded by a horde of soldiers. "They were after something, or perhaps trying to stop something? Whatever it might have been, every single one of them sided against this being."

"So?" Errogan grunted, not the slightest bit interested.

"So," Zarus said, "look where they're standing. On a single world. One."

Zarus drew his focus down the line to the depiction of Errogan's explosion and then on to the last of this wall's mosaics. Two separate worlds shown side by side, a single white ball floating between the two. On one side, a symbol with two lines rising and falling, curved about one another as a typhoon. On the other, a double-peaked mountain mirrored by the roots of a noble tree. Two distinct emblems. "This must be how Fawllhä was torn apart into Armiria and Eroz."

The original world Yath Ha created at the beginning of time. At that, Errogan shut his mouth and stepped closer to the story of glass while Zarus moved on to the adjacent wall.

It took a moment, but he eventually determined what happened next in the story. He looked over the glass, the color bleeding onto his face from the falling sun outside. "There was a war, some time after I would suspect. Five different sides, both worlds..." he spoke to himself more than his companion. Errogan responded nonetheless, looking at both worlds with a bridge connecting the two.

"Looks like this was after they found a way to travel between the worlds, after Olru and E'ral gifted the mortals the means to survive the world torn asunder." He paused, thinking. "The Crimson War?"

Zarus considered for a moment. The Crimson War: a conflict amongst each race, shedding blood for centuries. Though the details of ancient history were shaky on how the original world tore apart, the gods blessed their beloved mortals with the gift of what they needed to survive after the calamity.

That was a story even he had heard as a child—although the foolish humans thought it was how the two continents on Armiria were torn up, not two separate worlds.

One group asked for magic drawn from the heart, so they could rely on themselves when all else failed—the humans.

The next did not ask the gods for the ability to draw power from any-thing, only for the ability to adapt and survive in their new environment. Appreciative of their humbleness, the gods granted this group the ability to change their forms at will—the shifters.

The next group asked for power they could well from their own minds, much akin to the abilities the kaetha possessed. While Yath Ha did not gift them the freedom their Divine Helpers had, the gods still gave them the ability to well magic from their minds. This was the arrogant request of the demons.

The final group was the greediest. They asked for their very lives to be linked to the power of their new world. Lives and souls made magic themselves, fueled by the soil. This blessing was granted, but made them weak to elements of the very world they wished to draw their existence from. And thus the fae came to be.

Lastly, the dragons of old. The only beings not created by Yath Ha, but instead Mynil, the kaetha tasked to create holy beasts during the War of the Divine at the beginning of time. The dragons asked for nothing. What more would a holy monster created for war need?

On the canvas of stained glass, Zarus found five separate clusters of mortals at battle with one another. Two worlds submerged into a war devastating enough to nearly wipe out all life. And in its conclusion, the bridge between worlds was severed. All travel between banned. "For a war so devastating, it's shocking that most of the humans today know nothing about it." He was about to leave for the next mosaic, but something gleamed in his peripheral. He looked back, but the dying rays of the sun didn't lie.

Off where the demons assembled in their lines on the world that must have been Eroz, stood a dark mirror, tall and broad. A familiar sight, one he hadn't seen in years. Errogan cleared his throat, dragging Zarus's attention further down the tale.

"That white light is here as well," Errogan gestured to the Crimson War's end. The two circles depicting Armiria and Eroz were blank, nothing to fill them except a fine black line dividing both in two, the tunnel between the realms gone. Where the bridge once sat, there instead floated a white ball.

Zarus skimmed the pictures on the next wall until he found the white ball in the last mosaic. "Certainly not difficult to find the common theme." He made his way across the room to the final piece.

Three main works covered the wall. The first, a scene of fire and destruction. War and desolation. Two worlds plagued with a glass so dark, not even the daylight behind shone through. A shadow running down Eroz and Armiria like oil sliding down glass. The second showed the same, except there were two mortal figures standing between the worlds. In the center of one mortal's chest rested the white ball of light. The dye of the glass was lighter around the figures. The light pierced through it with more ease. Finally, the remaining scene was the simplest. Barely any detail compared to the masterpiece every other scene showed in this triptych of mosaics. There were no worlds, only clear white glass. A blank page. Zarus stared at the sudden shift in the story. Errogan scoffed.

"Did they run out of time? Where's the end of the story?"

Zarus said nothing. He studied the wall. The sunlight dipped below the horizon, and the glare of torches flooded the room, exchanging the clarity of daylight for an eerie sheen. No longer did the colors of the glass shine onto their faces. Their own shadows draped over the walls. Zarus's shadow shrouded the white glass.

A blank page.

Zarus released a sigh, rubbing his exhausted eyes. "It's a history book," he said as he dropped his hands to his sides. "Whoever the people were that made this, they took a liking to this ball of light. I don't know what it is, but it sure was important to them." He turned around once more to face the final wall, the last scene of white nothing.

"So, what about this one?" Errogan asked as he traced his stare. "Nothing like the last three has ever happened in history."

Zarus's eyes fixed unblinking. "It hasn't happened yet. A blank page to be written on."

Standing side by side, the White Cloaked Reaper and Shadow of Evenfall stared not at the blank page, but the one next to it. Two worlds drowning in darkness. A shiver wrapped around Zarus's spine. He resisted the urge to stir.

"Let's move on," Errogan finally said, breaking the grimness. "We'll tell Eretimis about this when we return north, but we have yet to find those archives." Before Zarus could say a thing, the white-haired demon strode through the archway they entered through. It was hard to say, but Zarus wondered if Errogan also felt the dread this mosaic instilled inside him. He supposed he would never hear if it had.

Zarus took one last look at the prophecy, then followed.

"I'll try to find any mention of a linked power in these two events," Zarus said, meeting Errogan's side. "There might be something out there if it played a part in both conflicts. For now, I think that the caster might give me some keywords to search for." He took a sidelong glance at Errogan, who was already smiling madly.

"You know, I was hoping you'd say that," he mused, a sadistic hum in his tone. "I'll bet he's even looking for us right now."

Zarus faced forward, thinking about the blank page one last time. The two figures standing between the worlds shrouded in shadow. Then a sharp curve met his lips. "Let's not keep him waiting."

***

His old quarters sat mostly empty. A chair before the fireplace, a bed in the corner, a small desk tucked behind the door, and two bookshelves on either side of the window. Nothing decorated the bare walls, only a throw rug before the cold hearth and the stains of his blood that would not come out. Only the things he carried up the tower five hundred years ago. However, a rainbow of faded books stacked on the shelves. Rows of two or three in front of each other, laid horizontally and piled atop one another. Leather bounds, parchment, scrolls—there was even a stone tablet somewhere in there. Anything he collected while he worked for Eretimis from political records, archives of magic theory, and entertainment to distract him from where he was. And history accounts.

Zarus laid on the bed for the better part of an hour after Errogan made his leave. He stayed there until restlessness bade him upright. Sleep was hopeless. He wandered the depths of his memory until he remembered every detail of that temple on the Meldii Plateau. The temple that revealed the white ball of light in each mosaic. No matter what Zarus and Errogan twisted, what they cut and tore, the caster in charge of protecting the temple did not break. He clung to silence so loyally, it cost him his life.

They informed Eretimis of the mosaics, and though the bastard hid it well, Zarus saw his eyes widen when the Tyrant heard its description. The Tyrant leaned in closer to soak up every word. Eretimis had been in a rather good temperament after hearing of it, despite Zarus channeling the Pits of Ashnagz for not mentioning the caster. Nearly four hundred years ago...

While Eretimis acted as though the white light meant nothing, Zarus poured himself into every history book he could find of the Crimson War and the Dividing of Fawllhä. Only tales and legends of the Dividing of Fawllhä were scribbled down; nothing other than there used to be one world and then a disaster made it two. Too long ago for anyone but the gods to remember. However, the Crimson War, though over five thousand years ago, was rigorously detailed. Demons kept the best records, after all, full of detail down to the eye color of enemy leaders. Still, there was no word of the white light. Nor of the dark mirror Zarus saw in the mosaic. Both were mysteries to him, or had been for the next four hundred years after visiting the temple.

Now, Zarus hunched over his desk, the stack of books towering over his head. A lone candle illuminated the corner, barely enough for his eyes to read the dramatic handwriting of the scribes of old.

The Divine Powers of Old. After searching through his collection, he found something useful. It caught Zarus's eye in the fortress's library centuries ago—the section of the once-temple dedicated to the god's right hand, the Kaeth Lhaerem. The small leather cover caught his eye in the vast library one night while sleep evaded him. It should have been eradicated when Eretimis first seized control of the temple, before even Zarus worked for him. Somehow, the ancient title survived the burnings of gods-mentioning books. Admiring its tenacity, Zarus kept the work from his mentor and carried it to his personal study. He never read it, but never tossed it out either.

Zarus flipped the frail pages. It must have been late into the night, for even the guards posted outside his door fell hushed, lulled by sleep's temptation. Most of the book's information was brief, to the point, and limited in its knowledge. No one understood the gods, after all. It wasn't until he was halfway through that Zarus found something in the small handwritten book.

The Infinite Key'. There was only a single paragraph written about this *key*, barely taking up a full page.

'A drop of the power of the two gods, Olru and E'ral. Yath Ha condensed their power into a source of energy, planting it into Fawllhä before they created the New Life. It provided the world with the power it needed to flourish. All, even the kaetha, were forbidden from using this power. However, the former kaeth, Anöwe the Sin Caster, sought it out for his dark will. He told the New Life of this power in his attempts to lead them away from the Divine's light. Once Anöwe fell to the Divine and

the New Life was punished with mortality, rumors of the Infinite Key still spread around Fawllhä. One unknown, ruthless mortal eventually found it, and despite the efforts of Fawllhä's inhabitants, he used the Key in an attempt to destroy the world. Failing, Fawllhä instead tore asunder. All knowledge of the Infinite Key's location has been lost ever since.'

The power of the gods.

Zarus read the paragraph once more. Then again. He flipped through the rest of the book, but only found explanations for the Divine's plethora of powers and abilities. Not another mention of the Infinite Key. He exhaled slowly, rubbing his temples. Errogan's warning from earlier that evening sounded in his mind like an echo in the abyss. The image of the mosaic's final scene flashed through his thoughts. The white light was submerged inside one of the mortal figures, fending off the dark.

Eretimis, the Dark Tyrant, was searching for the Infinite Key. Zarus didn't know how long he had been after it, but given how quickly his interest piqued all those years ago when Zarus and Errogan told him about the mosaics, Zarus would bet his tongue it had been for a while. Yet more importantly, after all the tests, all the drains, and the effort to keep him alive over the last two months, it became more than apparent.

Eretimis believed the Infinite Key was inside of Zarus.

His head swam. For whatever reason Eretimis believed this, Zarus hadn't the slightest idea. But if—the *smallest* if—this suspicion proved true, then Zarus was Eretimis's key to unrivaled power. No foe would stand a match against him. No one could check his power. A tremble took hold of Zarus's hands. What would the Dark Tyrant do with such power? Was there anything he *wouldn't* do?

Zarus swallowed hard, his throat as parched as his spring of magic had been only a few weeks before. He had no problem breaking through the very walls that held him prisoner right then and there. Even at partial strength, Zarus's magic could crush the fortress's empty wing like it was nothing. Eretimis knew he would stay on his leash, so long as the Tyrant held Rin in his grasp. That's where the issue arose.

Zarus Lowwenth could either flee from the fortress and spare Armiria and Eroz of Eretimis's malevolence, or keep Rin Nowell a hair's breadth from unending torture in the depths of the Dark Tyrant's dungeons.

The thought pushed away his desire for sleep.

Chapter Twenty

A ferocious chill crept through the window. Brisk enough for Zarus to cast a flame in the fireplace, enough to sit in the chair and use the flicking flames as light to read.

The Divine Powers of Old could have been written by anyone. Whoever the being was, they must have devoted their life to studying the Divine Pricks. There wasn't a detail left unspoken of the Attendants, nor Yath Ha. Zarus studied every page two times over to make sure he hadn't missed a note, the ancient ink in danger of wearing away for good. However, amid the anecdotes of divine appearances and preferred fragrances, the Infinite Key wasn't mentioned again.

Zarus groaned, rubbing his straining eyes as he rose to his feet.

He tossed the script onto his chair. None of his other books had a lick of information about this *key* either. He found it hard to believe that such a boundless source of power had been forgotten. Even if it were only myths and tales, something about the Infinite Key should have remained. Unless a destructive tyrant wanted to keep all knowledge of it to himself...

Pacing back and forth before the hearth, Zarus's nerves iced with the storm outside. Or maybe it was the frost crackling on his fingers. Whichever, his stomach twisted with every step. He resolved to keep Rin safe, but would he even be able to do that when Eretimis used whatever divine power rested within him? If it rested at all. Zarus scowled at the thought.

"You don't even know it's in you," he muttered to himself, turning away from the frosted window and wiping his brow. "Eretimis has been wrong before—"

"I wonder what should happen to you if he is."

Zarus jolted upright. The frost on his fingers sharpened to ice as his hand raised to defend himself. He did not find Errogan, the Twins, or even Eretimis standing in his doorway.

"How did you sneak in here?" He didn't lower his hand.

Nessriq leaned against the frame of the entrance, the hall behind empty of guards. Her long arms crossed below her bust, where the waves of her unbound hair draped over her red tunic. "I didn't," she said bluntly. "You were too distracted to notice me walk up the stairs and open the door."

He parted his lips to deny, but it was true. Zarus waited for the female to act. Attack, lead him to the throne room, talk. Yet the demon did none of these. She simply watched him with brown eyes that shone copper in the firelight. Curiosity rested in her expression, not violence.

Slowly, his hand lowered, but the ice remained. And he was lucky for it. The moment his arm fell, Nessriq rushed toward him.

Zarus managed a step backward, allowing himself an extra heart-beat to throw the magic on his fingers like daggers at the demon. Nessriq swatted them away, hindering her enough for Zarus to summon a wall of darkness. It erupted from the floor in waves of black and the deepest red. As he prepared himself for another rush, Nessriq remained on the other side of the wall. There was no flicker of opposing magic. When Zarus caught sight of her, she wasn't looking at him, but at his magic. In fact, it took him a moment to notice the hand that she held within the dark mist.

The darkness dropped to the floor, whooshing against the walls until only traces rose to the ceiling like crimson smoke.

Nessriq held her hand up between them, twisting it and studying the damage. Zarus was in no mood for games, and the intensity of his magic made that clear. Her light brown skin dried grey. It cracked, flaking as though blistered by heat, and falling to the ground as dust until the redness of muscle and veins shone through. Blood broke through the worn tissue along the back of her hand. The burn trailed up her arm like a stain on cloth, but stopped midway along her forearm. Her veins twitched with her pulse between the cracked skin.

Once her skin stopped crumbling, Nessriq dropped her hand without so much as a flinch and smiled. "You're quick to the point, Zarus Lowwenth."

"And you're slower than a glacier," he grumbled, although he failed to hide the confusion from his expression. She barely flinched.

Nessriq suddenly rolled her eyes. "Why should I have a point?"

Zarus furrowed his brow. "You're the one who came to this tower."

The demon spun around on her heels and perused the bookshelf behind. "You started talking."

"You attacked *me*."

"I'm sure it's nothing new to the Shadow of Evenfall."

Vexation stole his good sense. "What's stopping me from ripping you apart?"

Nessriq glanced over her shoulder, placing the book back onto the shelf in the wrong location. "The affection you hold for Errogan."

Before Zarus could grind his teeth, Nessriq turned away from the books and gazed at the content on his desk as she strolled past it. "That window is frail. You could easily jump out of it and end all your suffering."

Zarus sucked in a deep breath. "And?"

Nessriq cut him a curious glance. Curious, but not soft. "And yet you sit here like a dog for the sake of someone else."

A throb drummed in the back of Zarus's head. Prisoner or not, his business was his own. This Hraesan demon had no reason to stick her nose in it. Zarus tapped an impatient finger on his leg while Nessriq paced the perimeter of the room. "Has Errogan filled you in on the local gossip?"

Once Nessriq made a full round of the quarters, she finally faced Zarus and loosed a smile. "No, Errogan has made his opinion of my presence quite clear. The smallest things truly do set him off."

"I'd be careful how idly you talk about him. His bad side isn't one to fall on." He could sense her amusement from a mile away.

The demon waved the comment off with her corroded hand. "Yes, yes, I've heard all about the Flames you would raise for him. Both to others *and* yourself." Questions bubbled in his throat, but Nessriq continued before Zarus could voice them.

"The White-Cloaked Reaper's reputation is well known on Eroz. I expected a great general when I came to this dull world. You can imagine my surprise when I found a simple brat doing His Majesty's petty chores instead. The Wraith Sisters said little to me when I arrived, but they made sure to fill me in on Errogan's latest blunders. In fact, bringing you back to the fortress seemed to be his own damnation. He's been a whipping post ever since. It's refreshing to know even the famous have no place in the Dark Tyrant's army without the strength to show for it."

A whipping post? Zarus gritted his teeth. No wonder Errogan kept lingering in this tower. It was probably the only place he could escape his humiliation.

Nessriq's stare was unfaltering. Her taunt was clear as the day that never showed in the north, but more importantly, her searching was apparent as the dark gloom swirling overhead.

She studied the room too closely, brought up names too casually. New to this dull world. New and looking to learn more about the famous. He glanced at her hand trickling blood onto his carpet.

"Does Eretimis know you're meddling in his affairs?" Zarus asked, making his way to the open door.

Nessriq arched her brow, following too quickly on his heels only to be stopped once Zarus met the door and faced her. "You admit to being his affair?"

"You're meddling in things you don't belong in. A unique trait in us demons. Most of us are more likely to react before thinking, but you seem to think it through ahead of time." Zarus crossed his arms and leaned against the slim of the door. "I don't care what you stick your nose in, Nessriq of Hraesah. Just know that people who stick their noses in *my* business typically end up dead. Or worse."

With nothing more said, he flicked a nod toward the open door. "Give Eretimis my regards."

Nessriq watched him with indignity for a moment before catching herself and smirking back at him.

"As I said, you're quick to the point. Allow me to return the gesture." She leaned in close, holding his stare. "I don't care about you, Errogan, or your names. If you get in my way, I'll kill you. Whether of your own doing, or under His Majesty's influence."

Zarus could have rolled his eyes. This female was nothing more than a whelp trying to make her mark. "Eretimis doesn't like dissidents. What's your stake in all of this if you don't buy into his divine right to tyranny? You're too smart to believe in his lies."

"I believe in his power. So long as I stay on top, that power will favor me."

A sigh escaped his lungs, and he swung the door open wider to further his point. "You can keep his favor."

The female's lip nearly twitched. "You and Errogan will be nothing more than names forgotten in history before long. Neither of you is of his use now."

Despite himself, a chuckle seized his breath.

"Yes," Zarus mused, "I've heard a human is giving us a run for our money now. I've heard more about him than anything of your merit. How come you haven't gotten rid of him yet? Afraid he might bite?"

Nessriq huffed a laugh through her nose. "A demon with no presence would know a thing or two about cowardice, right, Zarus?"

Annoyance tugged his stoic resolve. The clatter of armored feet sounded down the staircase. "If you're that interested, I was born without one. Now get out before I fillet any more of you with my magic."

Nessriq stepped outside the doorway as the next guard watch ascended the stairs. "No one is born that way." Her smile could have sliced leather. "Only cowards and criminals wipe their presence. Your reputation didn't disappoint, Zarus. We'll be seeing—"

Zarus slammed the door.

The antics of children were of no interest to him. Prattling on about power and names. He wished he'd torn Nessriq to shreds from the moment she arrived. Loosing a sigh, he fell back into his chair and reopened the *Divine Powers of Old*.

He supposed the demon could have been more insufferable. At least she hadn't mentioned Rin.

Chapter Twenty-One

"She isn't a child. She can take care of herself." Even while Feyne spoke, he didn't sound confident.

"She's never been to the city, Feyne," Genesis argued.

"We don't even know how long she's been gone. She could be downstairs eating breakfast right now."

"I already looked. The inn keeper said she walked out the door nearly three hours ago. Said she had her blade with her."

"You don't think she ventured to the temple, do you?" Tatsuo asked.

"I don't know, but it's a start."

"Genesis, stop," Feyne demanded. "I know you're worried, but we need to let her be on her own."

Genesis stood right on the other side of the door. "Why's that? So she can get robbed at knifepoint? Or worse yet, caught up in whatever malfeasances you claim run rampant nowadays. Perhaps even attract Eretimis's eyes."

"She's not foolish; she knows to watch her back."

"I never said she was foolish. But it's not safe out there—"

Rin knocked on the door. There was a brisk moment of nothing. She cast an uncertain glance to the fae behind her. After an eternity, the door swung open.

Genesis greeted her, the pale of worry already subsiding from his face. "Nice of you to join us, Nowell." She smiled at his concern.

"Well, this is certainly cute, but am I allowed in? Hallways are too intimate for my tastes." Vi didn't wait for an invitation and pushed past Rin and Genesis, smiling wide when she saw the shifter lounging in the alcove below the window. "Sniffers," she greeted, genuine in her tone, "it's nice to see you as always."

"*Sniffers*?" Tatsuo snickered from the bed.

Feyne ignored the *narikaah*. "Why am I not surprised that you ran into each other?" His eyes flicked between Rin and Vi, but ultimately a friendly smile spanned his face. "Have you two made friends yet?"

Rin opened her mouth to explain they had just met, but Vi spoke first. "Why of course, dear. And what a friend to hold onto, Feyne. She speaks so highly of you. Says you wanted to chat with me about something?"

The shifter nodded. "Have a minute to spare?"

"As long as you have a minute to owe." Vi took a seat on the bed next to Tatsuo. She kicked her legs up, acting as if her shoulder wasn't severely burned. The brown leather of her pants faded around the knees. Her white blouse billowed at the sleeves before they tucked into long leather gloves. A traveler's garb. "I feel like I'm required to spare a second if you put in effort to *look* for me." She leaned back on her hands. "To what do I owe that honor?"

Rin's legs almost buckled beneath her. She had been up and moving for hours, and the sleepless night was catching up. After closing the door, she walked to the satchel of supplies and looked for anything to clean the fae's shoulder.

Feyne leaned his elbows onto his thighs. "Well, Vi, I'll get right to the point: I need a favor."

***

The *slosh* of her boots was hard to ignore. Rin didn't think her clothes had been completely dry ever since she stepped foot out of the Pit over a month ago.

Kah'Vi and Feyne worked out the details of their deal while Rin used what limited supplies available to clean and wrap the fae's shoulder. The story of how they met earned a shrug from Feyne, a laugh from Tatsuo, and a few questions about the man whose bits Vi squashed from Genesis.

Vi would be Feyne's ears and eyes throughout the city, and Feyne shared a tip he heard many months back that a gang of thieving demons settled on her favorite route to Damrok. Tatsuo nearly choked learning Feyne traded in deals so casually with a fae, to which Vi cast him a mischievous smirk, talking to the *narikaah* while the group departed the inn. Apparently distrust earned her attention, because Vi hadn't left Tatsuo's side on the entire walk across town.

"Scar treating you well?" the fae asked, her expression feigned an innocence her eyes didn't reflect. She was searching. Feyne's composure stumbled momentarily.

Vi led the group while Tatsuo, unable to shake her from his side, reluctantly walked in step.

Rin met her other side from behind. "So Vi, where are you taking us?" The change of topic earned a glare from the fae.

They walked for at least an hour before turning down a main road. As the morning drew on, more people gathered in the streets. Most walked, some rode in carts, and a few carriages rushed by. Some drivers seemed intent on running Rin over, seeing as they almost did. The houses they passed didn't look so run down; the streets were clean, though not polished; and the people walked a little higher, as if a different neighborhood meant security.

Vi huffed, leading the pack in the ethereal stride of a fae. "If you lot need a safe place to stay without a job to sustain it, then there's only one place to go."

It took a while to wear the fae down since none of them were eager to make more deals with someone notorious for getting the better end of such things, but Rin eventually attained the living quarters they needed. Was she happy to exploit the kindness she gave to someone she'd just met? No. Was she a little proud to remind Vi that she offered her jacket to the fae on the street so her burn would be covered from prying eyes? A little. Rin saw it as helping someone in need, but Vi saw it—bitter Rin understood it as well—as protection for protection.

Rin looked up as they approached a brick townhouse whose green roof gave the vast fields of grass outside the city a run for their money. It was tall, it was narrow, yet it was probably the nicest structure she had seen in Xandra yet.

Vi didn't bother to knock. There was a delicate *hiss* of the door handle, the metal burning red beneath her touch. Rin winced, expecting a waft of molten flesh, but the leather gloves the fae wore were thick enough to keep the heat at bay. To Rin's horror, the girl walked right into the house without a sound. Tatsuo followed in after, huffing a sigh of relief given the moment of space. Feyne eyed the house suspiciously, subtly sniffed the air, then shrugged and waltzed in.

"I don't know about you," Genesis muttered from her side, "but my father raised me with much better manners than this."

Rin nodded, half-expecting all three to be kicked out on the street any moment now. Though nothing happened. "My Da's heart would fail if he knew I walked into a stranger's house without permission…" She pursed her lips, wondering how many times his heart must have already failed in the last three months… She banished the thought. "Sorry, Da." She walked up the stone steps.

What greeted her eyes was a foyer that stretched far to the back door of the house. Dark wooden floors on light walls, a table here and there with some form of art or plant or trinket decorating it. A chandelier loomed overhead, flickering with a hundred candles and illuminating the arches leading to unseen chambers. The narrow staircase to her left led to a balcony on the second floor. And within the walls of the home swarmed an ocean of people. Clad in armor and carrying weapons. Daggers, swords, axes, even a flail. So many people that Rin about gave up on finding her friends. Genesis stood at her back, sure not to lose track of her in the mass of strangers, and Rin made sure she didn't slip away from him.

"Where are we?" Genesis asked over the buzz of overlapping conversations. He eyed the crowd, looking from weapon to weapon. An edge entered his posture, one Rin was feeling a bit herself.

"You, my friends," Vi called from the top of the balcony's edge, "are in the humble abode of Elyot Iver." A wide smile brightened her face, white teeth shining through like snow.

Rin couldn't help her jaw from dropping. Elyot Iver, the heroic leader of the New Light. A man she had only heard about in stories, and she was now standing in his very house. Without knocking. Her tongue dried a little.

Rin and Genesis pushed up the stairs. She wasn't certain, but she had a well-founded guess that the people gathered about the house were members of the New Light. Most acknowledged them with a nod. Some ignored them. There was a mix of everyone in the house; men, women, young, old. By the time they reached Vi, Feyne and Tatsuo on either side of her, Rin was staring excitedly from one person to the next, one blade to the next.

"How do you know Iver?" Feyne asked Vi, turning around from the balcony's railing.

"She and I go back," Vi replied. She spun around on the heel of her boot and began walking down the long hallway upstairs.

"She?" Genesis scrunched his nose, "I thought you told me a man named Elyot led the movement."

Vi sighed, not deigning to look back when she spoke. "Don't you know where all great men come from, kid? Their mamas." She glanced over her shoulder, stormy eyes dancing with smugness. "My memory is useless right now. Would you care to give me your name again?"

He met her stare, saw the dance in it, and hesitated. "No," he said carefully, "you may not have my name. But you can call me Genesis."

The fae huffed a sigh. "Feyne, where did you dig up these people? They're far too smart for my liking..." Rin honestly couldn't be sure, but it sounded like a jest. "Well, Genesis," Vi shrugged, "go downstairs in the kitchen. You'll find a woman named Kara. Ask her for a basin of water and a rag, then come meet us in the back room up here."

Rin watched the aggravation build up in Genesis's jaw, but he nodded. Smart enough to keep his soul, but also smart enough not to argue with Vi, especially when they truly were indebted to her. Genesis split from Rin's side and made his descent to the kitchen, lost to the crowd before long.

"So, you're taking us to see Elyot Iver's mother?" Tatsuo asked.

Vi nodded, her stride giving the group a wide berth from those few who roamed the second floor. Even within closed walls, she walked like she owned the room. "Indeed, I trust that woman more than anyone in this world. She'll take good care of you. There's something you'll want to see first, Sniffers."

Feyne frowned. The way Vi smiled at them, the way she waltzed across the room with a swagger to her gait, Rin grew suspicious of her intentions. Though Vi seemed trustworthy enough, even Feyne's expression held a fair deal of concern as they followed.

The hall curved, leading to a door. The fae was hiding something. That much was apparent when her smile turned feral. When she twisted the doorknob, softly pushed the hinges open, everyone was standing on guard. But all that met them the smell of spices and embers, one that swiftly caught Feyne's attention.

A round of suspicious glances exchanged between her and Tatsuo, but the shifter's focus pulled him through the doorway. The clatter from downstairs did not make it around the corner, and an eerie tranquility resonated within Rin's ears as she stepped into the room.

Two windows brightened the snug quarters, the daytime sun seeping through the far pane. An extravagant fireplace dug into the wall to her left, the mantle stuffed from corner to corner with plants and art. Beneath the window across from the hearth rested a bed, and before the bed was a woman in a wooden rocker. Lines of age wrinkled her brown face, stretching down her neck, slipping out from beneath the sleeves of her gown onto her hands. A braid held her thickly curled hair over her shoulder. Chestnut eyes flicked away from her book and up to Vi as the fae approached the elderly woman.

"Kah'Vi," her sweet voice hummed, a bright smile replacing her ruminative expression, "I didn't think I would see you again until after you ventured to Weslyc. Who have you brought?"

Vi opened her mouth to respond, a smile that harbored no mischief or arrogance spanning across her face, but she didn't get the chance.

Feyne didn't wait for an invitation. He ran through the room once the second draft hit them at the door and slid down to his knees before the bed.

Feyne gaped. He reached toward the covers tentatively but halted. Disbelief? Awe? Doubt? Rin couldn't be sure what paralyzed the wolf.

Rin's heart skipped. Frozen in place, unable to budge from where she stood beneath the doorway. Feyne's cheeks lined with tears. He squeezed the delicate hand that did not grip back. She slowly forced herself to walk toward the bed, dropping to her knees as well.

It can't be...

Rin stared in disbelief.

Scarlette Draelin lay beneath the covers in the bed, her chest slowly rising and falling in deep sleep.

Chapter Twenty-Two

Scarlette's eyes were closed, her expression as peaceful as a summer breeze. But it was not sleep that stripped her once warm cheeks of their color, nor was it a dream that made her deep red hair stick to the sweat lacing her forehead. She lay still, yes, nearly as still as the dead.

A scant breath rattled Scarlette's chest. Feyne hadn't taken his eyes off the girl, clutching her hand in his own like their lives depended on it. Rin didn't blame him. She was afraid this was all another dream.

She shook her head. "How?" She cast Vi an astonished glance.

Errogan's shadows had pierced through Scarlette's chest. She bled out in Rin's arms. No breath in her lungs, no rhythm to her heart. She shouldn't be here... she shouldn't be *breathing*.

How?

"That's what I want to know," Vi shrugged, wiping the wonder from her face. "With wounds like hers, her heart shouldn't have been beating, much less allowing her to shift around in the desert sun."

"She was walking?" Tatsuo asked from where he leaned against the window.

Vi shook her head. "I'd have devoted my life to Yath Ha right then and there if that were the case. I thought she was dead at first—like the rest of them." Rin winced at the words. "Then she shifted when I walked past her. Still does now and then, like she's searching for a way out of herself."

"She's stuck." The words were barely a whisper on Rin's lips. Her gut clenched. "In one of my first lessons with Ma, she told me probably the most important rule for a white mage to know." She caught the arch of Vi's brows at the title but ignored it. "Taking life is easier than saving it. The body can heal, but it's up to the wounded to decide when they will return. *If* they will return." She sucked in a breath.

It was Feyne who spoke, a desolate noise. "The body can only take so much."

Rin nodded, digging her nails deeper into her palms.

"She's warring with herself right now, deciding between the natural course of death or the ounce of magic holding her together." Rin nearly jumped when the elderly woman spoke. She had been so quiet the whole time.

"Why not finish the job then?" Vi's question was cold.

Rin could barely meet the stare. "I..." The words lodged in her throat. "I don't know how."

A sullen silence slithered into the room. Rin's eyes burned, her heart strained against the weight pressing on it. She should have been able to do this; she had done it before.

What's wrong with me?

"Is anyone going to explain how this even happened? I mean, Feyne, I was on my way to tell you that Eretimis's forces have been assembling in the North, and I'm met with a bloody desert of death and ash! How the Flames did it come to that?" The fae's stared until someone answered.

"Vi, there are some things better left unsaid," Ms. Iver said softly, leaning in to look at the thanatoid gleam of the girl beside her. The fae's demand fell in check with the woman's words. Feyne quietly replied.

"Eretimis found us."

It was all he said—all he *wished* to say.

A bitter scoff filled the air. "What did you expect?" Vi crossed her arms. "I've been telling you for years that you're treading water far too hot to touch. You never listened to me."

"*Kah'Vi,*" Iver said, hard as steel.

Vi went on. "No, you couldn't help getting in his way. A thorn in the side of the Dark Tyrant. How many others did you drag into your games?" A fury rose in her voice, one fueled by disdain and contempt. She spoke through clenched teeth. How many members of Base did Vi know? "Was it worth it, Feyne? Is this the world you imagined when you set out on this mission to help everybody?"

She had more to say, more to dig out, but Tatsuo had enough. No one realized he made his way across the room until he grabbed hold of the fae's arm. She nearly bit the dragon's head off for it too, but something in his expression—something so uncharacteristically stoic that it sent a chill through Rin's bones—held Vi's tongue. Hurt faded to contempt, and there it stayed. Tatsuo released her arm.

Rin glanced at Feyne. His body looked like it would crash beneath the pressure.

A warm stream trickled down her cheek. Rin barely held in her sob. She needed to find that power, needed to grab a hold of it and force it to listen to her command. How was she supposed to do that when every time she thought about reaching for it, she was scared to—

A draft rustled from behind, a few of her stray hairs catching in it. The door clicked shut a moment later, and Genesis met her side, water basin in hand.

He stopped short when he caught glimpse of Scarlette back from the dead. His curious glance shifted to Rin. She shrugged and showed him the open palms of her hands. Rin was relieved that he looked at her with concern and not pity. She recalled how Zarus reacted to her pity that first night, and now, she didn't blame him at all for it.

"She doesn't look good..." Genesis finally said; stating the obvious, but Rin read between the lines. She ran her hand back through the fray of her overgrown bangs.

Magically saved or not, it wasn't enough to fully pull Scarlette out of her coma. Everyone knew it.

"We will accomplish nothing by standing around and moping." Ms. Iver finally broke the silence. "This girl's been fighting the natural course for over two months now; she's strong. And to me, it sounds like you already know what you need to finish the work." The woman cut a knowing glance toward Rin, chestnut eyes soft in the daylight.

"Young man," she placed a wrinkled hand on Feyne's shoulder, drawing his attention away from Scarlette for the first time since he entered the room. "Wipe your tears. She is safe here; she is still fighting. Take solace in knowing there's still a chance." Years bring wisdom, and this woman looked to have plenty of wisdom to spare. The shifter stared hollowly, but heeded the woman. He climbed to his feet once more, taking a deep breath.

"Vi," Feyne said, regaining his resolve, "I need to talk to you about some rumors you might have heard recently."

The fae raised a brow, a sly smile returning. "Color me interested, wolf boy. Would the walls of my quarters suit you?"

Feyne nodded, wordlessly following behind the fae as they went off to speak on the matters that drove him to Xandra in the first place: who betrayed him. Before the two disappeared, Vi glanced at the elderly woman still in the rocker. "Aava, would you mind entertaining my guests until I return?" Without giving her a chance to reply, Vi exited the room, Feyne with her.

"Aava?" Genesis repeated, turning his attention to the woman by the bed. He squinted his eyes, as if trying to find something that didn't quite belong.

Aava fell silent a moment, as if only then noticing Genesis. There was a pause. She leaned in, looking the once-prince up and down, and locked in on his eyes.

"No..." She tried to get up, to walk toward Genesis, but old age affected her more than it did him.

Genesis walked to her and dipped on one knee. "Aava Knaidel..."

"You know," Aava's voice wobbled, lips curving into one of the most joyful smiles Rin had ever seen, "you're thinner than I remember, Masquarem."

He looked at her all over again, from eye to lips, hair and hands, but a beaming glee cracked through. He cupped the woman's cheek in his hand, softly holding her as an expression Rin had never seen appeared on the prince's face.

"Seventy years... it's been seventy years since I looked upon your face," he said. A tear streamed down Aava's cheek. She rested her frail hand over his. "And I get as much joy from seeing it now as I did seventy years ago."

Tatsuo took it upon himself to ruin the touching moment. "Old friends?" the dragon asked.

Genesis looked over his shoulder at the two of them.

"This old coot, my friends, is none other than Aava Knaidel. Member of the Royal Guard, and my best friend in the entire kingdom all those years ago."

Rin's eyes widened. Tatsuo raised a single brow. A second passed, and his smile broke off into horror as Genesis caught wind of his words and whipped his stare back to Aava.

"Flames, I didn't mean that!" he struggled for words, shaking his hands in denial. "No, that's just what I would call her because she's a year older than me—"

A bellied laugh escaped the woman. "I think it's safe to say that age was kinder to you than me, Gen." The old woman took Genesis's cheeks in her hands, looking over every detail of his face. "Yath Ha damn me, you haven't gained a single wrinkle. The spitting image of the day it ended..." She stared a moment longer, then pulled Genesis into her arms in an embrace. He leaned into it and rested his head on her small shoulder.

"I thought you would be gone," he whispered.

"And I thought you were dead." Aava was the first to let go. The joy did not subside, but a grim shadow fell over her features. "So, tell me, Your Highness, is there a story behind this, or have you discovered your birth parents were part of the Divine themselves?"

Genesis's smile dragged. The man out of time drew his gaze back to the woman sitting in the wooden rocker, a lifetime between them. "How much time do you have?"

***

To her credit, Aava Iver, once Knaidel, did not bat an eye when Genesis told her what happened at the end of Zelenia's fall, nor when he told her of Eretimis's existence and the demonkind. She was, however, taken aback when she inspected Tatsuo. From the talon-like nails to the pointed ears on his head, Rin was quite surprised others hadn't stared awestruck at the *narikaah* by that point.

"Don't be mistaken," Aava said to Tatsuo. "I was aware demons exist thanks to Vi, but I've never met one of your kind before. To my understanding, they were all…"

"Waste-sniveling bastards?" Genesis suggested.

Aava frowned but shrugged as she patted the damp towel over Scarlette's brow. "Along those lines."

Tatsuo smiled at the woman, holding the water basin for her while he perched on the edge of the bed. "To be fair, I'm only one-fourth demon. It's probably been a century since I've come across one of us that isn't a…" he glanced at Genesis.

"Waste-sniveling bastard," Genesis repeated from the far side of the room.

"Yes, thank you," the *narikaah* nodded. "There are good demons out there, like there are good humans. It takes a little longer to find them since most are on Eroz or fear Eretimis's wrath."

"Wrath for what?"

Tatsuo frowned, lowering his voice. "Siding against him. He labels us *sympathizers* for valuing all life rather than the demonkind, a crime usually punishable by death." His reptilian eyes grew solemn. "Most of the demons that saw Eretimis for the monster he is fled to Armiria when he assumed complete power. Some figured it out later and ran. They all became traitors to everyone else who fell victim to his influence."

Rin chewed the inside of her cheek. Zarus once mentioned Eretimis used the excuse of taking back lost land to convince the demons to invade Armiria hundreds of years ago. He said the Tyrant always had something else on his agenda. She couldn't help but wonder what Eretimis sought after so long. She also wondered if it was simply devout loyalty that kept the demons wrapped around his finger. After centuries of not achieving their goal, they had to have grown suspicious, right? Were they truly that loyal, following *that* blindly?

Aava took a moment to mull it over. "I suppose that's not too different from what's taking place in Nokomic right now. Those who side with the New Light are always at risk of danger. The Resurrection's influence is wearing thin, but it still runs strong in this city. Openly stating your opinion for justice could very well end with your body found in the gutter."

The woman thought it over, tapping her fingers on the chair's arm. "Support is better given under the cover of night, for everyone's sake."

Rin furrowed her brows. "How is any of this discreet? I mean..." she fumbled, "everyone here is part of the New Light, right? How do they keep their identities hidden when everyone is cramped in here? Surely, it's known this is your son's home."

Aava looked into Rin for a moment—not *at*, but *in*—with thoughts unknown to watching eyes. Perhaps she had misspoken? She opened her mouth to apologize, but the woman chuckled before she could.

"That's a very fair point; one I agree with, child. There usually isn't a crowd here. No one knows who lives here except the neighbors, who thankfully favor us, and we carry out our business somewhere a bit more *discreet* nowadays.

"Elyot's second hand, Gillan, gathered this bunch last night so they could apprehend one of the leading criminals of the city. They operated their business in this neighborhood, and Gillan thought it would go smoother if they ran it from here. However, that figurehead of the Resurrection had already fled by the time they got there. Everyone is waiting to leave one by one, so it doesn't draw attention."

Rin thought for a moment. "Jonathan De'Rina?" she asked.

Aava raised a curious brow. "That would be the one. Have you heard of him?"

"Well, yes, but only after I met him... sort of." She shrugged. "Last I saw, he was unconscious and bleeding in an alley in the southern part of town." Rin thought about Vi's bloody work of the slave seller. "I'm almost positive he won't be walking either."

Aava blinked, once and then twice. "I'm glad Vi got her piece of him. He'll be found and brought before Damrok in no time, but Gillan should know where you left him."

At that, the woman rose to her feet. Honestly, Rin didn't expect a woman of her age to stand that easily, much less walk without hindrance. However, for once, it would seem Rin wasn't the shortest person in the room. "Come, all of you. I'm sure that you'll want to meet her. Elyot trusts her to run operations while he's away. It's never a bad time to make friends."

Rin nodded as everyone followed behind, but she frowned when Scarlette caught her eye. "What if she needs something?"

Aava paused her step as she passed in front of Rin. Not vindictive, but bare truth assaulted her ears as the woman spoke. "What she needs will not be found in this room, child."

Chapter Twenty-Three

S orrow and joy, mourning and rejoicing. Once alone, Rin's sobs broke through her emotional dam and tears streamed down her face.

The rest of the day had been as unbelievable as the morning. Aava introduced them to Gillan Thrassen: a woman who preferred to keep conversations brief and her expression tethered. She was second in command of the New Light. It was only after Aava said they were all welcome to stay in her house that Gillan said they could call on her. After Rin told her where the slave seller was left in the dirt, the second in command nodded her gratitude and ran to gather a search party. Afterward, their sweet host sat them around the hearth in the house's great room.

Feyne and Vi were still nowhere to be found, but Aava chatted their ears off for as long as she could. She answered questions, and told stories about what Genesis was like growing up that had the prince's eyebrow twitching.

Upon further conversation of life after Nokomic's fall, and a bit of detective work, Rin learned Aava sat on quite a sum of wealth. Being part of the royal guard gave her the training necessary to fend for herself once chaos unfolded in the streets and the ability to teach others her trade of combat. Aava was hired to teach self-defense to civilians wishing to protect themselves. While teaching the people of the city, and even some from beyond who sought her expertise, Aava also worked as a healer around the whole kingdom. No user by any means, but she was well-versed in the way of medicines. Everything she had learned while training to become a knight served her once that dream was crushed. She gave back to her city as much as she could. In doing so, Aava became a sort of saint to Xandra. Bonds strong as iron formed—Vi being one of them. And after avoiding it all evening, Rin eventually asked about the Temple of the Divine.

"The Resurrection tried to burn it down," the woman explained, planted in an identical rocker to the one upstairs. "Religion suggests order, and order involving beings they could not control was not something they were interested in preserving. The fires were extinguished, but for years, the temple was another indication that you disagreed with the Resurrection's rule. People avoided it. Eleven years ago, the temple was Elyot's first priority. It was important for the people to praise Yath Ha in peace. They repaired the damage, and it's in as fine a shape as it was a lifetime ago." She cast a warm grin at Genesis with the last sentence.

He smiled back, but Rin saw the strain in it.

By the time all the soldiers left, it was well past twilight. Aava finally made her way into the kitchen and helped the cook prepare dinner. While knives chopped and ovens burned, Rin had very little appetite. Her head pounded on the walls of her mind. While Tatsuo helped to keep the fire stirring, and Genesis was off catching up with Aava, Rin snuck off to the bedroom offered to her.

The house was beautiful, full of life and memories. The quarters weren't large, no bigger than her room in Aresan, but the bed was lush, and the blazing fireplace warmed the air. Exhausted after another sleepless night, she lay silent in bed.

Rin wiped her eyes for the hundredth time, burying her palms into the sockets. It hit her all at once when she closed the door. The last three months, her absent magic, finding Scarlette... She hugged tighter around her knees.

She was lost, more lost than she had ever been, and she didn't even know *what* she was trying to find her way back to. She was about to double over into her pillow when a knock sounded on her door.

Rin jumped upright. Her gut twisted knowing that there was no hiding her emotions, but she wiped the tears away anyway and straightened her hair and clothes. She might be a bawling mess, but at least she'd look presentable. Rin cracked the door open.

A pair of sapphire eyes stared back at her. "You're not getting away that easily, Nowell. Aava isn't done embarrassing me."

Rin searched for a smile to offer but found nothing. "I needed to lie down." She couldn't hide the tremble in her voice, her swollen red eyes. Her friend's expression sobered.

"Rin," Genesis said carefully, "what's wrong?" She could barely stand to look at the austere gleam in his eye, so Rin sighed and swung the door open wide for him to enter. She found her spot on the bed again, this time lying down.

Genesis took the cue and shut the door softly after he entered. He took a place on the other side of the bed, facing her though she faced the other way.

The sole window in the room looked over an overgrown garden shrouded in darkness. Once vibrant flowers were wilted, dead and curled for the season. She watched as the wind picked up and swirled a pile of fallen leaves along the ground, stuck in the current and unable to break free. Silence paralyzed her tongue. She grabbed tighter onto the pillow under her head.

Genesis's voice broke the seal. "You saved her life, Rin." Her chest tightened at the words, silent tears creasing her eyes. "Scarlette is alive because of you."

"She's in a coma because of me. She was attacked because of me. She's half alive because I can't finish the job. The rest are dead because I couldn't figure it out earlier." She squeezed the pillow, hoping to calm the shake in her hands.

"Eretimis ordered the attack," Genesis countered. "From what Feyne said, he's had Eretimis's attention for years. Whoever betrayed Base, whoever sold them out, that's who you should blame. But Rin, I promise you—I swear on the grave of my father—that you did not do this. You *or* your magic."

Rin furrowed her brow and glanced at the prince. The denial failed to make it to her lips. She turned over to face him.

"I can't control it, Gen. I can't summon it, and I can't stop it when it comes freely. It almost killed all of you in the desert. Is it really so far-fetched that I made Scar worse? She's stuck in a coma, and I can't get her out of it."

"Scarlette was dead. I think it's safe to say you did the opposite." He locked eyes with her. "You know no one is forcing you to go to this temple, right? We're here to support you and whatever decision you make."

"I know, but..." *Three months.* She had barely known these friends of hers for three months, and yet they stood so strongly at her side. "I'm letting everyone down if I don't go. I'm letting Zarus down by not taking the steps needed to save him, I'm letting you and Tatsuo down for dragging you out here, and now I'm letting Feyne down for doing nothing as Scarlette dies..." Her throat clenched.

Genesis watched her for a thick moment. "What's causing your doubt?"

"I'm scared." She didn't hesitate. She knew the answer, knew that he knew. What stung was how pathetic it sounded. "Terrified, actually. What if I don't get an answer? Worse yet, what if I do? What if I actually get a response from Olru and E'ral after centuries of no one hearing from them? I—"

She shut her eyes tight, a wave of uncertainty pressing down onto her chest. And down she fell, further and further into that weight. Until a physical weight added to it. One on her hand.

Rin opened her eyes to find Genesis's hand atop her fist.

"Erin," Genesis crooned. She traced her glassy gaze to the serenity of the ocean in his eyes. "This is your life; you can do whatever you want with it."

The hum rang in her mind, a siren in the void; ever echoing, ever calling. She knew exactly where to look now. The whirlpool of magic raging. Genesis's hand gripped tighter around hers. She broke the trance of her magic and grasped back, tight enough to turn his fingers white.

"I found it today," she hesitated. "My magic isn't in my heart; it's in my head. I could have taken hold of it this morning, it was right there..." Genesis remained silent, letting her speak. "I could have. But I wouldn't. I'm afraid of it. In the desert, in the Pit... all it does is attack. I can't keep my eyes shut, knowing it's right there, waiting. What if it strikes again?"

A silence thick as wax drew on, the pause tangible as she waded through foggy thoughts.

"If the gods tell me to use this power? I don't know if I'm able to. The last victory was pyrrhic. With all these visions and dreams, no step closer to doing what I need to do... I'm afraid what comes next won't even be a victory."

"You can only rely on luck so many times," Genesis agreed, trailing off as well.

"I've relied on it too much as it is," Rin nodded, biting her lip. "I don't think I have enough left in the bank to get Zarus out."

She expected to hear Genesis's refute, that she was being crazy and that everything would be okay in the end. Nothing filled the gap between them.

Rin propped her head up with her hand. "It's something I need to figure out before we go talk to the gods, I suppose."

Genesis nodded, his stare still latched onto the shadows of the room. "I understand how you're feeling. Unable to have a say in what's going on... I get it."

Rin looked up to him, saw the ghosts masking his features. Of course he understood. How pathetic she must sound complaining when Genesis had his entire life stolen from him and turned into something only torture could produce. What had been going through his head all day after meeting Aava, after seeing exactly what he was torn away from?

"Genesis, I didn't mean to—"

"No," he cut her off, dragging his stare to the light, "I'm not upset. But please believe me when I tell you that you're not alone, trying to figure out all this unfamiliarity." The candle on the nightstand cast a warm glow on his skin.

"I've been trying to understand since I was taken prisoner—Flames, since I met Zarus. So much changed so quickly. It's still changing. I'm completely overwhelmed by it sometimes." He scoffed at the admittance, running his hand through his hair as he searched for the right words. Tension crept into his shoulders.

"I'm seventy years lost, and I have no idea where I fit into this world anymore. My kingdom is in shambles. My best friend's son is leading a civil war to reassemble it. I wish my magic would let me control my own emotions sometimes." His voice strained, an anger tugging at his tongue—one that he had held under control for so long that finally came loose.

Rin squeezed his hand, bringing his focus back to her.

"I don't know what I'm here for anymore, but I'm not searching for it by myself. You all have helped me so much the last few months; you, Tatsuo, Feyne, your mother... and now your guidance led me to Aava." A meek smile found its way to his face. "I'm not alone, and neither are you. If anything else, you can always seek counsel from me."

Despite everything on her mind, despite the magic still squirming in her head, and despite the tears still damp on her cheeks, Rin smiled. Something in her chest eased. It didn't disappear; everything was still exactly where it had been before Genesis walked into her room, but all the obstacles didn't seem so daunting right then.

"Thank you," she whispered, using her free hand to dry her eyes once more. A yawn slipped past her grasp.

Genesis frowned. "You really need to get some rest. How long has it been since you slept?"

Rin rested her head on the pillow. "Before we arrived in Xandra, hardly on the road."

His frown deepened. "Why didn't you mention it? I could have stayed up with you."

Her mind drew blank. He would have stayed awake with her?

"I—" she fumbled, "you needed to rest. Whenever I can't sleep, I look at the stars." She closed her heavy eyes, smiling as she saw the celestial tapestry behind her lids. "It's one of my favorite things to do, and lately I haven't had the downtime to sit back and watch the night sky, so it's the bright side of not being able to sleep. Although," she frowned, opening her eyes, "winter is coming fast this year."

Genesis listened to every word like she told him a story. Until finally, a smile warmed his face. "Why don't you close your eyes? I'll wake you when supper is ready."

At the mention of supper, Rin finally noticed the scent of herbs and seasonings downstairs. Her stomach growled like Feyne when Tatsuo irked him one too many times.

Rin shook her head, fighting back the veil of fatigue. "What if something happens and I lose control in my sleep?"

The prince looked down at her. A moment of consideration passed, when finally, he kicked his legs up on the mattress and leaned his back against the headboard.

"Well," he said with a sigh of relaxation, "I suppose I'll just have to stay awake and make sure you sleep soundly."

She frowned. "What about Aava?"

He loosed a shrug. "Eh, I waited seventy years to see her, what's one more hour?" He flashed a grin her way, tossing a blanket over her shoulders.

Rin stared at the prince with heavy eyes. Part of her wanted to protest, but the other half was already asleep. She rested her head against the pillow, falling into a dreamless sleep. Exactly how she wanted it.

Chapter Twenty-Four

A slew of profanities bounced around the hall. "You're bluffing."

A smirk laced Zarus's lips. "Open this door and prove it."

"You arrogant bastard," Errogan growled behind the door, "there is no way in all of Ashnagz and Lyhrëon put together that you have three purebloods. I just played two pures. No. Damn. Way."

"Well," Zarus shrugged for no one in particular, "if you don't unlock this door and show me that personally, then we'll agree to disagree."

"That's not how the game works!"

Zarus stifled a laugh. He didn't know the last time he'd played *Gallows*. While the card game was much easier to play when seated across from your opponent, able to see how many cards they place facedown and bluff their way to victory, playing from behind a door was a decent mental exercise. Keeping track of how many cards Errogan claimed he put down at least gave him something to do to pass the time.

Another week and a half gone, another week and a half confined to his room. No more tests, no more meetings. That was when Errogan wasn't hanging around his door. This was the fifth time in two weeks the demon had found his way outside of Zarus's room, sticking around long enough for a conversation or two. Zarus wasn't sure whether Eretimis was still assigning the prick trivial tasks like guard duty, or if Errogan intentionally sought his company. Whatever the answer, each time Errogan walked up to the door, his demeanor changed. Nessriq's words proved true; Eretimis was treating Errogan as a whipping post. The resentment became clear. Enough that the demon who still claimed to enjoy Zarus's suffering sought normalcy through his old friend; an escape from the demons that he worked with and for.

"I take it you're done playing?" Zarus asked. He leaned his head against the door he sat with his back against.

"Yes," Errogan grunted as he shuffled about. "You are impossible to play against."

"Here I thought you said this was going to be a challenge, E. Guess you're not as good as you say you are."

"You're not in much of a place to speak, if you ask me," the moonlit demon huffed.

Despite the unusual amusement in his tone, or the light-hearted mood, Zarus's laugh faded. The surrounding walls became a little more real, the fortress a little more imminent. "You're right, I suppose."

Eretimis had yet to mention the Infinite Key, if he would even mention it at all. Errogan picked up on the change of tone.

"I still don't get it, Zarus," his old friend said a bit too tenderly, but he caught himself. His voice hardened with the next word. "You can break this wall down; I have no doubt of it. I saw the aftermath of what you did in the throne room three months ago. You have your magic back. Nothing is keeping you inside these walls."

Zarus stared out the window across from him.

"Why are you still here?" Errogan asked, but it sounded more like a scoff.

Silence swelled Zarus's tongue. "It's the least I can do."

"For her?"

"Yes."

Zarus knew Errogan wouldn't understand. Flames, he didn't even understand it himself until recently and didn't blame anyone for questioning his sanity for surrendering his life for a human. But that didn't matter. Because she was closed in these walls with him, taken prisoner *because* of him. So, if the world had to suffer a little in order to keep Rin from Eretimis's mastery of agony, then Zarus would submit to that demand.

"What makes her worth your sacrifice?"

Was that disdain? Zarus almost couldn't tell through the apathy. He exhaled deep, wiping his face of exhaustion.

"Look, Errogan, I don't expect you to understand, but it's not that shocking. It's the same thing I would have done for you three hundred years ago."

What met him in response was a bitter laugh, jarring and abrupt. "Oh, please, three hundred years ago you would have left me out in the frozen wastes just so you could claim the kill."

Confused, Zarus opened his mouth to reply, then closed it again.

"Did you attain a head injury in the last few centuries? Actually, head trauma would explain the sudden shift of attitude... Because from what I remember, you were a part of me." Zarus didn't care to conceal the contempt in his voice. "Or am I the one who hit my head?"

"Burn in the Flames, Lowwenth," the demon grounded, a visceral ire trailing through the door.

"See you there, Errogan."

Errogan continued. "You turned on me. You brushed me aside so you could be number one, and you have the *right* to ask where I hit my head?"

Where is he getting this nonsense? Zarus's eyes narrowed. What had Eretimis fed into Errogan's ear while he was away on that mountain?

"You were the only person in this world that I trusted, Errogan. You shared my joy and pain, and I yours. And now after you tumbled down that ravine, it's like that doesn't call forth any memories for you." He shook his head, tried to keep the melancholy from his tone and kept himself centered. "I'm done arguing."

Something between a grunt and a laugh escaped Errogan's throat.

"You betrayed that friendship all on your own! Diving into that ravine was the best thing that ever happened to me! I don't care about your denial, and I don't care what happens to you from here, but you're being foolish. No one—not that girl, not me, not *anyone*—is worth more than your own freedom. I mean, you even saved that prince's life instead of your own!"

Zarus considered this. There was merit to it for sure, although he only saved Genesis Masquarem because he couldn't keep his head upright, much less find Rin and save her himself. Although in the end he didn't play his cards well enough...

He could leave right then, and his life wouldn't be any different. Rin Nowell would become another memory lost, and time would roll on, just as it had with Errogan. It was tempting, so tempting that Zarus contemplated it for a single moment. Until he also realized how easy it would have been for Rin to disregard compassion when they met. She could have used the free shelter, then left him fallen before the mirror without saying a word. But she didn't. She didn't leave him when he was so overwhelmed by his pain that he needed to use the mirror as a drain for his magic, and she didn't leave his side when he was retching at the base of the mountain with that silver blade in hand.

"That might have been the case at one point, but not anymore. If it spares her even a fragment of pain, then I'll be here serving Eretimis with my own free will."

Errogan scoffed.

"You're a fool, Zarus. A damned fool." The anger fled Errogan's voice, leaving him sounding tired and trampled. "Eretimis is ready. He's finished with his plans for you. It won't be easy, believe me; it will be the worst thing you ever experience."

Zarus's brow furrowed. *This is different from the usual mockery; this is a warning.*

"You've caused his liege one too many annoyances, old friend. He'll make this one hurt. You might want to try to repent to those gods you hate so much. For her sake."

Zarus's thoughts muted against the buzz in his head. The voice that was not his voice tried to speak once more, a chill wrapping along his spine, but he silenced it.

"Where do the depths of your loyalty end?" There was no judgment. Zarus had none, nor did he deserve to wield it. Simply... bewilderment? Errogan had always broken his back to please Eretimis, but now it seemed like he was severing his spine in two.

Errogan's words were a ghost's breath through the door. "With my life."

Zarus scrunched his nose. "You truly owe him that much?"

"I owe him my life."

"Just because he took us in doesn't mean he saved us, Errogan." Zarus's blood boiled knowing he once thought the same thing.

"That's not what I'm talking about... I wouldn't be here without the Dark Tyrant—I would be *nothing*."

There was a time when Zarus knew Errogan like the back of his hand. That time had long since passed, but something deep in his gut told him this stretched beyond what Errogan ever shared.

Zarus shifted. "So, what now?" The question sat heavy in the air.

"Now we both come to terms with our decisions."

Errogan made his choice, so had Zarus. However, Zarus's gut clench with what came next. The dusty connection to the gods sat quiet in his head, and he was sure of one thing. He needed to brush up on his prayers.

Chapter Twenty-Five

Zarus balanced on the edge of his last nerve.

The presence of others typically dampened his attitude, yet Zarus's skin crawled off while seeking the Divine's presence. His teeth ground together, his head pounded feverishly, and all together he wanted it to be over. Which was not as bad as he expected when he closed his eyes and reached his rusty prayers out to the gods.

Yath Ha they were called. The two creators, Olru and E'ral, responsible for writing the history of existence. Their helpers, the kaetha, were lesser deities that acted as counsel, warriors, messengers. There were hundreds of kaetha, possibly even thousands, all wielding a chip of the gods' power in themselves, but there were only four known by name to the mortals.

Lhaerem, Nraessa, Vulyn, and Mynil.

They were the Attendants, closest to Yath Ha. They used to walk freely through the land of Fawllhä. It had been countless millennia since those days, days before Zarus, even Eretimis. Yet it had been centuries since Zarus dared speak to the Divine. He used to frequent temples and shrines a lifetime ago, before he realized how cruel the all-knowing all-powerful Divine were. He sat on the edge of his bed, eyes closed, fingers digging into the wooden frame, wondering if he should be on his knees or not.

Each thought strained his mind, a recoil from his better judgment. The temperature of the room fell, his hot breath puffing into the air. Frost stiffened his fingers, his magic raging against the tension in his mind.

Perhaps asking the gods for help made him a hypocrite, but perhaps that meant nothing. And perhaps his mind was searching frantically for anything to distract him from reaching out.

Olru and E'ral, I ask for your benevolence. Spare Rin from the hands of Eretimis. Please allow me to find some way to get her free from his reach...

Nothing.

Zarus closed his eyes tighter and reeled his focus in.

Creators, I am seeking your guidance. I don't know what I should do. I don't know what I can do at this point. Rin's life is in danger because of me. I owe it to her to find a solution. To get her away from this place and from Eretimis's interests. Please, I—I beg you.

He tried not to snarl at the thought of it.

I need your help. I'm lost. How am I supposed to help her when I can't even find my own way away from him? Show her mercy, please, and tell me what to do!

Zarus sat in silence, the muscles in his neck taunt with stress. That was the thing about these gods the mortals loved so much. They were always too busy to reply.

He waited and waited and waited. Listening to the wind whistle outside, the muffled chatter of the fortress's crowded halls. Nothing stirred. Nothing answered. There was no echoed call in his mind. The gods who'd pestered him over the past three months finally decided they wanted nothing to do with him.

Zarus expected nothing more from the Divine high on their thrones of Lyhrëon. They'd left him to rot too many times to count.

But Rin? Zarus bared his teeth at those lazy beings, watched as ice crept along the room in a thick, rigid sheet. A draft pushed away from where he sat, extinguishing the flame of the sole candle.

It became a different story when they abandoned Rin.

Chapter Twenty-Six

"I was hoping you two would have left the fortress and spared me the displeasure."

"I wonder, Zarus," Raia mused with an unnatural tilt of her head, "did that sharp tongue come installed or did it take every century you're worth to forge?"

Zarus regarded the wraith with contempt. "I suppose there are some things you will never know."

"Perhaps..." Tesyl spoke from behind, "but it would take little to see how long it remains."

Zarus sent a shard of ice spiraling upwards from the ground of his quarters, where the second wraith idled. Like morning mist dissipating in the sun, Tesyl disappeared into the shadows before it struck. The darkness surrounding her sister stirred. The Wraith Twins stood side by side a moment later, blocking the door to his room.

"Come now, Tesyl," the eldest sighed, "this one won't play so easily into our hands."

"No, I suppose not," the younger shrugged. "The other is more amusing."

Zarus bit down on his tongue. It would help neither him nor Errogan to jump to defenses. Instead, he took a moment to size the two sisters up and down, searching for their objective.

A feral smirk widened Raia's expression. She swayed with the shift of shadows set by the fiery hearth. "You need not worry, pet. We're not here to steal your magic again."

Almost in the same breath, her sister picked up the thought. "Although against our request; the Dark Tyrant needs you standing this time. No more depthless spring to quench our thirst…"

They both hummed in unison, offering their own twisted smiles. "For now."

"You wouldn't have any luck this time around," Zarus warned, eyes narrowing at the beings who stood across from him.

Raia gasped, uttering a feigned disbelief.

"What's this? A backbone to be found? I thought Eretimis removed that already?" Her cadaverous leg slipped through the slit of her billowing skirt, carrying her in a stride across the room that ended at Zarus's side. Her grey complexion drained the vibrancy of the light. Dark hair fell limp at her back, intermingling with not one glint of the firelight, as if the entire source simply didn't reach her.

Tesyl followed suit, only finding her place on the other side of Zarus. The younger looked the same in the fire, only her shoulder length hair swayed with her step as they encircled him. "You know how dangerous such a thing can be, Zarus. It doesn't affect only you anymore…"

Zarus calmed his mind before the twitch reached his lip. Instinct clawed at his insides to tear the wraith's throats open. However, they were right. He clenched his jaw and held his tongue. Raia tilted her head to the side—taunting. He glimpsed the scarred handprint across her skin. He caused that. It might not have meant much, but it left a curve on Zarus's lip to know the wraiths broke—eventually.

"Shall we be on our way then?" Lost in thought as he was, Zarus couldn't pin down which twin had spoken.

He finally blinked. "Where might that be?"

Raia released a shrill laugh, shaking every nerve in Zarus's body. "Do not forget that *you're* the pet, Zarus. You don't ask questions."

A flash of teeth slipped his composure, creeping up before he could contain it. *One more time, if she calls me that one more time—*

His thought was cut ajar by a grip on his jaw. Tesyl twisted his head to face her. "Look now, sister dear, I think you've angered him. Growling like a mutt who lost his bone. Do you know what happens to mutts that disobey their masters?"

Raia smiled. "Why, they get corrected, Tesyl."

He narrowed his glare, letting his magic run as ice to Tesyl's hand, the bitter chill frosting her fingers. She pulled them away before he could snap them off one by one.

"I think I know exactly the punishment, Raia." A manic twist of her features spanned Tesyl's face. One could call it a smile. "We could catch that little worm of a girl, that human—"

"You'd lose your arm before you laid a hand on her," Zarus growled.

"Is that so?"

"I've scarred you once. I can do it again." His temper escaped him, but despite the open invitation to retrieve Rin Nowell from her dungeon cell, the twins remained at his side.

Raia and Tesyl were never ones to miss an opportunity for torture. They practically drank the misery of others. Yet here they remained, within the four bare walls of his little room, stuck with only his disdain for them to feed on. The Wraith Twins never chose the route of passiveness. The route of empty threats. Zarus realized no one had made him bear witness to Rin's torture, the one thing keeping him in the fortress. Did they need her unharmed? Eretimis should've jumped on the chance to display what would come if Zarus disobeyed.

A grim conclusion settled in his mind.

Zarus paused the notion and brought his stare to Raia and Tesyl. The twins were always ones to play games as well, and their tricks often left their victims verging on death. Or in his case, waking up on the throne room floor. Besides, the risk wasn't of his life, but Rin's.

"Don't make us wait, Zarus. You know how much we hate waiting." Raia sighed from his right, linking her arm around his.

"We have a surprise waiting for you," Tesyl added, connecting arms with him as well. "And this time you might not make it out all in one piece."

Raia stood on her toes and pulled him close, her lips a fragment away from his ear. *"You certainly won't be the same afterwards."*

Zarus tensed. He wouldn't be able to yank his arms free if he tried. "What might I be after this?"

Both twins smiled, both leaned in closer so there was no air between the words and Zarus's ears.

"A monster."

They stepped forward in time with one another, escorting him on either side in all his reluctance.

Zarus scoffed before he could care to catch it. He had been Eretimis's prized monster for nearly five hundred years.

Chapter Twenty-Seven

"We're almost there."

Rin pulled her gaze from the slick stone of the street to the buildings around her.

The day had finally come. It had taken weeks of preparation. Weeks of Rin determining what she would do if she was given an answer. Weeks of practicing her magic with Genesis, learning why it was in her head instead of her heart. Weeks of reading books to Scarlette, and combat training with Aava. A sense of urgency grew in the back of Rin's mind. She approached Genesis and told him it was time. The Temple of the Divine couldn't wait any longer.

The day couldn't have been worse for it.

The downpour halted to a misty trickle. They waited out the first brush of rain in the morning, hoping a break in the clouds would eventually roll in. Yet they would have to make do with the dark skies. The rain held off for a few minutes, but the storm resumed its flood when they were too far from Aava's house to turn around. The bitter droplets soaked Rin's core with a chill so violent it ached her bones.

She chewed the inside of her cheek. The tremble wasn't only from the cold. Walking the central street of Xandra northward toward the

Temple of the Divine, she couldn't help being crushed beneath the roar of her magic.

The hum in her mind deafened. Rin was rather unnerved to know that it was not from her anxieties over the temple. This sickening feeling, her magic... it only started once they hit the major streets of Xandra's northern district. The north was the most populated area of the city, but it wasn't as dangerous as the southern end. More people meant more eyes, and since more and more eyes were siding with the New Light, the Resurrection was less likely to strike in broad daylight. Which was exactly why the warning in Rin's mind concerned her. She knew if she voiced this, the others would see it as her nerves breaking free. They would insist on returning home and doing this another day when she was ready. However, Rin wanted nothing more than to get this over with.

In order to distract herself from the phantom cry, Rin watched Genesis. The prince seemed to be lost in thought too. Eyes flinching from one building to the next. It was when they roamed past a parkway filled with adolescent trees that Rin spoke. "Anything familiar?"

He didn't tear his gaze from the park. "I played here with my father when I was young. This park is the only thing that looks the same."

"After the downfall, most structures were ruined in the chaos," Feyne said as he led. "Nearly everything needed to be rebuilt."

Genesis looked from shop to shop. "Gillan mentioned that the entire northern edge of the city was newly constructed."

The shifter went on, his proud stride granting them a generous berth through the street. "Most of the damage from the temple fires was on the inside, so the exterior is as recognizable as the marshes of Damrok."

Tatsuo's brow furrowed. "Are the marshes recognizable?"

"If you've seen them before or were told what they are."

Before Rin could question the logic of that statement, Genesis's jaw clenched. She traced his gaze to the sea of mingling citizens hoarding the temple by the hundreds.

***

Rin didn't know if the crowd sparked joy or disappointment. Hundreds upon hundreds of people stood around the holy temple, waiting patiently to be next inside. If it was this hectic outside, she could only imagine what the inside looked like.

"That's a lot of people," she muttered, staring wide-eyed from the distance they stood.

Genesis huffed, planting his palm against his forehead. "None of us thought to consider it was the holy day."

"To be fair, I've lost track of how many days we've been in Xandra," Tatsuo mumbled.

Drenched and freezing, they all watched the bustle of people waiting for their time in the temple from beneath a canopied storefront on the opposite side of the square. The shower's intensity grew, yet none of the pedestrians left. Rin's heart sank as another twenty people gathered in the line.

This was supposed to be *the* day. She had finally prepared herself for it, and this is what she got... She rubbed her palms into her eyes.

"You'd think the weather would keep them at home," a voice said from behind the quartet, "but nothing keeps them away since this place opened back up." Rin glanced over her shoulder to find a young man named Aiden: Elyot Iver's son. To Rin's envy, the man remained completely dry with something looking like a parasol in his hand.

Rin wiped her drenched hair to the side. "How long does it stay like this?"

"On the holy day?" Aiden's eyes rounded as he thought about it, wiping his stubbled chin in a feigned thought.

Rin found he was a bit of an egotist, sometimes an ass, but kind. The type of man who knew where boundaries lie and liked to prod at them anyway.

"The last person will leave right as the sun sets. I'll be here making sure there's no issue until then." Rin noticed the hilt of a blade poking out beneath his cloak.

Not only did her heart sink down into her stomach, but it also did somersaults along the way. It was only midday.

"Does the temple close at sunset?" Genesis asked, turning around to face the hazel-eyed Nokomai.

Aiden's curly brown locks shook with his head. "No, Your Majesty."

Genesis frowned at the title, but Rin chuckled. Aava might have been introducing Genesis as the lost prince, but was clear the prince did not want to be known as anything other than Genesis. No formalities, no honors. He was only a man who *used* to be a prince. Aiden, along with many others, didn't believe his grandmother, but saw the irritation it stirred in Genesis all the same.

"The streets clear at night because of the horrors that rise when the sun falls."

"Night is when the Resurrection resurrects," Feyne sighed.

"Exactly," confirmed Aiden with a snap of his fingers. "Civil duties end when the day does, and that's when I'll be patrolling for danger. Not only that, but the city's been a bit disgruntled by all the sudden disappearances too. People go out, they don't come back. Keeps the streets clear of mischief after hours, that's for sure."

They had been told about the disappearances early in their stay. A deep thought fell over the bystanders. Aiden stood oddly amused by it but flicked his watchful stare to the temple now and then. He might be a prick, but he was an honorable prick.

"Rin," Tatsuo was the first to break the silence, "what do you want to do?"

All eyes fell on her; in the exact way she hated most. She sucked on her teeth for a second, shifting her weight back and forth. The longer the task remained unfinished, the heavier it would weigh. But asking everyone to come back after nightfall? She couldn't ask them to put their lives at risk—

"We should return just before the sun sets," Feyne said, finally breaking his stare from the temple and turning to face the rest of them.

Rin blinked twice. "Are—" she stuttered. "Are you sure? There's a reason everyone goes home at night." They successfully kept to themselves so far in the city. Did Feyne want to waste that cover for her?

The shifter shrugged. "We'll take them if they give us any issues. Besides, holy day or not, I bet this place is usually quite busy."

He glanced at Aiden, who nodded in confirmation.

"I think it would be easier for you to pray if you were by yourself, anyway."

Rin glanced at Tatsuo and Genesis, her heart drumming. Tatsuo spoke through a yawn. The back of his jaw revealed sharpened teeth, causing Aiden's eyes to bulge. "Rin, I'm here to assist you however you need, but anything would be better than standing in the rain waiting."

Genesis folded his arms and leaned against a post holding up the canopy. "It would give us the privacy and time you need. The decision is ultimately up to you."

Rin knew Aiden listened to their conversation while he pretended to focus on the crowds. Aava and Vi were the only ones who knew she was a white mage, since she slipped the information the first day they met, but it remained hidden from everyone else. And she intended to keep it that way. Between being hunted by Eretimis and targeted by the Resurrection for seventy years, everyone knew hanging around users was dangerous. They couldn't afford the spotlight.

She lowered her voice. "We'll come back at night and continue on with our business."

What could go wrong? She tried to convince herself as her stare settled on the mass gathered before the temple. *It's only the Resurrection we'll run into; you know, the group of ruthless criminals. Maybe even Eretimis's demons will be out here... nothing to worry about at all.*

"Well, I'm starving," Rin sighed, flicking the sodden fray of her bangs out of her eyes again. She direly needed to find a pair of sheers and cut them at some point. "Let's head back."

She promptly said her farewells to Aiden, who overexaggerated his surprise of their departure as if he wasn't listening to their every word. The road to Aava's house was fairly simple.

Rin laughed too airily for the distress she was under. Between Tatsuo's and Genesis's tales of old injuries, it was a surprise that either of them were still walking.

"Were they magic healers? That wound doesn't sound like something a nonuser could patch up."

Genesis weighed his answer. "Yes and no. We had hundreds of skilled healers in Nokomic when I was around; some were users, some not. Both were highly skilled in their craft. Nokomic was one of the last places users could be at ease with their magic. It was viewed as a gift here." Suddenly his expression tightened. "I assume that changed when Eretimis attacked. I heard the guards at the fortress discuss how many users Eretimis had hunted over the years. How they were becoming harder to find."

"Once a blessing to help the lands thrive and keep the people guarded, then suddenly turned into fuel for a witch-hunt." Feyne said. "Users were no longer welcome in society after they started bringing trouble wherever they went. Most retired the use of their abilities, some went into hiding."

Rin contemplated this for a moment. Having to keep part of yourself hidden to avoid ostracization, leaving everyone you love to keep them safe... She held tight to the leash of her mind. She didn't want to think about her mother right then, not with all the other things piling on her plate. Her next step cast her foot down into a puddle, splashing upward to the knee of her pants.

"Aside from the fact that an army of demons is hunting me, that's also why I would rather keep word of my magic quiet." Rin wiped the exhaustion from her eyes.

She started running every day with Genesis again, but for whatever reason, her head dulled with fatigue. In fact, her step swayed with the sudden weight tugging at her body. "Magic is great and all, but when people are so scared they would kill you for it—" Rin's tongue froze.

The rats scrambling at the far end of the path drew her eye to the mangled body on the ground.

The stench of iron smothered the air. Blood flowed into the sewers. The body had been left to rot. Mauled and shredded and left in bits, Rin caught glimpse of the claw marks along the flesh. A long, precise slice across the abdomen spilled onto the cobblestone, the digested contents of the soul's last meal splattered through the crimson. Two slashes marked the body's calves. A strike to keep prey from running. Her eyes watered.

Feyne crouched down next to the body. He ran his fingers carefully over the ground, where deep scratches marred the stone walkway.

The world fell to a hush around her, a buzz growing in her head.
Find shelter, child. Flee.

It was the first thing Yath Ha had spoken to her in over a month. Her magic raged against the chill climbing her torso. Everything fell still, Rin hit the ground.

Chapter Twenty-Eight

A thousand needles scorched her head, red hot and sizzling against her skin. Rin couldn't think with the phantom blaze burning her mind to ash. She grabbed her skull, dug her nails into her scalp.

'*Rin!*' she heard from above—a whisper compared to the wailing of magic that buried her.

Rin bared her teeth and pried her eyes open. A frigid wind reminded her of her wet clothes. The world stilled, shrouding her in confusion. Genesis's arms held her, his hands emitting a calming purple aura. Tatsuo and Feyne lay on the ground, limp and panting like stones gathered on their lungs.

"What—" Rin hissed at the stab of her throat. "What happened?"

Genesis hesitated. "You crashed to the ground."

Rin forced herself to glance at Feyne. Her throat tightened. "What about them?"

Genesis fell silent, his breath leashed. She tried to look at him, but his arms held firm.

"Genesis," she said quietly, "let me see."

He held her for a moment as Feyne and Tatsuo stirred. His arms loosened, allowing her to sit up and see the violet hue fade from his hands and eyes. His chest was a healer's nightmare.

His jacket blackened at the scorched edges. A hole burned through his shirt where she had been pressed. His chest... Blood and melted skin oozed from the burn. The stench of molten flesh roamed thick in her nose.

She whispered, "I did this?"

"You stopped it," Feyne coughed, his voice hoarse and crackled.

"Not until I lashed out at each of you!" Rin cried.

"You *controlled* it, Rin," Tatsuo gasped for air.

She shook her head. Suddenly, a thought occurred to her.

Rin checked the alley, studied the roofs and the corpse. Something had her magic on edge before finding it.

It wasn't a moment later that she heard footsteps approaching from behind.

Four humans blocked the alley exit. Feyne and Tatsuo were on their feet in seconds. Genesis was dazed and slow moving. The burn was worse than he let on. She helped him stand.

The man who led the group spoke first. His nose sat at an awkward angle, a scar lining his lip. His scowl stretched for miles.

"Looks like we've caught our killer, men." His voice boomed over the alley. The skies hid behind the clouds, casting a cool, stark light onto the city. He huffed a satisfied sigh. "Here I thought that one of the other factions had turned on us... To think this whole time, it was just some damned user."

Rin's stomach churned. They saw her fit of magic.

She kept her voice strong. "What are you talking about?"

The leader looked past her, amused that she was the first to speak.

"The disappearances," he said too softly for Rin's liking. "People missing from all over Xandra. It started only a few weeks ago, and I'll be happy to deliver the head of the user responsible to my boss. Especially finding her towering above her most recent victim—one of our own." He gestured to the body behind.

Rin quite liked her head on her shoulders where it belonged. The moisture fled from her throat, and she resisted the urge to rub the base of her neck. What would happen if she slipped one more time? Her gaze flicked sidelong to Genesis's reddened, charred chest.

"Sorry to inform you, but this fellow was like that when we found him," Feyne said, drawing the man's attention.

"I appreciate the intel, but it doesn't matter to me," the stranger shrugged. "Poor bastard's been dead for at least a day, a fool could tell you that. The fact is I now have someone to blame for it." His hideous features contorted into a smirk "People like a face to go with blame. Lets them sleep a bit more soundly. The Resurrection needs a boost of influence."

Rin snarled at the greasy smile the man threw her way. Even Aiden mentioned disappearances. Was this what happened to those who never ventured home? If it wasn't the Resurrection killing the missing... She forced her stare forward. The bile scratching the back of her throat wouldn't settle if she stole another glance of the body. She couldn't be blamed, could she? They had no evidence but their word... and a body blanched by her magic.

Tatsuo's growl vibrated her chest. "You'd forsake the blood of an innocent just to get people on your side?"

A bellied laugh rumbled the alley, stinging Rin's ears like the buzz of wasps. Each of the man's subordinates had the same humor as him.

"Kid, if you even have to ask that, then get the hell out of my city." The curve of the stranger's lip was anything but joyful.

"*Your* city?" Genesis spoke lowly; a deathly breath carried in the wind. "I don't think this pig understands who he's talking to."

All eyes shifted to the prince and the dark aura of his hands. There was something in his voice. A rage so still and stoic.

The man did not whimper at the sight. His smile deepened. "*Two* users? I get to behead *two* users today? Flames, Druvisk might very well kill his second right then and there and promote me!" A round of coughs exchanged between the man's lowers, to which he stuttered on his breath. "*Us*, I meant *us*."

Rin's chest tightened and hollowed all at once against the symphony of her rattling head. It wasn't until someone behind the man spoke that the fog suffocating her head cleared.

The woman's voice was nothing close to sweet. "We have orders to bring them to Druvisk for questioning, Darius, we can't kill them here. Even if they're users, someone might still see."

The woman was more put together than her associate. Much older than Rin. Her copper eyes almost looked *friendly*, her posture welcoming. Looks were deceiving. "Killing a kid in the middle of the street won't sit well with the people, Darius."

That scowl found Darius's face again. "We don't work to *sit well with people!*"

"Exactly," Feyne growled, taking a step between Rin and the strangers. "Who do you work for? Racline? Hewlson? Druvisk?"

The woman regarded Feyne with calculating eyes. "Druvisk."

Tatsuo *tsked* under his breath. "Assassins..."

Druvisk. Rin supposed he was another leader belonging to the Resurrection factions, like De'Rina. But assassins?

The woman resumed her stare at Rin. "You can wipe that expression from your face, girl. You're not dead where you stand. Not yet, at least. Our boss wants a word with you. In fact, all the Resurrection has been wanting a word with you ever since you stepped foot in Xandra. An anonymous tip was sent out for the light-wielding user. Someone's looking for you, girl, someone willing to go to the extreme to find you. All of you."

So they're not here because of the body...?

Rin's heart panicked. The Assassin Guild of the Resurrection was interested in her. Who on Armiria searched so intently for them? Someone pulling strings within the shadows.

Rin swallowed hard. Her resolve shook, threatening to fall out of place and leave her exposed. Yet she found the hilt of the blade strapped to her side. She swallowed the dry spit teasing her tongue and unsheathed her scimitar. Beside her, purple aura thickened, fire blazed, and a flash of light blinded.

The assassins were remarkably composed after watching Feyne shift into a beast more than half their size. Their shock faded, but they didn't catch wind of Tatsuo's spear manifesting within his grasp. He waved the weapon's tip toward the grey skies, a blaze rising between the assassins and Rin's friends. Three assassins stumbled away from the heat, but the fourth unnamed man was not so quick. He ran headfirst into the inferno, little more than charred bone and flaking flesh when he emerged through the other side. His cry was short. The burnt husk of a man fell to the ground. The remaining three assassins stared in horror as the flames died, even Rin stared at the unnerving glower Tatsuo wore. When he fought, he became something entirely different from the gentle soul she knew.

Feyne fought against Darius, while Tatsuo faced the nameless assassin desperately trying to dodge the flames at his feet.

Genesis watched Rin's back and she returned the gesture. The smug female assassin didn't falter when Genesis jabbed his short sword into her shoulder. She predicted where the prince intended to place his feet and swung her chained-sickle for his legs.

Genesis anchored his foot and leaned forward. His blade cut between him and his opponent, but the woman's sickle swung below the sword, wrapping around the blade. The chain pulled taut, yanking the hilt right out of Genesis's fingers. The sword rattled against the ground.

Rin swooped into the assassin's blindside, her scimitar striking her opponent's abdomen. The woman's face twisted as a stain of red formed along her shirt.

Rin ducked below the woman's fist and grabbed Genesis's sword. She safely fell back to his side, but the assassin didn't halt. A promise of death in her eyes, she charged for Rin. Her chain swung for blood.

Rin's breath caught in her throat. She didn't have enough time to dodge the sickle. She braced herself for the Divine Vulyn's guiding hand. But Vulyn ran late.

Rin peeked her eyes open, finding a dark haze gathered before her head. The magic licked against her skin. The woman's chain fell limp. A twin haze formed around Genesis's grasp, a line of blood trickling down his hand. Both auras faded, leaving the severed sickle in Genesis's hand.

This woman might not have cared when Genesis summoned his shadows before, but she certainly cared now that her chain was missing its lethal swing.

"Do you know what it's going to take to fix this, kid?"

"Believe me, nothing will be left to salvage if you keep this up." The faintest grin lingered on Genesis's lips.

It was then that Rin caught glimpse of the third assassin fallen on the cobblestone. Tatsuo joined Feyne against Darius. The fight was over.

A scowl found the woman's face, tearing any poise she might have possessed to shreds. "You might want to change your tone before I shove my fist into that pretty mouth of yours."

"You're hurt," Rin said levelly. "Leave now and—"

Rin's jaw snapped shut as a screech echoed off the alley walls.

A sickly light enveloped Xandra in response.

An unnatural shriek sent a shock through her core, all the way to her head. She jumped at it, and with her, so did her magic. Like lightning sparking in the dead of night, it flashed in and out in a matter of seconds.

Rin's mouth gaped. She grabbed hold of her magic and reined it in. But the burst still got the better of her, and everyone paid the price. And what about the scream? Where did it come from?

Rin didn't dare look at Genesis, nor Tatsuo struggling to drag himself near her. And Feyne? Feyne didn't move. Not once, but twice they were subjected to the violence of her magic. It stole the vibrancy of the alley. The roads faded, the colored roofs dull. The female assassin standing before her tumbled down to the ground, blanched and dried. Her magic threw Darius back. Even her own skin stung with needlelike pricks.

She bit back the sharp pain, wrapping her hand around her scimitar and standing. Whatever caused that ungodly screech was still out there. Rin took two steps toward the assassins rolling on the road before the world fell out from under her feet.

Her head buzzed with the impact. Her arm twisted in the socket. Fatigue seized her body and mind at once. Darius overcame the temporary blindness and climbed to his feet. The female assassin hovered over her, chain in one hand, Rin's scimitar in the other. Her friends still didn't stand. Rin cursed as she looked up at the woman.

Disdain twisted the assassin's face, spitting at Rin's feet. "Keep that evil to yourself, demon."

Rin grinned, dazed. "I know a few who you'd offend by calling me that."

The woman's brow arched but didn't pry into Rin's rambling. Rin's attention shifted to Tatsuo, held still beneath Darius's boot. To Feyne, not a muscle flinching.

Genesis's skin was ghostly; too exposed to her recklessness. Yet the prince's attention was not on her. She traced it to the end of the alley. Rin caught a brief glimpse of a four-legged creature stalking before it disappeared into a blur. Her eyes raced to find it, but heard Darius's scream a breath later. She witnessed the gore before the weight of the world barreled into her chest.

The air ripped out of Rin's lungs. Her bones reverberated with the shock of the ground. She tried to rub the white splotches from her vision, but she was pinned to the ground. Hot breaths puffed against her face. Daggerlike teeth hung inches away.

Shouts sounded like thunder in her tender ears. Beneath the pressure, it almost didn't register that a four-legged monstrosity hovered atop her. Almost.

The beast's teeth were sharper than daggers. Its eyes empty like grey, murky water. Powerful legs held her shoulders down, muscles bulging through greyish green flesh stretched so thin it seemed like it might tear apart. Its chest was twice her width. Its paws honed rigid claws thicker than her thumb. Barely anything but muscle and bone. The hairless being snarled, and she was stuck in a staring contest with it.

Rin refused to take a single breath. Because the monster had not yet lunged for her throat, unlike Darius's. Fear paralyzed her. Something froze the beast as well. Not even its stare flickered against the frigid breeze. It looked at her soul as if it were a book. She realized the murky eyes were reading her story. A thrum of power stirred inside her head, pounding on the inside of her skull.

There was a drag of steel, a reflection of light, and the monster searching Rin's soul recoiled with an ear-splitting yelp. Genesis carved her scimitar into its side. Blood black as oil splattered across her face. The prince pulled her off the freezing ground before she heard the howl. The female assassin raced to Darius's side, but the behemoth of a beast left nothing for her to save. Two other beasts appeared at the end of the alley, chasing an adolescent boy who tumbled to the ground in a fit of gasps and blood. Tatsuo pushed to his feet again and charged the two beasts with his spear, keeping them away from the young man. One slipped the *narikaah's* guard, and Genesis retreated from Rin's side so it didn't pounce on Feyne's unconscious body.

"You!"

Rin jumped out of her daze. The female assassin pointed a sharp finger at her.

"You did this! You summoned these beasts!"

The assassin charged her. Rin prepared for the assault, but an arm suddenly wrapped around her waist, yanking her to the side. The assassin tumbled to the ground. The motion stole Rin's breath, and when she looked to see who it was that pulled her, she found a figure clad in a white cloak.

"Who...?" Rin opened her mouth to question the newcomer, when the figure turned and offered a sidelong gaze.

The lilac stare held the gravity of twelve years. Luna's braid rested over her shoulder, draping out of the cloak like fresh honey.

Without a word, Luna leaned toward the assassin, caressing the woman's cheek as her nails dug into skin. The assassin snarled, but before she lifted a hand, her face turned grey beneath Luna's touch.

Grey and sickly green, until finally the skin deteriorated like a dry leaf. The aroma of the Pit's hollow air danced around the alley. Decay.

The assassin screamed as her body decomposed around itself, crumbled away to dust under the freezing rain. Luna did not remove her hand until the assassin's cries ceased. Her veins bulged, taut and exposed to the crisp air once the skin crumbled back just like her skull. Every piece of flesh, bone, blood, and tissue saw the light of day. Until nothing but dust remained.

So, this is Ma's magic...

Rin stared in disbelief until the beast who first tackled her stirred, circling mother and daughter alike.

Chapter Twenty-Nine

"What are these creatures?" Rin shouted. Her head stirred. Where had her mother come from? Why did she arrive with these beasts?

Four beasts stood before them, and Rin barely registered the young man cowering on the ground as Genesis and Tatsuo retreated to her side with Feyne's body in tow. To her relief, the wolf's eyes crept open.

Genesis handed back Rin's scimitar, his short sword rolling in his other hand. "They won't be alive long enough to find out."

As if it understood, one of the four beasts lunged for Genesis. Its claws scratched the steel of the prince's sword as he blocked. Genesis held firm to his ground. With a growl of strain, the creature tumbled back, landing on all fours.

"I've never witnessed something like this," Luna said calmly, except Rin recognized her mother's tension.

She had pulled back the white hood, keeping her eyes on the creatures. The monsters stared them all down, although the grey eyes focused on nothing. Rin watched their nostrils flare, the tilts of their narrow heads with the slightest noise. The beasts circled, and Rin stood back-to-back with her companions in the middle of the alley.

"Any suggestions?" Tatsuo grunted, whirling his spear as if to warm his joints.

"Aim hard, aim well," Rin muttered.

In a spare moment, Rin glanced down at the cowering man below. The gash on his arm was enough to stir the breakfast in her stomach, but it was the fashion of the wound that twisted her gut.

"Gen," she whispered.

Rin gestured to the gaping flesh, and the prince matched her graveness. The orientation of the slash was the same as the one on the corpse they found.

Rin knelt and offered the young man as much of a smile as she could, but it was enough to drag his attention away from the howling beasts. His disheveled curly brown locks fell over his rosy face. The emblem on his tunic caught her eye—the same woven knots carved into the steps of the temple. *Too young to be a priest*, Rin thought, *he must be a shrine hand*.

"You'll be okay," she smiled. "We're the best people you could have run into."

"I'd rather not have met you at all if these had to be the circumstances."

Rin could have laughed. "What happened before we got here?"

The shrine hand opened his mouth, but one beast snarled at Tatsuo and pounced. The dragon adjusted just in time, lodging the guard of his spear across the beast's mouth. He wrangled back and forth, unable to throw it off by himself. Feyne joined the struggle and slashed the creature's spine, warranting something between a snort and a gargle as it retreated to its pack.

Rin forced herself to look away, keeping her tone level. "My name is Rin. What's yours?"

The young man barely flicked his eyes to her before they rushed right back to the monsters inching closer. "Gavril," he said meekly.

"Where did these creatures come from, Gavril?" She did her best to sound like her mother, hoping that calming nature passed down to her and not her father's inability to hide what he was feeling.

Her fingers were white against the blade's hilt. She couldn't hide that.

"I was walking home from the temple," Gavril explained.

The stalking creatures growled, scraping their claws on the cobblestone.

"Something was wrong, like a nail pressed into the back of my head. It attacked right when I turned onto an empty road." His brown eyes lined with tears.

Blood leaked from his arm. Rin saw the flays of torn flesh hanging limp at his side. Whatever these things were, they stalked him before attacking.

"Well, that's enough convincing for me," Tatsuo muttered from behind. "Are we good to kill them now?"

One of the beasts howled deeply. The monster leapt, picking whichever prey was closest. Genesis barely held his ground. The prince gathered his balance and threw the creature back with his blade, but it became clear these beasts hunted as a pack.

Two more creatures flanked the prince, snapping wild jaws at his arms and legs. Before they mauled Genesis, Luna reached out her hand. Rin's spine shivered against the sensation of her mother's magic. The beast on Genesis's right met the same agonized fate as the assassin. Genesis pulled back the moment a tower of red inferno erupted into the remaining creature.

In moments, her friends scattered across the alley. Rin jumped to her feet as Genesis picked a fight with the beast calling the shots. She intended to aid him, but Tatsuo's cry pulled her attention as another creature settled its jaw around his arm.

Rin sliced into the stretched skin of the creature's back. Black blood welled from the wound. It instantly retracted its jaw and freed Tatsuo, but the sound of sizzling skin ensued.

The stench of burnt flesh hit Rin's nose. The beast's lip curled, its nostrils flared, showcasing a jaw that could rip the life clean out of her body in an instant. Yet instead of attacking or retreating, the slash she inflicted along its back slowly grafted together. Before she cursed the sun and moon, two hands wrapped around her shoulders, and Rin staggered backwards.

The sway of her head eased, and Rin found Tatsuo's spear advancing toward the beast that had lunged for her blindside. The creature was faster than the others, like a viper waiting to strike. The drumbeat in her head amplified.

Both beasts prowled back and forth before them, then both lunged for Gavril. The shrine hand froze in the middle of the street. He could do little more than cover his eyes from death.

Rin's heart pounded. She couldn't even shout. Instead, she did what any sensible person would do: threw herself after the monstrosities of death. She wouldn't let another person die! The itch in her mind swelled, and for once, she didn't fight it.

Light reigned across the alley. Not down from the heavens, but out from Rin.

The hum of magic sang inside her, finding its way out and reveling in the escape. Her breath hitched. Light flooded from her hands. For the first time since learning of the foreign power, Rin directed the magic through her will. It sparked and simmered. With each flicker, the warmth ebbed, but she didn't let it go. Even when she chased after the two beasts.

The monsters were nearly as tall as she was. Yet they recoiled and writhed under her light, stripped and blanched beneath it. Such monstrous strength, yet such painful cries. Rin threw her hands before her face and ran for Gavril. The creatures screeched against her touch, carving a path between them.

The shrine hand didn't flinch against her light, but Rin didn't know how long she had before the creatures worked around it. And what of the third beast? She flicked her gaze to Luna, Genesis, and Feyne. It was fighting them, unaffected by the light.

Rin hefted the young man to his feet with a grunt. Her muscles burned. The growls of snapping maws raged behind, but she dragged the Xandrite beside Tatsuo before the beasts overcame the burns.

Rin released Gavril's arm, forcing his legs to take on the weight of his body. "How did you do that?" he gaped like a fish, watching the light slowly fade from her hands.

"Frankly," Rin panted, "I have no damn clue. But I would really appreciate it if you didn't tell anyone." She sucked in one last gulp of air.

"No damn clue, huh?" Tatsuo asked from her side.

By the time the beasts ceased their wails, their burns had already simmered shut. Only the scar remained. As she opened her mouth to suggest a plan, a boulder smashed into her back. At least, it felt like a boulder.

Rin caught her balance before she tumbled over, spinning to find Genesis already on the ground. His forehead leaked like a crimson faucet. The third beast buckled its hind legs, ready to pounce on the fallen prince, but Feyne and Luna stepped into the opening between them. Refusing the go near her mother's decay, the creature pivoted, redirecting its leap to the side and snarling at the deathly magic.

Rin and Tatsuo helped Genesis to his feet, only to find that he could barely put any weight on his leg. "Well, Nowell," he muttered, "got any other brilliant plans up your sleeve?"

Luna's monster gave up and retreated to its pack as Feyne guarded their huddle.

"Actually," Rin smirked, "I do."

Her eyes locked on her mother. She understood what her daughter intended immediately. Their blades couldn't kill these monsters. Rin sheathed her scimitar.

"Are you sure about this, Erin?" her mother asked. Rin nodded.

She didn't know what had changed from that morning, but it was as if something clicked into place. Rin refused to die before meeting Yath Ha, before helping Zarus. For the first time, she saw the power inside her as the only means to live. The faint glimmer of her hands staved off the cold.

Luna's hands emerged from the heavy wades of her cloak, ready to end this.

Both Genesis and Tatsuo were bruised and beaten.

"Stay by Gavril," she breathed.

Then she turned to Feyne. "If any come near, corral it back to us."

The wolf's head nodded.

Rin swiveled around on her heels, feeling the ice forming with the sun's fall. While the giant pack leader roared its might, she embraced the warm light fluttering within her body. Its pounce was swift. The world before her succumbed to a vibrant flash.

The creature hissed against the light, tumbling away. It scraped at its blinded eyes, allowing Luna to advance unnoticed. Her touch on its back was all it took. The beast writhed. Death masked the air, the stench tearing Rin's eyes, and she could have sworn the other beasts writhed with it. There was nothing left of the creature to heal.

The two remaining beasts regained their composure, no longer thrashing with their fallen brethren. They watched, assessing as if they had never seen one of their own die. It was the bulky one that threw caution to the wind, labeling Luna as the primary threat. With another flare of Rin's light, they made quick work of the nightmare. Yet Rin blinked twice, for when she looked into the beast's eyes as it decayed, she found the murk had faded, replaced by the clarity of a green eye. No pain, no rage. All until it was gone.

The final creature screeched, its body contorting until it was the last one alive. It watched and waited, knowing what had come of its pack, and it did not make the same mistake. The beast lunged. Rin readied her power, but when her light sparked to life, the creature closed its eyes. It soared past her, aiming for the prince and *narikaah* guarding the helpless civilian.

Rin and Luna cursed in unison. Much faster than the last two, but the creature toppled off its path as Feyne rammed into its side. Luna threw herself forward, reaching for the creature's back, but it sensed the mage. The beast bucked its hind legs, throwing Luna across the street.

Rin cried out. The creature wrestled against Feyne, regaining its ground and throwing the wolf backward onto Tatsuo with the slash of its lethal claws. It barreled into Genesis, knocking him over and pinning him down. The prince thrashed against the weight, but it was too heavy. Shoulders pressed onto the icy ground; Genesis tucked his legs beneath the monster's torso. He couldn't wedge it off. The beast roared.

Tatsuo shoved Feyne off and sprinted to the prince's aid. His bleeding fist slammed into the creature's head, flames erupting through his knuckles. The monster jolted to the side, convulsing against its blistering skin—skin that didn't heal. Genesis trudged to his feet. Luna was still gasping on the ground.

Think, dammit! Rin ground her teeth together, but her foot slipped on the fresh ice covering the street and flipped her onto the cobblestone. Her head rattled as she lifted her cheek from the ground. Despite the sting of torn flesh on her face, Rin's eyes brightened with an idea.

"Hey!" she shouted, climbing to her feet. "I'm not finished, you ravenous rat! How pathetic to have a jaw like that and not have killed any of us!"

Everyone gawked at her nonsense. The beast also looked at her. Its murky eyes narrowed as it realized she stood alone.

"I'll leave the grace of Ashnagz's paradise and descend into its Pits so I can beat your hideous self in the afterlife too!"

Rin screamed madness, but the beast was intelligent. It watched her hands for light, sized her up and down. Cold sweat lined her back. She slowly rested her hand on the hilt of her blade, the beast riling in response.

Its claws clenched down, cutting through the ground like sand. The creature sprang forward with a roar, eyes closed, the burn on its face wrinkling with the action. Rin waited. Her mother heaved a cry. Even Gavril finally jumped into motion and called out her name. Rin didn't move until the beast was an arm's length away and its jaw unhinged to snap her neck.

She leapt out of the way, drawing the scimitar as she went. The earth quaked as its bat-like feet hit the ground and slipped out beneath it. The ice cracked as its claws tried to grab hold, but it tumbled hard, crashing into a brick wall on the far side of the street. Rin ran for the beast, casting a soft light from her hand on the ground to avoid the reflection of ice. Without a moment's hesitation, she channeled the thrum of power pulsing through her mind.

A wave of light challenging the sun. She watched as the creature of nightmare shriveled against her magic. Grey skin blanched, cracking and drying as she poured out every ounce she could find. Its very soul burning. Rin didn't cut off the flow of magic until the rage faded from its eyes. Like a candle blown out in the night, the late afternoon light enveloped the world again.

The lanterns took rein. The beast lay in shambles against the alley wall. Stretched skin threatened to peel apart. None of it healed. It loosed one final growl as she approached. However, as the other had, the beast's eyes cleared to blue and became rounded and full of suffering. A plea for a merciful end.

Rin paused, surprised. An entirely different being from the one charging at her moments ago. Its entire body convulsed. The silent pleading faded, replaced by the snarling rage that fueled the creature lying on death's doorstep.

Rin's heart rebelled when she raised her hand after the softness she witnessed. The blue eyes turned grey again. Whatever shred of consciousness it had wouldn't hold out for long against the beastly rage. Rin raised her blade, hand trembling, and slit the creature's throat.

Chapter Thirty

R aia and Tesyl flanked Zarus, giving him no chance to slip free. A smugness resided in their stride, knowing something they had not deigned to share. Something that had Zarus raising a brow when the unpleasant duo marched him right past the throne room.

He noticed the unusual buzz of the fortress. Even with hundreds stationed at the fortress on a typical day, the halls never rang. Everyone had their duties to fulfill; everyone had their assignments. Why was a building stuffed full of the most obedient beings in this world singing with chatter and life? Zarus pondered that until they came to a pair of double doors opened wide. The courtyard beyond was bittered with ice and snow. He hissed against the unusual clarity of the world, but after seeing the harrowing mass of shadows over the fortress, he realized he had been cooped indoors for too many months. He was in Rin Nowell's company when he last witnessed the light of day.

Zarus's skin stung against the gusts. He caught sight of the masses gathered within the wide stretch of the courtyard. It was a circular hollow in the fortress carved of weathered stone, opening wide so that hundreds of thousands could stand within. What was once likely used for ceremonies and rituals for those damned Divines was now used for the occasional announcement, and only if that announcement required all the demons in the land to be present. It rarely did. The last time Zarus saw the yard in use was when Eretimis announced he was moving troops into the western continent of Armiria—half a millennium ago.

Exposed to the extremes of the unforgiving North, not one soul dared to flinch against the winds. Hundreds of conversations roared at once until a figure appeared on the pale ivory balcony overlooking the courtyard on the far side of the circle. Five hundred conversations hushed, a flame blowing out from a wick.

Eretimis stood above his masses. From the moment he stepped out, Zarus knew this was no mere announcement. The Tyrant wore his battle armor, the polish of black metal reflecting against torches and braziers. The edges of his hair frayed like a shadow. Behind him, Errogan stood to his right with none of the vulnerability he'd shown earlier. In fact, the White-Cloaked Reaper appeared to be his usual malicious self upon that ledge. Nessriq stood to the left of the Dark Tyrant. And almost imperceivable, a new face stood. Tucked behind the Tyrant, he stuck close to the door. Even Zarus saw his violent shiver all the way from the other side of the yard. The middle-aged human was doing his best not to freeze in the Northern Wastes.

Zarus listened hard to what was so important that every demonic soul was required to hear it, but as Eretimis opened his mouth to speak, the twins yanked him away.

He snarled at the pull of his limbs but moved on. There was no use fighting the Wraiths. They wished to give him just enough to drive his curiosity mad, and they succeeded. Zarus growled to himself about it when Eretimis finally spoke.

"Too long have we demons idled! Too long have the humans ruled what rightfully belongs to us—"

Stone and wood-worked walls muted the speech as his escorts forced Zarus around a corner.

***

The laboratory. Zarus was not expecting the laboratory. His body tensed with the memory of being held down as his arm was sliced open. The serum still haunted him. His eyes searched the dim room while the Twins made their exit.

"Enjoy it while you can," Raia crooned, a feral smile cracking her lifeless face.

His gaze narrowed. "Enjoy what?"

Tesyl sounded a chuckle, a cat choking on its own tongue. "Life before the throes."

The Wraith Twins faded into shadow, the door shutting where they once stood. Zarus wondered if they even bothered locking it. He hated to say it, but he didn't know what to expect. From what Errogan warned and the twins taunted... frost lined his back. The table full of blades and devices of torture caught his eye. Then the flash of glass bottles, all holding their unique mixture of suffering. Zarus sucked in a deep breath, trying to ignore the suffocating aroma of herbs and poisons.

Whatever it is, whatever Eretimis forces you through, you can take it.

He didn't believe his claim, and his resolve shook at that realization. The ice cracked. His mask slipped. Zarus did not know what Eretimis had planned for him, but it was a fool's death to do nothing but wait.

See the truth, impenitent child. Escape these halls and flee his grasp.

The gods still gave a damn. For once, Zarus agreed with the Divine and made quick work of searching the room. He scoured drawers, pulled back curtains that hid no windows, pried the corks from bottles. All he found was a small vial in the empty drawers. He stuffed it into his pocket after wafting the scent to make sure it was a strong acid. He halted his search once the doorknob clicked.

The Tyrant entered, still in his armor. A shadow in the lantern-lit room. Even Zarus couldn't deny the visceral fear it struck in him.

"That was quite a crowd." Zarus kept his voice flat.

"A grand turnout." Eretimis smirked, clearly pleased. "The better half of the demons on Armiria made it in time to hear."

He called everyone back? Zarus narrowed his gaze. What could be that important?

"Must have been quite the show with a crowd full of demons *and* humans. So, tell me, when did Eretimis the Dark Tyrant decide humans were worth listening to?"

Eretimis watched Zarus with an unblinking gaze, searching far and wide for the prisoner's intent. The Tyrant severed their stare and walked to the wall arrayed with devices of torture. Some were blades with unorthodox curves, other utensils that had one grotesque purpose. Zarus had seen all the instruments in use.

"Tools are made to be used, *uhlandyi*. It does not matter what form they take."

A snarl tugged at Zarus's lip. He was no longer Eretimis's student, his *uhlandyi*, no matter how many times the Tyrant insulted him with the title. But he had no room to fight it.

"It matters to most." Zarus kept his eyes on the demon and not the tools he hovered over. "How did the masses take it when they discovered a human was in their midst?"

"The same as when they heard you risked your life to protect one of the same." He didn't even care to look at Zarus when he spoke. "When they realized it was not an attempt at humor, they listened. The human is an asset at this time, so I will use him as I see fit while it lasts."

As you do everyone else. Zarus wondered for a moment. If he was of use to Eretimis, the human must be quite ruthless. He could have asked more, but they were the only souls in the desolate laboratory.

"Why am I here, Eretimis?" Zarus asked aloud.

"Because you chose to save a life rather than take one. Because you defied me three hundred years ago and thought you were above paying the price. Because you never seem to make the right decision." Finally, Eretimis looked over his shoulder. "The list goes on, boy."

Zarus bit down on his tongue. "Why did you bring me to this room?"

A malevolent grin met the Tyrant's lips. He struck a chord, and he knew it. "Because you are a tool, Zarus, and the usefulness of your current condition has run out. You have gained too much of a conscience, too much of a voice."

"I've always had a voice," Zarus growled.

"Then you made the mistake of using it. Mistakes are for the weak, and I do not enlist the weak."

A scoff escaped his throat, thick and loud in its freedom.

"*I never enlisted.* You dragged me here against my will!" Zarus's fist slammed onto the stone table beside him, the rock splintering beneath his touch.

A rawness gripped the air, enough to cloud the breath before his lips. Little by little, Zarus's composure shattered.

Eretimis inclined his head, a sharpness taking hold of his shadowed features. "Watch that tone, boy, unless you want to see blood shed today—"

"Will I now?" Zarus interrupted. "Wouldn't that be something worth seeing! Because from what I can tell, you're pulling these claims out of nowhere! Tell me something, oh *honorable* stain on *all of existence,* how—how on every dying breath of those slain for you—are you going to shed the blood of Rin Nowell when she isn't even here? What magic will you conjure to execute that, what ties will you pull, what soul will you sell to draw out this delusion of a lie *any* longer? I've had my suspicions, but now you've cleared any doubt. So go ahead! If you truly are hellbent on forcing me to my knees again, poor blood on the ground before me before I even *consider* it!"

Zarus snapped. Every ounce of patience he collected crumbled away above the absence of his facade. '*See the truth.*' Too long did he hold his eyes shut at risk of being blinded. Too many times had they threatened Rin, too many times they dared mention her name. All with nothing to show for it.

Eretimis's silence droned on, his stare so sharp it cut through the very breath in Zarus's lungs. He read the Dark Tyrant like a book. Zarus was well beyond trembling under that stare. His teeth bared, a bitter laugh cracking his scowl.

"Do you have nothing to say? I saw through your pathetic lie, broke free from your trivial control *again*, and you have nothing to say?"

Eretimis was motionless, a statue in the deep night. His silhouette blurred as the shadows tugged along his body, the rest of the room fading of color. Yet it ended sooner than it started.

The fray of darkness returned to its natural sitting so quickly, Zarus would have missed it if he had blinked. Eretimis slipped. Zarus had successfully awoken the beast trapped inside the Tyrant's poise. Because Zarus saw it from the moment he first laid eyes on Eretimis. From the moment he turned Zarus's entire village on him; Eretimis's true nature. A beast clawing to free itself of the shell the Tyrant chained it inside. However, the hush prolonged.

"I am disappointed, Zarus. After all this time, after so many years of teaching, you still cling to foolishness like a child clinging to its mother."

Zarus dug his heels in. He wouldn't take the bait, no matter how loudly his magic raged.

The Dark Tyrant's voice shook the room, reverberating through his bones. "You want blood?" Zarus's gut twisted at the words. "Very well. Remember something, *uhlandyi*: this is yet another decision you have foolishly made."

There was no smirk, no flaunt of victory in Eretimis's tight expression. Zarus may have pushed him over the edge, but the Tyrant chose when the beast got released.

Zarus swallowed hard. The callousness of the Dark Tyrant's expression twisted into a sneer.

"*Errogan.*"

Chapter Thirty-One

Errogan's hair was dull in the lantern's glint, his eyes the same. He walked into the laboratory, face still flushed from the winds outside.

Zarus's heart dropped. The room went as silent as his thoughts. The Dark Tyrant smiled at him in satisfaction.

"Stop this," Zarus begged. Confusion arched Errogan's brow. The demon didn't know what awaited him inside the laboratory. "This is between you and me, not him."

Errogan's jaw tensed, understanding sinking like a rock. His entire body froze, not allowing a reaction to betray him. Not an flick of dread showed, but Zarus knew the panic swelling behind Errogan's expression. Eretimis's smile deepened.

Zarus bit down hard enough to well blood. *You made it worse.*

"No, Zarus. As usual, you fail to see the weight of your own decisions." Eretimis shrugged, the edges of his form faded into the slightest blur. "Attacking me when we first met created more than you know. Running away from my service hindered my reign over this realm. Defying me over and over again affects all those around you, not only yourself."

Eretimis's hollow gaze dug into Zarus's skull. "Perhaps I have been too merciful in my biddings. Perhaps I have not done my part to teach you what it means for everyone else when you disobey my word."

Zarus dug his teeth into his tongue. *Nothing.* Falling to his knees would do nothing to help Errogan. Begging for forgiveness would do nothing to appease the Tyrant looming before him. Zarus's blood chilled, then boiled. His heart thudded a storm. *Don't do this.* He wished so desperately to plead, but he couldn't. He couldn't even bring himself to move a muscle.

His mind blared, raging like a thousand instruments all out of key and time. The passing moment blurred. Eretimis had dragged Errogan before him. A masterpiece of agony contorted Errogan's face, yet not a single grunt made it past the demon's lips. Years of mental calluses built up for such an occasion. Even calluses fade.

Grey scale doused the throne room as Eretimis's magic stole every shadow in the chamber. The magic formed a shell around Errogan, his dull silhouette visible. Eretimis stood motionless as he cast the ferocious power. Zarus's lips pulled back from his teeth as the shell collapsed inward. Errogan's howls echoed off the walls. The Tyrant's narrowed stare eased, the shadows subsided as the magic dispersed; the stolen color soaked the room once more.

Grey faded to red. Errogan's face was barely discernible through the gore. His gashes delved deep enough to reveal stark white bone. Crimson pools flooded around his body. Errogan's stare traced to Zarus, something of a plea slipping past his control.

Zarus's teeth clenched so hard his ears rang. If he fought back, Eretimis would only make it worse for Errogan.

The Tyrant looked at the battered demon at his feet, a shadow slicing through Errogan's back. The demon's teeth bared against the strike, red staining his mouth, eyes rolling back against his will. Whatever happened three hundred years ago, Zarus didn't care. He did not care if Errogan hated him.

Errogan's cries grew hoarse, his body convulsed with each strike. Zarus pinned his crimson stare into the Dark Tyrant. He never saw it clearer than he did then: he simply did not care what it meant for himself anymore. He conducted his yearn for blood so perfectly, so precisely, not even Eretimis saw it coming.

The room chilled. The shadows gained even more depth. Ice and darkness combined into one and spiraled with lethal intent.

Zarus gritted his teeth, but he didn't have the time to collect himself. Every ounce of magic Eretimis unleashed on Errogan suddenly turned back on the Tyrant.

The flash of power was direct. The magic struck the Tyrant's heart, but Eretimis didn't fall to Zarus's shadow-ice. Instead, they both stared at the red hue of shadow magic.

Zarus looked past the crimson glow coursing within his magic and narrowly evaded the swarm of shadows Eretimis summoned. He was a breath away from the stone table that was sliced in two.

"A little more practice, and you might hit me," Zarus taunted.

He hoped—*prayed*—that Yath Ha might shed some favor on him. He needed Eretimis away from Errogan. A plan formed in his head when the color of the laboratory suddenly sucked away.

Eretimis barely flinched. He stole the room's shadows, wearing it like a cloak upon his shoulders, a hood over his head. Not even the Tyrant's hollow gaze pierced through.

Zarus's shadow rippled beneath his feet. He jumped off the dark pool before it swallowed him whole. Before he hit the ground, Zarus reached down and touched the shade with a frostbitten hand, a mirror of ice crystallizing over the pool of consumption. He lunged off the ice and for the Tyrant, putting Errogan's unconscious body behind him.

Zarus reached for Eretimis's face beneath the shadows, his icy nails ready to tear the demon to shreds. But he was forced aside. The Tyrant's shadows surged over him. Zarus delved into his pocket and shattered the stolen vial into the darkness. The acid fizzled against the dissolving magic.

He shifted his weight and circled behind Eretimis. His movements were quick and precise; enough to land a blow on the Dark Tyrant's back. Zarus stomped down, a path of ice stretching across the floor and reaching up Eretimis's legs while Zarus summoned enough darkness to drown out the sun. The wave bellowed toward the Tyrant. Rather than fight against the ice on his legs, Eretimis ducked below the shadows. Zarus pulled the magic back before it consumed Errogan's unconscious body. The Tyrant shifted his weight, shattering the ice encasing his legs.

Zarus narrowed his eyes to keep track of the demon. The room's monochrome lanterns flickered against the unnatural dark. Black and grey surrounded everything. He pinpointed an advancing blur. Zarus held out his hand, a wall of ice towering from floor to ceiling in the Tyrant's path, but the shadow rammed through the barrier. Ice shards sliced Zarus's cheek.

He advanced toward the billowing shade that was Eretimis, frost biting one hand and a mist of crimson-hued darkness in the other. His only choice was to strike before he was struck.

The nip of frost absorbed into the shadows as Zarus collided with Eretimis. No blades, only unrelenting magic. Zarus's crimson shadow clashed harshly with Eretimis's depthless void. Each strike of his magic raged against the thanatoid pull of Eretimis's. The Tyrant tried to wield Zarus's as his own, but Zarus held tight to his power.

The absolute pull of the shadows, the emptiness intertwining through the air, and the dead silence all registered at once in Zarus's head. Realization clicked amid the violent magic. Zarus had the upper hand. The Tyrant hadn't landed a single blow, and blood still poured from his wound. Eretimis was on the edge, perhaps even over it. The battle was life or death, and Zarus knew the Tyrant wasn't thinking straight. Possibly for the first time in two millennia. A strike through the heart was enough to send the Tyrant tumbling off that precarious edge.

Zarus focused on the movements beneath the shadow cloak. Eretimis fell still, halting his step so abruptly that the shadows pulled away from his body. For a fraction of a second, Zarus caught sight of the Tyrant's eyes burning with rage. His normally poised expression tainted with the desire for blood.

The shadows surged, stretching out from the Tyrant. Zarus threw himself down and covered Errogan's body. A dome of ice crackled to life around them as the wave hit. Zarus's magic groaned with the impact, threatening to shatter as the shield had, but he bit down. He held it in place with everything he possessed and watched the laboratory torn to shreds beneath the pressure of Eretimis's attack. The floor rumbled, the walls shook, the cabinets and tables crumbled. Zarus didn't let his grip slip until that wave finally passed. And when it did, he didn't hesitate. If Eretimis wanted this to end in death, fine. Zarus didn't intend to end it any other way.

Zarus summoned forth a handful of darkness, its misty tendrils flaring around his palm. Concentration and adrenaline beaded down his brow. The magic stretched his limits, but he did not buckle. He lashed back at the magic, forcing the mist in his hand to take shape.

The power struggled to keep form. A shadow-forged dagger met his gaze. He shattered the dome of ice protecting himself and Errogan. Eretimis was still in a craze, the shadows pouring out from him. They hit Zarus and Errogan like the gale of a storm.

Zarus groaned against the magic, forcing his step one foot at a time.

"K-keep trying," he growled, gaining another step, "you can't hold me back anymore."

The force was too powerful and depthless. Zarus was slipping. He gritted his teeth, narrowed his eyes.

He forced his body to lean into the current, raising a barrier of ice that divided the room in two. Only this ice, it was different. Frost and crimson shadows frozen in one like a kaleidoscope. The barrier groaned and cracked as magic battered against it from the other side. Heaving breaths filled his lungs. His heart thundered in his chest.

The Dark Tyrant's attempts to break through the ice were feeble. Even after he stretched his grasp, after Zarus saw the shadow beneath his very feet stolen and sucked under the wall of ice, the barrier endured. His crimson magic was the only color within the laboratory, and it had the Tyrant abandoning his strategy.

Zarus kept calculating. He barely took a breath before Eretimis barreled into the ice and crashed through the wall. The looking glass fell. Zarus met Eretimis head on.

Zarus gripped the hilt of the shadow-dagger. His teeth bared, flashing a wicked snarl that bellowed deep in his throat. He lunged for the Dark Tyrant. The dagger met its mark, piercing straight into Eretimis's torso, slipping through the shadow cloak and the obsidian armor beneath. Zarus's head was on fire; the will it took to keep the blade sharp enough absorbed his focus. He twisted it until the dark grey liquid pouring out of the Tyrant's side drenched his hand. He ripped the phantom blade free. Eretimis's grip on the shadows slipped.

The cloak thinned enough to see Eretimis's armor, some shadows returning to their natural positions. Crimson dripped to the ground. The muted colors bled into the room as the Tyrant's blood poured out. Zarus saw nothing but rage in his dark eyes. Before he could react, a tendril of darkness slithered out from the shadow returning to Zarus's feet. Fast as an arrow, the tendril aimed for his neck. Zarus grabbed the tendril, stopping it in its path.

Clarity filled his mind. Enough to force his will over the magic in his hand and make it submit to his control. When Zarus finally released the limb of shadow, Eretimis no longer guided it.

Zarus sucked in a deep breath. Without flinching, the shadow magic slithered around Eretimis's neck. The Tyrant's eyes widened, full of fury and hatred, his hands gripped at the tendril. Zarus tightened it. A snarl pulling back Eretimis's lips as his legs buckled, sending him to his knees as he scraped for a hold on the magic. Zarus grabbed hold of the Tyrant's head, one hand on each side, and dug his nails in, cutting through skin and drawing blood.

A hiss slipped past Eretimis's throat. As Zarus gripped the Tyrant's skull, understanding bloomed in the Tyrant's eyes. More shadows escaped Eretimis's grasp; more color poured into the room.

Zarus forced the Dark Tyrant to look him in the eye as he formed a spike of shadow and ice. This was it. This was *finally* it. The moment Zarus craved all those years. He was going to kill Eretimis. Every guard or demon who could stop him was off preparing the orders Eretimis gave them in his announcement.

Exhilaration danced along his skin. It was his magic that Eretimis was always after—killed over and over for. So, it was his magic that Zarus would give him. He leaned in—close enough to feel the wheezing breath of the Dark Tyrant, close enough for the Dark Tyrant to hear his growl.

"Blood will be shed."

Spittle leaked from the sides of Eretimis's mouth with nowhere to go as the darkness suffocated him. The spiraling spike above his head solidified, hardened into the edge that would take his life. Something flickered in Eretimis's eye that arose with death staring him in the face. Something Zarus didn't give a damn to figure out. The spike crashed down, aiming between the Tyrant's eyes. Zarus awaited the sight of blood.

But blood never came.

The spike froze midair, tearing away from Zarus's control like flesh from bone. His control over his own magic paused. The disconnect shuttered through his head like a hatchet splintering wood. Even the tendril wrapped around the Tyrant's throat fell to the floor. No matter what Zarus did to regain control over the magic, nothing worked. And his frustration must have been apparent.

Of all damn times, why in the Flames—
Not now, child, not yet. The key is still missing.

Zarus nearly screamed at the gods in his head. He could have killed them. Tore their Divine selves apart one by one until there was nothing left but strands of holiness. Eretimis's scowl faded, replaced by a tug of the lip that might even be called relief. Something shifted in the corner of Zarus's eye, bruised and broken.

"Sir," Errogan groaned, looking up through moonlit strands stained crimson. "We... we need him unharmed for the procedure—"

A hail of shadows splintered into Errogan's chest, pinning the demon to the ground.

Zarus made the mistake of looking at his old friend.

Whatever halted his magic was not a mercy granted by Zarus, and Eretimis didn't return the favor.

Too late, Zarus saw the shift of the tendril protruding from his shadow. The jab didn't skewer him, didn't even make it all the way to his back, but it hit exactly where it needed. Zarus cursed through his teeth, falling to his knees. He pressed his hands hard against the stab wound oozing pools of red onto the floor.

Bitterness overcame him. The shiver reached his spine, coursing through his mind until his blood was ice.

Inches. He was *inches* away from ending the Dark Tyrant's life. Inches away from settling all the scores and ending over two thousand years of torment. It slipped through his hands within seconds. All because his magic hesitated. The same hiccup as the last time Zarus held Eretimis's life in his hand.

Nothing more than the gods themselves spared Eretimis. They were the only ones who possessed the might to stop him. How would he have to suffer for it this time? A scowl twisted the pain out of Zarus's expression, bitter as he looked at the Tyrant he once again knelt before. The beast no longer raged. Eretimis stared at Zarus, empty eyes cutting deep into his soul. Uncertain eyes.

"You never cease to surprise me, *uhlandyi*. Just when I think I have seen everything..." An exhausted sigh escaped the Dark Tyrant's lips. He looked tired. "Your shadows changed. The Twins informed me you possessed the Fallen's Mark, but I did not believe you carried such raw power until now."

Zarus almost lifted a brow. The new form of shadow magic he possessed was of no interest to him then. He kept still, teeth grinding. His heavy breaths tasted of iron.

Eretimis studied Zarus like a speck of dust.

"I suppose it does not matter. Not now." He cast an unamused glance at the blood seeping from Zarus's abdomen. A frown marked his lips.

"That will have to be taken care of before we proceed." The Dark Tyrant stared for a moment too long, as if expecting Zarus to rise to his feet.

Zarus was in no condition to move. His vision blurred along the edges. A bloody laugh spat from his lips.

"Wouldn't want to lose your Key now, would we?"

The Tyrant's expression fell. His hollow eyes slid to Errogan's motionless body pinned down by shadow magic. "How would you know of such things?"

Errogan will be blamed no matter what I say.

"You're not as sly as you think."

Neutrality reclaimed Eretimis's expression. "Both of you continuously act out of turn..." He turned away, the obsidian armor reflecting the lanterns.

Zarus bit down on a snarl. "Flames! What did he do wrong?"

Eretimis cast an uninterested glance at Errogan's bleeding form.

"He questioned me."

The Dark Tyrant strode out of the room looking worse for wear. The clanking of armor sounded in the hall, feet stomping to investigate the ruckus in the laboratory. Mere minutes since Eretimis entered the chamber... Zarus coddled his wound; Errogan barely had a breath in his lungs.

Inches away.

A wet cough broke his thoughts.

"Y-you're a fool," Errogan breathed. He glanced at Zarus, a ghastly gash above his eye staining the entire side of his head. "You've given him another edge over you."

Zarus watched him as Nessriq filed into the chamber with a flank of demons. They staggered against the remnants of magic and gore. There wasn't a mock to be found in his old friend's words.

Chapter Thirty-Two

The stench made its way through the alley shortly after the body decayed. The rain from the day turned to sleet, freezing still as the night settled and chilled.

Rin's eyes leaked like a faucet. She kept still next to her mother, watching intently. Four bodies of beast and human decayed, only one to go. Rin watched the mangled corpse decompose until nothing remained.

"Erin, I—" Luna choked, the words catching in her throat. Rin glanced at her mother. "I should have never let you step foot out of that door without me by your side."

When Luna spoke again, her voice was without tremble. "I left Aresan to protect you and your father, and when the moment came to protect you from harm's way, I hid. Living in fear so long... it took something from me. Something I pray to Yath Ha that you will help me bring back. Erin, if you believe nothing else, then please, I beg you believe this: I am so sorry for not protecting you. I'm sorry for making you go alone." She reached for Rin but hesitated.

"Mama..." Rin started, but the words trailed away.

What could she say to that? Nothing would tell Luna how happy she was to see her. Instead, Rin wrapped her arms around her mother and did not let go until she hugged back.

"I love you."

Luna resumed her work on the body shortly after they pulled apart, and Rin took a seat next to her wounded companions.

"Remind me again why you're going through the effort to dispose of them all?" Genesis asked. Rin cast a sidelong glance at the prince. His chest was still tender, Luna having grafted the new skin mere minutes ago.

Luna didn't respond until the last flakes of flesh disappeared into the air.

"They'll be reported as missing, but nothing will remain to trace back to Erin." Her voice was back to the usual hum. Luna explained she had witnessed the blast of light while searching for Rin at the temple; it's what led her mother to them. The entire city must have witnessed it.

Rin pulled her legs to her chest. In the aftermath, Rin remembered what the assassins said.

Someone was searching for her. Someone desperate enough to enlist the Resurrection's aid. Genesis sensed her dread. A hand wrapped around her own, squeezing tight to bring her back to reality.

"We'll figure this out," he assured.

"I still don't understand how you knew your plan would work..." Tatsuo huffed, changing the topic and flexing the blood into the veins of his freshly healed arm.

Feyne snorted a huff of his own, his large yellow eyes rolling across his canine head as if the answer were obvious.

Rin fought off sleep while she spoke. "They sourced their magic through each other; that's why they shrieked when another died." The toll of her magic emptied her energy stores, and her head and eyes became heavy. "Like the soul-collector back in the Lennaels."

"When you struck the last one," she yawned. "The burn didn't heal."

The wind's lonely howl filled her head. After rubbing her eyes clear of sleepiness, a mortified shrine hand was staring at her.

"Who—who *are* you people?"

Everyone looked at Gavril, who was currently under the care of Luna's working hands.

The group of outcasts exchanged glances until finally Rin opened her mouth.

"Rin Nowell, novice user who has no idea what she's doing."

She offered a wide smile and outstretched her hand until Gavril finally shook it. A meek smile met his face.

"It's nice to meet you, Miss Nowell, despite the grievances. Would you give me an explanation as to what in all Yath Ha's holy world just happened?"

A grin slipped Rin's lips at what she couldn't decide was a blaspheme or not.

"Well, yes, and no. I think we all just found out how the people who disappeared over the last few months died, but I don't know if I can tell you much more than that."

Gavril looked into her eyes, searching for the lie. "My youngest brother has been missing for a week."

Damn her for speaking so idly of death. She offered her condolences, and Gavril accepted. He turned toward the rest of them in the corner of the dark street.

"And what of you?"

"Genesis."

"...Luna."

"I'm Tatsuo, the biggest, baddest *narikaah* around."

"*Narikaah*?"

"Part dragon, part demon."

Gavril's brow creased in confusion.

Rin pinched the bridge of her nose. "Gods, this is Tatsuo, the biggest *dork* around. And that's Feyne." She gestured to the giant wolf guarding the alleyway. "He'd be stark naked if you wanted him to talk."

"What an odd bunch…" Gavril muttered to himself, poking at the newly wrapped bandage on his arm. "It would seem I owe you my life. If you ever need anything, you can find me at the temple." A smile spanned his face.

Rin suddenly jumped to her feet. "Wait! There is something you can help me with."

The shrine hand dipped his chin for her to continue.

Staring at the cloudy sky, past the blanched alley, Rin decided she had a handful of new questions to ask the gods.

Chapter Thirty-Three

No choirs filled the halls, no masses, no priests or priestesses filing in and out of the temple chamber. Rin only passed a single female shrine hand that smiled at her along the hall. The Temple of the Divine was nothing like she expected. Then again, she was in a secluded room that Gavril had snuck her into.

When Rin requested a quiet place in the temple away from the crowds still gathered outside, she expected Gavril to take her to a small room, branching off the main sanctuary. She was not expecting him to sneak her beyond the restricted offices and sleeping quarters. She questioned whether it was appropriate for her to be back there, but Gavril only waved her off and gestured to the fresh skin where his arm had been torn up. At a certain point, the shrine hand made it clear that Rin was the only one allowed to follow him into the depths of the temple. Tatsuo, Genesis, and her mother were reluctant to leave her, while Feyne opted to return to Aava's home and inform her of their encounter with the Resurrection immediately. The empty space made the silence of the ancient building settle deep in her bones. It was only when Gavril stopped at two large wooden doors that he stepped aside.

"This is the original sanctuary," he explained as he unlocked the iron bolts.

"And I mean *original*, from when the temple was first constructed at Nokomic's founding. By the way..." Gavril's eyes shifted away abruptly. "I'm heading home now, but if you ever need anything else in the city... you're welcome to find me."

Rin's eyes widened when she realized he was blushing all shades of red. Without another word, the shrine hand ushered Rin into the chamber, then closed the door behind her.

Rin had never seen the temple with her own eyes. Her father dubbed the eastern roads too dangerous for her to make the pilgrimage. The pearly stone of the towering walls glimmered in the streetlamps outside. The cobblestone leading to the temple looked woven together, carved into a stunning work of decorative knots. However, this far inside, the walls were bare. Exposed beams arched the ceiling above, and creaking boards sat below with only a few flickering candles to guide her step.

Deep breath, Rin. Just take a deep breath.

She took one step into the empty chamber. A draft carrying the musk of time welcomed her. Restored or not, this building was one of the oldest in the entire kingdom of Nokomic, and here she was, on a journey to ask the beings for which it was constructed for guidance. Rin's heart thudded.

Her step down the aisle of pews was careful not to disturb the waxy silence. One by one, she passed the shrines along the pale walls. Two on each side, one stained glass portrait for each of the Divine Attendants.

A bundle of leaves, branches, and the last bloom of blood-orange flowers gathered upon the first shrine. Above the stand, the emerald green glass depicted fiery red hair, a faceless female cloaked in forest green with an arrow in hand—the kaeth, Mynil the Adventuring.

Across the aisle, a portrait of a male's raven strands, dressed in black and violet, as faceless as the first. He held a skull in one hand, scrolls in the other. Vulyn the Balanced. Smoke still trailed from the edge of the incense resting on the shrine—the same incense burned at funerals.

Further down the wall sat a shrine opposite to Ashnagz's ruler. The faceless portrait of Lhaerem the Knowing showed a male with dark skin and brilliant blue and white garbs. Blond hair long and flowing. The head of the Attendants: a leader and trusted advisor to Olru and E'ral. A kind yet steadfast soul, wiser than any mortal hoped to be. Nothing rested on his shrine, for people only left their words and confessions. No one could hide their intentions against his unwavering convictions, not even in their dreams depicted as a river of lilac mist flowing out of his hand.

Rin's eyes finally swept to the shrine next to Mynil's. A midnight backdrop hosting a faceless female garbed in navy blue, snow-white hair flowing around her body. Countless plants spread about her shrine. Unlike Mynil's offering, the greenery consisted of blooms which only grew under the pale moon. Nraessa the Bright, the kaeth most favored by the mortals.

The quiet was a warm hug after a cold trek. Rin held her shoulders higher than she had in weeks. Her faith had always been personal. She devoted time each day to speak with Yath Ha despite their silence for centuries, but the unanswered prayers had been difficult as of late. Especially since they actively spoke in her head lately. However, this silence was not harrowing. The hum of her mind was at peace. Before she realized it, Rin's foot found the first steps leading to the altar atop the dais where Yath Ha stood.

The statue carved of pale stone towered over her with a watchful presence. Veils draped the humanoid figure; its shoulder turned to the sanctuary. On both sides of the head, a blank face was molded, covered by a draped hood. Two in one. The symbol of Yath Ha, Olru and E'ral.

No one had ever laid witness to the gods to know what they appeared as, or no one wrote it down if they had. Humankind was left guessing what the Creators looked like, unlike the kaetha, who took many forms. There was always something about this depiction that sent a shudder along Rin's spine. Personally, she doubted the Creators took on a humanoid form. She also doubted that anyone would see it with their own two eyes.

Just a deep breath.

Rin closed her eyes. She fell to her knees, a wave of nausea sweeping over.

Vulyn's Pits, I'm going to be sick…

Something within her stirred, something deeper than blood, deeper than bone. A breeze sounded in the depths of her soul. Two ethereal voices spoke, overlapping.

Peace, child, for we are with you.

Rin nearly choked on her spit. She might have come here to ask the Creators questions, but she didn't think she would get a response so quickly. It was refreshing to learn that the temple truly served as a connection to the Divine. That was until she realized the conversation started with her cursing one of the kaetha.

She swallowed hard. The presence wasn't suffocating, nor did she feel dull amidst their glorified light. A shadow had not cast over her, but a light shined upon her.

Rin took one more breath.

"I—I don't know what to say. I'm trying to keep my head up, trying to figure out how to do all these impossible tasks, but I'm lost. This power is too grand. I can't use it to help anyone. Even today, I hurt them before saving anyone. These visions that you keep showing me;

I don't understand what I can do about it." She reached out to the idol, softly touching the stone of its bare foot slipping out beneath the cloak.

"Yath Ha, I'm begging for your help. Show me which path I'm supposed to walk down; show me what you want me to do so I give back to the people who time and time again laid their lives down before mine. What is this power? Why am I unable to do this by myself?"

Light and life thrummed from the statue, coursing down her arm and warming her chest like rays of the morning sun.

You were never meant to do this by yourself.

The task falls to the Two Chosen.

Divine Mortals born to direct the path of all realms.

Rin opened her eyes expecting to see a phantom deity standing before her, but all she found was the statue.

"I don't understand," she whispered.

You will learn in time.

Like an arch of lightning touching still waters, a shock rippled up her arm from the idol. A yelp escaped Rin's lips. She nearly recoiled against it, but bit down on the flick of pain and kept her hand on the figure.

Our time wanes, child. His power holds strong.

Rin opened her mouth to ask what on Armiria any of that meant, but a draft heavy with time dried her throat. The gods spoke first.

Find the demon trapped in the corrupted temple. Free him from the Dark One's grasp. Your answer lies with him, and his with you.

Ice spread throughout her fingers, climbing up her arm and seizing hold of her shoulder. The presence inside the idol was changing. Growing colder and colder with each passing second. Their time was running out.

"Wait, I need your help! What do all these visions mean? What do you want me to do!" She pleaded, opening her eyes as urgency seeped into her core.

Save the demon, then seek us out where the tainted power has not yet reached, Alentye...

The warmth bled from the altar. Rin threw her other hand upon the idol, her eyes clamped shut against the ice running up both limbs. Her teeth gritted in a fit of fury and pain.

"Please..." she cried.

Chapter Thirty-Four

A speck of watery light waded around the corner, bright enough to glimpse the unconscious demon in the cell across the dungeon.

Zarus had dug into one nerve too many to be cast into the filthy dungeons with a maimed abdomen. He still possessed some shred of usefulness after the affray in the laboratory, else the healers wouldn't make rounds to close his wounds. They never once touched the cell across from him, leaving Errogan unconscious for days in his own blood. The Tyrant wanted nothing to do with him. Zarus made it clear if the healers refused to work on Errogan, then they would find themselves without teeth if they tried to work on him. They eventually complied, but he knew it wasn't of his own convincing. The threat of not carrying out the order to prepare Zarus is what pushed them to heal Errogan's wounds. They all saw what became of the White-Cloaked Reaper after he displeased the Dark Tyrant.

The dungeons were dark and damp. Zarus hadn't gotten used to the stench yet. No longer in his own company, no longer with himself and his thoughts, the dank halls echoed the wails of countless prisoners. About the worst place to be locked for days on end. However, he wouldn't have wished to be anywhere else. He had eyes on Errogan and knew he was alive. It left nothing to assumption. Like the assumption that Rin was being held in the fortress…

Foolish.

Zarus sucked in a deep sigh, leaning back his head to stare at the abysmal ceiling. He wasn't able to lie down with his hands bound behind his back. Apparently Eretimis didn't want him attempting any more portals.

Somewhere down the hall, a fellow prisoner screamed. Another pleaded for their life. Zarus rubbed his temples. Naturally, no one found it worth their time to investigate the cries of the dungeon-crazed, so no one batted an eye when Zarus began muttering amongst himself a few days ago.

"You realize you have no permission to be in my head, right?"
What we say must be heard, child.

"I'm sure there's someone else in the world who would much rather hear it."
Our words are meant for you.

His head pounded from the chaos of the dungeons. His patience dwindled. Why, after everything these invasive gods had done, would he want to hear what they had to say?

"Your desperation disgraces your reputation," he growled at the shadows of the cell.
Desperation speaks volumes to those with sense.

Now that—however much he hated to admit—piqued his interest. For as mighty as the gods claimed to be, pleading with him was a far stretch. Whatever they needed, Zarus found himself curious. He cursed himself to the grave for allowing them to know.

The not-voice of the gods echoed off the walls of his mind, two hums as one.
You need to unite with the human girl.

No shit. Zarus seethed.

"I weep at the brilliance of your counsel, Divine. Should I also open my eyes in the mornings, or perhaps take in air to live?"

You should hold your tongue and heed our words.

A laugh scoffed through Zarus's cracked lips, rumbling a sharp jolt throughout his torso. He stifled the thrashing through bared teeth.

"Leave me to suffer in peace."

Do you not wish to find her?

"Of course I do," he snarled at the voice in his head, earning an inquisitive glance from the guard making their rounds.

"And I would have already been on my way to find her if you had just let me be!"

The scene played again: the spike of magic about to burrow into Eretimis's skull, the finale of their centuries old conflict, all tumbling to a halt because of the gods. This was all *their* fault. It was *always* their fault.

We intervened to save no other than you, child.

"I could have killed him."

It is not so easy to kill beings of such corrosive power.

The words caught him off guard. "What is that supposed to mean?" Was there truly no way to kill the Dark Tyrant?

Do not take this task on alone, child, for you shall fail over and over if you try. Find the girl, give her guidance, and you shall find the truth.

"How in the Flames am I supposed to find her when I'm unable to kill the tyrant holding me here?" Irritation seeped into his tone.

He took his only chance of breaking free, and the gods squandered it.

Patience. And faith. Fill the void of doubt with kindness.

Zarus fell silent. No explanation needed. He'd known what his ticket out of the fortress was from the start.

"I don't think you realize how impossible that is."
Faith, child. Faith will set you free.

Goodbyes were unnecessary. His divine company left the dungeon. Always at his side when unwanted, never when called upon. Zarus hissed a sharp sigh, holding as still as he could to keep his wound from reopening. Magic or not, it would take many sessions to heal. Time before Eretimis subjected him to whatever procedure had been mentioned before he fell. Time to find a way out.

Zarus's stare pierced through the darkness, finding where Errogan stirred on the damp ground.

Faith.

The word bounced around his head for a few moments before he ultimately huffed one last sigh. He had to find which words wouldn't set Errogan into a frenzy.

Chapter Thirty-Five

"You know," Zarus croaked, his voice rough, "I can drown out the cries and moans of the crazed, but I don't think I'll ever get used to this smell."

How long had it been? The days merged together. The guards didn't care enough about the prisoners to take their rounds routinely. Even the healers came and went on no particular schedule. His abdomen was in much better condition, but he still had a way to go. From the grime coating his skin and the smell wafting off his body, Zarus knew the days were stretching on.

"It's worse than the sewers of Ravyhs," he rambled aloud.

The noise in the cells had mostly dozed off. Zarus sat upright, hissing at the tenderness of his gut.

"You'd think for such an advanced city, they'd have better waste systems."

The hoarse voice across the dungeon grunted. "Of all the shit that happened in Ravyhs, *that's* what sticks with you?"

A weight lifted from Zarus's chest.

"I remember the blood and torture as well, but the smell in that sewage labyrinth is what sticks out the most."

His finger tapped endlessly in the pause that followed. Until a sigh full of exasperation huffed through the dark. Errogan's muddy white hair came into the murky lantern light. The tissue around his left eye swelled nearly shut, the scar on his temple hid behind layers of bruises, and a gash scabbed at his lower lip. That was only his face.

"I think that's putting it lightly," the demon said in a tone so short, Zarus would've missed it if he blinked.

Zarus chose his words carefully. "It was one of the messier missions. Humans seldom gather word of demonic dealings."

There were few humans who recognized the existence of demons, fewer who knew anything about them. So, when scouts in the south intercepted a letter talking of a threat named Eretimis, addressed to Melde's Prime Archon from a counselor, interest stirred within the fortress. Zarus and Errogan were the ones selected to investigate the claims. It seemed like a lifetime ago, but not long enough to forget that their escape plan was trekking through stretches and stretches of shit.

"Did anything ever come of that letter?" Zarus asked, never having cared enough to read it himself.

Even with proof, one man was not enough to shed light on the existence of an entire race hiding in the north. The Archon wasn't quite stupid enough to tarnish his reputation with talks of myths.

The Moonlit Bastard was quiet at first, but it seemed days of starvation and thirst worked in Zarus's favor.

"Nothing but talk of an otherworldly threat. Something about assembling troops in case the legend of Eretimis showed up at their doorstep."

Zarus frowned. "Well, that's disappointing. After all that excitement, you'd expect some strange bit about his past to be in there."

"Your time with the humans raised your standards for their potential," Errogan grunted.

"Do demons still ignore that no one knows where he came from? I mean, he holds all the Seats on the Council, yet he appeared out of thin air one day. We know no more about him than the humans whispering his name."

Errogan cast him a tired glance out of his unbruised eye. "Why does it matter? Eretimis challenged one of the five Council members. He beat them and took their Seat, then did the same with the remaining four. Those are the rules of succession. Who cares where he came from?"

Zarus couldn't be the only one who thought it was odd. "The rules of succession in Hraesah call for an official battle of the duelists' choosing. No death, only dishonor. It's public. It's official. Eretimis won the first Seat fairly, but he ambushed the second two Seat Holders in their own home and killed them because they disagreed with his proposals. I don't think that falls in line with the law."

An amused scoff rang through the hall. They were alone in that moment, but hushed voices ensured the conversation didn't make it back to his liege. "Our society isn't built on such sportsman ideals, Zarus."

Not anymore, it isn't.

Errogan continued. "Furthermore, Amerthen and Sarhania Radorhé's guidance led us nowhere. They refused to allow us into Armiria. Once they were out of the picture and the two remaining Seat Holders forfeited their positions, things began to progress."

Progress? The Tyrant has barely left his stronghold the for entire two thousand years he's been in Armiria.

"We've laughed at kings who single-handedly damned away their kingdoms, Errogan. Do you want to be part of such a damning fate as well?"

Errogan wasn't foolish enough to blaspheme the name of the demon race's self-appointed god, even if he saw the question for what it was. Especially then.

"No matter where he came from, Eretimis holds all five Seats in the Council. He controls every aspect of Hraesah. Even if one demon defeated him, he would still hold the other four. There's no getting around that, but there's a reason no one in the last two thousand years has pulled out a book of laws and held Eretimis accountable. The Radorhés' deaths left a statement. What's with the sudden interest in politics, anyway? Didn't you once say the Council of Hraesah is '*an over-glorified shit spewer*'?"

"Over-praised, actually," Zarus corrected.

He couldn't do anything as the conversation died. In fairness, it didn't quite matter. No one was robbing Eretimis of his titles. No one was stripping him of his armies and troops, of his warships and throne. No one possessed the power to challenge his power. And a dabble in politics was still a brush with the plague. It shouldn't have bothered him. Zarus kept telling himself to forget the whole notion as the pace of a guard sounded down the walkway. He knew he wouldn't let it be forever.

A chill settled in the dungeon.

"Well, for everything that's happened, you're at least better company than the maddened demons around us."

Errogan flicked a brief nod to him, and nothing more. Zarus carefully stretched his arms still bound behind his back until voices murmured down the hall. Footsteps headed their way. It was before the healer ever reached Zarus's cell that Errogan's eyes locked on him. He rested his hand carefully over his bruised eye.

"Thank you," he whispered.

Zarus offered a brief nod. The demon had been unconscious every time Zarus forced the healers to work on him. Apparently, he healed enough. When the healer arrived, so did Nessriq to retrieve Errogan.

Chapter Thirty-Six

Zarus snapped his jaw down. He didn't care about causing another scene, but he didn't want to reopen his wounds by tearing the limbs off the healer beside him either.

"I would suggest not doing that again," he growled, a vein strained along his temple.

The young healer flicked her copper eyes at him.

"And why's that?" The challenge in her voice was clear as day.

Zarus knew that he would waste his breath if his aggression spoke for him. Without a response, the demon brushed her hair over her shoulder and continued to press her olive-toned hands against his abdomen. Elief, the healer assigned to him, never cared about his curses of pain. She didn't put a second thought onto him and found words a waste of time. While her hands checked for any reopening, he couldn't ignore the pain.

"So, tell, what's in store for me next?"

Elief cast him another dull stare, as if deigning him a single thought was as tedious as reciting herbal remedies backwards.

"You're out of my hands after today, Lowwenth. What happens to you next is of no concern to me."

Zarus stared at the ceiling. Elief brought one of the hall's lanterns into his cell for a light source, but that was all it offered. Nothing would take away from the nip of the ground against his bare back as the healer examined his wounds. His hands had to be unshackled from behind him in order to be worked on, but Eretimis didn't trust them to be free. The guards instead locked them in special iron bindings that covered his hands and prevented him from moving his fingers.

With nothing to do while Elief's trained hands continued along his abdomen, Zarus let his eyes trail across the dungeon. Silhouettes lay slumped on the floor in their cells. Some he could see breathing; some he wondered if they were breathing at all. He supposed he was counted as lucky. He spent so little time locked down there—the place where countless rotted away for much less than what he'd done. And he was being healed. The rate at which Elief closed his wound was impressive, but what came afterwards? Healing only brought more suffering, not freedom. His eyes lingered on the vacant cell across the hall.

"You shouldn't worry for him." Elief's voice was a pickaxe through his thoughts.

"And why's that?"

The sharp retort earned him a heavy glare and a jab of the healer's hand where the bruises were the most tender. After he cursed her to the grave, Elief gestured to the empty cell.

"You have enough problems to worry about. You shouldn't adopt someone else's along the way."

"Here I thought you didn't care about me."

Another jab. Another hiss.

Elief sighed. "It's foolish to worry. Besides, His Majesty doesn't waste tools. Errogan is too valuable to throw out, especially right now."

Zarus propped himself up using his elbow. Tools could always be replaced.

"What's so important now?"

The healer's stare deadpanned, forgetting she was speaking with a prisoner in the dungeons. "His liege has plans for the near future. All hands on deck. He needs his tools assembled in perfect place right now. From this world and the other."

Silence filled the thicket of air between the two. Finally, when he closed his eyes against the flickering light, he remembered Eretimis's announcement before their fight. Standing atop the balcony, the Tyrant spewed something about humans ruling Armiria for too long.

"He's planning to invade human territory."

Elief nodded, retracting her hands from his skin and pulling out a tin of salve.

"After nearly two thousand years."

Eretimis had been on Armiria since Zarus could walk, maybe even a little earlier. And all this time, he'd been waiting, watching. Secretly searching for the Infinite Key to assist him in his conquest. If the Dark Tyrant was ready to move his forces out into the world and make his grand presence known, then he was damned sure he had that Key locked in place.

Zarus's stomach churned at the unknown of what awaited him the moment Elief left his side. Was it truly possible that the Key rested in him? It was a notion he hadn't much time for in the last few days. Zarus loosed a sigh. There had to be more information about this godly shed of power. Eretimis knew more about it and probably burned all the texts he found about it after reading them.

"I suppose it won't be long before the Pits of Ashnagz manifests around us then."

"Perhaps," she breathed, applying the salve generously to his scarred tissue. "But that's why the demons are here. That's what they've been waiting for all these years—a rightful place in this world as well. The Crimson War took away our kind's land here. They want it back."

"What's so wrong with Eroz?" He asked, folding his arms behind his head.

"What's wrong with the plains compared to the sea?" Elief countered, wiping her hands clean of the pale ointment. "People prefer to live in different areas. That's how it is."

Zarus spoke through a yawn. "Seems like an excuse to run away."

He should know; he was the leading expert on running. How many demons wanted out of Eroz? Not everyone liked Eretimis, especially after two millennia of waiting on him to fulfill his promise and massacring the governing system set in place countless millennia before. The demon colonies on the eastern continent of Armiria proved it for the better part of five hundred years. Even if the demonkind fled to Armiria, would they be safe from his rule? Something told Zarus that Eretimis wasn't leaving this world anytime soon. For those who wanted freedom—those smart enough not to flee with the sympathizers—was this the correct solution? It all boiled down to what Eretimis's intentions were, and Zarus knew that no one was safe from them.

"Everyone has their reasons to run, Mister Lowwenth. Isn't that why you've been missing for three centuries?"

Zarus cast a glance at the healer, her calm tone and busied hands. "You know who I am?"

"A face like yours isn't easily forgotten. I worked on you before, many years ago. When you returned from raiding Arwyrn."

"That was nearly five hundred years ago."

For a brief second, a flash of a smile brightened the female's face.

"My memory is not one to underestimate. Besides, everyone knows who you are, or at least your name." She thought about it for a moment, recalling the encounter Zarus couldn't bring to memory. "For a city of scholars, Arwyrn left you beaten."

"A city filled to the brim with scholars is smart enough to learn to defend itself. Especially one teeming with users."

Elief nodded. "I think Master Errogan took on more of the damage. I remember him barely able to walk on that leg of his."

A smile broke his scowl. Zarus chuckled as he recalled the sight of the demon limping on the leg he nearly lost for the three days after they returned. Served him right for engaging so recklessly. The humor subsided, replaced by the remembrance of the conquest.

"Arwyrn shouldn't have been touched. We had no right to destroy such a place."

Elief glanced toward him, a brow arched at the suddenness of the statement.

The lantern cackled its opinion.

"You should be mindful of what you say," Elief warned, her eyes caught by the shadow of a guard passing the corner a few cells down.

Zarus wanted to shrug and claim nothing more could be done to him, but he knew it was a fool's statement. Meeting Rin awakened something in him—an appreciation for life perhaps. Eretimis would use it against him to all ends. It wasn't only his life to worry about anymore.

In a hushed voice, he started again. "Burning knowledge is no better than cursing your Tyrant's name."

A spark of offense flickered in Elief's eye, but it subsided after a moment. Her expression sobered, her voice flattened.

"I'm shaky on the details. What was Arwyrn exactly?"

Zarus noticed the shift but didn't comment. Everyone wore a mask in this place.

"Arwyrn was a place of learning in southern Weslyc, a sanctuary where scholars could study. The entire city was a library. Different streets for different subjects. Different buildings for specific topics. History, medicine, literature, agriculture. Over a millennium of Armiria's history lived in those streets, archives stacked so high toward the domed ceilings, you couldn't find the tops. The halls spanned as far as this fortress, maybe even farther, full of accounts and texts written by hundreds of thousands of hands. You could get lost for days if you didn't know your way around. A city built on knowledge.

"Scholars made pilgrimages there, but a good sum were magic users. There was a section of the city dedicated to the history of magic, techniques, practices, theories. It's where a majority of the human users learned to master their skills."

Zarus could tell by Elief's slackening expression she knew where this was going.

"It was a threat to Eretimis. Magic users were a force that could oppose him." The words were vile on his tongue. "He ordered the city burned down."

A pregnant pause numbed the air. So long that Zarus expected nothing more to be said on the subject. However, the healer parted her lips once more.

"That would be the same as someone coming to Hraesah and destroying Grekur."

Zarus blinked at the sadness hinting in her tone.

He had never seen it with his own eyes—any of Eroz for that matter—but the Chambers of Grekur was a tower where the demons kept their archives. Grekur made Arwyrn's texts look like children's books. The demons had their talents, but one of the most praised was record keeping. Anything you ever wondered about, you could find your answer within its walls. It was a history book towering leagues into the sky, but held much of the same topics as Arwyrn—only more detailed. An encyclopaedia built in the heart of Hraesah's capital. Not only relating to the demons, but also the fae, humans, shifters, even dragons from all ages. There's a myth that whenever something is written down in Hraesah, a second copy spawns in Grekur. It's rumored to be the place where Eretimis learned to open portals between worlds. And since the burning of Arwyrn, it was the place where information about the Infinite Key remained. Zarus always wished to see it, but he never got the chance to step foot on Eroz.

He gathered himself before he picked up his thoughts.

"That's exactly what we did."

We. He led the attack. He tried not to snarl at the truth.

"Those were the glory days of human users, and every day since, it's been a struggle for them to learn their craft."

Zarus could only think of Genesis, of Rin. They could have benefited from Arwyrn's banks more than anyone else. How had he damned them in helping demolish it?

"Burning the Tower of Grekur would strike an outcry of war," Elief commented.

Zarus clicked his tongue. Realizing that Elief collected all her supplies, he sat up, struggling to pull the remnants of his shirt back over his body with the iron covering his hands.

"The bastard has committed countless atrocities against humanity, yet it seems he still swayed the favor of one."

An airy huff hissed through Elief's teeth. "There are certainly some deliberation over that. People don't want the beings they believe are beneath them in their ranks."

"Who is he?"

Elief pulled at the tips of her umber curls with a slender finger as she spoke. "No one, from what I've heard. Just some Damrian that caught wind of the Dark Tyrant. Not even a user. He must have something of value though. I hear he's been trying to work on something in Xandra."

Her stare slid back to him, though her focus remained mostly in her mind. "Rumors aren't as fine a source as others, but they're all I have. The demons here—they don't have all the details." She shrugged.

Zarus ensnared her gaze with a grim realization.

"You should take your own advice. Your words betray you, Elief."

The female opened her mouth, but Zarus spoke first. "You're the only demon who doesn't associate themself with the others here, with their cause. Words speak wonders."

They. Their. It was those very statements that earned Zarus an eye on his back when he lived here.

"Like you said, Eretimis needs all his tools in line. Watch your step so you don't stumble out of it."

Elief stared in silence. He watched as she forced her breath to remain even, but the warmth drained from her face. The girl stuck to her ground.

"I don't know what you're talking about, Lowwenth," she said too quietly.

"I think you do." Zarus didn't care to know what this female was running from, why she sought to live in Armiria away from Eretimis, but he could tell that she wanted dangerous things.

"How's that?"

"You don't use my name as an insult."

Her brows arched over her narrow eyes, so he continued.

"I'm not a fool. I did a damn good job of keeping the origins of my family name to myself while I lived here. Yet when I'm dragged back, it's all anyone calls me. I assume word spread after I left that humans raised me?"

Elief nodded in confirmation. It was something Zarus noticed right away during his imprisonment. A past he kept to himself was suddenly common knowledge amongst the ranks. He wondered if Eretimis himself came down off his mighty throne and spread the news to his subjects. Or possibly the Wraiths figured it out. Maybe even Errogan told.

"The name Lowwenth is of humankind, and it seems I was correct to assume the demons here wouldn't take kindly to it once they learned its origin. Yet you don't use it as a curse."

Zarus asked himself why he was telling this female all of this. Maybe he could save her the same mistakes he made while working under Eretimis. Spare her the same hardships. She knew the risks of taking the most dangerous path to get away from the Tyrant. She probably planned to leave for the colonies. Honestly, Zarus admired it. What a dangerous thing: to live. He wanted the same thing.

He dabbled in unwanted territory. Elief picked up her satchel of supplies. In fact, she made it all the way to the iron bars before she paused and looked from side to side for any listeners.

Quietly, she spoke without even looking back.

"My brother was labeled a traitor. He voiced his disagreement with Eretimis's decision to kill sympathizers in a tavern one night. One drink too many. The soldiers broke into our house the same night and dragged him into the street. They took him away, flogging him as they went. I never saw him again."

She inhaled deep, then glanced over her sharp shoulder to meet his gaze. "It was only after I enlisted here in hopes of fleeing Eroz that I learned his fate. They tortured him, demanding to know who else was plotting against the Dark Tyrant. When they received no answer, they hanged him from the trees outside the capital. You've never been to Hraesah, Zarus, but you know a life of hiding and treading dangerous ground. Yet still you ask why I would want to escape it? Like Anöwe has dealt you all of Ashnagz's cards, none left for the rest of us."

There it was—that spark of fire leading so many in silence. He opened his mouth to protest, but she went on.

"Funnily enough, the demon that dragged him from his bed pretended to be the infamous Shadow of Evenfall. Your reputation precedes you, Mister. My brother pleaded for death on sight when he heard it." Elief paused for a moment.

Something of humor lingered on her tongue. "When I heard I was assigned to heal you four hundred and twenty-two years ago, I very well intended to kill you. But the male who stole him from me that night looked nothing like you. Just an impersonator spreading fear. You're lucky my memory isn't one to trifle with, Zarus Lowwenth."

Zarus wondered how decomposed his body would have been by then if her memory proved less reliable.

Chapter Thirty-Seven

R in stared at the pale pink sky with disgust. The bitter chill of winter played with her hair. She cast a sidelong glance at her mother in the brisk dawn light, whose wind-chilled cheeks gave away her own discomfort.

It had been a week since she summoned her magic and wielded it without fail, since the gods told her to save Zarus, and since she convinced everyone she hadn't heard incorrectly. It had also been a week since Rin left Aava's house.

Her mother huffed. "I admit, it's colder during the mornings in the city than it was in the plateau."

"You think?" Rin retorted.

"Not to pick sides," Genesis tuned in from the bench behind, "but standing around complaining won't warm us."

"Oh, bite me."

"Why don't we spar and see who wins?" His sapphire eyes danced with challenge, hands tapping against the wooden blade at his side.

A warm light buzzed at Rin's fingertips, dim enough that it barely illuminated the Iver Estate courtyard around them. She couldn't help smiling as her power fluttered around her hands.

Rin held her light in place. After an entire week of mastering the ability to bring forth her light, she had not yet used it during training. She narrowed her stare, but someone else shouted first.

"Kick his ass, Rin!" Vi called from the balcony overlooking the courtyard. "Put that boy in his place."

"Show him who's boss, Red!" Tatsuo chimed from the doorway behind.

Genesis rolled his eyes. "No one's going to root for me?"

Without replying, Rin lunged.

The light flickered from her hands, fading into the morning mist as she twirled her sparring sword. Genesis caught the assault head on. His weaker arm didn't even budge. Rin twisted her body to the side, allowing Genesis's weight to stumble forward. He caught himself and slid his foot in front of hers. She leaned into the fall, rolling into the leaves plastered against the ground, but halted the motion as she landed on her knees.

The prince adjusted his blade so the pommel faced upward. Rin noticed the shift of his feet before his body followed. She pivoted on her heels to follow Genesis's momentum, and kicked a fallen branch in front of his step. The prince tumbled to the ground with a mouthful of dirt and leaves. He flipped onto his back, face bathed in mud.

Rin leapt while he was down and pinned him. She heard Vi's whistle from above, but ignored it. "Who's biting whom now?"

Genesis's muscles shifted beneath her. All too quickly, he hoisted himself upward, throwing her backwards. Her head shook with the roll. Genesis towered above her when her head settled. She lifted her arm to whack her faux blade at his ankle, but her hand was empty. Rin searched for her sword.

Genesis wielded his spar weapon in one hand, dangling hers from the other.

"You were saying?" he taunted, tossing her blade in the air and catching it firmly in his hand.

Rin's teeth ground together. The prince's taunt riled her anger. She sprang to her feet, lowered her aim, and threw herself into the solid wall that was Genesis Masquarem. Genesis hit the ground with a *thud*. Rin's bones rumbled but she ripped her blade out of his hand and bonked the dull stick into the tip of his nose.

"I think I'd call that a win," Tatsuo murmured from Luna's side. Even Vi was leaning over the edge of the railing dumbfounded.

Rin climbed off Genesis and offered him a friendly hand.

"You almost had me there," she smiled.

It was an effort not to laugh at the sheer surprise smothering his face, but Genesis eventually smiled back.

"Flames, where did that come from?" He took her hand and lifted himself up.

Rin shrugged. "Instinct?"

It was no mystery that Rin had gotten a fair amount stronger in the last few months. She had asked Aava to help her with her form after dinner each night. Her strength was her saving grace against the Resurrection. She trained behind closed doors, not to get ahead, but to learn exactly what she needed to do differently. However, her smile fell short once she saw the line of red trailing down Genesis's head.

Softly, she touched his temple, wiping the blood away. "Maybe I took it too far..."

Genesis gently lowered her hand.

"You've done worse before," he smiled. "Besides, it looks like we're even."

The warmth on her chin didn't register until then, but Genesis wiped the blood away before she could reach for it.

"You must teach me where you learned such cunning, Miss Nowell. Or has it always been there?"

Rin laughed. "You just have to tackle things head-on."

"Are we done for the day, or would you like to watch your daughter kick my ass once more?" Genesis asked Luna.

"Once more! Once more!" Vi chanted.

"Ah, let him be, Vi," Tatsuo waved, falling in line between Genesis and Rin. He wrapped an arm around her shoulder, pulling her close into a hug. "That was one Flame of a victory. Rin needs to celebrate!"

"Aye," smiled Luna as she walked over and examined both cuts, "but save Genesis's embarrassment for later in the day when the shops in town are open, Tatsuo. They still have the rest of their lessons for the next few hours."

Rin nearly groaned. Ever since the temple, her lessons had turned from magic theory to research. Not even Luna knew why Rin's magic welled in her head. Books would be her answer. At least that's what her mother hoped after countless trips to Xandra's library. But fear had destroyed most of the books about magic.

"Are you sure she can't skip today? I mean, she *did* just win. I think that deserves some sort of reward," Tatsuo pleaded on her behalf.

Rin would have been touched at the notion, but she knew his effort wasn't selfless. The only beings that used magic welled from their minds were demons. Tatsuo inherited his magic from his father's demonic heritage. Unfortunately for Tatsuo, Luna enlisted his help during their lessons to see if the specifics of demon magic rang familiar with Rin. For instance, did she also have mental barriers to break down to reach her magic like demons did? To everyone's surprise, Rin understood demon magic far more than human. It didn't explain why she was the sore thumb sticking out of the human bunch.

Rin pleaded with her mother, weaving her fingers together in a prayer against her heart. "I'll put in twice as much work tomorrow."

Luna's expression almost looked amused. "We both know that's a lie, Erin."

Rin's shoulders slackened. It was worth a shot. "Sorry, Tat," she said, nudging the dragon.

"Looks like you're stuck in class with the losers," Genesis mused, picking his blade off the ground. "Try to keep up."

"Oh, bite me—"

Rin couldn't quite get the words out before Aiden slammed the courtyard door open. Everyone's attention swept to his heaving breaths, the drained color of his face. His lips opened and closed.

"Scarlette."

Chapter Thirty-Eight

No one cared to remove their muddy boots. Rin certainly didn't care to change out of her filthy tunic and pants before she ran upstairs. They raced into the bedroom where Scarlette had been stuck for months. Despite her doubt, beyond her disbelief, there she was.

Her hair plastered to her face, the color sapped from her cheeks like water out of the cloth on her forehead. Sweat beaded down her skin. Scarlette's condition had taken a turn for the worse in recent weeks. Barely shifting in her sleep, breaths short and forced or barely there at all.

Luna immediately went to work on Scarlette when she arrived a week ago, but nothing made a difference. Her mother didn't know what caused the comatose either, and was hesitant to delve too deep into the wound on Scarlette's chest for fear it would tamper with whatever magic Rin used. Yet despite all odds, Scarlette's magenta eyes were open, seeing light for the first time in months.

Feyne hadn't left her side all week, ever since Luna first examined the aura-reader and gravely said, *"I'll do what I can."*

The shifter leaned close to Scarlette, holding her weak hand. Tears streamed down his face. Scarlette was *awake*. Rin looked at each of them and made sure she wasn't the only one confused.

Vi was already standing against the far wall, arms folded overtop one another. "When did she wake?"

"Two minutes ago," Aiden said, standing in line with Genesis and Tatsuo in the back.

From her rocker, Aava glanced over her shoulder and met Rin's stare, gesturing for her to come near with a silent finger.

"She is awake because of you, young lady." The woman's voice was sweet, praising, but all Rin did was stare at Scarlette's sickly face, the frail arm she couldn't even hold up on her own.

Sitting this close, Rin realized Scarlette was speaking, saying something so faint she couldn't hear. Feyne had his ear to her colorless lips, and by the time Rin heard the words *attacked from within,* Scarlette's eyes slid to Rin's.

Scarlette parted her lips, and Rin nearly winced at the hoarseness in the words.

"I'm told I owe my life to you."

Rin's eyes welled with tears. Her body was iced down to the bones. For all the joy in the world of seeing her friend alive and speaking, Rin Nowell's chest emptied. She bit down on the hum in her head.

A sharp clearing of the throat sounded from Vi's direction.

"I believe I'm due some of the credit, Scar." Scarlette's smile turned to Vi, and it was when the attention was no longer on Rin that she let go of the breath locked in her lungs.

"I guess I'll thank you as well," Scarlette smiled, masking her exhaustion. "Although I'll take your word. I don't remember much until a few moments ago."

Luna spoke up as she met Rin's side. "What do you remember?"

Scarlette glanced at Luna, to Aava, Genesis, Aiden. All of the people who had not yet been introduced.

"I remember fighting, falling... there were voices. Someone else had been there."

"Errogan," Tatsuo murmured from the back of the room.

"No," Scarlette's brow creased, "not him, someone else."

She closed her fatigued eyes, reddened by the fresh air. Weaker, quieter, she eventually spoke. "Genesis?"

The prince glanced at Rin before anyone else. To him, Scarlette had been dead before he arrived at the scene in the desert. Rin tried so hard to push all thoughts of that night out of her head. The heat of the fires, the warmth of Scarlette's blood. Drowning beneath her magic's touch. Her stomach churned again.

"It's nice to properly meet you," Genesis said.

"Be sure to mark it in your memory," the aura reader smiled.

"Not to sound unhappy with the current twist of the day," Tatsuo said, taking a seat near the fire, "but would it be too much to ask about that night?"

Feyne shot a deathly glance toward the dragon. "Talk of Base can wait. She just woke up—"

A gentle hand squeezed the wolf's forearm. "Some things can't wait, Yreyshin," Scarlette said, her smile subsiding.

"There are things you need to hear." Scarlette closed her eyes, resting her head against the pillow below. "It started not long after you left to find Luna. Maybe an hour after I set out on watch, I heard steel clash near the cistern's entrance."

Rin recalled the layout of the bunker, the water supply that flowed into it from the highlands. A long tunnel led into the cistern, and at the far end was one of the many hidden entrances.

"I found the watchman posted outside dead, the lock on the door lying in the sand."

"Someone broke it?" Genesis asked.

Rin answered for the scholar. "It was unlocked."

She lowered her chin, recalling Feyne's talk of a traitor. A chill ran down her spine. Had Feyne truly gambled her fate so recklessly? The shifter must have had a similar thought, for his face crumpled, eyes full of regret.

Scarlette slowly nodded. "A member of Base led the demons into the bunker. I don't know how long they were down there, but the bell went off before I could do anything. I tried to go down the waterway and cut them off, but they blocked it. Completely blocked off the exit behind them. I couldn't break it down. Smoke was already trailing out. There was no alarm, Feyne. They attacked us from the inside while we slept."

Rin remembered the sand in the well; the boulders piled in front of the other doors. Every entrance, every hole someone could use to get free... closed for good.

"I looked for a way in, but... I eventually ran into four demons. No one from Base was with them."

"One of them was dead by the time I showed up," Tatsuo added.

Rin's eyes widened. Scarlette fought off four demons by herself.

"I wasn't far, just at the edge of the plateau. I ran back when I smelled it," Tatsuo said, guilt coloring his voice.

Aiden raised a brow. "The smoke?"

Tatsuo shifted his solemn gaze to the human. "Demons."

Aiden scrunched his nose accordingly. Of course, this was all new to him, just as demons had been new to Rin a few short months ago. When the young man looked to his grandmother, she merely nodded.

A heavy pause stuffed the room. Someone sold Base out to Eretimis. That was the only explanation for the betrayal, the carnage left behind, the reason Scarlette had been left for dead. No one she met could have done it. They all joined Base so Armiria could thrive. It had to be someone else, one of the other members that Feyne said wasn't at the bunker.

"Whoever it was, whoever betrayed us," Scarlette said, "they must have gotten stuck in the flames."

Rin spoke without thinking, "Or someone who wasn't there."

Scarlette and Feyne shared grim expressions before they turned to her.

"As I told Fido when you first arrived in the city," Vi stated, ignoring a glare from Feyne, "I've kept an ear out for news of the remaining members. No one's turned up dead. No one's lurking with any unruly crowds. As far as I know, the other members don't even know Base is in ruins."

Rin raised a brow at Feyne. "You didn't tell them?"

"I wasn't risking it."

"But what if they go looking for you there?"

Feyne sighed, resting his elbows on the bed and his head in his hands.

"They won't. They always kept to their own territory. Besides," he added before Rin could protest such a selfish move, "Scar and I were the only ones in the bunker who knew where they lived."

Rin's shoulders hung low. "I guess we'll never figure out the mystery. Whoever betrayed Base fell with it."

Scarlette nodded, speaking in a low tone, "It's better that way. For their sake."

Rin cast a glance toward the young scholar and knew that it was not the shifter that she referred to. Scarlette fought off four demons alone. Scarlette killed one of them.

"There's something else. Something I tried to tell you before I blacked out, Rin. Errogan," Scarlette spat out the name. "I read his aura."

Rin furrowed her brow. "Why would you do that?"

"Because I have seen nothing like his power before."

Tatsuo shook his head. "Pureblood demons can wield darkness," he explained softly. "It's called shadow magic. Humans might not see it often, but it's not uncommon."

"Well, that's just the thing," she pressed, exhaustion bordering on exasperation. Scarlette propped herself up on her elbows unsteadily.

"He's not a demon."

The words blew through the room like an unwelcome draft in winter. Rin blinked twice. "Come again?"

"Errogan is *not* a demon," Scarlette pressed through clenched teeth, her face reddening with effort.

Luna urged the girl to lay down. The healer wrapped her honey hair into a bun, as she often did when she went to work, and hovered her hands above the young woman's chest. Right where Errogan's darkness struck her.

Rin shook her head. "That doesn't make sense. Zarus referred to him as a demon."

"If not demon, then what?" Genesis asked.

Scarlette shook her head, damp strands of hair falling to her pillow.

"I don't know. Nothing I've ever seen or studied, and I've studied it all. The first layer of your aura tells what species you are. Always. There's no exception to that rule. I've seen humans; I've seen shifters; I've seen demons and studied that of fae. Errogan's aura doesn't fit with any of them. He's something new. At least new to the eyes of aura readers."

Feyne rubbed his brow.

"And how long have you lot of readers been around?"

She paused for a moment, taking a deep breath, "A long time. Very long time. The scrolls I taught myself with were part of the city of Arwyrn."

There was a shift in the corner. Perplexity lined Tatsuo's face. "He wields shadows. Only demons can do that."

Rin scrunched her nose again. "Genesis has darkness in his magic."

Genesis shook his head. "Summoning is a different sort, a human sort. It's not the same shadows that the demonkind handle. Not as empty."

He was right. Genesis's magic filled the room with energy, Zarus's and Errogan's drained it like a leech.

Rin frowned. "What about dark magic? You told me those twins you fought possessed it."

"It could be dark magic, but it's not like any I've seen," Tatsuo commented. "Dark magic is a knock-off of shadow magic, but it drains life to use it. Errogan, though soulless, doesn't have any of the symptoms."

Curious, indeed. Rin bit the inside of her cheek, a headache welling in response.

"All things that we can discuss further another time," Luna finally interrupted.

She glanced at Rin, eyes as lively as a cemetery. Scarlette's face was wan as the dying harvest outside the city, her breaths short and forced. She needed rest. And a healer.

"For now, I ask that everyone leave these quarters and give Erin and I time to work."

Rin's eyes widened. She pointed a questioning finger at herself, and Luna's smile eased the lingering uncertainty in her heart.

Chapter Thirty-Nine

"**W**hat's drawing out such a long face?"

Rin glanced up from the hand her head rested atop. "Hm?"

"Erin, I was gone for many years, but I still know when something's wrong."

Rin sighed through her nose. She straightened up from where she leaned on the edge of the bed, the rising sun kissing her face.

It had been little more than an hour since everyone left. Vi told Tatsuo that he slouched like a fish and needed better posture as she strode out, so the dragon chased after her with some comeback. Aiden walked his grandmother out, asking that the woman please shed some light on what in the Flames everyone was talking about. Genesis offered Rin a pat on the back before he left, claiming that he agreed dawn was a gods-awful hour and crept back in bed. All that remained of the crowd was Luna, Rin, and Feyne—who refused to leave and took a seat in the rocker by the fire. His head had bobbed back and forth until finally, he graced the room with a choir of snores. Luna and Rin had been sitting in silence for a while.

"For starters, my arse is numb," Rin remarked as she shifted on the wooden chair.

Luna stifled her laugh, careful to keep her hands steady. Scarlette's chest rose and fell softly, peacefully, but she was far from healed.

"I used to bring a pillow with me whenever I worked."

Her feather-light smile lasted only a moment, receding into the well of her concern as she glanced toward her daughter. "I think I know what's bothering you."

Rin raised her brow.

"I promise that you didn't do this to her, Erin."

"So I've been told." Rin's stare fixed on the gaping wound in the middle of Scarlette's chest. There would definitely be a scar.

Her mother looked forward. Compassion hovered in the air between them.

"Did you know I was fourteen when my magic started showing?"

"Isn't that a little old for magic development?"

The fact that Rin remembered something out of *Oh Blessed Are We of the Gods: A Magician's Handbook* riled her head with unbridled rage or pleasant surprise.

Her mother nodded. "So long from what's normal, my family assumed I wasn't a user."

Rin nearly scoffed, "Wait a royal minute, are you telling me they expected you to be one?"

A smirk laced Luna's lips.

"There was speculation. My sister's magic showed its face when she was four."

Rin didn't know what awed her: magic ran in her family, her mother was a late bloomer, or the fact she had an aunt. The questions stirred, all battling to be the first asked.

"I, er—" she scratched the side of her head. "Family trait?"

Her mother found more whimsy in the question than Rin did.

"No, magic is still as rare to us as it is to everyone, but out of the rare, it isn't uncommon for myths and conjectures to arise. Most people believed that if one sibling had it, the other would too."

"What started that?"

Her mother shrugged. "People pushing all of their children to be let into magic schools most likely. They were prestigious, and everyone wanted their kids to go there. If you could convince someone you were a user in the old days, you could convince them of anything. Unfortunately, I couldn't convince anyone of anything, and I was not accepted into Gamillon."

"Gamillon?"

"It was a small school for users in Croft."

Rin tried rubbing away the early morning from her eyes.

"I thought the last magic school in Nokomic was destroyed in Zelenia."

"Only the last official school. Gamillon wasn't as grand as the Ancient City itself, but it was one of many underground schools established after fear of users stirred when Zelenia fell."

Her mother paused her thought as she brought one of her hands over Scarlette's brow, the other tracing a line over the scholar's heart.

"Instead of learning to harness magic, the underground schools taught users how to hide their power. My sister went there after her magic appeared." A smile tugged on Luna's lips.

"I remember how the rooms would rumble and quake whenever she would get excited or angry."

Rin would have smiled at the memory, asked more about her aunt, but she knew better.

Luna's voice fell flat. "Yulane was four years older than I, so joyful and loving. Not a mage, but a talented caster. She was eighteen when the Resurrection burned the school."

Suddenly, the winter chill bit a little harder.

"Why…" Rin said, unable to be shocked by cruelty anymore.

A heavy breath loosed from her mother's lungs, calming the tremble of her voice.

"The power of magic poses a threat to everyone in power; whether it be tyrant, king, queen, or group of criminals… Eretimis is only one challenge users face on this continent."

Luna closed her eyes.

"My mother and father hadn't received word from Yulane for a long while and got worried. We took a trip to see her and bring some joy into what we thought was stress of the academy—"

"You don't have to say any more." Rin offered.

After a moment's silence, her mother's eyes slid open. Tears barely kept back.

"I discovered my magic when we found the ruins of the school. It happened too fast for me to remember, much like when your power showed itself in the desert. I slammed my hands against the ground and wailed. My magic ate away at it. Everything I touched was wiped away. The entire street began to wither."

Rin's chest beat hollowly as the desert night played over in her head. "How did you stop?"

"I couldn't. It wouldn't have stopped if it weren't for someone hitting me on the back of the head. I woke up on the ground of a barn, my parents in the other room pleading with the owners to let us stay the night. They broke me out of the holding cells in Croft and ran away with me."

"How did they manage that?"

"My father was a soldier of Nokomic before the kingdom fell and he turned to smithing as a career."

"Oh," Rin mumbled. Suddenly, her mother's combat skills made sense.

Luna continued, "My parents stayed away from big cities after that, and magic schools, but they found a mentor to teach me. I've never seen someone as shocked as when my mentor discovered I was a white mage. The power only appeared when I least expected it. I thought she was going to have a heart attack."

A grin stirred on her mother's face. Rin smiled back.

"The point is, Erin," Luna said a bit more present, "I blamed myself. I blamed myself for my late magic. I felt I should have been with my sister to fight by her side, and I blamed myself for not having known I was a healer so I could have saved the people I hurt when my magic destroyed that street in Croft."

But none of that was your fault. The words numbed her tongue. Rin ran her hand through her ginger strands dancing in the sunlight.

"What did you do?"

"I trained and grew stronger."

"And?"

"And I blamed myself even more once I realized my true potential." Luna sighed through her nose, cutting the flow of magic to her hands and stretching her arms.

"The stronger I became, the more I knew I could have saved my sister. I hated myself for it. Not only that, but my magic did the exact opposite of what a healer is supposed to do. It destroyed as much as it saved. I took life out of things, made them rot and decay. I was afraid of it, of what it would do to the people I loved. The more I feared it, the worse my control of that power became."

Another deep inhale.

"I worked through years of hate and fear before my mentor taught me I couldn't control it until I controlled my hate and fear. Instead of seeing my power as a curse, I should see it as the gift it was and use it to help people—as was the original intent of human magic." Luna turned to Rin and grabbed her hands.

"Your magic is a blessing, Erin. Only you were given it, and it's up to you to decide how to use it. In order to take control, you need to stop fearing this part of yourself. Your magic kept Scarlette alive. Your magic is healing her now, even if you don't understand it."

Rin had witnessed her mother's magic, felt the air in the Pit. How long did it take her to master that destructive force? How long before she accepted it as part of her? A tightness grew in Rin's chest.

Luna squeezed tighter.

"You've gotten so much further this week alone, Erin. You're summoning your light at will, cutting it off on demand. You learned to do that all on your own. How many lives have you saved by using it?"

The words severed Rin's stare, turning away from her mother and looking at rust brown stains.

"This bandage should be changed," she mumbled, letting her hands work free of thought.

Luna helped hoist Scarlette's torso up as Rin switched out the bloody wrap for a fresh one. Once they finished cleaning the wound, Rin stood from her chair and walked to the water basin in the corner.

"Twenty-eight."

Luna looked up, the distortion rising from her hands cutting off. "What's that?"

Rin sucked in a deep breath and looked at herself in the mirror above the basin. "Twenty-eight people dead because I didn't understand my magic."

The names replayed across her mind. Every face caught in the burning bunker, every body she passed. Rin bit down until her jaw was sore.

"They're dead because of me, not even a proper grave to honor them, and I'm left haunted by the power that left them for dead!"

How was she supposed to move on and accept that? An entire group of living, loving people—gone.

"I don't trust it—don't trust *myself* with it. The gods could have given it to anyone in the world, yet they thought I was the best fit."

She turned away from the basin and ran her hand through her hair. "They must have needed something to laugh at."

An airy chuckle tore through the silence, gradually increasing into laughter. Rin's brow creased at her mother's sudden fit.

"Oh, child," Luna said with a sweet tone that dug up memories. "If only you saw yourself the way I see you. You are stronger than you know, Erin. Not everyone could make it through what you have, the handicaps you placed on yourself."

Luna's expression dropped, eyes falling to the side.

"I'm the one to blame here. I left you when you were eight, assuming you didn't have magic. And then I didn't teach you as much as I could have when you found me."

"Are you forgetting how many filthy old accounts and techniques you had me read? I still don't think the dust is completely out of my lungs. Oh, and by the way, where the in the Flames did you get all those writings, anyway? Was it really *that* necessary to drag them across Death's Yard?"

Luna blinked twice before another chortle stole her voice. "I'm glad to see your hatred of it is as enthusiastic as mine was. Honestly, Rin, I'm surprised you learned anything from those books. I doubt anyone in the last century has learned from the old texts of magic."

A sunken feeling settled in Rin's stomach. "You didn't intend for me to learn anything?"

Luna bit her bottom lip, her fingers dancing on the post of the bed. "No. I intended for you to stay as far away from magic as possible."

"Because you didn't think I could handle it?"

Her mother scoffed. "Lyhrëon, no! Erin, I wanted to keep you safe from the world, not yourself! A white mage is a target. I wanted you to live a life of freedom, not running."

The words cut short. Luna leaned her elbows on her knees as she rubbed the strife from her forehead. "I was trying to protect you from a life like mine, but I was wrong. I hid the key to your success. I am so sorry for the suffering I caused you."

Rin was silent. For all she was worth, an emptiness tenfold swallowed her heart.

"So you're telling me," she began after a long moment of thought, "that you had me read *The Armirian Proposal: Anaphorious's Essays of Foot Form and Movement* as busywork? You're saying that there was no point in reading *five hundred pages* of which way some old rooster shitting user preferred to place his feet while casting his trivial little spells?"

A sheepish grin drew on Luna's lips.

"Perhaps..."

Rin bit down on the laugh rumbling in her chest. "I'm going to need some time to get over that."

A spell of laughter erupted from Scarlette's bedroom soon after. Even Feyne stirred in his recliner until finally Rin and her mother calmed themselves.

"Look," Rin cut through the fit, a smile lacing her expression, "I won't sit here and place blame on every person who could have done something different. We're here now, and that's what matters. Besides, reading all that crap did help."

Luna's eyes widened. "You're joking."

Rin shook her head. "No. Every one of those texts led me to the conclusion that I'm the oddball out of human users."

"Still no luck?"

Rin bobbed her head. Reclaiming her chair by the bed, she sat on it backwards, balancing on two legs.

"It's when I search the depths of my mind that I find my magic."

Luna pursed her lips at the mystery. "It's still hard to believe. For ages, humans drew their magic from their hearts."

"That might have been true for a few hundred centuries," Rin shrugged. "But for whatever reason, my source is misplaced, and the gods didn't answer why. I will say though, knowing where that ocean lies makes it easier to avoid drowning in." She laughed it off, but Luna sensed the truth of the statement.

"How much can you use before you get to that point?"

Was the feeling of drowning in your own mind exclusive to her, or did her mother know the terrifying sensation as well?

"I summon it lightly, barely taking a step in the waters, but can't use it during training for anything other than a taunt. I don't know what it would do in a fight without the threat of death clouding my judgment."

Rin offered another smile, and this one Luna accepted.

"You can keep above water by treading it, dear."

Luna leaned back in her chair, clearly needing a pillow beneath her rear as well. "Magic is a part of us. It will act to protect us if we're in harm's way. All it takes is a bit of practice to overcome that instinct. And seeing how your duel went with Mister Masquarem today, I think it's safe to say you're getting the hang of quick-moment decisions. By the way, do you plan on attacking all your opponents like that, or did you make a special exception for the prince? You two spend a lot of time together..."

Rin's face burned hotter than the damned Flames. Her mouth gaped open for a heartbeat.

"It was tactical thinking." She nearly smacked her hand against her forehead.

Luna's implying smirk was relentless. "Perhaps save this tactical thinking for closed doors next time."

Rin buried her face in her hands, shielding against the sight of her mother's smile. "You know, if we're making suggestions, why don't we take a moment to talk about how you and Da should have been behind closed doors that one night when I was five. You know, when I stayed up late drawing you a picture of our family and was so excited to show it to you, but you took my prolonged silence as a go-ahead to get down on the living room floor and—"

Her mother's face instantly matched the blush of Rin's.

"*You were silent for four hours*, how were we supposed to know you were awake!"

"The candle in my room was lit!"

"*Anyway*," Luna continued through a tremendous effort, "Tatsuo has some interesting insight into the magic. I think it's best that you keep working with him to figure out a system that works for you."

Tatsuo had poured hours into assisting her. Going over demonic techniques of summoning magic and the different types of it. Honestly, the types were all similar to humans': they cast spells, but also possessed natural abilities like mages. What baffled Rin was that demons barely had limits. A human's limit lingered at the extent of their physical strength. All a demon had to do was break their own mental barriers to widen the banks of their power. Easier said than done, but it was still as unbelievable as a human drawing magic from her mind.

She had yet to meet with him today. He mentioned something about practicing meditations to calm the mind, things his father did to collect focus before summoning incredible amounts of magic. Frankly, a bit of relaxing and thinking about nothing didn't sound too bad.

Rin yawned as she leaned onto her mother's shoulder. "I don't think there's much more to do right now, Ma. The wound needs to rest before we try anything else."

"Aye," Luna nodded, stretching her back, "and the medicine needs to sit. Why don't you find Tatsuo before he hides from you again?"

A smile tugged at her lips. She'd never forget how the *narikaah* hid underneath the kitchen counter to avoid studying with her a few days ago. Rin hoisted herself off the chair, kissed her mother on the forehead, and left without a sound. She rounded the corner to Tatsuo's room, pondering how lucky she was that the *narikaah* inherited his father's demonic magic, and not his parents' draconic abilities.

Chapter Forty

Rin stared at the back of her eyelids for too long. It wasn't until her head dipped down that she felt a nudge on her shin.

"If you want to do this tomorrow, I won't argue," Tatsuo pleaded a little too desperately.

Rin cracked a smile without opening her eyes. "I already told you that you don't have to do this with me. I'm okay if you show me what to do and leave."

A sigh dramatic enough to blow away the heavens sounded across the floor. She finally opened her eyes, already having a steadiness in her own mind. Tatsuo's expression was far from content.

"No, you might fall over and die of boredom at any second, Red. I need to be here to resuscitate you should that happen."

"I appreciate it," she replied. The form wasn't difficult; it was similar to the meditation her mother showed her months ago. It was quite shocking to hear that some demons sat meditating for hours on end before needing to summon incredible amounts of magic. Rin didn't think she had more than two hours in her. What wasn't as surprising was that Tatsuo was not, in fact, one of those demons.

"Did you know Vi could sing?"

Rin peeked her eyes open once more, concentration cracking like ice.

"It would not surprise me. I've heard human tales of fae voices and their power. Have you heard her sing?"

Tatsuo nodded, his braid sweeping up dust on the ground like a broom. "When we went into town the other night. She took me to a tavern, and some acquaintances coaxed her into a tune. She has the best voice I've ever heard."

"I didn't know you two went out," Rin mumbled, catching Tatsuo's shrug before closing her eyes.

"Now that Fuzz Face never leaves Scar's room, I have no one to spar with. We ran into each other one day, and she invited me to talk to a—what did she call them—*news holder*. After that, we hung out for a while."

"Doesn't that sound exciting," Rin teased, a knowing smirk trailing to her lips. Her eyes remained closed, but she knew the pillow was being thrown in her direction before it hit her.

"Exciting is the right word. I never know if she's leading me down a dark alley to stab me or show me a hidden treasure of Xandra," he admitted. "I have yet to trade my soul for a song though. Probably..."

"She's certainly your type."

"You know my type?"

Rin scoffed. "I've walked around this city enough times with you to know your type, Tat."

"Oh, and what might that be?"

Rin smirked, peering through one eye. "Anyone who can kick your butt and rub it in your face."

Tatsuo's stare blanked. He blinked, searching for a retort.

"I mean, you're not wrong. Fearsome women, but gentle men, I suppose. Xian was never the asskicking type..."

"Xian?"

"The young man who stole my heart when I was no older than you, young one."

Rin's eyes opened. "You fell in love?"

The *narikaah* nodded.

"We met a while after my parents died. I was still living in Dìghao on the eastern continent. He was human, but damn he was a catch." The dragon nearly choked laughing before Rin said anything. "He was a fisherman." Tatsuo's eyes closed, a smile of remembrance warming his face. "It's so long ago, it feels little more than a fairy tale now."

Rin smiled, dropping her focus.

"How come you never mentioned him?"

His smile faltered. "Because my parents were dead, and I wouldn't sleep until they had been avenged."

Rin opened her mouth, but Tatsuo spoke first, "Xian didn't want me to go after Zarus. He wanted me to make a life with him and move forward."

The dragon dropped his stare, shaking his head as a shadow fell over him.

"I wouldn't listen. I only cared about paying the debt due. Rage is blinding, Rin, so blinding that you won't even notice when it pushes away the ones you love. Xian and I parted ways when I moved west." Despite himself, Tatsuo smiled, "He was a good man. I'm sure he made a life with someone better for him."

Rin's heart squeezed. She would never understand how this *narikaah* stayed so strong. Her respect for him was unrivaled. The conversation turned into silence, and she searched for her focus once more. She inhaled deeply, then let out the excess focus.

"So how's Scarlette doing?"

His voice rang like a siren against the quiet meditation in her head. The dragon did not care for this reflection of power one bit.

Truthfully, Rin wasn't sure. Ma hadn't mentioned whether Scarlette's infection worsened or improved.

"I think it's about the same as last week," she considered, "The infection isn't what's keeping her down."

Rin gave up on reclaiming the tranquility in her mind. She relaxed her shoulders and used her hands to prop herself up as she leaned back. The hearth beside them roared, warming the air enough to sit comfortably on the cool floor. Winter had finally come, and it came with a vengeance. "She should have been dead, and her body knows it."

A sullen hush conquered the room for a minute as Rin's eyes lowered to nothing in particular. Scarlette was a fighter, that was for sure.

"You'll find the right answer," the dragon said, a flame dancing proudly around his fingertips. "You always have something up your sleeve."

"Ma thinks I'm helping Scar's situation somehow." Rin shook her head, rubbing her eyes. "But I haven't done a thing. Even if I have a handle on it, the only magic I summon is harming, not healing," she reflected, basking in the fire light. "I'm getting the hang of light, but healing still evades me. It resonates differently than my light's hum. It's more of a song than a buzz. More structured."

"Confidence spills into every aspect of our lives, young one," Tatsuo said in feigned wisdom. "Maybe believing in the buzz is affecting the song as well."

Rin shrugged. "More pieces to the puzzle."

"It's a good thing we've gotten good at solving those," Tatsuo laughed, embers floating to the slitted pupils of his eyes. "Have you thought about how we're pulling off this master scheme yet?"

Rin's gaze sobered as it met Tatsuo. Last time she asked, he was as clueless as she was on how to break Zarus free.

"I have some ideas, most worth dumping down the chamber pot though," she sighed, laying down on the rug. "From what you've told me, the weather around the fortress will provide enough cover for us to get there, but it's after that stumps me."

How were they meant to sneak into the lethally guarded stronghold of the most dangerous being in the world?

"Would've been nice if Yath Ha had given me a few more hints on how to go about this."

She rubbed the sleep from her eyes. It was only midday, and Rin could've slept for ages.

"How do we find our way through a maze without drawing attention to ourselves?" It was a rhetorical question, Tatsuo merely voicing his thoughts, but it still sounded as hopeless as meditating next to the dragon.

"We can cover our scent with clothes," Rin thought aloud, "or blood if necessary." She tried not to grimace at the memory of leaving Hilyan's Peak with Zarus. "But that also assumes we're able to get inside and steal their clothes... Why don't we just knock on the door? I'm sure he'd love to host our company."

Tatsuo humored her, chuckling quietly. "We need a way to know where everyone is before we see them. I don't know about you, but I can't see through walls very well."

Rin smiled, but deep thought interrupted the sentiment. The fire crackled, engulfing each log with such fervor, it had nearly burned through the entire pile. That's how they would have to be—quick, precise. No room for error. The thick aroma of burning logs took her back to Aresan, where she and her father would spend their nights reading and relaxing after a hard day of work. She hadn't yet had the time to write to him. Hadn't risked sending a letter to her home. It killed her when she wondered what her father was doing right then. She was all he had, and it had been months since he heard from her.

Tears welled in her eyes. *Soon*. She would return home, and she would be back in the rocker before the mantle. Rin doubted he would believe half of the things that she had been through—probably refuse to believe the other half for his own peace of mind. She exhaled a smoky breath.

Rin's eyes shot open. She blinked away the daze, disbelief holding her tongue.

"Rin," Tatsuo called, nudging her boot with his foot. "You alright?"

She looked at the *narikaah* slouching on the floor.

"What is it?"

Excitement bubbled in her stomach, rising all the way to her face. Rin bit down on her bottom lip, teeth peeking through in a smile.

"I have an idea." She jumped to her feet and ran down the hallway to gather everyone.

Chapter Forty-One

His shoulder smacked the stone, his head hitting next.

Zarus groaned as he climbed to his feet. Dastardly shadows danced around the cell.

"Never should it be claimed Eretimis the Dark Tyrant doesn't hold a grudge," he growled as he rolled his shoulder back and forth.

"You still have not learned." Eretimis stood between him and the cell door, two guards posted on the outside.

It was the first time the Tyrant had trekked to the dungeons to pay Zarus a visit since they nearly killed each other. It was also the first time Zarus had seen Errogan since Nessriq collected him days ago. Rightfully so, his old friend refused to look directly at him to avoid setting off the Tyrant's wrath.

Zarus assumed the reunion would come eventually. But this? Woken up and dragged to another part of the dungeon where only echoes of his fellow prisoners trailed. It was not expected.

"Are you going to monologue at me?"

Dark, depthless eyes pierced into Zarus's skull. "I have grown tired of our banter, Zarus."

Without warning, a shadow slithered around Zarus's neck, forcing him to his knees. He tried to unravel the phantom rope, but the darkness wove too tightly to manipulate. Eretimis didn't intend to give him another edge. Which was precisely why Errogan was in their company. Insurance that his prisoner wouldn't act out of line.

A curse tangled Zarus's tongue. Little more than a sputter made its way out before his head swayed violently. Like a ship amidst the storm, the world rocked around him.

His ears rang. Every sense Zarus had blared at him to fight back, but he killed that instinct until his vision blotted out the light. Black splotches and white stars took over. Right before he slipped away, the shadow magic vanished. He doubled onto the floor.

Heaving gasps stumbled into his lungs, spittle flying to the floor as he struggled between coughs. Zarus wrapped his hands around the chill the darkness left on his neck before he crawled to his knees. Eretimis towered over him.

"Your will is stronger than I anticipated, Lowwenth. You freed yourself of my serum and challenged me time and time again."

The Tyrant slowly lowered himself until he was eye-level with the prisoner still gasping for air on the ground. Little more than a whisper, little more than a threat, he spoke slowly. "I am going to take everything that makes you *you*, and burn it to ash."

Zarus had little more than a beat of his thundering heart before the darkness enveloped him.

***

"Zarus!"

His eyes barely opened before the light stung them.

"Zarus, come inside. It's time for supper!"

Like ice shattering over a frozen lake, his eyes cracked open. So distant, so faint, like listening to someone speak underwater. Yet his ears weren't playing tricks.

That voice.

Zarus forced his eyes to look around, forced his mind to focus on the dark, nothing he found himself submerged in. He pried himself off the ground as it bent beneath his step. He looked from side to side. There was nothing. Until a spark of light erupted.

A maelstrom of color twisted into shape. Tall, thick trees as high as the clouds towered around. Green soaked the sky. Birdsong sang through the air. A forest that blurred just beyond his field of vision. It had been a lifetime since he'd laid witness to the evergreens.

Zarus stared in awe. The path cutting into the thick wood ran perpendicular to him, narrowing from the forest's trail into the home blurred by distant memory. Disbelief jarred his gut, and the world swayed with the motion.

The woman's head stood at his shoulder. Brown hair scrambled into a bun, flour wiped across her warm cheek. She stood under the doorway smiling at him.

"Zarus, sweetie, come inside. You can go back out later." The sweetest voice he had ever heard echoed through the seams of the scene, her tone distorted and faltering every other syllable. A man suddenly walked up from behind the woman, putting his hands on her shoulders. It was odd. Zarus couldn't find any details in the man's appearance. Even his voice came and went in waves.

"—ome ins—de, —on. —e'll wal— throu— the wood— —ater."

Zarus couldn't understand his words, but knew them by heart. He stumbled, not knowing what to say to the ghosts of his past. "I can't hear you, Father—"

The ghosts did not respond. The world around him stuttered, and rain began to fall. Both the man and woman drained of all life until everything around him faded into monochrome, and then black. The rain didn't stop. It poured and poured as another scene rippled.

A cemetery surrounded him. Instead of two bright faces, Zarus stared at a single headstone. The moss trailed recklessly along the edges, covering the top with vines. It nearly covered the names too, but Zarus always scraped it off every few weeks. How many years had it been? How many years since they passed from the plague?

Search in Peace Adram and Marine Lowwenth

Beloved Father and Mother

Loved in Life and Beyond Death

May Vulyn's Hand Guide You

Zarus's breath hitched. The rain poured in falls, yet he never found himself to be wet. How long since he stood in this very spot, mourning his parents? The very humans who found him abandoned in the forest and took him as their own. Was it possible the gravestone was still in the ground, or had time ripped it away too? Shame bled into his soul. He never went back.

"What would you have thought?" Zarus asked the weathered stone.

"Would you have called me a monster too?" No matter how long he stared at the names carved in time, nothing but the rain answered.

Zarus didn't flinch as the world bled dry before it shuttered and faded.

***

What would it be like to tread through that hall of twisted memories?

Zarus had stopped struggling. Eretimis's darkness seeped through his skull and corrupted his mind. The demon appeared to be asleep.

Eretimis stood above his prisoner, eyes closed in the finest focus, still as the dead as he worked. The mental connection had been placed. The Tyrant's ties to Zarus's mind were strong as steel.

The calm Zarus wore under the sedation of sleep... How long until it was permanent? How long until Eretimis wiped away everything inside his mind, made him into a blank slate?

Will you even remember me, Z?

Silent, he stood. Still, he watched.

***

The hush of the dead's resting place roared. The sound twisted until Zarus stood in the blanket of a blizzard up to his shins. He couldn't see through it. There was a sense in the air, one that burned his nose like incense of the temple. It instilled hatred. It infused fear.

He forced himself against the treacherous winds, trudging through the mounds of snow working against him. Until he found himself in a clearing. Her ginger strands rebelled against the wind, emerald eyes searching for any ounce of help. The girl was near blue, a step away from freezing, a step away from death.

How in all of Armiria had she even gotten up there?

The Lennaels were a formidable host, Hilyan's Peak worse so. Zarus watched her struggle, watched her cry out against the winds and ice. The world itself damned her, and she fought against it with every ounce of herself. She stumbled into the clearing, catching glimpse of his shadow amid the storm.

"H-hello? I think I'm lost... would you happen to know a path that leads down this mountain?"

His mouth slipped open, but he caught himself. A human treading this far in a storm like this? Impossible. Zarus's eyes narrowed, his mind sharpened. She had to be a scout, a spy of Eretimis. It was the only explanation... He would wait—see what she had up her sleeves—before he made any decisions.

Just as Zarus made to move forward, to size this human up and determine what she knew about him, the scene of white, green, and red paused. A silent moment between thoughts. The girl faded, then the entire world twisted into black.

Zarus braced himself for the rush of life to spread around him. Waited for the world itself to unfold and take him somewhere unexpected, but it never did. He heard a stream brabbling nearby. He smelled the sweet air, even felt the grass tickling his arms. Yet darkness encased him, and through it, he saw nothing. Until he realized someone was beside him.

"Are you going to lie there all day or are you going to help me?"

Zarus's eyes shot open like lightning amid the storm. He shielded his face from the sun's radiance and blinked away the tears as he looked at the green world.

A forest? Had he been asleep in a forest? No, his eyes adjusted, catching glimpse of the red fruit growing in the lush patches around him. Summer strawberries. Finally, he turned the other way and saw someone walking up the path through the field.

"I hope you slept well, because I've been slaving away for hours finding something for us to eat." The words weren't malicious, nothing of a bite to them.

The male laughed them off as he sat beside Zarus. His white hair eclipsed the sun, his eyes a dim pale blue.

"From the looks of it, you've come back fairly empty handed," Zarus groaned as he hoisted himself up, rubbing the sleep from his eyes.

"Oh? Well, Z, I'll be sure to eat everything I found and let you scavenge for yourself if you keep complaining."

Zarus laughed, propping his arms in the grass, feeling the warmth on his face.

"Let's fight over them and see who wins."

He smiled with closed eyes, enjoying the day. However, everything fell silent. The world around hushed; no breeze whistling, no brook rushing, no retort from the demon.

Zarus opened his eyes. Black, grey, white. No color, no life. He turned to his friend but found a statue of the male. Frozen in time, his stare a thousand years away.

Zarus clenched his jaw as he waited for everything to fade, everything to be taken away. Like his friend, the world froze. Stuck. Flickering in and out but never leaving.

"How many memories are you erasing?"

Zarus jumped at the words. It was like a voice in the back of his head, but the words were his friend's. Except his friend's lips did not move.

"As many as I can stir."

Another voice, a voice like running oil through his veins. Zarus tried not to shift against it. The colors of the world suddenly flashed in and out. Barely even there, but he saw them as they tried to fade.

"No," Zarus ground out, holding tight to the surrounding memory.

It was a memory, one that someone was trying to steal from him. He hissed at the sudden pounding of his head, pressing a hand to his temple. He looked for something, anything that he could dig his nails into.

"You're taking all of them? That's madness!"

Zarus's old friend was still frozen, but the iris of his eye lightened. Blue seeped into the grey like ice thawing with the first rays of morning sun.

Errogan.

Zarus pressed harder into the memory, straining his mind to think of something else... the smell, what did the world smell like? Pain thundered through his skull. Zarus grabbed his head with both hands.

"S-stay out." He fought the bite inside his head.

He pushed it out until he felt the warm breeze of midyear rustle through his hair and the sweet fragrance roam into his senses. With each breath of memory, with every bit of the scene he remembered, that nail drove deeper and deeper into his mind.

Zarus cried out at the hammer sending it further down. He nearly buckled and let the memory slip away entirely, but resisted until he had a handle on the hammer with both hands. Zarus pulled it free from the nail's wedge. His head writhed against the invading force. The power pushed tenfold back when Zarus barred it from the memory. The force snarled as it realized it could not slither back inside the memory, so it redirected its bite.

"Keep your tongue still before I remove it, Errogan!"

The strawberry fields around blew away like smoke from a candle. There was not black, grey, or white. There was simply nothing.

Zarus turned to Errogan, but even the smoke casting his memories had blown away. He bared his teeth, bracing himself for the next battle over his mind. Yet for all the power he possessed, nothing prepared him for the spreading fires.

Obsidian smoke choked his lungs, searing heat blazed against his skin. A sweltering panic seized Zarus's heart. The fires raged, nothing to be seen through their thick smog, but he didn't have to see to know where he stood. The gravel crunched underfoot; the screams violated the night's serenity. The wails were not cursing his very existence anymore, not spitting on him and throwing him into the street to die.

Zarus forgot about Dreya Village before his subconscious did. He had run to the closest town for help as he bled out after his village attacked him. But he did not receive help. Already, word of what happened in his home village spread—skewed words based on fear and falsehood. The people of Dreya had prepared for him. They built the stake before they saw him stumble across the horizon. Never once did the humans ask him for an explanation. Monsters received no such luxuries. Monsters deserved none.

Even his memory did not give him the entire story, but Zarus knew the town was trying to burn him for a crime they did not understand.

Yet they understood waging war on him was a mistake.

His ice lashed out at the mob. Then something stirred. Something like a shadow, but not cast by any source of light. The crowd of humans didn't know what to do once the force unleashed. It fought off the fire, creating a barrier between Zarus and the flames, forcing them the other way.

Zarus clenched his teeth against their cries. How many cries had he heard throughout his life? How many pleas from those who had been so intent on killing him? Too many. They all deserved to perish. Humans were made to follow, never lead. Made to be used. Damn them all.

Zarus did nothing as the world faded into monochrome tones. The flames stilled, the cries distorted and silenced. Those humans had served their purpose. They probably did not question the hand that led them to their very deaths.

That was exactly what caught Zarus's attention. Only one being survived the slaughter of his home. Only one being had the strength to fight back against him and walk away. The hand that intercepted Zarus from the very beginning, that trailed to the nearest town and spread falsehoods about him so he would be rid of long before he became a threat.

The same hand had a hold of his mind.

Zarus looked into the depths of darkness overtaking his memories.

"Get out."

A splash of color bled into the fires. Zarus closed his eyes, letting a darkness of his own envelop his body, heart, and mind. The magic, so cold it burned, stung every inch of him as it searched. He didn't falter against the shadows until he found the bit of magic Eretimis embedded in him.

The nail split through his mind, the hammer pounding down down down. Zarus held tight to his own shadows, but he needed more, something else to stop the hammer. Frost consumed the hammer's head. Spreading until it sealed the entirety in a layer of ice so thick, not even winter had a hold on it. The hammer pushed to be free. The memory drained into the bank of his mind, trembling like a lake disturbed by wind as something new unfolded. Nothing stirred in the dark void. Nothing manifested into view. Only words to his ears, only warmth around his body.

Singing. Singing sweet and hushed. A lullaby filled his head, stilling the quake of the hammer, soothing the pain of the nail. Zarus focused on the words. A female voice he didn't recognize, but one so familiar.

> *"In your heart, I'll carry you on*
> *Away from this storm you slowly drift upon*
> *So rest your head, child, let your worries be*
> *And be sure to think of me."*

Distant, a male called from another room, "Arha, the meeting starts soon. We should get going."

Another pang of nostalgia echoed in Zarus's chest.

"I'll be right there," the female replied. She whispered softly, as if leaning closer so only Zarus would hear, "I'll see you tonight, my love."

Zarus stilled; his magic steadied. The sweet tune remained in his head, lulling the tension from his mind. Who had ever sung to him in such a way that affected him so deeply? A shift of the hammer pulled Zarus away from his reflection. He turned his attention back on the darkness miserably squirming into the back of his mind. Zarus broke the magic's tie, crushing it to dust.

The surrounding void stirred.

Chapter Forty-Two

R eality closed in quickly. Fury was the first thing Zarus heard upon waking.

"I wasn't the one who let him slip away!"

"No, you were the one who raised your voice and brought him back to reality."

It didn't take long for Zarus to find the ache in his head. His thoughts stuck to the sides of his skull, huddled in half-formed clumps. It was like waking up from a sedated sleep. He groaned as he brought his hand to his temple. Zarus bade his eyes open. Instead of a Tyrant ominously standing over him, he found an argument.

Errogan raged like the winter winds.

"You're full of waste!"

Even Zarus's eyes widened.

"The only reason I'm down here is because you told me to be. If you thought I would meddle with your plans, then why don't you shove the request up your ass next time!"

A greasy silence trickled over the dungeon. Even the howls of the crazed fell short of Eretimis's wrath. However, Errogan wasn't as good at getting under the Tyrant's skin as Zarus was, and Eretimis held his resolve with an iron fist.

"I assumed you found your senses after your outburst in the laboratory, Errogan. I was incorrect." A chill ran down Zarus's spine at the irate calm that concealed Eretimis's words. The shadows in the room trembled—his only tell. The flame in Errogan's eye did not back down.

"It was a fool's whim to overpower his mind." The Reaper stood against the Tyrant, not a care in the world for the repercussions.

Eretimis didn't bat an eye. Only the shadows raged. "I had such high hopes for you, Errogan." His voice was little more than a sigh. "I should have never listened to you and gotten rid of the original."

Zarus tried to piece the conversation together through the fog of his thoughts. Whatever Eretimis meant, whatever purpose his words served, it worked. Errogan's expression twisted. He bared his teeth against it, snarled right in the Dark Tyrant's face.

"*I'm the perfect being* you *made.*" Errogan seethed.

There was no hesitation in Eretimis's response, only cold steel slicing through a facade.

"You are a disappointment. Ever since I allowed you to be on your own, you have brought me nothing but failure. Spare me your whining and leave my presence." An order. One final warning.

Errogan stared. Zarus wasn't sure if he was holding his tongue or for once didn't know what to say. At long last, his head shook. Errogan caught himself before he idled too long, before he earned more than the cut of words. Nothing more said, nothing more risked, the White-Cloaked Reaper collected himself to the best of his ability and begrudgingly bowed before his Dark Tyrant.

Errogan cast Zarus a wary glance as he turned around and walked out of the cellar into the dungeons.

Zarus expected hell to rise the moment Errogan was out of sight, but it would seem the demon dug his nails deep enough after all.

The Tyrant seethed under his facade and stalked off into the shadows without ever looking at Zarus. The bars slammed closed behind him, and the two guards followed.

Despite the memories Eretimis dragged him through—memories he fought for in the spans of his subconscious—all Zarus could do was stare. Uncertainty settled in his chest. Old questions resurfaced. New mysteries riled.

Who are you, Errogan?

Chapter Forty-Three

The wind beat against the windowpanes, rattling while Rin faced the uncertain stares.

Her mother spoke first. "Erin, I'm not sure if that is the best—"

"It will work."

"But Rin," Genesis shook his head, "that leaves so much room for things to go wrong—"

"It *will* work."

"This is Eretimis's fortress. People don't just waltz in," Tatsuo tried to explain.

"Look," Rin said to her friends, "I know it sounds mad in its simplicity, but that will work in our favor."

Genesis inhaled an uncertain breath. "What if they have it closed off? Zarus said the inhabitants of the fortress didn't know about the crypt passage, but we drew a lot of attention to it when we tried to flee."

Rin shook her head again. "If there are guards posted at the gate, then they'll be too far from everyone else to alert Eretimis before we attack. We'll be quick about it. Gen and Tat will tell us if any demons are at the gate. Feyne will smell if there are more the further inside we go."

The only other option was to build a full-fledged army and invade the fortress. Finally, when silence had settled for well more than it was welcome, Feyne spoke up.

"Why do you need me if you have them?" He gestured a nod to Genesis and Tatsuo. "Their senses will tell you who we're coming across better than my nose."

"Their senses aren't as good as your nose, Fuzz Face," Vi said to Feyne.

Tatsuo shook his head. "Things like walls and severe weather can block presences. They're only the touch of an aura, so if you cover one up—"

"You can't feel it," Feyne murmured to himself.

He sat next to Scarlette's bed, holding her hand in his own while the scholar slept.

"I don't know, Rin. We're basing our lives on our ability to be quick and discreet. Neither of which we've ever gotten the hang of."

"We've done the impossible before, remember?" Rin pleaded.

Feyne's eyes narrowed, his expression taut. "Yes and look where it got us."

Rin's eye traced Scarlette's limp hand in Feyne's own.

Genesis walked to her side.

"So that's how it's going to end? You're going to let all those people in Base you called friends simply fade? Did their deaths mean nothing to you?"

"Don't you *dare* talk to me about loss, prince," the wolf snapped. "I'm needed here right now."

Tatsuo's laughter spat across the room. "You belong in the Wastes, Wuflan! You give all this big talk about making the world a better place and helping those in need, but when it comes down to it, all you do is make the selfish choice. You were selfish to bring Rin to Base. You were selfish to hide there was a traitor amid you. Maybe we should talk about how much of a *risk* that was?"

Rin held up a hand toward the dragon. "Tatsuo, please stop."

The dragon took a heated step forward.

"No, Rin! He put your life in danger so he could learn a little more about the Dark Tyrant, and now he has the *audacity* to deny you the very promise that wrapped you up in this mess?" Another disdainful laugh spat out from the dragon. "Did you ever intend to help free Zarus, or did you say whatever was necessary to make her give you the information you wanted?"

Feyne's deathly stare dug into Tatsuo, a fight looming in his golden eyes. Tatsuo didn't budge.

"Feyne," Rin said softly. "Please, we can't do this without you. You're the only one who can guide us through the fortress without being seen."

Feyne's sense of smell would lead them through the fortress. Nothing else. What else could they do to free Zarus? Genesis and Tatsuo's senses could only go so far.

"He'll most likely be in the dungeons, far below Eretimis's feet."

Rin tried to recall the mental map Genesis described to her. "We only have to slip into the lower levels. We won't have to engage."

Feyne's black-flecked eyes bore into her but he remained silent.

"We need you."

"Rin, I—" Feyne began, but Luna walked up from behind him and placed a gentle hand on his shoulder.

"Give him time to think it over, Erin," her mother said.

It was his decision to make, his life to risk. Yet still... Did their promise mean nothing to him?

Scarlette needed him alive when she healed. Rin understood that. However, taking time to mull it over... they didn't have that luxury.

"I'm won't force you into this, Feyne," Rin murmured, "But I can't wait for Scarlette to be healed before I go. We've spent too much time idling. Zarus has been there for too long; I can feel it."

"Do you remember how to get back in?" she asked Genesis.

Genesis studied her for a moment, searching her eyes. Until finally, he knew there was no changing her mind. She needed Zarus. End of story. He nodded.

"I can guide us through." His tone was less than convinced this plan would work.

She didn't care. She turned to the dragon. "Tat, are you able to sense someone before being seen?"

Tatsuo hadn't calmed down, but dragging his attention away from Feyne eased some of the tension.

"It's hard to say. The fortress is old; its thick walls meant to keep the inhabitants safe. It would be difficult, but with enough focus I could give us some warning."

"Rin, this is madness," Luna protested, stepping across the room to grab her hands. "We can wait and think of a new plan."

Rin squeezed her mother's hands. "Yes, it is madness. Almost as foolish as leaving home to find you, accepting a stranger's invitation for shelter, or befriending a dragon who tried to kill me out of revenge, and fighting off assassins and monsters in the streets of Xandra. We have nothing else, so madness is going to have to keep working for us. Because the alternative is losing Zarus."

Luna looked deep into her daughter's eyes, looking for any sign of common sense. Rin blotted the sense out.

"You don't have to come," Rin uttered, but Luna silenced her and kissed her forehead.

"There is nowhere that I would not follow you."

Rin swallowed hard as she looked about the corridor. Fear and uncertainty smothered her friends. She stifled it. They had work to do.

Chapter Forty-Four

Zarus was grateful Errogan had caused such a scene with the Dark Tyrant. In the heated argument, Eretimis had stormed away and Zarus remained tucked away from the masses of the dungeons. Isolated in his own section of the prison, only echoes to offer him company.

A groan slipped through his lips as he adjusted the iron gloves on his hands.

"You sound like a bilious oaf."

Zarus swung himself around in disbelief.

"Yet you've come all this way to check on me. I'm flattered."

Elief sighed, making sure no one had followed.

"Don't make me regret this."

Despite himself, Zarus couldn't help smiling as the healer quietly pulled a key out from under her top skirt. She made sure not to let the hinges of the door screech as she entered, closing it until it was just shy of clamping shut. She took one look at his dazed composure before she raised a dark brow.

"Gods bless Eroz, what have you done since I left, sir?"

"I think *Zarus* will do fine," he sighed, letting himself fall against the back wall of the cellar. She nodded, careful where to tread with the newfound familiarity.

"Sorting through memories," he finally admitted. He had spent the last few hours picking through disassembled memories, making damn sure they were all in place. But he could never be certain.

Elief scrunched her nose as if something tickled it. "You're being held prisoner in Eretimis's dungeons, and that's what you spend your time doing?"

Zarus groaned as a nasty sway seized his head. "Why are you even here?"

"By the looks of it, you need my help."

"Word spreads that quickly, huh?"

"It doesn't." She paused, sucking in a breath.

"I received a summon in the middle of the night saying you needed urgent attention." Zarus opened his eyes long enough to share a glance with the demon as she pulled supplies from her satchel. His gaze narrowed in conclusion. "It would seem I was wrong; your concern wasn't wasted, after all."

He couldn't help the edges of his lips from twitching upward. That must have been where Errogan pardoned himself to after he left the dungeons.

"I'm surprised he knew who I was. I didn't think he was conscious during the times you forced me to work on him."

Zarus smiled. "You have to be careful with him. You never know what he's paying attention to."

"He's struggling," Elief said, working through her satchel. "I can see it in his eyes... I figured you could use these."

She tossed him a set of fresh clothes.

"It's... much appreciated," he whispered.

An understatement. He hoisted himself free from the wall, but needed her assistance since his hands were bound. Together they removed the pathetic excuse for a shirt he had worn for the better part of three months and exchanged it for the warm undershirt and tunic the healer provided. She also tossed him a pair of pants, with the demand he figured out how to put those on after she left. In no time, Zarus used the scrap shirt as a pillow as he laid back on the floor. Elief sat beside him, hands hovering above his forehead.

A few minutes passed, neither of them saying a word; Zarus thinking and Elief working. Zarus glanced at the healer as her hands shifted above him. She chewed her lip.

"You look like you've been stuck in a Tyrant's stronghold."

A feeble attempt to pull her out of thought, but any mirth in his face fell flat once the healer flicked her stare to him.

"The toolbox is organized."

Slowly, he propped himself onto his elbows. He looked into her grave eyes and wondered how much fear swam beneath the surface. Freedom wasn't easy to come by these days.

"All assembled?"

A still nod.

"How long?"

"Two months until they hit Xandra."

Another pause.

Zarus sighed through his nose, closing his eyes. Two months, and Armiria would never be the same. Did he plan on doing it exactly as he had Zelenia? *No*, this wasn't just an experiment. He wouldn't call every demon from here to the other side of Armiria back if it was only to destroy one city—

An uneven breath caught Zarus's attention. Elief hovered above him, her hands shaking, the whites of her eyes as red as his own. But her face was solid—hidden behind the curtain of her dark hair—a resolve that hadn't broken. Still, watching as everything she hoped to run from invaded her planned life of peace, the healer had to be silent. Her emotions might betray her in this corrupted fortress.

Zarus opened his mouth. To offer condolences, to try to soothe her pain, to tell her to be careful. He didn't know what he planned on saying, but he knew no words would help. So he closed his mouth, rested his head on the tattered shirt beneath him, and put an iron-bound hand on the healer's forearm as she tearlessly wept.

Chapter Forty-Five

The morning sun did nothing to warm Rin. A pale, lifeless light illuminated the horizon, not even lighting the cityscape stretching for miles behind. It had been months since she stepped foot outside of Xandra. All those months feeling cooped inside the city's range, yet Rin's stomach twisted as she looked at the path below. The tended road ended, and the wild grasses grew over its span.

"The dirt can't be that interesting."

A piece of metal smacked into her cheek. Her mouth opened to bite Genesis's head off, but a glimmer in the dirt caught her eye.

A single copper piece.

"Coin for your thought," Genesis mused.

Rin almost returned the smile, but her chest knotted. "This is going to work." No one asked, no one dared it, but Rin wasn't sure if she had convinced herself yet.

She heard Tatsuo and Luna quietly chatting ahead, both of them more of a morning person than she could ever muster. Truthfully, Rin never fell asleep. She was awake all night—the first clear night in over a week—staring at the stars pointing north. It seemed like time lunged forward after the day she convinced everyone to do the impossible. Everything poured into the mission in which all their lives were on the line. She was the very hand that hung them.

Rin didn't dare glance to her side, didn't risk looking at Genesis for fear he shared her doubt. "This is going to work," she repeated. "It has to." Another bitter gust forced her to adjust her scarf. Winter bit particularly harsh this year. How bad would it be near Nokomic's northern border? How treacherous was it in the Unclaimed Lands of the north, where no kingdom cared to declare ownership?

"I was lucky enough to get a free ride out of the north without the trek through the snow," Genesis stated. "And you know what?" He made sure that Rin looked at him before he went on. "Zarus better remember how to make that portal, because I do not fancy the idea of making this trip again."

Rin's laughter burst from her lungs as a snort. Genesis at least seemed to enjoy the sight.

"I'll let you be the one to make that request," Rin finally breathed, wiping the line of silver from her eye. She calmed herself, but her smile never faded—his either.

"It won't be long," the prince said, glancing at the blotted sun, "we'll have that grumpy demon at our side in no time, and then all of Xandra will know the pleasure of dealing with Zarus Lowwenth."

She wanted to believe him, wanted to stare into his sapphire eyes radiating in the young sunlight and feel his words as a promise.

"How do you know that? Without Feyne... There's so much un-certainty about what we're walking into, Gen. Even if he had come. I want to believe that I'm making the right decision. Zarus has been there too long." She shook her head, the wind dancing through her hair. "How are we going to pull this off?"

Genesis was silent, looking ahead as Tatsuo and Luna walked fur-ther along with packs hoisted on their backs.

"Because I trust you, Rin. You know in your gut that we can't put this off any longer. I trust your instincts. We're all going into this with complete commitment. So stop doubting yourself because you're probably the most dangerous one of us all." The prince brought his stare back to her. "And I mean that in the most endearing way."

A weak grin made its way to her lips. "Careful what you say, or I'll burn you again." The humor barely made it into her voice. She closed her eyes, forcing the tension from her mind.

"Feyne is needed in Xandra; he made the right decision. We'll make-do without him." Before Genesis could reply, she forced a glacial breath into her lungs, resulting in a raging cough.

Genesis frowned as Rin lurched over her knees. "You're not doing too well today, are you?"

Rin swooped up the copper piece and chucked it at his head.

A smirk curled his lips, but Genesis narrowed his eyes. The smile straightened, his attention stolen by a sound too far for Rin to hear. However, she could tell by his face that someone pursued them.

Rin laid her hand over her scimitar, his on his broadsword. Dusk still laced the world. The rolling fields outside Xandra offered nowhere to hide. The moment she heard the footsteps storming in their direction, her eyes rounded as she found the shifter running up the path.

"Feyne?" She caught glimpse of his golden eyes, quickly sheathing her blade. "What are you doing here? Is everything okay?"

His huffing breath was his only response. The shifter held Rin's stare until understanding lowered her brow. He had made a promise. She smiled at the wolf. Feyne lowered his head, a sharp exhale puffing around his nose before he turned toward Luna and Tatsuo.

Rin remained still for a moment. Until finally, she could breathe normally again. This would work. There was no other option.

Chapter Forty-Six

"Let me go! I'll cut that expression right off your face, Eretimis, I swear to Ashnagz's Flames!" Zarus yelled as the guards yanked his chains forward. He couldn't break free.

"No, Zarus," the Dark Tyrant stated plainly, "you would never do such a thing to Errogan."

Anything. Say anything to push him over the edge! Dammit!

Zarus's lips pulled back in a snarl. *"Anöwe's Whore."*

The edge of a chain slashed into his back.

Zarus's vision blurred as iron tore into his scars. He stumbled, landing face first on the stone floor, and directed his leer to the guard swinging the chain.

"Watch it, scum," the guard's guttural voice echoed within his helm.

"Do I need to drag you there myself?" the Tyrant asked, never looking back.

The guards pulled Zarus to his feet, pushing him forward before he attacked.

Defiled bastard.

Down the hall he was dragged.

***

An understanding settled in Zarus's soul as he followed the Tyrant into the stretch of the fortress. If he didn't find a way out, he'd be better off dead.

His arms were bound, his tongue just as tied. All his efforts would be redirected toward Errogan. Yet the longer he waited, the lower his chances of surviving. Of finding Rin. Of unfolding the mystery the gods placed on them. Time was running out, and he was alone. No healers, prisoners, or old friends to help him out of this one.

The guards holding his chains yanked Zarus under the archway at the bottom of the stairwell and into the dank chamber Eretimis stood in. A similar sensation to the dread Vulyn had instilled in Zarus coursed through his mind upon entering the wreckage of Lhaerem's library. Zarus wondered if Eretimis felt the presence too.

Eretimis stood beyond the light's glare, collecting various items from a table. Vials? A cold sweat dripped down Zarus's whipped back. He would never forget the control serum.

Zarus forced down the dread in his gut. Eretimis hadn't looked his way since they stepped foot in the corridor; not when Zarus fought back against the guards attaching his chains to the bolts on the ground. Not even after one was dead and the other left the once-divine library.

The ancient library rested in ruin. Overturned shelves, burned pages. The Tyrant burned everything that once honored the kaeth Lhaerem. Zarus pulled his chains as far as they would stretch, as hard as the strength of his wrists could take—Eretimis locked eyes on Zarus.

"How many years have you kept the Infinite Key hidden from me?" His words were sickening. Zarus kept his eyes on the Tyrant, never once letting the chains binding his arms fall slack. He forced himself to breathe, but even his focus subsided as Eretimis stepped forward, conquering the silence that reigned between them. His voice burned to ash.

"I suppose it does not need to be said," the Dark Tyrant sighed. His stare pierced through Zarus's soul like a nail. "All that matters is I finally have it in my grasp, after two thousand years of searching." The void in his eyes twisted Zarus's stomach.

Zarus backed away from the excitement in Eretimis's expression, but the chains didn't snap. Two thousand years. Had the Infinite Key truly been the only reason the Dark Tyrant stepped foot on Armiria? He swallowed the thought. "Was this always your intent for me, or was there a point you actually thought you could keep me docile under your command?"

The Tyrant studied him. "I thought you held the potential for greatness. You saw that humans are a sin of existence, and I believed you would work with me to cleanse this world of filth, Zarus. I was wrong."

Zarus spat his laugh. "Don't waste the time I have left with lies, Eretimis. I never bought into that patriotic cry for Hraesah. I know you never cared about lost lands, and I know you laugh in the face of justice."

"Yet you stood by my side for five hundred years through your own free will."

"You chained me at your side by manipulating my pain."

"How many times were you singed by the Flames of Ashnagz? How many times was I the one to bring you back from death's door?"

"How many times did *you* send me there!" Zarus yelled through his teeth. An infamous temper burned in his chest. "You deprived me of my life, you ripped me away from everything I knew, and you turned the only person who ever mattered to me against me! And now you have me chained to the ground, acting like I clamped them around my wrists myself."

Amusement grew in Eretimis's eyes. "You alone pushed Errogan away. You came to me, asking to be taught alone. Did you ever think of what it would mean to harness your depthless power and leave him behind? I have no room for the weak, boy. My mistake was listening to Errogan when he said we did not need your service anymore, that he was strong enough for the both of you. His scheme to dispose of you was the first sign of his weakness. Taking you on a mission where my hunters would kill you instead of killing you himself... yet I believed him that you could not be trusted. I should have realized his bluff when he fell into Mortality's Edge and not you."

Zarus's throat tightened. The Tyrant didn't allow him to reply. "Life is not without consequence for you, even for me. Beings of our kind face the edge of the world every day from the moment we are born, and only a handful keep from falling into the depths. Steel is not forged in sunlight, Zarus. I made you what you are. I granted you a chance to hold on to that edge when you tried to jump over it time and time again. I am the reason you are alive and able to curse my name. At least Errogan has enough sense to understand that."

His ice melted. Zarus could have burned the fortress to ash and cinders with only a glance. Yet the chains were demon made, and the raw, blistered skin beneath promised he would not get loose. Where were those gods now? Where were their kaetha? Perhaps the legends were wrong, and they fell into damnation while Anöwe the Corrupted ruled over Lyhrëon.

Zarus leered at the demon. "Tell me, Dark Tyrant, what do you plan to do with the Infinite Key now that you've found it."

The Tyrant was still as stone, yet the vials he held shifted in his hand. The slosh of crimson caught Zarus's attention. "It is ironic how hard you fought to free your mind from my magic, Zarus. The process of throwing away one's memories, clearing their minds of everything they used to be; it is a mercy. They become moldable, numbed to the sensation of being torn apart and rebuilt."

Zarus clenched his jaw. "What are you going to do to me?"

A malevolent smile, a complacent malice. Every alarm blared in Zarus's head, every instinct roared.

"I am going to build you anew."

The shadow magic creeping in the corners of the dull room evaded Zarus's senses. Yet it was not shadow magic that struck him. It was the cold, life-draining touch of dark magic.

Eretimis's magic rushed in a swirling mass around Zarus. He tried to send out his own wave to block it, but the unnatural course swept it away. The dark storm hit. Zarus dropped to his knees. The power laced his skin, burning like poison until there was nothing left to engulf. The magic seeped through every pore, unraveling the strands that held him together. It started outside first, then worked in. A million shards of glass. His eyes and nose burned with the Flames; his throat bled dry.

Zarus could do nothing but scream.

He crashed to the ground, wrapped his arms around himself, dug his nails deep into his skin until blood ran down his arms. Nothing—*nothing*—took away the sensation of unraveling. Zarus cracked his eyes open through his contorted face and looked at the demon towering high above. His head splintered again and again, a mirror shattering on the floor. He couldn't fight back. Yet he could see, and what he saw twisted his gut far before the magic reached it.

The Dark Tyrant held the vial of crimson and crushed it in his hand. Glass shattered, but not one drop of blood hit the floor. It hung in the air, mixing with the dark magic surging around them. Once liquid, the blood now carried as mist in the whirlpool of magic suffocating Zarus. Eretimis stood amid the storm with little regard for its current.

And as that hellish mixture of blood and magic touched him, the door slammed open.

Zarus stifled his cries long enough to stare at the demon barreling through the doorway. Even the magic flow around him seemed to skip a beat, but Eretimis reeled in his indignity. The guard dropped to a knee and spoke above the roar of magic with earnestness.

"My liege, intruders have entered the fortress!"

A scowl twitched at Eretimis's expression. He turned around, leaving Zarus to writhe as he spoke. "Yet you choose to interrupt me rather than bring me their heads."

The demon hesitated, but he continued without trembling, "Sire... the human girl is with them."

"The human girl..." Eretimis repeated, his attention removed from Zarus altogether, but the magic still raged in a whirlwind.

A thoughtful silence ran through the outcry of Zarus's misery. The Tyrant smiled at him over his broad shoulder. "To think she came all this way for nothing. We might as well let her see our prized prisoner before he dies. What do you say, Zarus?" The torture drowned him out. Eretimis walked toward the door with orders on his tongue. "Call in the Twins. Their magic should sustain the process. Have them finish the rest."

The sentry rose, following fast in line behind. "What of the invaders?"

The Dark Tyrant never paused his step. "I want the girl. Kill the rest."

Chapter Forty-Seven

The wind practically tore her skin off; her fingers burned with every movement. Not one inch of her body was exposed, yet nothing was safe from the icy snow. Mid-winter froze the wastes of the north, and with the harsh wind blowing off the Abandoned Wings, Rin would have preferred the Lennaels.

Two months trekking north. Two months of grueling exhaustion. Yet the ice hadn't torn them to shreds in the desolate tundra.

Rin stared. She expected a temple—somewhere the Divine were once revered—but the stronghold looked like a prison spanning deep into the Frozen Wastes. The knots in her chest reached her gut as she looked at the massive walls of the fortress; so tall that the clouds masked the tops. Decorated in ice and snow, the sharp spires jutted skyward, bridged by walkways midair and sections of the structure larger than the temple in Xandra. Larger than a city: an empire.

The gate of the crypt lay on the other side of the barren clearing, its frozen stream stiffening beyond the fortress. Despite the hellish cold, Rin lay low behind a gathering of rocks jutting out of the ground like broken bones. No one spoke or shivered against the violating winds. Each of them remained breathless as they studied the gate crumbled by Zarus's magic.

Tatsuo's voice was low, yet no one had trouble hearing him because everyone hovered close to the warm dragon. "Why would they leave it unwatched?"

"Pride will do that," Luna muttered, never taking her stare off the gate.

"Who would be foolish enough to sneak in?" Genesis offered.

It was like being in the castle on Hilyan's Peak all over again. Although, the stiffening joints and exhaustion were the only similarities. Something picked at Rin's nerves.

"Where's the sun?" It was high morning, yet not a glimmer of light shined.

Genesis shook his head, his complexion ashen. "It's always dark here. Eretimis corrupted holy ground, and the world never forgot it. Just look at the trees."

"Dark oak," Tatsuo murmured.

Rin looked at the storm of darkness swirling in the sky.

He blotted out the sun...

Ice chipped at her mind. Yet the hum resonated and melted the ice. Rin sucked in a deep breath. She didn't need the sun anymore.

The shifter prowled back to the gathering of boulders in a low stride. The wolf rounded behind their cover and nodded.

All clear.

With one more nod between them, Rin and Feyne led the invasion into the Dark Tyrant's fortress of ice and darkness.

***

While the crypt offered the welcome of a graveyard on a moonless night, Rin wasn't bothered by the impending doom. Vulyn's presence reassured Rin they weren't alone in the forsaken fortress.

From the moment they stepped through the crumbled gate, Feyne's nose caught the scent of two demons. Rin found footprints not far inside. Most likely, a watch had been set up after Zarus revealed the vulnerable section of the fortress. An encounter was inevitable. They walked fast along the shallow stream running through the chamber, weaving through the grid of graves lining the walls, guided by Feyne's nose and Genesis's memory. The prince would often pause his step, or redirect them a few paces. *He was only here once*, Rin reminded herself.

The prince stared at a staircase for a minute too long when the crypt suddenly flashed white.

Feyne rose on two legs, naked as a new born. The *ghren* could barely speak through his chattering teeth. "G-guar-ds. Com-coming."

Panic seized Rin's chest. She threw the extra fur-lined cloak around the shifter's broad shoulders. "How close?"

The wolf tugged the cloak tight as he breathed into his hands. "They'll be on our tail before we reach the top of the stairs."

"We could run back," Genesis suggested. His voice was as hollow as when they first met. "They might think we continued into the fortress and look elsewhere."

Tatsuo kicked at the layer of ice and dust on the floor. "Our footprints will give us away. We can't risk them alerting anyone."

Rin looked to her mother, but the woman merely stared down the crypt, waiting for something to emerge from the shadows. Rin huffed a breath, forcing her freezing fingers to bend in her gloves. "We'll fight them." She knew they couldn't sneak away from every encounter, but the scimitar at her hip weighed heavier than usual. Her magic hummed.

Feyne reigned in the tremble of his voice. "I suggest stealing their clothes while we're at it."

"Tired of the draft?" Tatsuo jested as he summoned his spear.

The wolf cut him a snide gesture before dropping the thick cloak from his shoulders. "Rin and Luna are reeking up the place. I'm sure that's why the guards are heading our way." The shifter resumed his beast form, and Rin had barely knelt to recover the robe before they heard armor clanking down the hall. She squandered the sickness in her gut.

The battle was swift, five against two. With the help of Tatsuo's fire, they caged the demons, leaving them with no chance of victory. They accepted death before defeat. After wrestling the armor off the corpses and stripping their garbs, Luna disposed of the bodies. Genesis led them up the pale stairs, the next step of navigating to the dungeons. It was as she ascended the hundredth step that Rin walked square into Tatsuo's back.

Thankfully, her mother stood behind her, catching Rin before she fell. They stood on a landing that split the staircase in four different directions: two in front, two behind.

Rin spun around to the *narikaah*. "Why are we—"

The dragon's hand covered her mouth. Feyne huffed, gesturing his nose toward the steps descending from the right. A conversation hushed by distance lingered down the stairwell, instilling a fine panic in Rin's stomach.

"Gen, which way?" she whispered, barely letting the words leave her tongue.

The prince pointed to the stairs leading upward on their left. Silently, they moved into the stairwell but stopped when their footsteps echoed too loudly. They were stuck. Rin closed her eyes tight, sending out a silent prayer to the gods who sent her there.

The conversation grew closer. Two demons descended the stairs together, male and female.

She sucked in a breath, closing her eyes to alleviate the roar of magic.

"It's quite a shame," the male said, little more than a sigh in his breath. "After hearing all those stories, I really wanted to see the legend for myself."

"By E'ral's tits, is there anything else you can talk about today?" The female's voice boomed through the halls. "You haven't shut up about that traitor for the last six days."

The first was quick to defend. "Can you blame me? I mean, it's *Zarus Lowwenth* for crying out loud! Half of us thought he was a myth until a few months ago."

His companion snorted at the remark. "The demon's a traitor. He deserves to rot in whatever hole His Majesty dragged him off to. Even the dungeons were too good for him."

The male considered, his voice alarmingly close. "Even if that's the case, I still wish I could have seen him. I've gathered it's like watching frost in the morning."

"Take a cold wash. We have actual work that needs to get done."

"Oh, piss off," the male hissed, "let me have my daydreams."

Rin's heart dropped dead in her chest as one of the demon's boots swung around the wall dividing them. She wore the clothes of a demon, but Rin wasn't confident in her ability to deceive anyone. She had dragged them all to their deaths—

A blur of red lunged down the steps, ramming into the duo before they rounded the corner. Tatsuo hit the female hard enough that Rin heard a *crack* as the demon crashed to the ground, cupping her nose as blood sprayed.

"Vulyn's Pits, I'm late for my shift," Tatsuo apologized as he stumbled away from the demons, blocking the group hiding in the stairwell behind.

"You're going to be concerned about more than tardiness in a minute!" growled the female bleeding on the floor. "What in the Flames am I supposed to do about this?"

Tatsuo rolled his eyes, leaning further into the wall with crossed arms. "Oh, go see a healer and quit making a disgrace of yourself. Watch where you're walking while you're at it. I don't need your blood on my shirt."

"Why, you little—"

Rin watched as the bleeding demon seethed, but the male demon nudged her back down. "Quit squealing, Hedran. We have time to see a healer." He glanced at Tatsuo, a smile lining his face. "I haven't seen you around before."

The demon on the ground rolled her eyes as she threw her hands in the air. "Gods, I give up! While you refuse to keep it in your pants, I'm going to get this mess fixed. And you," she snarled at Tatsuo, who yawned in disinterest, "watch your back before you find a knife in it."

Tatsuo rolled his eyes. "You'd sooner stab a wall than my back."

The female tried to lunge for him, but the male gave her a swift kick in the shin, warding her up the stairs they came from.

The male waited a second to ensure privacy before he took a step closer to Tatsuo. "Are you new here?"

Tatsuo swayed his head side to side. "You could say that," he shrugged, stealing a glance behind to make sure no one was in sight. "First week. I still haven't gotten the hang of things."

"Oh, you must be here for the invasion," the male droned. Rin's attention—and everyone else's—perked up right away.

"Uh, yeah, that. Just getting prepared for that," Tatsuo almost stumbled. "I was hoping to see the *legendary* Shadow of Evenfall before that, but I guess my luck is drier than I thought."

The male barely held back his groan. "I know, I missed him too! His Majesty took him off somewhere in the fortress. No one's quite sure where…"

The dragon leaned in a little closer. "Well, maybe No One could shed some light on the subject, and my luck could well up."

The demon leaned a step in, nearly face to face with Tatsuo, his voice little more than a breath. "Maybe so," he smirked. "Last I heard, they took him to the west wing. Eretimis himself led him there, so if you're trying to sneak a peek, let me know."

The male stepped back, following the bloody trail the female left along the other staircase. "Find me after your shift; ask for Raelen." With that, the demon chased after his partner. A thick moment of silence filled the landing, although Luna was the one to speak for once.

"You seemed rather comfortable."

Tatsuo let out a heavy sigh, dropping his hand to his hips. "You know, you could voice a little more appreciation. I did just save your asses."

Rin loosed a sigh of relief. The word *invasion* echoed in her mind. "So," she said wearily, "Zarus isn't in the dungeons…"

Feyne's flash of light blinded them all. "The dungeons were a straight shot," he muttered as Rin tossed him the extra cloak. He shook his head, teeth clenching. "We shouldn't have come so unprepared. If we leave now, we can avoid death, capture—probably a worse fate for you and your mother, Rin."

Rin bit down on the shout clawing at her throat. She kept her tone level. "There was no way to be more prepared, Feyne." She cast a glance at Genesis, who had barely uttered a word since he stepped foot into his seventy-year prison. "Do you know the west wing?"

The prince was silent, his radiant eyes cast downward as he rummaged through years and years of memory. He had been a prisoner here, Rin had to remind herself. He won't know every nook and cranny of this deathly fortress either. Gods, how could she be so foolish—

Rin snapped down on the thought. *There is no other way to do this,* she told herself. *The gods told you to save him. There was no time to idle and search for another way.*

Genesis's voice pried her back. "It's the far end of the fortress from here, and I don't know the way through these passages. We'd have to go by the surface."

Even Tatsuo's bright eyes were less than convinced. He leaned against the icy wall. "I don't know how many more demons I can dazzle, Red. Not all will be as bored as that one."

"Erin," her mother voiced, highest on the steps, "this is crazy talk. There's no way that we can maneuver this fortress blindly." Her voice was soft, sympathetic, but faith had drained it as low as Feyne's. "We can still turn back—"

"No, we can't, Ma," Rin said sharper than she intended. They didn't *understand.* "Did you all forget about the demons we killed back there? What happens when the next watch shows up to replace them? Even if we're long gone, they will still alert Eretimis. He'll probably cut us off before we cross into Nokomic! There is no going back now."

Her magic pounded on the inside of her skull, *begging* to be released. "There's a reason that male was disappointed Zarus left the dungeon—he talked like no one would see him again... There might be nothing to save after today. He's the only one who can help me, and we're the only ones who can help him."

Rin closed her eyes, refusing to witness their reactions. It was the truth, and every single one of them knew it. The gods themselves had claimed it. Whatever was different about her magic, Zarus held the answers.

The silence raged on. Rin forced her eyes to meet those of her companions. "I'm not forcing you to stay here. Our plan shifted. This is your last chance to leave unnoticed, so go if you're having second thoughts."

It wouldn't be long before the four of them realized how selfish she had been. And she wouldn't blame them. Yet no one made to move.

"None of you?" she asked in disbelief.

"Look, kiddo," Tatsuo crooned, "I already told you we're getting that grouch out of here. No one deserves to die in this fortress."

"Likewise," Genesis agreed, running his fingers through his ashen locks. "I made you a promise, Nowell. Zarus as well."

Rin shifted her eyes to her mother, standing behind the crowd. "You couldn't force me away from your side, Erin."

Finally, she looked at the shifter shivering beneath his cloak. He had barely been standing on two legs for the entire trek north. He held her stare, intense as the swarming darkness above.

She bit the side of her cheek. "What do you say, Feyne? Do you trust me?"

Rin's chest tightened as she gazed into his unsmiling eyes. "Of course, I trust you. I didn't follow you here to see the snow, you know."

"So then," Genesis asked, walking up the steps. "West?"

Rin nodded. "West it is."

"Then I suggest we get a move on," the prince stated as he turned forward. "We wouldn't want to make Tatsuo miss his date."

Chapter Forty-Eight

Tatsuo peered around the corner, signaling *all clear* to move forward.

Feyne walked behind him, nose subtly sniffing with every step. Luna trailed the back of the line, her observant eyes missing nothing of the sinister fortress. Rin fell in step at Genesis's side, even though it was like walking with a ghost. Every corner they rounded, every doorway they passed, the prince expected the Dark Tyrant to be there.

Rin's heart thudded when they delved deep enough into the fortress to hear the demons. Never close enough for details, but Rin heard them conversing, debating, bantering. Laughing. She didn't know what was worse: the fact she expected screams of terror and torture, or that the interactions of demons weren't all too different from those of humans. But every time she treaded down that stream of empathy, Rin had to remind herself what these demons would do if they found her. They were loyal to Eretimis.

Genesis silently directed their trail, but his memory proved foggy. The prince nervously wet his lips, staring at the end of the hall with no outlet. "I swear this was the route past the courtyard."

"Maybe if we trail back a little, it'll refresh your memory?" Rin suggested. A cold sweat licked her spine. Her fingers restlessly tapped against the stone frame of the window at the end of the hall.

"Take a deep breath, Genesis," Luna soothed. The woman was cool as an autumn night, but Rin felt a hint of decay.

"Whatever we wind up doing, we're going to have to backtrack." Rin bit her nail. "We're locked in a corner right now—"

Feyne's low, guttural growl reverberated through her bones. The beast's hackles raised as he prowled away from the dead-end, his nose huffing one breath after another.

"What's wrong?" Rin whispered. However, the wolf's snout sucked in one final breath before a snarl wrinkled his jaw. Without a word, Feyne sprinted down the hallway. Rin jolted at the sudden motion, but urgency flooded her veins.

What are you thinking! She thought to herself.

Lacking all caution, Rin chased after her friend. Yet when she rounded the corner, she ran into a wall. At least it felt like a wall.

Her ginger hair frayed in all directions as she hit the ground. Dazed, she looked around. Genesis's weathered boots stood at her side. She shifted her gaze across the hall and found someone else. The old Damrian captain's teal eyes narrowed on Rin, a sight she thought burned with Base.

Her blood chilled. Rin tried to blink away her hysteria as she looked at the walking dead.

"I knew you were nothing but trouble since the day Feyne brought you into that bunker, Rin Nowell." The Damrian's gravelly voice scraped her ears.

Bjarkh Grevik had been the traitor.

The curses boiled on Rin's tongue, but a bone-shattering roar shook the room. Feyne lunged at the captain with an open jaw. The shifter neither needed nor wanted an explanation. Bjarkh was the traitor.

Feyne didn't sink his teeth into Bjarkh's throat. Just before the shifter claimed the kill, he collided with a haze rippling in the air, and the traitor stood unfazed while the shifter tumbled backward. Soon, two demons rounded the corner at a leisurely pace and joined the traitor.

"I didn't think you'd find them, Grevik!" One of the demons clapped Bjarkh on the back as the male approached, but the Damrian kept his eyes locked on Feyne. "When you claimed the tracks outside were a shifter's... Well, it seemed too ambitious for a human to possess such skills. But look what this hunt brought us."

"Bastard," Rin seethed. "*Bastard.*" Genesis helped her up as Luna and Tatsuo joined her side. Yet when she unsheathed her scimitar and tried to run forward, Genesis caught her arm.

Feyne's growl struck her core. He paced back and forth before the Damrian, but never pounced. Rin looked back and forth along the hall. No fire burned, no decayed lingered, no flesh tore. She narrowed her gaze. The slightest ripple shifted in the air before the demons and Bjarkh. Rin suddenly remembered who she stood against, and searched.

It was nothing she could find with sight, but her magic combed the hallway until she found it. The magic barrier radiated from the demon at the front of the line. She also found her mother's magic beating against the invisible wall like a storm beats against a house. The barrier barred them.

Rin threw her magic into the wall. White light sizzled the barrier with a vengeance, but it didn't break.

She bit down to keep from buckling beneath the magic wall, looking Bjarkh in the eye. "*Why.*"

Bjarkh raised his grey brows, but his eyes didn't soften.

"Why?" he repeated. "Because the world needs change, and we're going to see Armiria has it."

A growl erupted from the wolf's throat. How many times had she heard Feyne utter those words around Base? Rin shook her head; something didn't sit right. Something about the emptiness in his stare.

"You're a damned fool," Genesis spat. "To think anything but ash will come of Armiria under Eretimis's hand."

Bjarkh's weathered eyes didn't flinch at the prince. "Change will be found in ash, boy."

"Then burn." Tatsuo's call was little more than a whisper against the blare of his flame. The fire whirled, cresting on itself as it smothered the wall.

Rin shielded her face with her arm. The bone-melting heat died down, the blinding blaze dimming to the few lanterns strewn about the hall. She drew her attention back to Bjarkh, the demons before him. Not even an ember crossed the barrier. Tatsuo squared his jaw, readying to send forth another blow when the demon on the other side sneered.

"Aren't you lucky that our Lord loves to hold sympathizers as company, dragon-born," the female demon smiled. Her blades swayed through the air. "You might even be lucky enough to hold an audience with him." The smile hardened, choked by the sadistic mirth Rin had seen on countless demons before. "I wish I could witness that hearing."

Luna took a step forward. The demons only barked their laughter at her attempt to break the wall down.

"No mortal magic will pass this barrier, human," the female flaunted.

A rumble, lethal and low, emitted from Feyne. *Nothing in, then nothing out.* The dark flecks in his golden eyes radiated, wedged into

Bjarkh's throat as he leapt at the wall. The magic screeched beneath his claws.

"You know, Feyne," Bjarkh said roughly, as if the very act of speaking was a push of his temper. He watched as the shifter dove into the barrier and bounced right off. "I don't think I ever told you about my family during the years of Damrok's campaign in the east. I met countless shifters before I ever ran into you, before you started wasting my time with your pitiful hopes of a better world. It's a shame that the hunt for shifters died down. They make for great sport. My daughter adored the pelts we made our coats from in those years. And what a hunt you've put me on all these months in Xandra. Yet the Resurrection could never have made it this easy. Walking up to the Dark Tyrant's doorstep and letting yourself in. Your recklessness finally paid off—"

All Flames broke loose on the magic barrier. Flames waged; death and decay intertwined to eat away at the life of the magic. And Feyne. Feyne didn't have fire nor decay. Right at the edge of that wall, he thrashed with all his strength.

Genesis never moved an inch. "Wasting time..." he breathed.

The words were little more than a hush. Yet Rin's mind rattled against them.

We don't have time for this.
Time draws near, Alentye. Do not fall into their trap.

The Divine voice finally broke through her rage. Rin whipped her stare to the demons laughing behind their magical defense, to her mother and friends wasting their power in vain. A pit settled in her stomach.

"Stop!" she cried, lunging forward into Tatsuo, yanking his burning arm back. "Stop it, all of you!" The flames died, the decay ebbed, yet Feyne did not back away from the wall.

"Flames!" Tatsuo hissed, nearly thrown off balance. Even Luna fought back against Rin's call.

"We need to leave this hall *now*," Rin pressed, yanking on both of their arms to run. "He's stalling us!" She threw a pointed glare in Bjarkh's direction. "He's keeping us here until backup arrive!"

The hall finally ran silent, and already the floor beat like a drum. Countless demons heading their way. Their attacks had masked the noise. Any moment, and their demise would flood the halls. Even as Tatsuo summoned his spear, as Luna withdrew the blade hiding beneath her cloak, Feyne sniffed at the air and laid low on his haunches, the sickening knowledge hit them all. They would not outrun this horde.

Rin's head pounded in her skull. She cursed the gods who persuaded her on this journey, cursed the cowardice betrayer hiding behind a wall of magic, cursed herself for ever believing she was ready to pull off such a wild scheme.

The shifter cast a betrayed glance at her. He demanded vengeance for everyone. The wolf stared at her a moment longer, heavy pants puffing in the frigid northern air, golden eyes gleaming in the torchlight as he looked ahead. The shifter's back was to her, a wall against the horde.

"Go," Tatsuo said from behind, taking a place at the wolf's side. "The three of you go. I'll stay with Feyne and give you time. Find Zarus; we'll catch up with you."

"The Flames you will!" Rin met his side, but a symphony of chaos echoed down the corridor, shouts and commands, steel and boots.

Yet Bjarkh stared at her with grave, heavy eyes and a straight mouth. "Sacrifices must be made, Rin Nowell." His tone was depthless behind the magic barrier.

Rin gritted her teeth. "We are not leaving you behind!" she screamed at Tatsuo.

Tatsuo snorted, grabbed her by the hand and tossed her backwards into Genesis's arms. "There's no time to argue, Red. Run! We'll hold them back!" Already, the dragon was facing the other way, twirling his spear in one hand, a flame flickering in the palm of the other. His eyes closed, drawing a meditative breath. Feyne lunged for the barrier once more. A roar of wrath stunned the room, shook the windows.

The first wave of guards rounded into the hall, barreling at speeds great enough to blur her vision. Rin let out a harrowing cry. She couldn't quell her magic. The ocean craved to devour.

The entire corridor illuminated in a pale light. Magic bathed the room, stripping the stone and hitting every demon around. It sank through the cowardly barrier until it fizzled into steam. The demons, the murderous human; they all fell exposed and blinded, but it never touched her friends.

Rin's magic raged as she turned away and forced herself to run away with her mother and Genesis. The flash would not hold back the army bellowing at the end of the hall, nor the demons blinded ten feet away. It stumbled their advance long enough for Feyne and Tatsuo to raise Ashnagz's Flames. Iron and ember smothered the air. Rin forced herself to run.

They would make it back to her. They had to.

Chapter Forty-Nine

The Wraith Twins stood just outside the library. What came as a surprise was when Eretimis cut his connection to his own black magic, and Raia and Tesyl picked it up without hindrance. The limits of dark magic were as harrowing as they were excruciating.

Zarus could have sworn another edge added to the magic when the Wraiths took over.

Zarus's body stung like glass embedded into his soul. His vision focused on the finest details of the ancient walls, then dulled into a haze. His heart thundered in his chest. Every whisper in the fortress reached his senses, then vanished with the wind. His nose burned, his eyes stung, his mouth was left metallic yet bland all at once. Reality flushed from his grasp in a whirlwind. The blood in the vial, the magic tormenting his very being... it all made sense.

A monster, they said. He would become a monster. How many times had Eretimis performed this process since he first attempted it with Genesis seventy years ago? Forcing his blood with another species...The magic boiled his core to form something new.

Another cry loosed, another metallic pang ran down his throat. Blood—he tasted the blood of his throat shredded howl after howl. Zarus's head split. Every thought and rivet of his consciousness echoed the deathly pound in his head. There was no point summoning magic.

The current of darkness would only sweep it away. Not even the invasive gods could break through.

The gods...

He would fail their demand. Another item on the list of failures. Yet Zarus winced at the thought that he might have failed Rin Nowell so greatly. Torn and divided and unable to break himself free to find her. To find whatever answers he was looking for in her. To bring her to a safety that Eretimis would never tarnish.

'All I want is the girl. Kill the rest.'

For months, Zarus had thought that the bastard kept her locked in the depths of this damned fortress. For months, he had been made a fool to believe the lie. And yet, that girl walked right into the impenetrable fortress. Who else had she come with? Who else was as naïve and reckless to walk into the gates of the Pits?

A bitter numbness settled in his chest. His thoughts broke down, eroded by the current of magic. His eyes looked, but couldn't distinguish what they gazed at. He heard the Wraith Twins cackling, but did not make out what they said. He tasted the blood lining down his throat, but couldn't tell if it was there at all. All around was the darkness cocooning him. All there ever had been was the isolation the shadows brought with it.

Cold.

Empty.

Nothing.

He had become nothing; the nothing would get him out of this, the nothing had gotten him into this, and the nothing would be his mark on this world. Two millennia. Two millennia and Eretimis had finally won. Now he would win Rin Nowell as well. Zarus remembered the terror lining the girl's face when they last saw each other. When he could not save her. Would she wear that fear again when Eretimis met her? The understanding that death was near. The same notions trickled into Zarus's heart.

'*Close your eyes,*' the darkness whispered, '*you have no use for them anymore.*'

The echo of laughter resonated in his mind. His face ached against the cold floor. But his eyes? He gave into the temptation. The world grew dark, his heart numb, and Zarus Lowwenth allowed his final failure to

Veil...

His...

Tomb.

The human girl is with them.

Six little words. A phrase so simple yet so wrong. Zarus's chest flickered.

Rin Nowell walked headfirst into the most dangerous place on Armiria.

His eyes cracked open, the light of the sconces burning them dry.

Rin Nowell banded together a group of lunatics and marched into the fortress walls.

A flicker. A flicker in his core, stretching to his mind. That was all he needed.

Rin Nowell came to Eretimis the Dark Tyrant's doorstep to save me.

Zarus gritted his teeth, fighting against every ounce of magic. In the beat of a heart, the blink of an eye, his magic swelled—spreading along his neck, down to his fingers and toes and heart—only bursting within himself once the pressure sickened him. His senses stifled, but as he forced himself to his knees, Zarus was wholly, entirely himself.

The dark magic began to calm. The calm before the storm. Too long had that storm been waiting. He climbed to his feet—limbs stiff and numb, ears ringing from teeth clenched together. He sucked a single breath into his lungs. Zarus Lowwenth looked through the stilling shadows at the two sisters with their backs turned to him. Their job assumed finished.

The thrum of magic traveled down to his core.

Impatient, hungry.

The human girl was in the fortress, and Zarus intended to find her.

One moment of focus was all it took for the pent up magic to ravage the ancient room.

Chapter Fifty

The Wraith Twins weren't blind, nor foolish. They thought Zarus had succumbed to the dark magic suffocating the room, but Raia and Tesyl felt the sway of magic before it tore them apart.

The eldest redirected Eretimis's discarded darkness, gathering it as a shield around her and her sister. The tendril of ice and shadow collided head-on.

Zarus sucked in the fresh air. His head was void of tension. The burst of his magic cleared Eretimis's black magic, whatever the process had been... he stopped it. A smile tempted his lips. No flick of the wrist, no snap of the fingers; Zarus motionlessly called forth the splinters of ice that had crashed to the floor, pulling back the mist of his shadows floating through the air. It swarmed around him, a cyclone cutting into the Hraesan cuffs on his hands until the shadows and ice sliced them clean off. His raven strands danced in the gust. Zarus stood in the middle of his magic's rage, letting it fend off the defiling shadow of the Wraiths.

"Look here, sister, the monster has some fight left in him." A half smile, contorted in malevolence on Raia's face. However, Tesyl said nothing. She held a pensive glare on Zarus's eyes. He should've been unconscious. He should not even be himself.

A single step forward, and a path of ice reached out from the sole of his boot, stretching all the way to Raia's sandal. The Wraith raised an amused brow at the spectacle. Her mouth opened, but Zarus didn't care to listen.

The ice below her sharpened at the whim of his thoughts. Spears of frost and snow jutted out of the path, aiming not to impale the wraiths but drive them back. Tesyl was the first to move, giving way for her sister's retreat. She immediately stepped foot into the veil of his shadows waiting behind. The younger sister's scream raised the hair on the back of his neck. Inky blood splattered on the floor like rain from the heavens. The Wraith seethed, throwing herself forward, but Zarus didn't let go of her. Shadow trailed into her lungs like smoke, thousands of granular ice fragments carried with it. He carved her insides with the ice as it entered her lungs and throat. Her blood poured out every line of her face, streamed down her eyes, welled in her mouth. No matter the screams, no matter the writhing, the Wraith could not escape his magic. Not until Raia lunged for Zarus.

A facade blown away. The eldest threw herself at him, intent on shredding him to pieces bit by bit. *"Let her go!"* the hag seethed. *"Let her go before you wish you never crawled out of that magic!"*

Zarus evaded the nails digging for his eyes. "How do you plan on doing that when you're missing half of your—"

But where his taunt paused, a writhing hiss began. A thrum of pain, a remembrance of Eretimis's magic; it pulsed in his head, flaring his senses, burning his thoughts. The world spun. His magic slipped away from the Wraith Twin, retreating to protect himself. Zarus forced himself upright, biting down on the throes tearing into his head. Until finally, the world stilled, and his senses eased. The dark magic wasn't completely eradicated.

Zarus flicked his gaze to the Twins, but already they were nothing more than a haze flanking him. Raia's hands leaked dark magic—the grey mist falling to the floor as it welled from her palms. The same magic they used to drain him all those months ago. Tesyl handcrafted herself a phantom whip with her black magic.

A cascade of snow floated throughout the nameless shrine. A shield of ice stretched up Zarus's shoulder, guarded from the eldest's draining touch. Crimson shadows in his other hand, he conducted the magic into the shape of a ghastly blade. Phantom though its steel might have been, he made sure it would cut through the two ancient hags.

From the second the Wraith Twins found his sides, Zarus ducked below the snare of Tesyl's whip, and blocked Raia's deathly grasp with his shield. His mind split down the middle, a battle in each hand. He whirled the phantom blade to strike Raia's exposed wrist. A tendril of misty shadow rose to guard his back from Tesyl's strike. Black blood sloshed on the wall, a hand falling to the floor.

Raia hissed as she grabbed the stump of her wrist. Zarus pivoted toward the elder, ducking below her strike at his face in the same motion. He slashed his blade down the wraith's body, but his arm reverberated with a wicked shock. Tesyl caught the downward strike with her bare hand. It cut through muscle and bone, but did not sever. The Wraith held firm against Zarus's efforts. He willed the shadows to sharpen along the edge, but he lost the momentum of the strike.

"Your pride betrays you," she *tsked*.

"I don't need pride to cut you down." Zarus narrowed his glare on Tesyl, slicing the sword out of her palm. She raised her whip in the other hand, aiming for his chest. Zarus couldn't ready his shield before a stiff lifeless hand slithered around the back of his neck.

Raia grounded in his ear. "How rude you are to take your eyes off me, child."

Zarus didn't feel an ounce of his magic stolen. The hand that hadn't been dismembered oozed with dark magic, but couldn't strip his power with the severed hand not yet sewn in place.

Zarus shifted against the eldest's weak grip, the ice encasing his arm slamming into her skeletal chest. The force sent her stumbling backward, but he also crashed into an empty altar behind, nearly splitting his head on its edge.

He couldn't ignore the splicing shock that paralyzed his body. Every nerve tingled—Eretimis's work not yet cleared away. For a brief moment, his vision shifted. Not clouding, but softening, like the edge of a sword growing blunt. His eyes wavered. When he saw clearly, Raia and Tesyl were standing over him. Heavy breaths worked his lungs. Sweat beaded his brow.

"Tell me, sister," Tesyl said slowly as she wiped away the blood at the side of her mouth, "have you ever watched prey eventually bow into the predator's hunger?"

Fire danced in Raia's wild stare. "Countless times."

Tesyl cocked her head to the side. "Now, Zarus, what do you think that means?"

They were hungry for his life. Blood-seeking, bone-snapping hunger. Zarus narrowed his gaze. One quick move was all he needed. One precise strike and he would find Rin.

The world rushed by, a whirl of pale stone and lantern light. Zarus summoned every ounce of shadow welling in his mind, all aimed at the hearts of these cackling wraiths. Before his attack ever reached them, though, the Wraith Twins' eyes rolled. They fell flat on the floor. Blood pooled from their bludgeoned skulls.

Zarus blinked, his adrenaline easing to a low murmur.

"You know what? That was satisfying." Errogan tossed the lead pipe onto the ground. An idle shrug bounced off his shoulders. "You know how to get under people's skin in the worst way, Zarus."

Zarus sucked in a deep breath, exhaling the burn of his senses. He glanced at the Wraiths prostrate on the floor before him, an unnatural sizzle emitting from their sunken skulls. As hard as it was to believe, the Twins were too distracted to realize Errogan snuck in.

The demon offered little more than a nod as he helped Zarus to his feet. No taunts, no retorts. Zarus walked to the exit of the ancient shrine before Errogan called out. "You're going to find her, aren't you?"

He glanced over his shoulder. The notion suddenly hit him that this demon saved his life. "Yes," he replied.

"You realize that you're racing against Eretimis to find her?"

Zarus faced forward. "Yes."

A pause stifled behind, too quiet in too clamorous a fortress. Finally, a defeated sigh escaped Errogan's nose. "Okay," he muttered, taking a place at Zarus's side. "Okay..."

Zarus looked to the demon at his side, to the twins behind. "Come with me," he blurted. "You can leave this place for good."

A humorless smile tugged at Errogan's lip. "You and I both know that's never the case."

Zarus's mind grew weary. *Why? What could Eretimis possibly give you?* He bit his tongue before he sent the demon away from him once more. "They'll know it was you."

Errogan lazily trailed Zarus's stare to the pipe, nothing more than a shrug finding his response. "I'll tell them I wanted the kill for myself."

A fragment of a smirk drew across his desolate face. "No one will have trouble believing that."

A grin made it to Zarus's expression, but faded against the tightness in his chest. "Errogan, I—"

The demon held up a silencing hand, moonlit hair shifting as he shook his head. "Go. You're already behind; Rin needs you."

Zarus bit down on his wince, swallowing it with the plea for Errogan to come with him. To escape. He knew Errogan would fend for himself. It's what he was best at. Yet the divide in his heart nearly tore Zarus asunder. Time was running out, and he knew the demon beside him would not budge—what a stubborn ass he always proved to be. Words weighed on his tongue, tying down any hope of a goodbye. After all that had happened, this is how they parted... Zarus shoved down the questions simmering in his head. Another time. There *would* be another time.

"Thank you," Zarus forced out.

Errogan only smiled, gesturing a nod to the doorway. "Run. Before it's too late."

Zarus nodded. While Errogan waltzed out the entrance, Zarus suddenly pulled him into an embrace. Startled as he may have been, Errogan did not fight it, nor did he let go until Zarus released him.

"Be careful," Zarus pressed. He held Errogan's gaze until the White-Cloaked Reaper answered.

A mighty grin flashed his way. "Always, Z."

Zarus would be back for his friend, but right then, he spun toward the exit and sprinted through the fortress. The human girl needed him.

Chapter Fifty-One

"Stop standing around before I smash both your heads together! We have intruders to find!"

The captain's voice boomed down the hall with vengeance. The demons chatting casually out of sight in the atrium scrambled for their attention when caught slacking off. An arachnid being and helmeted biped bolted down separate paths without daring to utter another word before their commanding officer chased them down. A nerve-wracking silence settled behind the door, two intruders tucked behind.

"Are they gone?" Rin whispered.

She held her breath as she waited for Genesis to return. The stomp of feet had dulled, but she couldn't find the prince through the gap in the door she hid behind. After what seemed like an eternity, he finally walked into the atrium from the hall.

"We're clear," he breathed in his own voice once more. It was uncanny, but Rin thanked every Divine she could name for Genesis's impersonation skills. He captured the captain perfectly enough to scare the idling demons without their second guess. She was glad they had heard the captain's voice barking commands not five minutes earlier, but supposed anyone shouting commands would have sent the two demons running against the frenzy the fortress had become.

The prince slipped into the unlit room Rin and Luna hid within. Genesis had yet to master presence sensing. Feeling the oncoming aura of a being further than he could see took time to perfect, half demon or not. And since their two trackers had stayed behind to fend off the army of demons, the three cut it dangerously close with any demons they risked passing. So close, they relied on hidden talents to save them.

The prince closed his eyes. He ran a hand through the stray hairs that had escaped the tie, pacing further from the door as his concerns swelled. The same worries plagued herself and Luna. Every demon in the fortress would be on their heels at any moment, even sooner if they stayed hidden in the vacant hall.

Rin bit the inside of her lip. She had an idea of how to pick up the fragments of their plan. She also knew no one else would agree. "We need to split up."

Both her mother's and Genesis's attention flicked to her. "Erin, one of us splitting away from you won't solve anything but more confusion. We'd still have them on our tail," Luna dismissed.

Rin squared her shoulders. "We're not getting anywhere like this." Genesis opened his mouth, but she spoke first. "That's why I'm the one who's going to go alone."

Her mother gaped.

Genesis looked about the same. "What are you thinking, Rin?"

Rin pursed her lips. "We're going to be found eventually. There are too many demons swarming the halls to avoid them forever."

Luna's voice picked up immediately. "That's exactly why we shouldn't—"

"*But,*" Rin stated, "my face is the only one unknown around the fortress." Her mother's mouth closed, a tight line drawn over her lips.

Genesis stilled. "Gen, every other demon we come across will probably know who you are. And Ma, Eretimis himself has been searching for you for years now. When they finally find us, there's no hiding." Rin closed her eyes for a moment. "I'll go on alone. You two need to head back to the crypt and find your way out while you still can."

"And what about you?" Luna asked tightly.

"I'll keep looking," Rin explained. "I'll search every nook and cranny of this place until I find Zarus." It sounded like lunacy—it *was* lunacy. Yet it was the only way for Genesis and Luna to avoid a life of torture. "We've already seen how their pride underestimates us. They'll think that we ran out of luck and retreated to the wasteland. They won't think to keep looking in the heart of the fortress."

Genesis considered it. His head shook. "Even with those clothes on, it's a matter of time before your scent overpowers, Rin. They'd be on you faster than you could react." The worry in his voice nearly crushed her resolve.

Rin shook her head. "I have this tunic and scarf." All stolen when they first arrived. "It will be enough to sneak by. Especially if—"

"We draw them away from you..." It was barely a breath on Luna's tongue. Her mother fell slack.

"You'll need my cloak," Genesis finally said. "It'll cover your scent more." He stripped it from his shoulders, draping it over her. Rin's mouth ran dry as a desert.

A shadow of a smile lined Genesis's face when he saw her confusion. "Rin, I don't think you're a fool. I don't want to leave your side, but you're right. I'll stick out like a sore thumb here. Better to split up and find Zarus than all three of us end up in the dungeons. Or worse."

Or worse. Rin's gut knotted.

Luna removed the gloves and overcoat she had taken from the demons, and tossed them to her daughter. Rin quietly slipped them on, pulling Genesis's hood over her head.

"Stick to the shadows, keep your hand near your blade," her mother instructed. "If you hear someone, if anyone comes to pass, walk with your head high. Act like you have a place here and do not for one second give them room to believe otherwise, Erin." The gravity in her eyes hitched Rin's breath. "Remember your lessons, use your magic and your blade if necessary. Make yourself one of them, but do not linger long enough to catch their memory. We'll lead them away, give you time to search. There shouldn't be a reason for them to suspect you while another human is running around."

Rin gulped the fear in her throat. "What will you do if they find you?"

Genesis glanced at Luna, an understanding between the two that ran in silent unrest. Yet the hush drew on.

"They won't find us," Luna assured. "But I hope you realize we are not leaving this fortress without you. The idea alone is as absurd as—"

"As wandering into Eretimis's stronghold?" Rin cut in.

Her mother's tone was as intense as the cold outside. "Yes."

Genesis nodded in agreement, rubbing the back of his head. "I said you're not foolish, Rin, don't challenge that by suggesting such foolish things. We'll meet back with you, and we'll all get out of here alive. You, me, your mother, Tatsuo, Feyne, *and* Zarus. I promise."

Despite herself, a smile spanned Rin's face. Warmth spread through her chest. She wasn't alone. She leapt forward and wrapped them both in a hug. They all put so much faith in her. One day, she would repay them. For now, Rin stood tall under the layers hiding her humanity.

The three organized a vague plan—which direction she needed to follow, and where to meet up after an hour. Neither would give in to

Rin's suggestion to flee if she hadn't found them by that point. She was leaving them for the wolves, but Rin reminded herself who she was dealing with. Luna Nowell and Genesis Masquarem were not two to be trifled with. Already, she sensed the faint nip of Luna's deathly magic in the air. Not fear for her daughter, but bait for the demons. Rin willed herself to keep still and let her mother and friend walk out the door. She waited until it was only her and her frantic heart beating until she finally stepped into the vast fortress.

All she needed to do was head to the west wing. Simple.

***

Rin nearly screamed as she found herself looped in yet another circle.

It seemed every five hundred steps she walked rounded her back to where she started. The halls curved and twisted, and if she didn't choose the correct direction, it was likely she wasted five minutes of her time only to start over. Thankfully, the ever-present gods kept her in their divine gaze. Rin hadn't crossed any demons. Nor had she been so lost that she couldn't navigate westward using her internal compass. With every room passed, it took all her willpower to peer inside. No corner left unchecked, no rock unturned. With her next step toward the opposite side of the hall, Rin heard someone walking behind the corner she'd rounded.

Her heart tore between running away and stopping altogether. A sickly sweat lined her back, the piled layers instantly becoming a burden. Rin didn't risk peering over her shoulder, didn't risk bolting down the hall and praying the next door was empty.

'*Make yourself one of them,*' her mother had said.

Rin couldn't comprehend how Tatsuo managed it with that male on the stairs. *Intimidating*, she thought. *Make yourself intimidating.*

One more deep inhale, and Rin opened her eyes into an aimless glare. The same neutrality she had seen so many times on Zarus's face. She took a moderate pace in the middle of the hall, swinging one hand idly at her hip while resting the other on the ruby pommel of her blade. It wasn't long until a *whoosh* of air rushed past, nearly slamming into her shoulder. It took every ounce of control not to flinch. Instead she stood firm, casting an unamused glower toward the demon zipping to a halt as they were forced to go around her.

"You're hogging the hall, girl," the demon hissed. The lithe figure moved more like a serpent than a human, turning in a fluid motion that nearly spun Rin's head. She didn't recoil, but hardened her stare.

"Watch where you spew your waste," Rin cut back, crossing her arms. *Authority, give them authority.* "Else you might be scrubbing your blood off the floor."

Their serpentine head cranked to the side at her threat. Rin forced her heart to remain calm as the demon stepped forward, standing nearly a head over her. "Foolish runt, don't you know us Serpenti haven't a drop of blood of our own in our bodies?"

Whose blood do they have then? Rin quickly came up with a few unsettling ideas. She stifled a shiver, rolling her round eyes.

"I don't waste my time with the details of underlings." She didn't give the *serpenti* a chance to reply before striding off, not wasting another breath. They cursed her from behind, muttering something about a *pure blood bitch*, but ultimately turned down a branching hall away from her.

Rin loosed the heaviest sigh once she was clear of the demon, leaning into the nearest wall as she rubbed her temples. *Gods, how do they talk like that everyday?* It was pathetic. Although, it baffled her that the demon hadn't seen right through her facade. Rin pulled herself together and continued on her search.

Rin bit the inside of her cheek as she neared an antechamber. Her path ended, splitting in two opposite directions on either side. There was a small window in the middle of the split, out of which she viewed two separate wings of the fortress. Genesis hadn't mentioned it before they parted ways.

She gazed out the window, debating whether to go right or left. Both wings towered higher than she stood. She couldn't see where Zarus might be, nor did she hear anything other than the distant chatter of thousands of demons.

The hum in her mind had been constant ever since she split apart from her mother and Genesis. The constant drum of fear hollowed her gut. So Rin let out some of the magic, directing its pulse down both sides of the hall and throughout both wings. She stood at the window staring so intently at nothing. It was difficult to navigate the stone walls, and countless bodies stood in the way, but she pushed her magic on. Leaving no corner unchecked, no crack unseen, no rock unturned. It was risky, allowing her light to hum through the air. Little more than a buzz, it spread through the hall as a flicker. Most would think it a trick of their eyes, but any ounce of light made a difference in the dim fortress. So she made it quick until finally—*finally*—Rin hit her mark.

Ice and darkness and shadow. The magic frosted her own, sending a shiver along her mind that spiraled into the depths of her consciousness. She'd recognize that ice anywhere, the sheer might of it, although left in splinters it had been. Zarus was down the left hall. He had to be. She bet her life on it.

Rin cut the flow of light and took two steps before someone spoke.

"Is the light show over already?"

Rin's blade unsheathed, cleaving through air so quickly she barely had time to notice the fiery braid or slitted pupils as she spun around.

Tatsuo swept backward as Rin pressed into the swing, redirecting it toward the wall. Sparks flew as steel struck stone, but the dragon remained unscathed.

"Pits n' Flames, Tatsuo, don't sneak up on me like that!"

He held his hands in an innocent gesture, letting out a low whistle as he glanced at the chip taken out of the wall. "You've gotten pretty good with that thing. Remind me not to get in your way during a battle. I have no interest in being fileted."

Rin blinked, her heart finally calming. "Tatsuo..." she shook her head. "W-what are you doing here? Where's Feyne?"

"Feyne's fine," he assured. "We held off the demons long enough for you guys to run away, then I put my own magic barrier between us." He offered a sly grin. "The fires kept them back long enough for Fuzz Face and I to book it. We found Gen and Luna a bit ago. He stayed behind to help with the distraction. Eretimis and most of his fools haven't met me before, so I won't let you roam this death maze alone." He flashed her a smile, but Rin couldn't help wrapping her arms around him.

She hugged tight, feeling as though she walked ten tons lighter. "Thank you," she whispered. Rin pulled herself together before turning her attention toward the left wing. "Zarus is that way."

Tatsuo trailed her gaze toward the twist in the corridor. A frown tugged his lips. His pointed ears twitched as he looked out the frosted window. "Of course it's the path ridden with them," he huffed, leaning his hands onto the windowsill. The dragon looked over the wintrous wastes and pursed his lips. "It won't be easy getting through."

Rin scrunched her nose. "You think the rest of this has been a walk in the park?"

Tatsuo cast her a sidelong glance. "Watch the sass, Red, or I might leave you alone again."

Rin blew a raspberry at him. "Leave, and I'll tell Vi every way to make you tick."

His smile instantly disappeared. "You don't have it in you to be that cruel... Do you?" Rin was already walking ahead. Before long, Tatsuo fell into step beside her.

Much to her grace, having Tatsuo along meant she no longer had to creep past each corner and hope it was clear. The dragon strode through the hall as if they were not, in fact, seeking to break one of the Dark Tyrant's prized prisoners out of the premises.

Rin kept close behind, doing her best to fit in with the demons they occasionally passed. Thankfully, no one gave them the time of day, but Tatsuo certainly laughed himself tearless after claiming Rin was too short to be a demon. She kicked the dragon in the shin. Yet, no matter how many demons they walked by, no matter how many even offered her a glance, Rin didn't pick up any suspicious eyes along the way. Perhaps it was that the halls grew darker in these parts, the air cooler. Or possibly it was the rushed steps and busy hands of everyone.

An invasion. Rin couldn't quell the grease lining her stomach. Whatever the invasion was, wherever it was heading, these demons had barely stopped running around. They prepared for war. A war that seemed to be close upon them. But with who? A shadow cast over her mind.

Rin turned left, finding a staircase wrapping itself up and down a narrow tower. She didn't take a moment to pause before descending.

After so long of silence, the little voice inside Tatsuo finally prodded his thoughts to life. "How are you so sure where to go?"

"I sent a wave of magic along this part of the fortress," she explained. "It trailed through the halls until it hit Zarus. I'm just following the path it took."

"You remember the layout of this place from that?"

"Apparently."

Awe settled in the slim pass.

"When did you learn to do that?"

Rin shrugged, keeping her eyes on the sinister shadows dancing on the wall near the torches. "Right before we left Xandra. Ma helped me figure it out."

Another pause, long enough that Rin cast a glance at Tatsuo. She found a dumbfounded stare. "I'm glad your lessons are paying off."

Rin loosed a grin as she hit the bottom step and veered right. "Me too."

The sentiment didn't last long. She certainly didn't know the exact layout of the never ending fortress, only that they were probably on ground level. But the room stretching before them looked like it could be a cellar. The stairs let out onto a wide square landing, an arched entrance on the opposite wall. Her breath clotted in her throat as she breathed in the stale air, forcing herself to walk through the darkness.

She delved into her magic and withdrew a ball of light that rose to the ceiling. It exposed old, brittle tables strewn about. The far wall held two shelves that should have been full of books and scrolls, but they were empty. In the middle of the shelves stood a marble altar, though nothing rested on it. No statue, no offering, nothing but a weight in the air. A shrine for a kaeth? Lhaerem, if she had to guess by the humble makings of the chamber. A prod in her head seemed to confirm it. Rin traced her stare along the walls and found nothing but ice. Ice and frost encased the shrine, splintering across the floor and creeping up the walls. Her breath clouded before her lips.

"He's not here," she sighed, a weight creeping back in her chest. "No one is."

Tatsuo met her side. "Then who does that belong to?" Rin traced the dragon's bright eyes to the oily, inky liquid pooling in the center of the floor. The warmth of her light didn't touch the black liquid.

"What is that?" Rin cringed at the liquid.

"Blood."

She scrunched her nose. "*That's* blood?"

"Dark magic does terrible things to the body..." Tatsuo mumbled. He looked over the chamber once more. No other exits or entrances. "Whoever was here, we barely missed them. Zarus too, probably."

Rin looked at the stairs, letting her light die. "We didn't pass him in the hall. He must have gone up." Tatsuo nodded, taking the lead. Rin offered the empty altar one last glance before Tatsuo called to her from the archway.

No one seemed to venture down this corner of the fortress, Rin realized. The entire end was as forgotten as the shrine tucked within. She quickly understood why as they found the top of the staircase and the towering doors that stood atop it.

Chapter Fifty-Two

The glacial draft forced its way through the gap under the ancient doors at the top of the stairs.

Rin tugged her cloak tighter around her shoulders. "Why does it always have to be ice? Why can't it be a cozy fire-lit cabin he runs off to for once?" she groaned, but she couldn't tear her eyes off the radiance of the entryway.

Ornate carvings danced along the trim of the frame. Simple redwood shaped the heavy doors, but the embellishments spanned from top to bottom. Carvings of stars, carvings of fire, carvings of sun and moon, even the little fireflies that find their way into Aresan during the warmest parts of summer. Any sources—*all* sources—of light rested on the mosaic. In the very center where the two doors met rested a lithe form. It's flowing hair intertwined with the rays from the surrounding suns, the reach of its gown blending in with the fires. A circlet of starlight rested upon the being's head. Nraessa, the kaeth who stayed in the mortal realm after the war against Anöwe. Whatever lay outside the doors, it was a tribute to her.

Tatsuo's caution leveled with her entranced stare. "Rin, for all we know, that blood could have been there for hours. We won't last outside."

Rin shook her head. "It was still wet. He had to have gone this way."

Carefully, she placed her hand upon the polished wood. A piece of the original temple, holy and divine, but only frost slithered into her hand. No presence like Vulyn's crypt. No sense of entity like in Lhaerem's shrine. Nraessa—one of the High Kaetha though she once had been—stayed with the mortals after the War of the Divine. Nraessa was forever trapped on Fawllhä's remnants, making sure Anöwe's power never stirred again.

Her hand slid to the iron handle, the glove barely staving off the nip. Before Tatsuo protested, Rin pulled the doors open. The empty rendering of Nraessa split, allowing a violating gust of wind inside.

Rin stifled a spasming cough. An open balcony welcomed her—wide enough to fit a cavalry of fifty riders side by side. A frozen fountain rested in the center below the dark sky. The wind seared her cheeks, but Rin's numb joints didn't matter once she saw the shadowed figure standing in the frozen hellscape.

Her heart leapt. Zarus was *alive*. His raven hair raged through the winds like a stain of ink against the snow. A wraith in the night, looking over the balcony's railing. Rin couldn't contain herself, couldn't help the smile from cutting across her face. He hadn't noticed her yet, his back facing her. She needed to be fast before he disappeared.

Rin ran into the blizzard, using her light to melt the ice under each step. She ran so fast that she didn't even notice when Tatsuo tried to grab her arm. Didn't even hear the panic of his shouts. However, Rin heard the thunderous *boom* as the doors behind her slammed shut.

***

The sound reverberated through her bones. Rin whipped around. The beautiful wood of the balcony's entrance bled black. A shadow stretched over it, a lock sealing her out of the fortress.

Blinded by the blizzard, Rin had failed to catch the details. However, standing right before him, a slick fear coated her insides.

Shoulders too broad to be Zarus's; hair black as night, but shunning all light just like the blood in the shrine. The heaving winds didn't affect him. Instead, a phantom breeze of his own caught the edges of his obsidian cloak. When he turned around and towered above her, higher than Zarus ever stood, charcoal eyes of the void stared back. Lifeless. Empty. She couldn't tell whether his faded skin was a trick of the darkness swirling in the sky or her own terror.

"After so long, girl, it is an honor to meet you." The same oily voice from the Lennaels.

Rin couldn't talk, couldn't breathe. She stared at the Dark Tyrant, forgetting every lesson she had studied. It all bled away under that stare, against his calm, lethal smile. Her voice shriveled. The siren of her magic muted against the shadow's corrosive touch.

The demon took a step closer, the shadows under his feet stretching her way. Her own shadow riled.

"I could not be more grateful for your arrival, Ms. Nowell."

Rin's stomach revolted at her name. This demon was nothing like the monster she had always imagined.

"You see, the *uhlandyi* I have taken under my guidance has recently defected my will. I think you might be the key I need to lock him in place." The Tyrant's smile twisted.

Rin's magic jolted as the shadows lunged. The world drained of color. Her hair faded from ginger to grey, the navy cloak around her shoulders like so. Everything faded except for the Tyrant—he already walked Armiria wrung free of vibrancy.

A wall of light blocked the shadow's grasp. Hissing, the shade dissipated until only a dark vapor remained in the air. Rin did not attack, nor did she budge. She stood still, eyes widened and unblinking and never moving from the demon staring down at her like an unsolved puzzle.

"Have you forgotten how to speak?" the Dark Tyrant asked. No words passed through Rin's lips. None were brave enough. His sway over the world assaulted her senses. Her light may have extinguished the shadow, but that's all. The world would wait for as long as he wished—as long as it took her to well up an answer.

Rin swallowed the terror. She pulled her wan expression back, soaking up a deep breath. "There is nothing worth saying." She tried to step back, but her legs anchored in place. Yet nothing more than her shadow sat below.

The Tyrant's gaze hinted at amusement. "Now," he mused, another chill running up her spine as he advanced a step, "that is not the case. I have heard so much about the human who thawed Zarus's heart for months now, and I am sure you have heard just as much about me. What better opportunity to separate myth from truth?" An invitation danced in his hollow eyes.

Rin gritted her teeth, squared her shoulders and looked up at the demon. "I know all I need to," she spat.

Her eyes strained to focus on him under the darkness storming overhead. Eretimis loosed a *tsk*. His expression fell flat of mirth. "Foolish human." He shifted like a phantom in the night. "It is clear you have not heard enough."

Rin's rigid guard kept her head from rolling off her shoulders. The shadows swarmed around the Dark Tyrant. Even the abysmal clouds coalesced toward the demon as if the entire world eddied to him. Rin nearly lost the Tyrant within the tempest, much less saw the scythes of shadow-make cutting through the air. She barely threw herself to the side before the shadows sliced off her head. Yet her own shadow acted as glue on the bottom of her boots.

Rin hit the ground elbow first.

Her teeth gritted. Bones still rattling, she conjured a blinding light. The burst thinned her shadow enough to tug herself free, but her light barely cut through the maelstrom of darkness.

She crawled to her feet before another blast struck. A ripple of white light spread across the ground with each step, blowing back the coursing shadows. The dark gusts overpowered the blizzard. Rin gathered all the magic she could muster around her hands, warding the corrupt smog from entering her lungs. No matter how much light she conducted, it only cast more shadows for him to wield.

Rin's eyes shifted—to the shadows, the ice beneath her feet, the being at the center. She was powerless, and her magic knew it.

A flame robbed of oxygen, her magic sputtered. What once was an ocean now offered a drought. The shadows buried her. The hum of her magic ceased, replaced by a bellowing void. Eyes open or closed, world up or down, she did not know. She lost the demon wielding the squall. A cry escaped her lips. Rin pried the last ounce of light from within and forced it onto the storm of shadows suffocating her.

Warmth encased her hands, dissipating the smog, but the Dark Tyrant snuffed out her power. The course strengthened. Rin's knees nearly buckled. Just when her feet slipped on the ice, and she was going to be swallowed whole by the storm, it stopped.

Rin crashed to the ground. Her head rattled, an echo of pain along her arm. The howling wind sounded so docile compared to moments before.

The snow calmed, fluttering gently on her skin. Puffs of air clouded at her mouth with each rapid breath. When her disheveled hair drooped in front of her eyes, she realized the color had returned to the world. Rin couldn't gather her thoughts. The darkness sucked the life out of her.

She opened her fatigued eyes to find black boots standing in front of her. Rin forced her stare up. A phantom breeze toyed at the ends of the Tyrant's hair.

She dug her nails into the frost coating the balcony and hauled herself to her feet. "Why not crush me?"

The Dark Tyrant raised a brow, as if the very question amused him. Rin bit her tongue to resist shivering beneath his stare. "How long have you wielded such magic?"

Rin wanted to pull the cloak tighter around her body and hide. "Not long," she admitted.

He studied her with narrowed eyes. So close. She stood so close to the Dark Tyrant. She saw the subtle exhale fogging at his nose, the stitches of his undershirt, the cloak crafted of the void shifting with his breath. No, not void—shadows covered him. Everything inside her begged to flee his presence. Everything but her magic. It did not rage, it did not bellow against him as it had moments before. Rin shuttered to find her magic swaying toward his dark presence.

The Tyrant remained silent for a long moment. "Tell me, Ms. Nowell," he said abruptly. "Do you know how the mortals received magic?"

Rin couldn't stave the furrow from her brow. Each word straightened the hairs on her neck, but something about them that sounded less like the Dark Tyrant, and more like the friend she searched to break free from the fortress. She narrowed her wary gaze.

"Yath Ha granted the mortals their preferred gift after the world tore apart," she said slowly.

"Precisely." An unpleasant note rang on his words. "Do you know where the gods drew the magic from before they imbued the mortals with it?" Rin refused to answer. "They crafted it from the shambles of the world. All magic wielders, no matter what race, received their magic from the same source."

She bit down on her chattering teeth. "What's your point?"

A wicked grin tugged on his lips. "All magic is from the same source, and it is that base that draws magic users together." Rin's magic suddenly tugged toward the demon like a starved bloodhound at the end of its leash. The magic swaying from the Dark Tyrant reached for her own. Rin's stomach churned.

"W-what in the Flames is that?" she stammered. The Tyrant never flinched.

"Only beings of great power feel the pull of their magic begging to unify. It wants nothing more than to be full."

Rin stifled the urge to retch on the boots of the male who held her fate. She could barely think against the magic revolting within her head, but a grim idea struck her. Eretimis read her mind.

"Do not waste your panic. It is not so easy to absorb the magic of another." The Dark Tyrant paced a circle around her. "I have no intention of stealing the might that courses within you, Rin."

"Then what do you want?" She was still alive. Either he or the gods needed her for *something*. She stayed still, not trusting her magic around him.

He spoke coolly from behind. "To offer help."

Rin couldn't keep the snarl off her lips. "The only thing you can do for me is stay away from the people I love."

"Not even act as a guide to harness your power?"

Rin whipped her stare to meet the demon striding along the corner of her vision.

He didn't watch her as he spoke. "Such a remarkable gift you have, Rin. Not just anyone can obliterate my shadows. How far do you think that light would stretch if you reached your full potential? You fought Errogan and won. You saved your friends from sure death in the blink of an eye. Yet still you strain to control it. How many loved ones have you injured in your lack of mastery?"

Her teeth ground together. She wanted to burn him in enough light to blanch the world. Yet she didn't possess the strength to cast that much magic. He certainly knew it.

Eretimis directed his dark eyes to her once he paced a full circle. "Think of what you could do if you learned to control it. Think of what you could do under my guidance."

A cold sweat laced her back. "I'm sure Zarus would have a thing or two to say about your teaching," she snapped, gathering the rebelling magic.

Eretimis's stare hardened as he resumed pacing. "Zarus caused his own fate. He struggles with obedience, and I do not have tolerance for the undisciplined."

Rin opened her mouth to shout, to remind him of the piles of corpses he raised, of how many friends she's lost to his dealings, but the Tyrant cut her off.

"You would never have this problem, Ms. Nowell. I know you would do nothing to warrant punishment. You seek to rule your magic, end the violence it stirs, and protect those you love with it and from it." His glance shifted to her. "Tell me, why are you so adamant to make an enemy of me? All I seek is to better these worlds."

"*Better* them?" She couldn't catch the snap of her temper. "You've ransacked this world!"

His demeanor didn't flinch. "All it takes is perspective, Miss Nowell. The worlds need to change—caught too long in the monotonous reign of the Divine. I understand the problem our worlds face, and I know giving these realms a fresh start is the only answer. There is no doubt in my mind that you can be the driving force of that effort. I can be your answer, the solution you cannot find on your own. I can give you the means to master the light burning inside of you."

Rin gaped. This demon was the embodiment of everything bad in the world, everything bad in the next. He had threatened her life from the moment he discovered her existence, caused so much grief and strife for everyone she cared about for decades—*centuries. A*nd he had the audacity to recruit her? He would guide her to Ashnagz. She would be dead before he gave the order to die! She seethed at the demon and his *better worlds.* How *dare* he assume she was that greedy—

"I admit I was wrong about Zarus." Eretimis spoke from behind once more. She willed herself to glance and caught the Tyrant's shrug. "I pushed him to his limits, expecting more from a demon gifted with the power of the gods. Now I see I misjudged his potential. The ancient power I sought dwells within you instead."

Rin furrowed her brows. "What ancient power—"

The Tyrant's lethal step directed toward her. Wind howled, ice groaned, and black consumed the balcony. Her magic flared. Rin cast a shroud of light to shield her, yet a shadow still pierced through inches from her heart.

Rin fell to her knees, all her breath stolen. A soft *drip* of liquid splashed to the ground. When she finally opened her eyes, not a scratch laced her body.

Rin dragged her clattered focus to the Dark Tyrant standing mere feet away. Blood flooded from his hand, a snarl painted finely on his face. A tether of shadows darted to strangle her. However, a wall of ice erupted from the ground to block it.

Chapter Fifty-Three

Frost nipped at Rin's cheeks. The shadow had reached for her throat, but crashed against the ice barrier.

Dazed, Rin found two crimson eyes raging through the snow beside her. The like-wraith pinned his glare on the Tyrant through the glassy ice.

Rin stared in disbelief, but Zarus never looked at her. His pale hand reached out, and she had to stare at it before she convinced herself it was real. The silent demon spoke in a low hush.

"I'll stand more of a chance if you actually help me."

Rin's face burned red. She snapped her gaping jaw, grabbing Zarus's hand faster than the winds thrashing against the barrier before them. "You realize I spent *months* planning how to get you out of this place, right? That I'm risking *my* life along with countless others to get you the precious freedom you always droned on and on about?" Even against her temper, Rin's lips curved upward.

Zarus finally glanced sidelong at her, a dark brow arching over nightmarish eyes. "Then what took you so long?"

She wanted to crack his cheekbone open with her fist—would have too, if not for the smirk tempting his face. No, instead she turned toward the Tyrant silently watching.

Eretimis hadn't moved an inch. His eyes dug deep into Zarus's skull, daggers staring in blind rage.

Rin kept her voice low. "Hiding any more tricks up your sleeve?"

"One or two," Zarus mumbled.

Rin glanced at him. His voice, his demeanor, his face. There was something different from the demon stolen from her nearly five months before. He looked drained of all color, his eyes darkened by exhaustion, and his body in a state of frailness only imprisonment brought on. However, Zarus stood taller. An energy coursed around him she couldn't feel before. Magic lined in might.

Zarus was no longer afraid of the Dark Tyrant.

Rin swallowed hard and turned toward the bastard demon. Her nerves raged. However, her magic no longer pulled. Instead, it begged to be released. The spring still bubbled deep in her mind. She exhaled any ounce of doubt.

Zarus was her friend, her answer. Nothing would stop her from freeing him.

***

Zarus barely contained the flood of relief as he stood next to Rin.

Eretimis had found her first, and Zarus never ran faster in his life when the shadows of the world seized. One moment later, and she would have been dead.

Or perhaps not.

Nothing about this girl reminded Zarus of the human in the Lennaels. Bleeding and panting, Rin remained collected. Her heart beat steadily. Stronger, taller. Most prominently, the ancient presence he had always sensed floating about inside of the girl flourished. A sea coursed around her, brushing against his own power and inviting it to dance. She stood uncrushed by its might; unfazed by the sheer grandness of it.

"What a touching reunion."

Zarus shifted focus to the Tyrant behind the wall. Blood poured from Eretimis's hand, but the injury was minor. Zarus had barely nicked the skin before he raised the ice wall.

"I suppose it's not the reunion you hoped it would be," Zarus grounded. This demon tried to make him a monster. This demon tried to rip everything away from him until he was empty. From bone and flesh to clay ready to mold. His nails dug into his fists.

Eretimis merely smiled. "It is not what I hoped for, *uhlandyi*, but we can still make the most of this meeting."

Rin stirred in the corner of Zarus's eye. "As if," her silvery voice grounded. "I have no more use in being here." Her emerald eyes flicked his way—a grin he had spent months missing. "I'm ready to leave. What about you?"

Eretimis's expression twitched, more aggravated than he would ever let on. Zarus couldn't help a spark of amusement stretching across his face. "Do me the favor of leading our way out."

Shadow swarmed. Eretimis dug his magic into the ice barrier. Pulsing, rippling, the shadow raged until it found a weak point and seeped into the cracks of the frozen wall. The shade worked through his power, twisting each fracture until it choked the ice. The wall shattered like glass.

Zarus evaded the shadow's strike. Eretimis advanced as he expelled another ripple of magic. The world stripped of color, and Zarus reached for Rin. But she wasn't there. A roar erupted from the girl's throat as she charged forward.

Zarus immediately shielded his eyes. The light blinded him, burning holes through his vision. He suppressed a hiss and peered through the gap in his arms. The shadows engulfed Rin, but a white light shone through its corroding veil. Darkness fizzled, extinguished like a flame.

Zarus saw the opening and leapt through it, forging a sword of reddened shadow in his hand. Eretimis's step deterred as Zarus jabbed the phantom sword toward the Tyrant's heart. He honed all his focus into sharpening its point. Zarus barely saw Eretimis unsheathe the sword hiding beneath his cloak.

"You forget one thing, boy," the Dark Tyrant parried the strike of the phantom blade. "You still have much to learn." Eretimis shifted his weight too swiftly, stumbling Zarus's step.

The Dark Tyrant charged at Rin, and she submerged the world in another burst of light. Eretimis's shadow veil masked his body, unfazed by the magic. Within a beat of a heart, Eretimis was on top of her.

Zarus lunged for the Tyrant and the human. Ice danced on the tips of his fingers. Dark mist laced his breath. Yet a tendril of his shadow slithered around his ankle. Anchored, he slammed on the ground.

The impact reverberated through his bones, rattling his focus. Rin reached for something under her cloak. Her hand barely grazed the ruby pommel before shadow fell over her. Yet Eretimis's blade did not strike. Rin Nowell stared in terror and disbelief, but Zarus smiled.

***

Rin froze as the ghastly blade raised above her. That was until the world ignited in flames and Eretimis faltered.

The hairs on the back of her neck rose as the balcony raged in grey and white flame. A vicious sizzle tore her from awe. She looked down, finding a layer of dark mist stained red and black wrapped around her body—the only ounce of color showing. Zarus's magic writhed as it blocked out the inferno. Through the mist, she saw the blaze fade pale blue. The Tyrant's shadows staggered against the flame, yet Eretimis didn't flinch against the heat.

The flames parted, and Rin peered into its berth. Blood stained the Tyrant's eyes, tension straining every muscle in his body. He did not move, didn't even blink.

"You know, Red, you should let me take the lead."

Humor didn't carry into his tone. The *narikaah* stood in the blue blaze, looking at the Dark Tyrant with solemn eyes. His hand balled into a fist at his side, and Rin had to squint to see the near invisible threads he held. The same spell he once used to paralyze Zarus.

Tatsuo's flames suddenly pulled closer toward the Tyrant, yet he didn't guide the magic. The shadow veil covering the Tyrant thinned as it absorbed the flames until shadow nor flame remained.

Tatsuo's arm yanked forward, the threads within taut and strained. The dragon pulled back with all his strength, but it wasn't enough. The Dark Tyrant flexed his arms outward, snapping the magic strands like hair. Tatsuo instantly released the magic once the Tyrant grabbed the rest of the bounds and tore them to shreds. The world slipped underfoot as Rin was snatched up. Tatsuo grabbed her, and jumped to Zarus's side, leaving the Tyrant to work through the remaining spell.

"I told you it wouldn't be as strong as last time," Tatsuo huffed, "I didn't have enough time to prepare the spell."

Zarus shook his head, a waft of shadows circling in the air around his hand. "Rin's not dead, so I think it did its job."

Rin last stood between these males ages ago. Zarus must have found Tatsuo trapped inside the doors to the balcony. Whatever seal Eretimis placed on it, Zarus broke through. She wondered what had happened to the like-wraith all those months. The dungeons were enough to break any being—human, demon. Yet he stood, a fire sparked in his crimson eyes.

"*Rin*," Zarus bit , dragging her attention back to reality. Both demon and *narikaah* stared at her.

"Hm?" she hummed, like there wasn't a Tyrant of death and darkness snapping through Tatsuo's magic before them.

"Did you get any of that?" She stared blankly for a moment before Zarus loosed one more sharp sigh. "I need you to work with me to drive him back to the edge of the balcony. Tatsuo will try to pin him with fire—" Zarus's voice cut short as he sensed the shift of magic. Rin felt it too as the world resumed its monochrome reign.

"Petty spells cannot restrain me," the Tyrant's voice boomed. His lifeless eyes looked into Tatsuo's very soul until familiarity struck. "I know you."

The dragon let out a bitter laugh. "You better know every line of my damn face," he growled, not giving Eretimis the chance to say another word. Tatsuo lunged forward, arm extended as his father's spear manifested in his hand. Zarus followed, the shadows in his hand taking the shape of a curved blade.

The hum in Rin's head roared as Zarus's magic sprung to life. She joined the two, but before she summoned her light, another wave of shadow rippled out from Eretimis. Tatsuo nearly blew to the side. Zarus skidded to a halt as he cut through them.

Eretimis wasted no breath. Forward he sprang, fading in and out of Rin's sight in the shadows he wielded.

She searched from side to side until she caught the stir of darkness near Tatsuo's shadow. Immediately, she summoned her light, evaporating Eretimis's magic before it could strike. However, light casts as many shadows as it kills. Another shade on the opposite side of Tatsuo stirred. The tendril wrapped around the dragon's neck. Rin bit down on the swell of panic. Light bathed the balcony, melted the snow falling midair, but it did not break through that shadow. Eretimis had compensated his power for her magic.

Rin screamed. She almost didn't notice the violet portal severing the dark tendril.

Another silhouette stepped out of the balcony's entrance. Blue eyes pierced through the snow. His scarred arm extended outward, a purple aura swirled around Genesis's fingers. The missing end of Eretimis's shadow protruded through the portal, fading to nothing once the prince cut the connection.

Genesis made his way onto the balcony as Rin ran to Tatsuo's gasping side.

Eretimis smiled, malevolent and bitter. "Has a life of freedom grown dull already, Genesis Masquarem?"

The prince narrowed his glare at the Tyrant. "There's no such thing as freedom when you're reigning terror on this world, Eretimis."

"Your adventures away have spoiled you," the Tyrant mused. "Perhaps I can remind you what imprisonment is like to those who have no worth to me." Shadows swarmed Eretimis's hand like a hive of agitated bees. He opened his palm to the ever-darkened skies, commanding the swarm toward Genesis, but Zarus shifted in the corner of her eye. He took a single step, and suddenly the shadows halted.

The swarm thinned and thickened. A tug of war over the cloud of death hovering in the air. Rin seized the opportunity and erupted a fountain of light. Within seconds, the shadows ceased.

Rin shivered as her magic rippled along her spine. Wings of pure light spread out from her back, twisting and turning in the wind. "You cannot win this," she said calmly, taking careful steps down the line between Zarus and Tatsuo.

Eretimis's facade cracked. His white teeth flashed a feral smirk.

"Do you know who you speak to, girl? Do you know where you walk? I am the lord who corrupted these lands. And if you are not careful, I will drag you down to the Pits of Ashnagz myself—"

The wolf pounced through the veil of snow like lightning. His claws stretched out, but Feyne only grazed Eretimis's chest before the Tyrant twisted out of the way. The shifter slid to a halt on the slick ground, teeth exposed and bared. Blood matted his fur. The Tyrant bared his teeth, his lethal step already directed toward the wolf, but he stopped, lurching over.

Luna Nowell knocked another arrow in her bow while Eretimis ripped the first from his shoulder. "Lay a hand on her, and you'll beg for Ashnagz before I'm done with you, Eretimis Havilurce." The words were a curse. Rin watched her mother at the doorway, the graceful steps she took as she circled around the Tyrant's backside. Her bow never lowered.

Eretimis's speech faltered. His eyes widened. The surprise only lasted a second before a snake's smile curved his lips.

"Cissrey Kingslin," he spoke with a spine-chilling hunger. "It was not even six months ago that I sent out a team of hunters to the western Unclaimed Lands in search of you. The cottage they found was abandoned when they arrived." Eretimis shifted his attention to Rin. "I suppose this girl would be your daughter... I might call myself a fool for not having deciphered it sooner. However, I would hardly call her a white mage." Something knowing twisted his expression as he glanced toward Rin. Her stomach revolted against it.

Luna—Cissrey—lowered her chin. "You've finally picked a fight you can't win, Eretimis. Listen to the girl and stand down."

The warning was hollow, full of empty words. Decay drifted through the air. However, she knew as much as everyone else that they did not have the time to waste killing this monster. A fortress swarming with his loyalists would be on their tails any moment. Eretimis knew it too.

Motionless, he stood, encircled by the only invasion party crazy enough to stand against him. Feyne and Luna behind, jaw ready and bow fixed. Tatsuo and Genesis on the side, spear directed at the demon and hand fizzing with the sway of summons. And who else to stand next to her against this force other than Zarus Lowwenth. Side by side, they stared into the empty eyes of the Dark Tyrant. A tension tugged on Rin's chest, but a deep breath cooled the swell.

"You're outmatched, Eretimis," Zarus finally said through the waxy silence, his voice broader than she had ever heard it. Eretimis's facade shuttered only once the words parted Zarus's tongue. Rage danced in his eyes. So well fettered it had remained until Zarus uttered the warning.

"Perhaps I have taken more of your mind than I thought, Zarus. I have stood against worse than this before."

Zarus's voice dug even deeper. "Not all at once."

A ghastly wind swiped Rin's hair in a violent dance. Yet the lack of color against the violent snow caught her attention.

"Perhaps I should even the odds." The Tyrant's nostrils flared.

With the raise of his hand, the redwood doors on either side of the balcony crashed open. Out flooded an army. Armed to the teeth with instruments of death, clad head to toe in armor, the demons poured. Bows rose from the roofs of the stairways. Yet despite the curses, the growls, the prayers, none of the intruders turned toward the gathering forces. No one dared take their attention off the Tyrant standing in the center.

"Quite the reunion," Eretimis smiled, glancing from side to side. "The White Mage, the Black Mage, the orphaned *narikaah*, the baseless shifter, the Shadow of Evenfall. And you." Rin fought the urge to recoil beneath his stare. A caress of magic shivered in her shadow. "Not quite a white mage, yet so much more."

Zarus seethed at her side. "End this incessant banter before I—" His threat cut short, replaced by a writhing growl as he clutched his head. The demon lurched, nearly doubling over before Rin caught his weight. His face blanched, then greyed, the discolor pulsating along his veins.

"Zarus!" Rin held him upright, but the demon's eyes locked shut. He grabbed at his face—clawing and digging into something she could not see until blood welled. When he finally eased, crimson dripped to the ground.

Rin ground her teeth.

Eretimis took a step closer to her. "I have so much planned for each of you." His voice violated her skin, oil coating every inch, ready to strike the match.

Just like that, the demons folded in. Her mother pivoted on her heels, aiming her arrow this way and that, warding off the nearest threat. Hackles raised and teeth flashed. Feyne offered any soul brave enough to near him a swift death. A fountain of curses sprung off Tatsuo's lips as a lick of flame hissed off his tongue. It was to no avail. Genesis's grave eyes met her own amid the demons.

Rin's head shook. The hum rang, her magic stirring violent waves. The power reached down her spine. It was an effort to keep upright, to keep Zarus upright.

Heat engulfed Rin; overtook her head, her chest, her fingers and toes. A wave crashed into her, one she had never known. Not in the desert, not in Xandra. Her head quaked. Yet all the power coursing within, trying to drown her in its cresting waves? She laughed at it.

Rin exhaled the might of the stars. Pale and burning and unrivaled. The luminescent wings emitting from her body surged in the ever-dark north. She grabbed ahold of the corrupted temple, lighting up the entire structure in place of the blotted sun. Stunned, the masses watched her; knowing, her companions flooded to her side with the distraction.

Eretimis's eyes widened beneath his cloak of shadows. An order barked from his throat—his attention divided. Strained, Zarus summoned a whirlwind of blackened ice onto the army. Shadows whipped to the Tyrant's grasp, but he was too meek. He had underestimated Rin, and for once, she smiled rays of starlight at the thought.

The Dark Tyrant snarled as he thrust the shadows forward. The attack was void of life, void of warmth. Yet Zarus stood tall, halting the void despite his discomfort. In the beat of a heart, the surrounding light erupted. Towering high into the darkness above, Rin conducted the mayhem into a sweet symphony of power. Tendrils of light flared around her, hissing against the shadows Eretimis tried to force past Zarus's control. A soothing warmth encased her against the Northern Wastes, and she extended it to her companions, shielding them from her magic.

The screams of the army terrorized the tundra. They cowered against the light, clawing their eyes, burning down to their very souls.

Rin kept the magic rolling, kept the light thriving as she turned to Zarus. The shadow that had fallen over his eyes faded, replaced by his crimson gaze. He was speechless, shocked. Even the rest of them; they had all witnessed her magic before, yet not this magnitude.

"Now," Genesis cut through the enchantment of Rin's magic. "We need to leave *now*."

Rin nodded, but panic seized her thoughts. The crypt was out of question. Even Zarus's worry showed until something caught the demon's red eyes. Zarus stared past her light in silent shock, but before Rin could trace his gaze and find anything more than a wisp of white hiding behind the doors of the balcony, a symbol flashed in the air. A portal lined with blue light opened in front of her a moment later. Shocked, but not questioning it, Rin looked at her companions.

She sent out another pulse of light as the six intruders jumped through the portal. However, she glanced back at the Dark Tyrant standing in the middle of the chaos.

He was the only one still standing. Fires had been lit in his hollow eyes, flames of shadow and shade warding off the light. His magic protected his vision, his skin, but Rin extinguished every ounce he summoned. The malevolence in his eyes cut into a twisted smile. Something amid the pain whispered, '*Until next time.*'

Genesis shattered her trance with a call of her name. He grabbed her hand and ran through the shimmering aura of the gateway. Zarus, however, stole one more glance behind the balcony doors before he dove into the portal and it hissed shut behind him.

The blizzard strengthened after the intruders escaped. So thick and so deep that no one noticed the break of sunlight through the swirling darkness above the corrupted temple.

Part Three

Invasions

J.E. Elliott

Chapter Fifty-Four

"**Y**ou've gone mad."

"Completely off your rocker."

"Have I? You believed Aava when she said I'm over ninety years old—at the very least, that I'm of the Masquarem name. But *this* is where you draw the line?"

Silence weighed on the room. Rin cast an uncertain glance at Genesis. He refused to let his composure slip and allow the New Light members to believe the meeting was a laughing matter.

Two months until an invasion. Zarus had been told that nearly half a month ago.

Thanks to the portal, everyone had stepped out of the fortress and into Xandra in one breath. The new year came and went while they were away, and two days passed since their return. Two days spent crammed in Genesis's quarters coming up with a plan, a proposal, and proof. They wasted no time after what Zarus told them. It all led to this meeting with the leaders of the New Light.

"What he means," Rin cut in, "is that as crazy as this sounds—as crazy as it is—we need you to put doubt aside." She glanced through the dim candlelight in the abandoned storehouse. "An army is coming to Xandra's doorstep."

"An army of *demons*?" Someone from the back called.

Rin bit the inside of her cheek and nodded. "If we don't prepare and spread the word, the city will be demolished just like Zelenia seventy years ago."

Another round of scoffs. Rin struggled not to stir beneath the shadow of disbelief. The office in the storehouse wasn't large, but the best they could find after Genesis told Aava to summon The New Light. Rin heard every curse and *tsk* under their breaths. Even Aiden looked like he was about to burst into laughter.

Someone—a face she had yet to meet—spoke first. "With all due respect, Your Highness, this seems unfair."

The prince nearly winced at the title Aava had taken up calling him. "Please explain, Ashai."

The man's expression pulled taut. Whether any of the New Light actually believed that Genesis was the crown prince from seventy years ago or merely a descendant of the namesake, Aava made it very clear she respected him. If Aava held someone in high regard, everyone respected them too.

Gillan's voice rose above everyone else. "When we opened our services to you, we meant for the betterment of Nokomic. Not against some fabled *demon army*." The second in command of the New Light narrowed her rich brown eyes, then shifted them to Rin. "We don't have time to waste on fairytales and myths. The Resurrection is rebuilding its defenses, gathering up the loose ends of De'Rina's absence. Not to mention, the cases of missing people are on the rise again. Whatever monsters you found near the temple, their friends have been tearing through Xandra tenfold. While you two were off playing in the north, we've been trying to keep this city safe."

Playing in the north? Rin's temper burned. "Excuse me, but—"

A shadow shifted at her side. A subtle scoff slithered off Zarus's lips, caressing the late night with violating nails.

"The improvidence of humans never ceases to prevail... You claim to trust and respect your kingdom's heir, yet raise accusing fingers when he warns you of a damning threat." His crimson eyes narrowed on Gillan's glower. "It seems Rin raised my hopes too high for the wisdom of humanity."

Zarus had stood so quietly until then, listening and watching. Was he debating whether these humans were worth helping, or studying the crowd before jumping in? Well, he jumped, and a cannonball of arctic waters drenched every member of the New Light.

Gillan's nostrils flared. "And what threat looms higher than the immediate shadow of the Resurrection, newcomer?"

Something of a smirk laced Zarus's lips. "The shadow of ignorance."

Rin rubbed her temples. *Gods on high, he doesn't know when to shut up...*

She shifted her stare to the other members of the New Light behind Gillan. All watched Zarus like he was—well, like he was a wraith in the night. A walking nightmare looking down on them and all they thought worthy to stand by. However, Rin paused her huff.

He's not putting the other species in a kind light...

She looked at Zarus, his ghostly skin offsetting the terror of his eyes. She caught glimpse of the shadows surrounding him. He placed a distinction between himself and everyone else stuffed in the small corridor. Instilling doubt that demons were merely things of legend. It worked.

Aiden shifted from foot to foot beneath the stare of the demon. Aava had explained the tellings of demons and otherworldly phenomena to him already, but stories and experience were two different things.

"Fine, let me humor you for one moment and ask you this," Aiden grumbled, finding solace in Rin's stare. "Say a demonic tyrant held Genesis prisoner for half a century and tortured to the point he's no longer human. Say there is a legendary army marching up to Xandra right now. What in all of Yath Ha's gloried writings are we supposed to do about it?"

Right now. Those forces were heading for the city as they spoke. So far, the element of secrecy graced them. Eretimis didn't know his invasion plans had been shared with Zarus.

Rin held Aiden Iver's gaze for a silent moment, her tranquil stare unyielding until the tension in his finally budged. "We stand against them."

Scorn met her words. If they didn't think she was crazy yet, that surely did the trick.

"And how do you propose we do that?" Gillan grounded.

Genesis stepped forward. "This organization has spent the last eleven years rekindling Nokomic's bonds with the powers of this continent. Years salvaging alliances over five centuries old. We need to call for aid."

Something in Gillan's expression lightened, but it vanished in an instant. Her grey and brown hair shook with her head. "One month isn't enough time to call for help. We'd barely have a handful of swords by the time this army arrived."

Zarus arched a dark brow. "You'd rather try death than have a fighting chance?"

Gillan held his stare, but her words ran dry. She didn't believe their alliances were strong enough to call on. How long had their fearless leader been off working on relationships with the neighboring regions?

Rin's gut knotted. Fear held their minds. It haunted their eyes as they looked upon Zarus. And fear led them to their demise...

"I understand your apprehension," Rin found herself saying. She stepped into the center of the room. "You believe our claims. You've all suspected something about us since we arrived in Xandra months ago. I can assure you, as someone who has faced the same fear and doubt, humans are stronger than you think. Humans are more resilient and adaptable than we've ever been told. Just think of this organization. You rose out of the ashes of a world the Resurrection burned down. You saw a need for action, and you each jumped to answer it with nothing more than righteousness in your hearts and drive in your minds. How high were the odds then? Xandra is safer than it has ever been in the last seventy years. All because you took a stand."

She looked from side to side.

"I've known fear like the rest of you. I faced the Dark Tyrant on my own and fought against his warriors with nothing but a blade in my hand while my friends lay fallen. I've seen what happens when you stand in his way." The memory of the Tyrant's shadows crawled on the edges of Rin's mind, raising the hairs on the back of her neck. "There is nothing but destruction waiting for this city if we idle. Eretimis will not give you the option of staying out of a fight that has nothing to do with you, believe me. He wants nothing but death, and he'll stop at nothing. We are the only ones who can keep him from this land. So take a stand, and change the course of this battle before it even starts."

Gillan shook her head. "How are we supposed to fight against this alone? How are we supposed to survive against such a certain fate?"

Rin had held tight to the thrum in her head. She almost stumbled once she let go. A golden light burst through the room. Shadow fizzled away. Nothing but her magic was alight, biting back the nip of the frozen winds outside.

"What cards do you hold in this fight? What power do you possess against such a formidable foe?" Soft swirls of her magic danced in the air, weaving around the members of the New Light.

"You have me."

Before any of their gaping mouths found an utterance, before Gillan could will herself to blink, Rin paused the magic midair. Like the flame of a candle blown out, the light ceased, and darkness returned.

***

The hinges to Aava's home screeched as Rin swung the door open. Light bled out from the foyer against the chill of the night. She was barely two steps inside the house before a blur ran down the staircase.

Tatsuo landed at the bottom of the stairs, skidding to a stop before he crashed into her and Genesis. Eyes wide, he asked, "What did they say?"

Rin took a moment to process the household. The warmth of spices lingered from the kitchen. Laughter danced around the parlor in the Iver estate. Her head swayed, sleep begging to guide her next step.

"Well?" the dragon pressed, his chartreuse eyes darting from her to Genesis. Neither had the energy to talk.

"They agreed to help," Zarus finally answered, filing in behind. His crimson eyes swept over the foyer as he closed the door. "Messengers will be sent out in the morning with the call for anyone willing to fight. Scouts are being placed north. We'll know as soon as Eretimis steps foot into Nokomic."

Tatsuo stared in disbelief.

It worked. They actually convinced the leadership of Nokomic that demons exist. Rin still couldn't believe it, although the smile stretching across Tatsuo's face eased her worry. Before she knew it, the dragon wrapped her in a hug and twirled her around like a ragdoll. Tatsuo's laughter shook the halls. A smile crept through Rin's exhaustion. Finally, her mother peered out of the parlor and met her stare. All it took was a simple nod, and Luna's expression broke into relief.

They actually did it.

Chapter Fifty-Five

Sunrise came and went by the time Rin wandered into the hallway the next day. The aroma of lunch lingered in the air. She lived off Feyne's hunts for the entire trek north... she would never take for granted the scent of fresh bread and berries ever again. Yet food had to wait.

Rin forced herself toward the door in the secluded wing of the house. Only after knocking thrice did she think to announce her name, but the hinges swung open before she uttered a word.

"Good morning," she hummed to the cold-eyed demon.

Zarus's room possessed everything that hers did aside from a vanity, but the curtains were pulled aside from the windows. Crisp light poured into the corridor, and Rin couldn't help but smile to see Zarus enjoying the freedom of sunlight.

"I think you mean afternoon," he corrected. It was almost as if nothing had changed about this male from half a year ago. Almost. A smile tugged at his lip. "Morning would have been five hours ago when the rest of us woke."

She rolled her eyes. "I'll be sure to leave an apology in my will."

Stiff, strained, but not unfamiliar.

It eased her concern to know Zarus was comfortable enough to sleep in a house full of humans. Anything was better than the depths of Eretimis's fortress, but she worried he wouldn't settle in the estate. Yet the bags darkening his eyes had eased over the last two days.

Rin's smile faltered when she remembered why she knocked on his door. She caught the day's peace before it fled for good. "We have a lot to do."

His serenity hardened. Zarus nodded without a word. "I need the layout of this city and everything that lays beneath."

Rin barely nodded before she spun around and moved down the hall. No, she did not have the layout of Xandra memorized, nor did she know if anything rested beneath it. However, she knew the woman who would. Rin was already narrowing down on Aava's door when she realized Zarus followed. She had forgotten how eerily silent his steps were, and nearly squealed when he met her side before the door.

"Someone needs to tie a bell to you," she grumbled.

"I'll leave an apology in my will."

Rin could hardly retort before the door swung open. A pair of sapphire eyes gleamed at her.

"I've been meaning to ask you, Lowwenth," the prince in the doorway sighed. "How come I can't sense when you approach? I've gotten half decent at sensing presences, but you always stump me."

Unfazed, Zarus replied. "I never had one."

"Is that even possible?"

"You tell me."

Genesis frowned at the unsatisfying answer. Zarus was an enigma. It didn't faze Rin in the slightest to learn he was missing something everyone else had. A faulty aura made sense, come to think of the stealthy demon. Nonetheless, she cleared her throat since Genesis still blocked the door.

He glanced down at her and smiled wide. "Look who finally joined us today," Genesis mused. "I contemplated starting a pool debating how long it would take you to wake up."

Rin blinked a few times. "How long were you hoping for?"

"My money would have carried me on into the evening," he smiled.

"Well," Rin leaned her hand on her hip, "I'm glad to have lost you your figurative money. Perhaps next time I'll throw the game if you split the profits with me."

"In your dreams, Nowell."

Rin smirked. Then Zarus cleared his throat next to her. "Oh, right," she muttered. "Follow me." She ducked below Genesis's arm propped against the doorframe, slipping past into the corridor.

Zarus glanced at the path Rin took. "Should I follow?"

A grin crossed the prince's expression. "If it would catch your fancy. We made pretty good friends in the dungeons, did we not?"

Zarus's glower didn't settle, nor did Genesis's grin. However, the latter stepped aside and allowed Zarus to pass without further prodding his temper.

"As good as ever to see you, Genesis," the demon sighed.

Rin smiled at the two of them before she spun around and nearly crashed into Aava.

"Good afternoon, Miss Nowell," the woman's voice hummed, a gentle smile to accompany it. "It's good to see you've woken up finally."

Rin returned the gesture. "I feel like we've barely seen each other since I've been back. Everyone seems to have managed well in the winter here."

Aava nodded, clicking her tongue as she rested her weight on her cane—a cane that she took up after Rin left. "We managed well, however the chill was unusually harsh this year. Almost like something was stirring the winds in the north." The woman cast Rin a grim glance.

Rin swallowed hard. The entire city would have to evacuate...

"Spring won't halt the winds, Ms. Iver," Zarus cut in. "We can only hope to gather enough forces to stop it before it reaches this city."

Rin frowned. "What are we going to do about these winds?"

The gears in Zarus's head were already spinning. "Is there a sewer system that runs beneath this city?"

They all stared blankly at him, as if he were a demon in a human city.

Aava eventually nodded her head. "This was the first city to be built with one in Nokomic. It runs in all directions and lets out a ways down from the city border."

"Keeping the streets of this place clean since ye olden days," Genesis nodded, his tone sweet and sardonic. "What's your point?"

Zarus didn't stir at the prod; his mind never stopped moving. "Eretimis likes to keep underground when possible. Fitting as it is, you really don't want him wandering around in the sewers. I've seen it happen countless times before, and it almost always works. Once he's in, that's it. The city is done for."

"So what do you propose, young one?" Aava asked. Rin nearly lost control of a chuckle after Zarus's reaction to being called *young*.

His dark brows fell flat from their arch. "Set up a constant watch over every sewer opening outside the city. Never let a moment go by where those entrances aren't monitored."

"And what if something sneaks through our watch?" Genesis asked.

"Hope an explosion seals the demons out." Zarus's eyes narrowed. "But I believe if the demons get that far, we're already on the brink of doom."

Rin shook her head. "Do we even have the numbers to keep a watch like that going?" She glanced at Aava, who looked no more hopeful than she.

"I'm afraid we are limited, dear. Elyot took a sum of his men with him to reach out to neighboring regions."

Rin sucked on the base of her teeth. Messengers went in search of aid only that morning... One month to gather enough people willing to defend Xandra. Rin's head spun.

Call forth the humans blessed with our gift, Alentye.

Alentye... that name again. The Divine had been ruthless in their interventions, but they might have a point.

"We need to summon the users of Nokomic..." She barely registered that the words left her tongue. So absurd that even Aava stared back with disbelieving eyes.

"Gathering the users of this land is a hopeless cause, Erin. I tried to summon their aid long ago when Nokomic was still in pieces. None of them tempted the wrath of this land's prejudice."

Zarus shook his head. "Not the wrath of this land, but the attention of the Dark Tyrant. If word of their magic got out, he would have been on their case in hours."

Rin slid her gaze to the demon on the opposite side of the room. Her own mother had been hunted like a stag when Eretimis learned of her magic. Eretimis was the reason Rin grew up without a mother, the reason her father's smile was never the same. How many other people did he force to live like that?

Rin groaned, massaging her temples as her magic buzzed.

Genesis sighed. "We can train swords and hands to aim better, but Eretimis's armies have us outmatched. We need a miracle to walk out of this alive, and anyone who's aware of Eretimis's existence knows it."

Aava looked over Rin with sympathetic eyes. "I'm sorry, but magic users learned long ago what happens when they announce themselves. We'll have to think of another plan."

Rin gritted her teeth. "We don't have time to think of another plan. We need all the help we can get, all the resources we can scrape up. One month to prepare for an invasion and alter the course of Armiria's fate. No one can stand out of this fight anymore, not magic users or ignorant humans. If they stand by and do nothing, nothing will stop Eretimis from dragging them to the fortress and experimenting on them!"

Genesis's frown still didn't budge. "I know, Rin, but..."

The prince rubbed the back of his neck. She couldn't help looking at his arm scarred by the serum. It no longer looked like the flesh was dying, but a permanent scar marred his skin.

"What can we do for such frightened people? Eretimis's terror reigns with him, and these users live with it every day. Do you really expect them to charge into battle because Nokomic needs it? A kingdom that damned them to begin with?" He nodded to Aava. "Their choice was made before you were even born."

"I don't expect their terror to lessen. Nor do I expect anyone to change their minds about hiding. But," Rin stated, snatching Genesis's stare with an iron grip. Even Zarus inclined his head to hear what she had to say. "That doesn't mean they won't listen."

Chapter Fifty-Six

"And just why in the Flames would I do that?"

Rin looked Kah'Vi straight in the eye. "Because a lot of people are going to die if you don't."

Vi narrowed her stormy gaze, the afternoon sun shining through her bedroom window casting a grim shadow over Rin. "People die every day. Why should tomorrow be any different?"

Rin knew Vi would be difficult to convince, especially since the fae appeared to be sleeping when she knocked. She grounded her resolve with Zarus next to her.

Her magic flared at her temper's prod, but Rin wrangled it. "Because we have the chance to lessen the casualties. Because the people of Armiria are completely unprepared for what's about to hit them."

"They had centuries upon centuries to prepare; it's not my fault they chose ignorance."

The storm looking down on Rin didn't falter. She didn't feel the need to squirm beneath it, but gritted her teeth. "You would leave thousands to fend for themselves?"

The fae stepped out from behind her bedroom door, wearing nothing but a black silk robe. "Look, Rin, I think your whole heroine act is charming, and it works for some people," she shrugged, "but this isn't my war. I've stayed out of Eretimis's way for this long. I don't intend to cross him now."

"Because you're afraid of him?"

"Because there's no stopping him."

"Not if everyone is too concerned about themselves to stand up to him." The retort slipped through Rin's restraint. She couldn't decipher this. Pride, fear, apathy? Rin didn't know what was holding this fae's mind so set.

Vi's expression fell less than amused. She leaned back against the doorframe again. "I heard what happened in the North." She cast Rin a sidelong glance, only then paying any mind to Zarus's silent presence behind her. "Not even you two could stop him—the ones your gods directed their attention on. Do you expect this time to be different?" Vi wasn't looking at Rin when she asked. She held Zarus in her gaze.

***

A cheap shot.

Zarus kept his face stoic. The fae no doubt knew his name, no doubt knew his history. And she no doubt knew he could not argue with her. Going up against Eretimis... Rin didn't understand it. Didn't understand the decades upon centuries upon millennia of wreaked havoc and destruction. This fae was right. He knew it better than anyone in all the worlds. Which was exactly why he stood there.

"I've cowered against him for too long," Zarus finally said. "There's nothing to gain in running when the inevitable catches up with you in the end."

"Maybe that's why he always finds you," the female bit. "It's not running you have to be good at; it's hiding."

Vi offered him a pretty smile, one only a fae spirit would call upon right then. "Call me a coward, call me afraid—I don't care. The way I see it, standing against Eretimis is a sure death, and I've taken quite a liking to life. Don't ask me to kill myself for the sake of people who dug themselves into the grave."

"What about us? What about Aava and all your friends in the city?" Rin hissed.

The fae remained unfazed. "I make my own choices. If everyone else decides to kill themselves, it doesn't mean I have to follow. Aava will be safe. There's no way Aiden will allow her near the battle."

Rin shook her head. "And how long will that safety last?"

Zarus struggled to find an argument, any counterpoint. He was so new to lending a hand, after all. He opened his mouth, but the fae stood upright. The black robe slipped off her shoulder in the motion, exposing a gruesome scar. Fae were masters of healing. Their bodies wove themselves back together. Only iron ever left a mark on them.

The female noticed his gaze long before he removed it. A bittersweet smile flashed his way. She did nothing to cover the scar. "Like what you see, demon? Live among wolves, and you're bound to be bitten from time to time."

The scars beneath his shirt stung at the sight. Over his heart, across his back, centering his abdomen. All of them. No, he wouldn't blame anyone for running. Humans—they were creatures of habit, and he was bound to meet their foolishness over and over on the path he chose. But that didn't mean they deserved to die. Looking at the girl next to him, he finally understood that.

An idea flickered in his head, casting a dangerous shadow of dread. Yet danger was nothing new to him. "Why not make a deal if you refuse to help with nothing in return?"

Zarus heard Rin's breath catch in her throat.

The fae held back her laugh. "You've only just gained freedom, and you want to make a deal with me?"

Zarus held his tongue, thinking about what he was going to say for once. "I assume you're leaving the city before the attack? While you run, seek out the users in hiding. Go around Nokomic and ask them to join the fight in Xandra."

"That's exactly what Rin just asked me, ghost boy. Was my mind supposed to change?"

Zarus sucked in a cooling breath, his temper lining with frost. "In return, I owe you a favor."

At that, the fae's interest piqued. Her eyes opened a little wider, her smile a little broader. "Any favor I want?" The possibilities danced in her eyes.

Zarus cut that dance short. "No. The favor cannot in any way, shape, or form endanger Rin." He glimpsed the girl's emerald eyes shift to him. "Whether it be an order to kill her or an order that will put her life at risk, I will not carry it out."

Vi's eyes narrowed. "How am I supposed to find these users?"

"You're the eyes and ears of this city," Rin spoke up, calmer. "If anyone knows where they're hiding, it's you."

The fae thought it over, her head swaying back and forth as the deal coursed through the air like magic. So thick and heavy it sat, Zarus almost coughed on it. Promising his life to a fae. He certainly had made worse decisions, but this would be new. The unknown formed a cold sweat along his spine. Vi drank his dread like wine.

"I'm sorry to tell you that my plans for fleeing don't involve all of Nokomic. But how about this? I will find as many users as I can, try to rile you up a good ole militia," cold cutting and sharp her smile was, "but only if they lie in my path. I'll tell them to inform their fellow user friends too, if they have any left. And in return, you owe me two favors with the same restrictions."

Rin frowned. "*Restrictions*? Is it so much to ask not to kill me?"

Zarus nearly chuckled. He kept his face blank and eyes cold as he mulled over the offer. Of course he knew what he was going to say, but only a fool let the fae be the last one to negotiate.

"Your *path* can't intentionally go out of the way to avoid users. You have to make an honest effort to find them and spread the word. All you have to do is speak. Anything beyond that is up to the human to decide, but *you* have to make the effort for them to hear it. After that, be on your merry way."

The female's long nails slowly tapped on her arm, counting the seconds away one by one. "And what if I refuse and leave without this deal?"

Zarus kept his brow still, his face hard as steel. "Then you miss the opportunity of having me under your wing."

It was quite simple. Zarus knew he was an asset and had no qualms about using it as leverage.

"My my," the fae crooned, pacing back and forth in the hall, "aren't we the self-glorifying type." Zarus would have rolled his eyes, if not for the fact he knew this female would only drag the negotiations out further if he had. Another moment's unnecessary consideration, and finally her stormy eyes brightened.

"I think that this sounds like a nice little deal. I have one question though," Vi said.

Zarus watched Rin's joy swell before it skidded to a stop. He didn't blame her, he wanted this conversation to be over too.

"Tell me what changed. Why do you fight for them now when they left you so broken and beaten?" The fae stared him down, searching for an answer in his unyielding eyes. Despite her haughty smile, he saw doubt. The need for a reason to care. Zarus was silent, the aeolian song from outside the only indication the world hadn't frozen.

The years flashed through his mind, memories of beatings and floggings and everything the humans had done to him from his sixteenth year on. Some he had forgotten about until Eretimis dipped into his mind and ripped up the remembrances like roots of a tree. He felt the strikes, the cuts, the fire burning his skin. Zarus's lips parted, but nothing came out. He had no reason to help the humans. He had no loyalty to them, nor did they deserve any. But there he was, standing alongside a human who pulled him out of the shadows.

Zarus cast the memories aside.

"Because," he breathed, "Eretimis has stolen too much."

Vi raised her dark brow. "So you fight to stop him, not save thousands?" she asked, disdainfully quoting Rin's claim.

Zarus didn't doubt his resolve. He stared straight into her eyes. "No one deserves to burn by his hand."

"And what beyond Eretimis? What other sympathies do they deserve?"

Zarus glanced at Rin, watched the way the human looked at the fae. *Empathy.* Was this how she looked at him when they first met?

"I don't know what lies beyond," he admitted, turning back to the fae. "But I'm sick of letting the opportunities to learn pass me by."

The fae studied him a moment more. No smile on her lips, no retort on her tongue. Before long—before that facade completely fell—her voice mingled with the air.

"It's a deal," she said softly, and suddenly a gust pushed through the air between them. A weight settled on Zarus's body, coursing through his veins like lightning. It faded before he could recall the sensation. The magic unfolded, the deal made.

"The name's Kah'Vi, by the way. Glad to make your acquaintance."

At that, the door slammed shut.

Chapter Fifty-Seven

"Thank you," Rin muttered through the silence of the hall. Midday buzzed throughout the estate as workers and visitors walked by, yet a waxy hush encased her thoughts.

Zarus cast her a glance. He nodded, his only response before the creak of floorboards somewhere in the distance stole his attention.

Vi slammed the door in their faces as soon as the deal had been struck, as soon as that foreign magic drifted through the air. Rin had never known the touch of fae magic, but as the brief weight settled on her shoulders like the entire world perched upon them, it made sense.

And yet, Zarus had gotten through to her...

"She would have been halfway across the continent and I still wouldn't have changed her mind," Rin found herself saying as she walked, not caring if Zarus wished to keep the quiet intact. "I don't think she even would have made a deal with *me*."

From his voice to his step, Zarus was silent as a shadow. However, he paused another moment before answering. "I didn't expect her to agree to my terms."

Rin raised a brow. "Is not harming me *truly* that much of an inconvenience to everyone?"

The edge of his lip curved. Zarus shook his head, keeping his stare ahead. "Having your name added to the deal makes you a part of it too, however loosely it may be. Not allowing my favors to put you in harm's way will carry over to her favor as well in a way."

Rin pursed her lips. "That sounds like a technicality."

"Fae magic is built on technicalities. It's like ink: it spreads further than originally marked. You just need to know how to manipulate it before you write a deal."

She considered this as they walked through the halls. "Is there any way the deal can be broken?"

The demon shook his head, not even his hair stirring. "Breaking the deal would put you in more danger by not gathering aid for the battle. Even if she decided she wanted out, the magic won't let her."

Rin's eyes widened. She never knew Zarus to be so cunning... but her tongue ran bitter to think Vi was trapped in their deal.

"Does she know that? I mean, I'll feel guilty if she—"

"She knows," Zarus said bluntly. Another pause. Conversations with Zarus were like finding a whisper in the wind sometimes. "She must think highly of you."

A smile almost made it to her lips, but Rin could barely help the sigh of relief in its stead.

"Thank the gods for that," she groaned, rubbing her palms into her eyes. When her vision cleared, Rin found Zarus had paled.

The demon froze at the mention of the Divine weaving their fate. They had barely talked about it, too busy trying to convince humans of Eretimis's existence. She asked him about the visions and voices, if he had had similar experiences, but Zarus withheld too many specifics until they had a moment of privacy. Or until he could no longer avoid the subject. The invasion was the only thing they talked about since leaving the North.

Rin bit the inside of her lip. "Zarus, I know this is a touchy subject, but you can't ignore it forever. Clearly there's something that we're supposed to do together."

"How far will talking get us?"

Something grim seized hold of Zarus's expression. Rin cast him a confused glance, but he continued before she could question.

"The gods need us for something, have kept their eyes on us for a while now... Something to do with fighting Eretimis, or stopping him."

Giving the realms a fresh start. The Tyrant's words echoed in her mind, raising the hairs on her neck.

"Beyond that, neither of us knows," Zarus sighed his frustration. "Riddles about keys and tasks, but I haven't been able to reach out to the Divine once to ask them what happens now. And I have a feeling no matter what we do, we're going to keep getting silence as an answer."

Rin inclined her head. "What do you propose?"

Another moment's thought choosing his words. "I think for now, this invasion is more important than what the gods are saying." Rin couldn't stop her brow from creasing over her crinkled nose, but Zarus continued. "After this is over, we should ask them directly."

"You're putting off the inevitable," she countered. "If Yath Ha is telling us something that can help, we should look for it. They told me my answers lie with you, not them. That *the Two Chosen* were meant to alter Armiria's fate together, not ignore that fate until it's convenient."

Zarus scoffed. "Armiria's fate was soured long before you or I ever rolled around, Rin. By letting Eretimis live, their power damned it long before we had a say. I like my odds better through my own choices, not what some Divine tells me to do."

Rin's jaw clenched. "Don't offer me backhanded insults because I trust their word. The only reason I saved you in time was through their guidance, Zarus. The only reason you're standing free right now. I was there—I saw what we did to Eretimis standing alongside each other. Do you think that was a coincidence?"

Something akin to offense sparked in Zarus's eyes, but Rin wasn't fazed. She had seen worse.

"Those gods come and go as they please into my own thoughts. They intrude my head but only ever help when it's convenient for them. I'm supposed to just give them credit for every achievement?" He barked a laugh. "No, Rin, I don't think it was a coincidence. But the gods aren't to thank for that. You and I wielded that magic, you and I brought him to his knees. As far as I know, the gods are just using us to get rid of a threat beyond their control. Why else would they need us mortals to do their work? What they command might have merit, but they're powerless without us."

Rin forced herself to take a long breath. Her fists unraveled, but her voice was taut. "So what do you plan to do? Promote yourself to Divine and take over the commands?"

The demon's glower ran unamused. "I plan to kill Eretimis during this invasion, and I hope you'll join me because apparently we can't do this without one another. Believe me, I've tried." Rin couldn't tell if his growl was directed at her or the gods. "After that, I plan to go to Eroz and seek the gods out whether they like it or not."

Seek them out?

"How do you plan to do that?" Rin asked more mocking than intended.

"I haven't figured it out yet," he brushed off, much to Rin's annoyance. "The fae's territory on Eroz was notorious for holding a deep connection with the gods in the past. Hopefully it still does. I just need to find a way there." He paused for a moment, as if a new thought occurred. "Would you come with me?"

Rin's mouth gaped at the sudden shift in tone. It had been months since she experienced the full onset of Zarus Lowwenth, and easing back into it wasn't an option.

"Of course I'll join you," she sighed, pinching the bridge of her nose. "Eretimis needs to be taken care of one way or another. But Zarus, if we agree to do this, you need to know something." She opened her eyes, and it took every ounce of willpower not to avert her gaze. "I don't have a complete grasp of my magic. What happened at the fortress... It's still new. So much has changed since we were separated. I really think it would benefit us both to sit down and talk for a bit before we plan the death of a tyrant."

She hoped he would be understanding, that he would agree to talk and they both could catch each other up on the last half a year. Rather than sympathy, Zarus huffed one of the most exasperated sighs she had ever heard before reluctantly nodding.

"Fine, we'll talk. It's not like there's an impending invasion to prepare for. We can talk about training you while we're at it." And with that, the Shadow of Evenfall headed down the hall, scaring the life out of the humans he passed along the way.

Gods help me, she thought as she followed the stubborn demon back to his quarters. There, both of their stories from the last six months spilled out. She told a dream that still didn't feel real, and in return, Zarus shared a nightmare.

Chapter Fifty-Eight

Xandra, Zarus quickly decided, was a death pen. He toyed with a few general ideas for the invasion, but only had a plan once he saw the city layout and weighed what this *New Light* offered with his own two eyes. Eyes that ached late into the night. Eyes that had been exhausted and overworked ever since he left the fortress, come to think of it...

He studied the schematics of Xandra for so long that the designs burned in his mind. What he decided?

The cock-wrestlers who built Xandra created it with half the brain of the very cocks they wrestled.

Built in an age of peace with no thought for protection. The city sat half a day's journey on horseback from the bottom of the Damrian mountains, guarded by nothing but open fields. No walls to surround it, no forts nearby to defend it or flee to. Xandra sat in the open of eastern Nokomic's hill country, completely and utterly defenseless. He made that point very clear at the meeting he led in the dining room the next night.

Another sigh left Zarus's lips as he slouched in the rickety seat. "I've done the impossible before, but this city is a disgrace to developers around the worlds." The lanterns burned in their sconces, the flicker of flame worsening his headache.

Luna Nowell spoke shortly. "Stop complaining and tell us what we have to work with, then."

Zarus looked to Rin's mother across the table. The woman was less than fond of him, he could tell from the moment they escaped the fortress. After spending two days scraping together their saving grace, he wasn't in the mood for her piercing stare.

"We're working with a shit show," he growled. "The only reason no one's seized Xandra yet is because no one wants to deal with its civil skirmishes."

Rin frowned before Luna tore into him. "I thought you said you had good news?"

"I do," Zarus grumbled. "I have a plan that probably won't get us killed in the first five minutes."

He could have sworn he heard a cricket chirp...

"Well, that's a good start," Tatsuo admitted from his left. It was the most Zarus had heard him speak since Vi departed the previous day. "Think we could stretch it to the first ten minutes? After that, we'll probably get the hang of things."

"What is this saving grace you're so sure of?" Feyne asked from Luna's side, a yawn quickly stealing his words. Zarus didn't know much about the shifter, but he gathered the wolf didn't like being woken up so late in the night.

The woman beside the wolf shifted in her seat, her magenta eyes falling to him. "I'm sure Mister Lowwenth didn't wake us all just to complain," Scarlette mused, offering him a sharp grin. "Let the male speak so we can start discussing details."

Impatience rested beneath Scarlette's smile. An impatience that stirred alarm in the back of Zarus's head. However, fatigue pressed into her, one that sleep would never cure. Zarus smelled the infection on her the moment Rin introduced them. Yet there she sat, participating in the saving of a city while death toyed with her soul.

Zarus had volunteered to develop the plan of attack, and after refusing everyone's insight, they grew restless as the hours counted down. He sucked in a breath. He opened his eyes, but before he could speak, his vision fuzzed. A wince slipped his grasp. The jolt lasted a moment. A moment that no one missed.

"What's wrong?" Rin asked. She made to stand, but Zarus held his hand up as he rubbed away the phantom shards.

"Tired," he grunted. *It can wait.*

The sudden bursts of optic pain started a week before, but he hadn't brought it up yet, and didn't plan to.

Zarus sucked in a deep breath before continuing. "Since the New Light's supplies and arsenal are stored in the eastern district, we need a system to efficiently transport supplies to each line of defense. Luckily, the road east leads to the bottom of a narrow valley outside the city. We should be able to hold the demons at bay on that path. But the remaining three roads entering from the north, west, and south are too far from each other. Our efforts would be stretched if we covered all of them, but we would leave a main entrance unprotected if we focused on only one or two roads. We could leave the narrow east road under thin protection. However, if the invasion reaches our supplies at all, then our best bet is to flee Xandra entirely. In order to keep Eretimis out of the city and away from there, we're going to need three levels of defense."

"Only three?" Tatsuo interrupted, doing absolutely nothing to mask his disappointment. "That's a bit... lacking, don't you think?"

Zarus steepled his hands against his lips. "I'm working with all I have," he admitted, "which I remind you is—"

"A shit-show," Scarlette repeated. No humor sat in her words.

An unsettling silence shifted about the dim room.

"Our defense will be based in the sewers." Another round of uneasy glances. Zarus ignored it. "Eretimis will send his strongest demons underground and tear the city down from the inside out. Hopefully we can keep them out before they ever get in."

"Well, it's a good thing I don't mind getting my boots muddy," Scarlette smiled. She was the only one.

Feyne rested his chin on his hand. "If we succeed in keeping the demons out, then we could also use the sewers for attack."

Zarus huffed a sigh of relief as someone else caught on to his brilliant plan. "That's exactly why the underground team will also pose as an offense. The sewers let out in a stream a decent way outside the city. They're the perfect hiding place for scouts. It also gives us the opportunity to attack the demons from behind."

"But that's assuming we succeed in clearing the sewers," Luna reminded everyone. The woman leaned into the table, the lines around her eyes mirroring Zarus's somber stare. "We're going to need a plan for when they get in."

When. Zarus withheld the sigh. So little faith they had in him. Centuries spent as Eretimis's prized strategist, and this is what he got. He could have groaned. But to be fair, he was *Eretimis's prized strategist for centuries.*

"*If* they get in, our goal is to block them off. I went and looked yesterday—the sewers are fairly easy to navigate, but it's still easy to make a wrong turn."

Rin wrinkled her nose. "Is that why you came home yesterday smelling like you played in the goat pens?"

"No, Rin," Genesis mused from his side, "he smelled because of the shit-show he's been forced to run around in the last two days. He simply played in the sewers to cut the smell."

Scarlette nearly choked laughing.

"*Moving along*," Zarus shouted, "many of the structural beams holding the ceilings wouldn't stand against an explosion. We'll cut them off."

The sway of ginger strands caught his eye as Rin shook her head, her expression grim. "That's too dangerous. We can't risk lives like that."

Zarus closed his eyes. "I think Tatsuo will be more than capable of lighting the fuse from a safe distance."

The *narikaah's* shoulders slackened. Tatsuo sighed, rather unenthusiastic about being stuck in the sewers. "What are the other defenses?"

"Ground and aerial. Our greatest advantage right now is surprise, and that's going to stay our advantage. If we set up a system of trenches around the city, we could attack more safely, perhaps even cut off the demon forces for a while. Every line of defense will also be used as an offense. We'll set traps and ambush the demons every chance we get—defeat them before they know what hit them."

Another pause. Zarus glanced about the room as everyone considered his plan. It was laughable, but all they had. When the recruiters returned with reinforcements, he would let himself breathe. Yet at that moment, Zarus wouldn't waste what may be his last few.

Feyne was the first to pull himself back to reality, but his stare wasn't directed at Zarus. His golden eyes flicked to Genesis. "Bjarkh was sure to tell Eretimis everything about this city and the New Light."

Scarlette stiffened at the name of the traitor. "They'll expect resistance once they reach the city. What's our headcount coming in at?"

The prince exchanged a hesitant glance with Zarus. "Eight hundred forty-two."

"Come again?" Tatsuo blurted, cleaning his ear with a talon.

Luna's stare widened. "Those are all the volunteers?"

Genesis slowly nodded, keeping his disappointment hidden behind a mask. "After we departed for the North, Gillan sent out more emissaries around the continent, thinning the hands left to help. What's really limiting us is the fear. Half of the New Light is out of the city right now, and the other half is being told they need to fight against an army of demons. I'm surprised we have this many willing to stand and fight at all."

Eight hundred hands were theirs to guide into battle. Only eight hundred hands of the New Light were in the city and guaranteed to fight against an army of demons. If the gods truly favored him and Rin, they would send the reinforcements they needed; they could come marching in slippers and nightgowns for all Zarus cared.

"How many demons are charging for the city?"

Zarus shifted his focus to Rin; her silvery voice as mirthless as the dearly departed.

Zarus thought about it for a moment, comparing the number of Eretimis's followers on Armiria from his time at the fortress to the masses he saw gathered during the Tyrant's speech in the courtyard.

"Anywhere between twenty to thirty thousand."

A bitter scoff assaulted the silence of the night.

"How are a band of humans supposed to ambush beings that can hear us breathe from the next room over?" Scarlette's voice was frail, cracking even as she spoke. "Not to be the one pissing on our only option, but these humans are equipped to fight humans, not a demon army. It's no better than sending a child to war."

Another long, deep exhale. The throb of Zarus's head faded, the pierce of his eyes too, but the work piled up. He looked at every being sitting around the table. Dull candles danced the shadows away, a chilled breeze banged against the windows. He wished he could keep the song of silence for just a few minutes more.

"We work with what we have," Zarus finally said. "I know Eretimis better than anyone. If you trust me, I will build our only chance of survival."

Genesis stared at him for a long moment, looking for any hesitation. When Zarus offered none, the prince took over. "We have weeks until invasion day. We use every damn *second* of that time to prepare."

Without another word, Genesis rose from his seat. "We'll go over the details in the morning with Gillan and Aiden. For now, everyone should sleep. This may be the last restful night you'll get."

***

"So, what do you think?"

Zarus figured the prince followed him to his bedroom door in hopes for a private conversation, but the vague question still irked him.

Zarus halted his step. "I thought I made it clear enough what I think."

Genesis shook his head, the mask fading. "I mean what you actually think."

Zarus studied the prince in silence. What he truly thought? He supposed Genesis had the right to know.

"Xandra should be left for dead. There's barely a fae's breadth of a chance we'll hold off the front lines, much less Eretimis himself. But if we abandon the city, Eretimis will have the entire north down to Croft. We could build a temporary defense in the ruins of Zelenia, but it's too far south to securely hold Eretimis back. We're stuck between the bastard conquering half of Nokomic and dying in a fool's battle."

To Genesis's credit, he only nodded. "I'm glad to hear I'm not the only one."

Zarus nodded, already turning around and heading for his room as another pang of phantom glass pushed into his eyes. His vision blurred. Sleep. He needed sleep.

"Hey, Zarus?" the prince called before he could make it another step. Zarus saw a hand reach for him, but it never grabbed him. Genesis paused. "I have a favor to ask."

Zarus glanced over his shoulder, too tired to speak.

The prince hesitated, causing Zarus to turn completely. "After Rin convinced them to help us the other day, Aiden and Gillan pulled me aside. They said neither of them were equipped to guide this battle. They don't know our enemy well enough—or even at all. They asked if I would lead the strike against the invasion."

Zarus knew his surprise didn't make it to his face. "That must be an honor," he murmured.

Genesis rubbed the back of his neck as his stare fell. "I accepted, of course, but..." His thought trailed.

"But you're unsure whether you have what it takes."

"Something like that," the prince sighed. He forced his stare back up.

Zarus watched him for a moment, but once he was convinced Genesis had frozen solid, he spoke. "What are you asking me, Genesis?"

The prince shifted his weight. "I want you to be my general. I need someone who knows Eretimis at my side, but I also need someone I can trust."

"You trust me?"

Genesis wrinkled his nose, much the same way Rin did. "I wouldn't have left the strategies up to you if I didn't. Look," he moved on, waving his hand, "I want you as my advisor, counsel, whatever you call it. I need your help these next few weeks. What do you say?"

Zarus blinked. Trust? His mouth hung ajar as words seemed to evade him.

"I, uh," he fumbled. "I think I can do that."

A smile spanned across the prince's face. "Gods, you don't know how much you saved me. Thank you," he beamed, bowing his head. The tension locked into Genesis's shoulders eased.

Zarus couldn't help a smile forming. He bowed his head in return. "I'll meet with you in the morning to discuss what I had in mind for defense lines. I'll need to know a few things about these humans helping us before anything is set in stone."

"Of course," the prince nodded, pacing back and forth in the hall. A window overlooking the street eventually stole his focus. "If this city falls, we lose half of Nokomic. I know that, but even if that wasn't the case, I don't think we could convince anyone to abandon it. This city has been a beacon of hope for Nokomic through the last decade."

Zarus considered this as he moved to Genesis's side, taking in the frosty street chilled in starlight. Spring would be upon them before long. With it came an army.

"Hope veils the truth," he muttered, catching a glimpse of his reflection staring back at him. "It's the reason humans are so rash."

The young prince looked up to Zarus through his reflection. "I don't believe so. It's the reason humans are so strong. Hope gives them the courage to stand against a demon army. Hope gives them the strength to wake up the next day."

"I've woken up plenty of days without a shred of it," Zarus retorted.

"No, but it's hope that lets you believe Errogan will leave Eretimis."

Zarus barely held back a frown. "What are you talking about?"

Genesis shifted to face him, unfazed by the growl. "Rin told me."

Zarus rolled his eyes. Of course she did. It's not like the conversation they had the other night was private. "That's no business of yours, Genesis."

"Perhaps," he sighed, glancing back to the window. "But we're guaranteed to see him again."

Errogan was bound to be leading the charge, or part of it. There, Zarus would be forced to make a decision. So would Errogan. His chest hollowed at the thought.

Genesis sighed. "Rin let him escape when we fought him in the desert, I'm sure she told you."

Indeed she did. She also spoke of the longing for a death in his eyes she could have given him. Zarus's blood chilled at the idea, something not even he had witnessed.

"I thought she had gone mad, but when I asked her about it, all she said was that she couldn't." The prince paused for a moment, thinking aloud to himself.

"Where are you going with this?" Zarus snapped.

Genesis nodded. "If Errogan truly feels tied to Eretimis, even if he wants out, then he's not going to give out mercies on the battlefield. No one else here will give him mercy either, not after what he's done to them."

Of course Zarus knew all this! Was this supposed to be some kind of warning?

"So I'm only going to tell you this once, Zarus: if you find Errogan on that battlefield," his sapphire eyes cut to Zarus, "then go to him and do whatever you can to stop him."

Zarus's eyes widened. He stumbled for words, but Genesis found them before he could. "If you think Errogan will leave Eretimis's side, then try to convince him."

Zarus didn't understand. "Genesis..." Errogan had torn him apart for years on end. His confusion must have shown.

"I know you didn't make the portal we escaped through," Genesis explained. "You were just as shocked as me when it appeared on the balcony. I saw Errogan tucked behind the doors. I saw him nod at you."

The prince huffed, glancing back outside. "Errogan is one of the worst of them, but if you can convince him to leave, then it's one less enemy to worry about."

Zarus followed his stare. "Not all of them are as jaded as you think."

"The demons?"

Zarus's stare pierced into Genesis until the prince's temper eased.

"Genesis, you just said you trusted me. Do you think I'm the only exception? The entirety of Hraesah was taken by him through murder and force. And it's through violence and deceit that he's kept his leash on the demon race. The only reason we know about this invasion is because a demon running from Eretimis warned me. You've only seen the radical loyalists he brought to Armiria. He fed them false promises and lies of conquering land lost during a war before any of them were born. There are countless demons who live in fear of him everyday. Countless demons doing what they must to escape him, just as the users of this world are."

Genesis crossed his arms. "Are you asking me not to fight back?"

Zarus's brow creased. "Of course not. All I mean is everything isn't black and white."

The prince's tension slowly eased from his posture. "Rin would say the same thing."

Zarus looked at the frost dancing ornate designs on the glass. "Rin understands people aren't a single page to be read. They're a book full of pages and chapters and lines. She helped me learn it too."

Genesis smiled, but sighed and rubbed the exhaustion from his eyes.

"Whatever happens next, this is going to be a long month." Without saying more, Genesis walked down the hall.

"Genesis," Zarus called out, stopping the prince's step. "Thank you."

He smiled, but it faltered as another needle-pierce pushed through his eye. The world fuzzed in and out of focus. Genesis watched him, then said a short farewell before trudging off.

Sleep. Zarus just needed sleep.

Chapter Fifty-Nine

T he meeting ended well over half an hour ago, yet the lanterns in the dining room flickered with conversation.

"I tried to convince her to stay, Rin." Slumped in his chair and distracted by the flame dancing on the tip of his nail, Tatsuo sighed.

Rin's tongue ran dry. "I didn't mean to make her go away that quickly." She shook her head, feeling utterly foolish for not having thought of this before she ran to Vi's door and asked her to leave the city.

Tatsuo extinguished the flame. "She was going to leave with or without the deal. She's probably the only being that can find those users too, so it works out..."

"But..."

"But," the *narikaah* sighed again, "I feel like there was something I could have said to change her mind. About this battle, Eretimis, about us."

Rin bit her tongue. Vi was dead set on leaving the city to burn. She took a moment to wipe the sleep away from her eyes. "What did she say when you talked?"

"That she didn't want to leave me, but she wasn't going to kill herself to stay with me," he explained. "She said that if I was going to risk my life because of some *stupid tradition*, she wouldn't follow."

"Tradition?" Rin asked.

The dragon rubbed the base of his palms into his eyes. "Dragons weren't created at the same time as the New Life."

"They weren't created by Yath Ha at all, right?" she asked.

He nodded, sliding his hands down his face. "During the Divine War, Anöwe tried to create his own life to use as an army. Without the Infinite Key, he had to resort to dark magic, which turned the beings into monstrous creatures who fed on blood and nightmares. They were labeled the zylk."

Tatsuo waved his fingers for effect.

"When the New Life opposing the fallen kaeth were forced to fend off the zylk, they were sorely outmatched. Already having a good sum of these monsters to worry about in Lyhrëon, the kaeth couldn't go to the New Life's aid. So Yath Ha disclosed the location of the Infinite Key to Mynil and tasked her with creating a band of holy warriors to defend the New Life."

"And then came the dragons?" Rin asked.

Tatsuo halfheartedly snapped his finger. "Then came my crew. Protecting mortals was considered sacred to the dragons. And I, being three-fourths dragon, take that honor to heart. Just like my parents..."

Rin let the words sink in at so late an hour. "Is that why you chose to stay and fight?"

The dragon blew a raspberry at her. "Of course not, Rin. I'm here because I care about you, and Zarus, and Genesis, and your mother, and Scarlette, and even that pain-in-the-ass Feyne. I'll never turn my back on people who need help, but not because it's in my blood to do so. It's what I *should* do. And there's no way I'm turning my back on my family." He paused for a moment, closing his eyes. "Which is exactly what I told Vi..."

"What did she say?"

Tatsuo twirled another flame around his fingers. "She asked me to go with her. I said that no matter where we'd run to, Eretimis would eventually reach us. I couldn't leave my friends to fight alone. I'm needed here... We argued for a bit after that, and she left the next day."

"Tatsuo," Rin's chest hollowed, "I'm sorry."

He shook his head, eyes fixed on nothing in particular. "The thing is, I knew exactly how it would go. It's the same thing that happened when Xian asked me not to leave. But I was so wrapped up in the thought of revenge that I didn't have the sense to see what I would lose..."

Rin's heart ached. "I'm sorry." There was nothing else she could say.

A weak grin formed on his lips, and Tatsuo pulled himself upright in his chair. "It's not your fault, Red. She has her priorities, I have mine. It hurts Vi couldn't accept that, but I am proud to be here."

She stared into his yellow-green eyes long and hard. The drive to protect wasn't in Tatsuo's blood. It was in his soul.

Rin sucked in a deep breath, pushing down the knot forming in her chest and combing her hair out of her face with her hand. "I think we both need a good night of sleep," she smiled, offering him a hand. The dragon took it.

"That's the best idea I've heard all night," he groaned as he stretched his arms high. "We've got a big day ahead of us, you know."

Rin couldn't help her frown. "I didn't think leaving Aresan would mean leaving my nights of restful sleep behind."

"Look at the bright side, Sunshine," he sang as a new nickname came to his mind, "at least we're not huddling for warmth in the Northern Wastes."

And how. Even her light did little to fend off the North's chill. Rin huffed a breath as she made way for the door. Tatsuo walked her to her room so she wouldn't topple over, and she truly thought that's where the night ended. That was until she closed the door, cast a dim light, and found Genesis lounging on her bed.

"I was starting to think you fell asleep on the table," he grumbled, half asleep.

"I was starting to think I'd get some peace and quiet for the rest of my night." She slipped her shoes off and tossed them in the general direction of the closet before jumping face-first into the bed beside the prince. "Can't this wait until morning?" The pillows muffled her words.

Half asleep, the prince spoke. "I asked Zarus if he would be my second in command."

Rin didn't bother opening her eyes. "How'd that go?"

"As one would expect."

"I told you you shouldn't have asked him when he was tired and grumpy."

"Yeah, yeah. He still accepted."

"Hurray." She barely whispered.

"Can I talk to you about something before you pass out?"

"Is it something that can wait until morning?" Morning, only a few short hours away. The clock ticked. She recoiled further into the blanket.

"I think you're right; something is wrong with him."

"He's an emotionally detached demon who spent the last three hundred years in isolation, six recent months of which he endured torture. Cut him some slack."

"You should have your mom check his eyes out tomorrow."

"Mm-hmm..."

"You should also get off the blanket so I can get under it."

Whatever Rin tried to say, it was incomprehensible. Her light slowly faded and darkness took over the bedroom.

Chapter Sixty

R in preferred training at night. Maybe it was the stars high in the sky, or the ounce of quiet while the busy city slept, but something about the setting helped her find her center. After days spent training and afternoons planning, her time at night with Zarus was a breath of fresh air.

A burst of light illuminated the courtyard.

"Is Genesis still pushing for the Resurrection's help?" Rin asked, sucking in a deep breath. She held the light still for a moment, then let the magic dissipate.

"Don't hold your breath. That only causes more stress." Zarus watched her magic with calculating eyes. A hand propped under his chin, he waited until she let the light go before he answered. "He's convinced that they would be a bigger asset than liability."

After he decided what he saw was satisfactory, the demon nodded, giving Rin permission to begin her next exercise.

"And what do you think?"

Zarus flicked his crimson stare to hers. "I think an army of thieves, mercenaries, and assassins would help our efforts greatly."

Rin closed her eyes, feeling the magic in her head whirl at her call. Another deep breath, and a light appeared between her and Zarus. When her eyes reopened, her magic had taken the shape of an arrow.

Or what was supposed to be an arrow, but instead looked like a sad twig broken off a tree. She pursed her lips.

"I thought I had it that time." The light faded.

Rin stretched her stiffening arms up toward the starlit skies. "What's Gillan's take?"

Zarus huffed, eyes rolling to the back of his head. "The woman nearly burst a capillary when Genesis proposed the idea."

"I can't say I blame her," Rin admitted. "Now that we're recruiting any civilians willing to fight for Xandra, do we really need the Resurrection? The people of this city stepped up despite hearing we're standing against an army of demons. Tatsuo's training sessions with the citizens are going well. Feyne is helping any stragglers catch up. And Genesis sent word out that King Aymon's heir was stepping up to run Nokomic." A shrug rolled off her shoulders. "To spend your whole life fighting against the Resurrection, then all the sudden be asked to work with them? It could cause a lot more problems than its worth."

There was a spell of silence. Rin looked to Zarus, whose brow arched high over his unamused stare. "Yeah, it must be terrible working with people you once hated. No one would ever survive that."

Rin rolled her eyes. "Okay, sassy pants, even you hated your life until recently," she chastised, although he knew it to be a joke. "All I'm saying is I understand her hesitation."

Zarus rolled his eyes. "Tatsuo is training farmers, shepherds, and stall workers. Genesis intended that announcement to stir inspiration in the nearby villages for a few extra volunteers—not the entire kingdom. We don't have time for hesitations. Without the Resurrection's help, we're working with unqualified fodder. It's foolishness."

"No, it would be foolish to rush into a decision like this without thinking it all the way through." Rin paced back and forth along the stone walkway. "Before I left my village, my dad warned me gravely about traveling the roads of this kingdom. He told me of the things he had witnessed in Croft before he met my mother; murder, arson, thievery. It was a nightmare. He was relieved to get away when he and Ma moved to Aresan. She ran from Eretimis, but he ran from the Resurrection."

Her father still had no idea where she was, no idea what happened to her. She couldn't risk sending a letter, not with so many enemies.

Rin forced the feeling far away. *Not now. Not now...*

"I mean, I only met Vi because one of the Resurrection's members tried to sell her into slavery. I nearly burned Genesis alive because a leader was after the bounty Bjarkh put out for me. They're not people to be mindlessly dealt with." She shrugged, turning back to Zarus. "There's no telling what they would do if they learned where the New Light stores their supplies. Their hand may help us today, but what about tomorrow?"

His nightmarish stare pierced deep into her. "Tomorrow isn't a concern if today is our last."

"Today won't be our last," she breathed, extending her hand in his direction. A swirling sphere of magic appeared in the center of her palm. "Not when you and I are here."

Despite himself, Zarus smiled as he looked at her magic. He extended his own hand, palm facing the night sky next to hers. A tendril of misty shadow spiraled down his arm and hand, playing with the flares of her magic. Rin cast more light to strengthen the shadow, and Zarus pulled back the darkness to brighten the light. Two sides of a coin.

"I assume my advice is working?" he asked, dropping his arm and allowing the mist to vanish.

"Night and day, Zarus, night and day," she smiled as her own magic faded. "Even from what Tatsuo suggested, your direction has made so much more sense. I don't feel like I'm reading half a book anymore."

"I understand," the demon said, not stirring at the frigid gale that brushed past. "I nearly killed myself when I first handled magic. I studied countless human forms that only caused me stress, and even when I learned I wasn't a human, my magic never worked like the other demons I knew. It's in my mind, but it goes beyond that. It stretches down to my entire being from there. I can feel it in my bones and blood and even my thoughts." He paused, his gaze falling to the ground. "Even if it isn't traditional, use what works for you."

Rin paced around a little more. The night was cool, but warm drafts from the house circled the courtyard. "When did you find out you were a demon?"

He shook his head, graceful in the shadows of the world. "My adoptive parents found me abandoned when I was an infant. There were no signs to indicate it until..." his voice trailed.

"Eretimis..." Rin muttered.

"The only other person I've come across who understood our struggle is Eretimis. His magic is the same. He's the only reason I know how to control it."

Rin went rigid with the words. Having something in common with Zarus? She didn't bat an eye. But the Dark Tyrant? A chill seized hold of her spine.

"What does it mean? Every other user seems to work under the same rules of their kind. Why is it different for us?" She fell back into a garden chair, an uneasy swell to her gut.

"I don't know," he said softly. "It's just another question."

A frown formed across her face. The gods had claimed Zarus was her answer. Apparently not all of them. She propped her elbow on the icy table beside her, leaning her head into her hand.

"You really think we'll find answers in Milganos?" she asked.

Milganos. Land of the fae. What trouble would they find there?

Zarus looked at her for a long moment. Sometimes he looked like he was simply an extension of the night. Then another gust of wind picked up, pulling on his raven hair with it.

"I doubt it," he finally said, taking a seat on the opposite side of the table. "I think it's the best option we have right now though. You and I are something different. It's just a matter of what that concerns me."

Understatement of the year. Rin lost herself in the stars before another notion came to mind. "Do you think it would be beneficial to go to the fae in search of an alliance?"

Zarus shifted to her, although Rin focused on the constellation she was trying to recall the name of. "I thought you felt guilty making deals with the fae."

She ignored his tone and continued on. "I don't think our problems with Eretimis are going to stop after this battle. Making a grand exhibit of his presence on Armiria is one thing, but it can't be the only thing. He's after more, and having allies could help. Whatever it may be..."

"Or whoever it may be."

They shared an uncertain look. Zarus had explained to her the sliver of divine power known as the Infinite Key. Explained what it was intended for in ancient times, how it tore the first world asunder, and explained that Eretimis thought Zarus possessed it. Until Rin fought him.

So many questions, and yet Yath Ha answered none of her calls. Rin might have learned to tread through the ocean in her mind, but sometimes she drifted aimlessly atop the waves.

"Eretimis planned this invasion when I was in his possession, when he thought he had the Key in his hand." Zarus was half in thought. "Whether me or you, he knows exactly where to find the power he seeks. But he was still after Xandra... I think he's finally putting his plans into action after nearly two millennia in this world."

Rin furrowed her brow, leaning her elbows onto her thighs. "Yes, but what are his plans? What is he after?"

Again, Zarus simply shook his head, so slowly Rin had to blink to make sure she didn't loose him in the shadows. "I don't know... Which is exactly why we need to win this battle."

Before she could say another word, Zarus's jaw snapped down on a writhing expression. He pressed his hand against his eyes.

She wanted to get up, look at him, and beg him to go see her mother. There was one thing Zarus didn't tell Rin when they exchanged their stories of the last six months. Eretimis dragged him down into the shrine at the bottom of the staircase where she had found so much of that black blood.

'*He tried to make me into his monster.*'

He hadn't explained more, and clearly didn't intend to. What pain he'd experienced since... Rin had a hunch it tied together with whatever Eretimis did.

She studied the demon in silence, waiting for him to cast her a glance, but he never did. She supposed the Tyrant's intent didn't matter, supposed that she could convince Zarus to get his eyes looked at anytime. They needed to keep Xandra from falling either way. Still, the knot in her chest pulled tighter.

Why did Eretimis murder thousands without batting an eye? Why he was so desperate for Rin's and Zarus's powers.

Her magic raged like a storm.

If this Infinite Key *will get me answers, I need to learn about it...*

Chapter Sixty-One

Rin knocked lightly. It was hard to tell when the injured were resting. Thankfully, someone shouted from the other side of the door.

"Come in," Scarlette called, her voice flat and far off.

Rin cracked the door open, catching a glimpse of the scholar reading a book while she laid in bed.

"Are you busy?" she asked a bit meekly. Her mother had managed to clear the majority of infection, but Scarlette's body held tight to the rest.

Scarlette's eyes flicked up from the texts, a smile stretching across her face. "I'm always busy," she murmured, sticking a slip of paper in the book and closing it. "What can I do for you?"

Rin took the seat beside the bed. "I had a few questions for you, and a mission if you're up to it."

The scholar's interest piqued. She placed her book on the nightstand. Rin glanced at the quarters in complete disarray. Books and scrolls mostly, but Scarlette managed to put her own personal touch on the room.

Scarlette finally sat herself upright, wincing as she did, but a smile found her lips. Rin's heart warmed to see her friend back in such a spirit.

"First of all," Rin began, "have you heard the term *alentye* before? The gods keep calling me it."

Scarlette's brow creased curiously. "It's Caenlin for *light*, which isn't too difficult of a puzzle."

Rin nodded. "Next: have you heard about something called the Infinite Key?"

Scarlette pursed her lips. "It was a shard of Yath Ha's power in the old tales I think. They placed it in the first world, Fawllhä, to enrich the land. You know, help the crops grow, keep the people flourishing, and make the world a happy place. Then some mortal found it and used it to tear the world into Armiria and Eroz. I've only found it recalled here and there. Although, it holds tremendous power, and if a certain demonic tyrant had that power in his grasp..." Scarlette clicked her tongue.

"Let's assume the worst of the worst," Rin offered gingerly.

"I could go on a bit more," the scholar said with a theatrical wave of the hand, "but most people would be bored with the details."

Rin shook her head fast enough to daze herself. "Not at all! Listening to you reminds me a bit of my Da. I loved listening to him go off about the topics he studied in Croft."

A smile crept upon Rin's lips. History, literature, some of the sciences, even politics he picked up from the merchants... her father could discuss them for hours before the fireplace. A soft remorse panged in her heart, although today she couldn't help but smile at the memory.

"When did your father live in Croft?" Intrigue flickered in Scarlette's eyes.

"A little over twenty years ago. He was a scholar at one of the schools when he met Ma."

Scarlette's eyes widened. "And you never thought to mention he attended studies at the largest school in the west?"

Rin offered a sheepish smile. "It didn't come up until now."

Scarlette scoffed at the excuse. "Well, Ms. Nowell, the rope of our friendship is severed to frays."

"I'll tell you about my dad when we have more time," Rin chuckled. "I think you'd like him, he was the top of his class and whatnot. Ma would know more."

The evil faded from the scholar's smile. "So what's this mission you're sending me on?"

Rin bounced in her seat. "Right: please help me find any texts that mention the Infinite Key. Knowing about it might give Zarus and I an upper hand. And who better to shove their nose in old dusty books all day than you."

"Hmm," Scarlette hummed, tapping a finger on her cheek. "I do like old dusty books. But my super powerful scholar magic only works if I get an offering to fuel it."

Rin narrowed her stare. "What type of offering are we talking about?"

"The severed heads of my enemies," Scarlette said sweetly as her god-touched eyes fell to Rin. "Or a pie from the kitchen. Either works. We can probably worry about the enemies in two weeks."

Two weeks. Just two weeks.

Rin grabbed hold of the bedpost, anchoring herself as her head swayed.

Scarlette scooted closer. "Rin? Talk to me."

Two more weeks and this city will be a battlefield... And there's still no sight of an army.

"I'm..." Rin forced out. "I'm fine." She couldn't find more to say, and Scarlette wasn't buying it.

The scholar slid her hand over Rin's. "We're going to make it through this," Scarlette promised. "Every single one of us is going to survive, and we'll make them pay for everything they did to us in return."

Rin was a ghost outside her body. She didn't want war.

Slowly, Rin nodded and swallowed. "This week arrived a bit fast is all..."

Scarlette nodded, not taking her hand off Rin's until she calmed down. The tension drained from her head, and Rin relaxed enough to smile again. They chatted for a bit longer until Feyne and Tatsuo's bickering filled the hallway. The duo walked in, debating who had won a spar—Tatsuo, who ignited his opponent's pants with a *little* flame, or Feyne, who shifted into a wolf and headbutted his opponent so hard they both fell unconscious for two minutes.

By the time Rin gently closed the door, her head riled in the hum of magic. The days flew by since returning from the fortress. She almost didn't remember her birthday was two days away.

Chapter Sixty-Two

R in's birthday came without any commotion. Her mother gave her a breath-seizing hug, but that was it. Rin didn't hate celebrations, but she certainly thought the impending invasion was more important. *Especially* when their scouts had yet to find the demonic army marching to Xandra.

Three days before, Aiden took a scout team to scope out the northern roads. He had yet to return. Rin thought about just that, walking the dark hall alone, when a sudden creak stole her attention.

Her eyes narrowed, tracing the origin of the noise to the parlor. No one else should have been in the house. It was the workers' day off, and everyone else had errands to run. They all invited her to go with them, and she nearly accepted Genesis's offer to grab a bite to eat, but Rin couldn't bring herself to. Not with the Resurrection still after her bounty.

No one had returned from their city ventures, she would have heard the door open if they had. Rin silently crept across the ornate rug and pressed her ear against the parlor doors. The room was as dark as it was silent.

The doors swung open.

Rin's heart stopped. She screamed. A flash engulfed the room. She punched whoever grabbed her and thrashed until those hands finally released. A *thud* rattled the ornaments on the antique shelves lining the grand room. She tumbled back, landing in the dark hallway with eyes widened. One candle sparked in the middle of the parlor, followed by another, then another, until the entire room was alight. Her heart fell to her stomach.

"Surprise..." Tatsuo muttered on the polished floor where he lay with a bleeding nose.

Rin looked from person to person. Silver streamers stretched out from the chandelier; navy blue bows hugged the chairs around every table. The warm scent of cake and roasted chicken filled her nostrils. Rin's mouth hung ajar.

Luna stepped out of the crowd and into the hall with a warm smile.

"Happy birthday, dear," she hummed, slowly helping her daughter to her feet.

Rin gawked.

Genesis poked his head out from behind one of the doors. "You didn't think we'd let your birthday sneak by, did you?" Rin wanted to laugh, but then she saw his eyes. And her mother's. Bloodshot, teary. Her magic rippled through the whole room.

Tatsuo was already on his feet, smiling with the rest of them, but his face blanched of color.

"I'm so sorry, Tat," she winced, "I thought you were someone here to kill me..."

Tatsuo waved his hand. "Don't fret it, Red, you had no way of knowing."

Rin narrowed her eyes upon second thought. "Why did you grab me like you were going to kidnap me?"

The dragon's eyes immediately averted from the question. "Well, you see..."

Zarus, tucked in a dark corner away from everyone, answered. "Instead of opening the door like we told him to, Tatsuo decided to drag you in like a prisoner about to be interrogated."

"What?" the *narikaah* shrugged, "I thought it would add to the surprise."

Feyne busted out laughing, clapping her on the shoulder. "See, Rin? Don't feel bad at all. He deserved to be blasted."

Rin loosed a chuckle herself. She couldn't help it, not when the shifter was so cheery. And when the tension fled her shoulders, the cheer commenced.

Rin wasn't dressed for a party. Her faded blue tunic still smelled of the day's rainfall, not even caring to wear shoes over her socks around the halls; but no one else dressed up either.

Luna sat Tatsuo down and healed his broken nose, and Rin worked through greeting and thanking friends and acquaintances. She chatted with Aava, punched Tatsuo on the shoulder, explained what her magic can do to a curious Gillan, and then dragged Zarus into meeting the home's staff and more members of the New Light.

She couldn't stop smiling. Between the cake, the food, and the people, Rin couldn't ask for anything more. Save her father. He always made a special event of the day for her. Taking a moment alone at one of the tables, Genesis caught her smiling over the memories.

"You look blue for the star of the party," he prodded, taking a seat.

Rin couldn't stifle her yawn. "I've had so much cake I think I might explode if I move."

The prince scrunched his nose, leaning into his chair. "If that's the case, then I'll leave you be. I don't need vomit all over my jacket."

Despite the urge to retort, Rin only grinned. "You know, if you told me a year ago I would be spending my next birthday surrounded by demons and dragons and shifters, I would have walked you to our local physician."

The prince nodded, leaning his elbow onto the table. "If you told me a year ago I would be celebrating my best friend's birthday while leading my kingdom into battle, I would have laughed in your face."

Rin dragged her eyes to his, practically glowing in the candle light. "I guess we were both pleasantly surprised." When he smiled back, all of the knots in her chest eased.

Her eyes wandered around the room, looking from friend to friend as they reveled in the jaunty music. A break from doom. When her gaze fell back to Genesis, something in his hand caught her eye.

"What's that?"

Genesis glanced down to the item wrapped in stiff brown paper on his lap. "A gift. For you. Since it's your birthday."

"You got me a gift?" she grinned.

She swore red stained his cheeks. "Yeah, er—we all did, actually. Since we spent all of our funds on supplies for the trip north, we had to join forces to get you something."

A moment of silence passed. Then another. "...Can I see it or do I have to wait until later?"

Genesis cringed, realizing he had been staring. Without a word, he extended the gift.

Rin took the rectangular package. She examined it for a moment before peeling the wrap.

"You know," Genesis murmured, "people tend to be more interested with what's inside rather than out."

After one or two obscene gestures, Rin carefully pulled back the paper. However, she had to cover her mouth to keep in the sob.

The book wasn't large, but it was thick enough to keep her busy for days to come. Bound in brown leather, cracking at the edges. *Stars and Constellations: Navigating the Night.* She brought her eyes back to Genesis, speechless.

He smiled warm, the tension flooding from his shoulders. "Now you can know what you're looking at when you can't sleep."

She didn't know what to say, so instead, she wrapped her arms around his neck and held the prince tight.

"Thank you," she whispered, basking in his warmth. "Thank you." It took a moment, but he hugged back.

The commotion of the party buzzed. At some point, Swahé—the girl who always made sure the curtains were closed tight when Rin overslept—hopped on the piano and Gillan pulled out a fiddle. The music flowed through the air, fast and rapid; perfect for the people dancing in the center of the parlor.

Silence rested between Rin and Genesis, but not awkward. She sat in bliss, and he swayed his head with the melody of the piano. Eventually, she found his fingers moving with the music.

Rin nearly jumped in her seat when it hit her. "Do you play?"

Without any warning, and to her very surprise, Genesis's expression fell mortified. He tucked his hands into his pockets. "Don't even think about asking, Rin," he begged. "I haven't played in over half a century."

Rin watched the prince, wide eyes brimming with anticipation.

"No, that is not fair. Do not look at me like that. Rin, this is ridiculous. *Rin*—"

After a minute of smiling at him, the prince let out a dramatic sigh.

"Fine," he groaned. "I'll play a song for you, but *only* because it's your birthday." Rin's smirk grew, but then something wicked sparked in the prince's eyes. "*But* if I play, then you have to sing."

Rin's resolve crumbled. "Wait, no, Gen. Wait a minute, you don't have to play. I was just joking, please—"

She scrambled for excuses, but the prince of Nokomic stood up.

Pulling her to her feet, his smirk deepened. "A deal's a deal, Miss Nowell."

Rin dug her nails into the rim of the table. She nearly took the tablecloth and everything atop with her. He led them toward the center of the parlor where the piano sat on a small pedestal. She tried to wiggle free, but they already became the center of attention. Genesis finally released her next to the piano, exchanging seats with Swahé.

All eyes locked on Rin and the prince. Genesis stretched his arms out, cracking his intertwined fingers. Rin opened her dry mouth to beg one last time, but the prince slammed his fingers down before she got out a whimper.

Fine. Ice threatened her gut as she listened, quickly recognizing the merry tune, and forced the lyrics of *Over the Falls with the Seer* from her lips.

Genesis wasn't expecting her pleasant voice, that was apparent.

***

Zarus watched the party from the same corner for three hours. Studied the same stain on the table cover for half of that. He stayed for Rin, but an hour of meeting new faces and chatting about nothing with people who stared at him with discomfort had driven his mind to a dull ache. He assumed they were uncomfortable talking to a demon. Rin had a different theory.

'They talk to Tatsuo, Feyne, and Vi everyday. It's not that you're a demon, Zarus. You're just a grouch.'

He couldn't argue with that, but he was trying to be on his best behavior, per request of Luna Nowell. Zarus thought he was doing quite well, especially when Tatsuo indulged in too much wine and tried to drag him out to dance. The dragon only suffered a sprained shoulder.

Another hour drew to a close, and since no one paid him mind for some time, Zarus decided he had stayed long enough. Quietly, he rose from his silver-wrapped chair and made his way toward the door. However, a clearing throat stopped him.

"She will want to say goodbye."

Zarus glanced over his shoulder to find Luna Nowell walking toward his side.

"She'll talk to me during training tomorrow." He turned to leave, but the woman extended her foot in front of his path.

Luna's cold eyes pierced him, the lines of her face taut. "It's going to happen sooner or later."

Zarus narrowed his eyes, taking another step. Another jolt of pain ran through his head, but he bit back the wince. "I don't know what you're talking about—"

"Oh for the love of the gods, stop avoiding me and let me see your eyes," Luna snapped. "Erin is worried sick about you."

Zarus's step faltered, just enough that Luna approached again.

"Let me see what's happening to you, and after, I'll never bring the topic up again unless you wish."

Zarus nearly bit off his own tongue as another surge of needles stabbed his eye. One he could not hold back. He lurched over, glad to be out of the parlor and in the shadows of the hall.

The dark magic Eretimis instilled not only blotted his vision, but dulled his mind in the same way as when the Tyrant invaded it. Zarus was no fool. He recognized the need for concern as far back as when it started on that frozen balcony. But dying in battle would cure the spikes of pain. However, knowing the next strike wasn't far off...

Slowly, he nodded. Luna returned the gesture.

"The infirmary will do," she said, making her way through the dim house.

She led him into the small medical chamber tucked out of the way. Nothing fancy, simply a closet for basic medical attention. Aava Iver's doors were open to anyone who needed sanctuary, after all.

Zarus sat atop the worktable, feeling as though a spotlight had fallen on him. He waited for the healer to finish washing her hands in the basin across the room. After she sat down beside the table, Luna examined his eyes.

Silence was nothing new to Zarus, but his patience thinned.

"So, er... how have you taken to the city? Rin mentioned you lived in a small village west of here." Zarus's voice scraped against his throat. Even he knew that was a pathetic attempt at conversation.

Luna didn't stop her exam. "It's no different from Croft," she replied tightly. "I lived there before Rin was born."

Zarus gritted his teeth. Luna did not like him, whether because he was a demon, he worked for Eretimis, or his existence involuntarily put Rin's life at risk. He supposed it didn't matter. While she looked directly in his eyes, he kept talking.

"I don't think I've ever been to Croft."

This caught her attention. Gently turning his head to the side, Zarus did his best not to recoil at her touch. Luna picked up something like a magnifying glass and held it before his face.

"You don't think?"

"No," he admitted, following his gaze wherever she directed. "Perhaps I have been there, but it was too long ago to remember... possibly before it was named *Croft*."

"It's been named *Croft* for nearly five hundred years."

"I've walked on Armiria long enough to live in Aelius."

As if Vulyn's Hand crept out of Ashnagz to deliver Zarus to the Lord of the Afterlife himself, a weight fell over the infirmary. A deathly and sickly touch, sliding down his back and strangling his throat. His head riled.

Luna's finger tapped against the table. "I've heard the stories, Master Lowwenth. Aelius, the ancient empire that spanned half the continent. Where users thrived and conflict ended. It was the greatest civilization in the world until the Shadow of Evenfall destroyed it."

Zarus gripped the edge of the table so tight his nails dug into the surface. "I've spent a lot of time on this world, Ms. Nowell, witnessed a lot of strife and grief. Yet still I didn't learn until recently that our ghosts are ghosts for a reason. We can't lay to rest what we insist on dragging with us."

"You may find it convenient to put such havoc behind you, but others will not find it so simple." Her words were steel cutting his flesh, digging until his bones ached with their truth. "Cut a stranger's hand off, and they'll never write again."

"I can't control the world," Zarus said, perhaps a little too quietly, "only how I live in it. I don't need a stranger's reminder of how I once chose to live."

Cold and hard she looked at him. "I do not wish to keep you from choosing a better life, Zarus. I'm simply warning you. Some people won't care how hard you try. Some people will only spit on the grave, not see the person who walked away from it."

Zarus studied the healer for a breath longer. Perhaps she did look at him with disdain, but he understood it wasn't him she was looking at. It was the pieces of herself she laid to rest.

The deathly weight to the air subsided. Luna hovered her hand over his eyes, a transparent distortion emitting from her palm. The magic tugged on his skin, raising the hairs on his arms. If it was anything like the demon healers he had encountered, white mage magic searched until it found something.

The frown growing on the woman's face didn't settle his nerves. Finally, after a line of sweat beaded down the side of Luna's temple, Zarus put the healer out of her misery.

"There's nothing you can do." He didn't bother asking, there was no question. Gently, Zarus lowered her hand.

Luna's confusion remained in place. "There's nothing *to* do." The healer shook her head. "Zarus, what exactly did the Dark Tyrant do to you?"

What did the Dark Tyrant do? Zarus's lip pulled back into a snarl. Like a wave crashing into his skull, the torment of his eyes stretched to his head. The memory played over and over. Every single inch of himself being torn apart and rebuilt by dark magic.

Zarus spoke as cold as the winter that had passed. "He performed some form of dark magic. He tried to erase my memories and create a blank page to work with, but I didn't let him." He paused, only then feeling the frost creep along his fingers, the breath clouding at his lips. Luna shifted beneath the glacial air.

"He used dark magic and a vial of blood. I don't know what the intent was..." Zarus pressed a hand against his brow, sudden exhaustion overtaking him. "It felt like he was ripping me apart piece by piece. I was thrown in the dark, left to rot before... before he put me back together." It suddenly became clear. Eretimis tried to rebuild him. But build what exactly?

Another swell of silence.

Luna scooted an inch closer on her stool. "How did you escape?"

He would hardly call it an escape; the stab of his eye reminded him so. He leaned his head against the wall behind. "I took hold of the magic he used against me, and I made it my own."

The healer leaned back too, exhaling. "I don't know about dark magic, Zarus, but your eyes are a very curious matter. My magic detects nothing out of the ordinary in them, nothing that it can heal. Yet something isn't right. A shadow lingers inside of them, and when the pain flares, the shadow thrives... I'm sorry, but I don't believe I can help. Eretimis used that magic to change something in you, and though it might not have done everything he wanted, a piece of that magic embedded."

Zarus listened with a steady head. Frankly, he wasn't expecting anything different. Eretimis hadn't won, but he partially succeeded. It was no different from any other experience he had with the Tyrant. Still, his chest hollowed.

Zarus opened his eyes and found Luna watching him. "If you're looking for tears, they dried out centuries ago."

The healer did not throw a retort. "If you said that you were able to take control of the magic Eretimis used, then perhaps you can do it again with this remnant. Try to suppress the magic. It could be concealed to a certain degree, one that might prevent the pain. Until you figure that out, I can give you a tonic to ease the surges."

Zarus nodded. Luna prepared herbs for the tonic across the room, leaving him to gather his thoughts. He needed to discover how to take hold of the lingering magic and force it back. Who knew, he might even figure out how to remove it entirely. Yet it would take time. An invasion still loomed over the city.

He uttered his gratitude as Luna handed him a bottle of the dark green tonic.

"Take it when you wake up, and it will hold you for the rest of the day. Tell me if the pain persists. Also..." Luna added, her mouth pulling to one side, "I suggest taking it with honey or the morning brew to conceal the taste."

Despite himself, Zarus cracked a grin.

Before he took a step out of the infirmary, a stampede raged in the house. People shouted, zipping past the doorway. A blur of ginger hair rushed around the corner and skidded to a stop.

"There you are!" Rin heaved. Luna ran to her daughter's side, but Rin barely caught her breath before continuing. "Aiden just returned with Elyot Iver and a handful of users." Her emerald eyes narrowed on Zarus. "Eretimis's army is three days away."

Three days. That was sooner than they anticipated. His expression flattened. However, Rin's stare faltered.

Luna cupped the girl's face. "What else?"

"I—" Rin choked. "Da's with them."

Chapter Sixty-Three

Chapter Sixty-Four

"He's lying"

Disbelief carved Genesis's expression. "What on Armiria are you talking about, Zarus?"

Rin's nose wrinkled at the very thought. "Why would you say such a thing?"

Zarus had approached her and the prince with a shadow in his eyes the moment the meeting adjourned. Something pried at his mind and he didn't waste a moment before dragging them both into the nearest empty study.

Zarus's expression didn't flinch, nor did his eyes tear away from Genesis. "No demon in Eretimis's army would have thought a living soul was dead. No matter how battered he was. Aiden Iver was the only one left alive for a reason."

A cold fire burned in Zarus's eye, one that melted the scoff right out of Rin's throat.

"Even demons overlook things," she disputed. Genesis shared her confusion, but his was not so calm. The prince had gone rigid, and Zarus sensed it.

Genesis's voice was taut. "Eretimis likes to spread fear. It wouldn't be out of the ordinary to leave a survivor and announce his arrival if he thinks we can do nothing about it."

The demon drew his lips into a straight line. "His hunters wouldn't mistake the living for dead. Eretimis is unaware we know about the invasion, and wouldn't spoil that with an announcement." Zarus paused, making an honest effort to speak calmly. "Genesis, I know Eretimis. I know how he works and the games he likes to play, but this doesn't sound right to me. Please, send out another search team, but keep it between us—"

Genesis almost barked a laugh. "Send out another team? The likelihood of this city being attacked at the end of the week is far greater than your hunch! Our hands are overflowing with the work that still needs to be done. I can't risk sending out another team when everyone is needed here."

Zarus narrowed his bloody stare. "Then send me. I can go alone and find the army for myself. If everything is how Aiden Iver said it is, I'll be back in two days."

Genesis snapped. He slammed his fist on the desk beside him. "Did you not hear me? I can't afford to send *anyone* out! Least of all you, Zarus! Or would you rather throw everything we've worked toward away and demolish the city ourselves?"

Zarus stood still as stone. Years of reinforced restraint held his resolve.

Rin was just as incensed by his accusation, but she couldn't afford to yell at the demon too.

"Zarus," she said calmly, "I don't think you need to worry about Aiden. He doesn't have a reason to lie about the armies."

Zarus shifted his stare away from the prince. Sure enough, the ice he crafted his words with thawed. The lines of his face softened.

"Rin..." The words were lost to his throat.

"You've been under a lot of stress lately," she said. "We all have. The bags under your eyes suggest you haven't slept much either. I'm not saying you shouldn't listen to your gut, but I'm asking you to deeply consider if you're simply on edge because of the situation at hand."

Zarus exhaled slowly. That was until he caught another glimpse of Genesis's fist on the table, and a scowl crept across his face. The dim study sat stiller than a graveyard, but the walls around Zarus darkened so that not even the moonlight cast through the window illuminated the shelves and desk.

"I agreed to work with a tyrant once before, Genesis. Make sure I didn't make the same mistake twice."

Zarus moved to the door amid the veil of shadows. However, Genesis charged for the demon in the same breath.

Rin's heart hammered. She grabbed the prince's arm and intercepted what was sure to end in blood. Zarus was already out the door before Rin swung Genesis face first against the wall. It seemed her mother's lessons still ran fresh despite the months that had passed.

"What in the Flames has gotten into you!" she shouted. His face pressed against the wall as she held his wrist in one hand and bent his other arm behind his back with her other.

He seethed. *"Let me go."*

Rin dug her heels in. "Not until you calm down."

The prince tugged to free himself from her, but Rin found herself with more leverage. Only when Genesis stopped trying to break away from her hold did she let go. Her heart beat like a drum.

A moment of quiet passed. Then another, and another. Until Genesis had finally caught the breath he lost in his rage. Moonlight drenched the room, his eyes glimmering like a torch.

"You're stronger than the last time we sparred," he offered weakly. However, Rin did not accept the jest. "Rin, you have to understand—"

She held up her hand.

Something moved at his lips, but no words came out. Rin turned around without a word.

"I'm sorry," Genesis said quietly.

She halted, narrowing her gaze on the dark grain of the door. "For what?"

The prince sucked in a deep breath. "For losing control of myself."

Rin peered over her shoulder to find Genesis staring out the door where Zarus had disappeared. He pressed his lips together in a straight line.

Rin turned toward him, crossing her arms against the chill of the study. "Don't get me wrong, he was an ass too. But you were in a foul mood from the beginning of this conversation."

He took a moment until he found a sufficient answer. "I'm seventy years out of date here, but Gillan, Aiden... They accepted me and placed their trust in me. Implying one of them is up to something so treacherous..."

Rin nodded, her stare falling to the floorboards. "Zarus came to you with a serious concern, and whether or not he's overthinking it, you tried to attack him."

A flicker of his anger swelled. "He compared me to *Eretimis*. Am I supposed to ignore that?"

Rin's nose scrunched. "Of course not! But you weren't just going to punch his face, Gen... We can't turn on each other so easily."

Hearing it aloud, Genesis sunk into the upholstered chair before the desk. "Suppose you have a point... He's jumping to conclusions. Years of dealing with the Dark Tyrant has left him scarred."

"Of course it has. Just like you. Things like that don't just go away; you know that more than anyone." She huffed a sigh, her head beginning to swirl. "I'll talk to him before I go to bed, try and calm him down enough to reconsider his claims."

It was the absolute last thing she wanted to do, but if it saved another argument, it was worth the lost sleep. She turned away, but a hand pulled her back.

"No," Genesis muttered, "I'll talk to him. Go sleep; you'll need it tomorrow when you catch your father up to speed."

Rin smiled, but Genesis held her hand.

He raced for something to say. "Thank you."

Chapter Sixty-Five

Distant thunder rumbled the walls of the hallway Rin walked through. She frowned when she glanced out the window. The dull morning brewed ominous clouds from the east. More rain.

"It's a good thing we finished the trenches yesterday," Genesis muttered from her side.

Rin huffed her agreement as they made their way to the great hall of the Iver Estate. "The ground was difficult enough to dig through," she said.

Despite Spring's arrival, each morning was greeted with frost. She opened her mouth to ask Genesis when he planned on leaving for the storage warehouse the New Light operated out of, but she nearly crashed into Elyot Iver when they turned the corner to the great hall. Genesis grabbed her elbow before they collided.

Rin straightened her tunic as she addressed the commander. "Master Iver, I thought I saw you leave the house already."

Elyot smiled, the lines around his eyes tugging. "I did, but came back for Genesis." A shadow suddenly cast over the commander's face. "We received word from Damrok this morning."

Rin felt Genesis tense at her side. "And?"

Rin knew the answer from Elyot's expression. "They're not sending aid," she breathed, sparing the commander of the strife.

"The same message we received from Melde," Elyot huffed, pulling out the letter from his jacket. "Damrok said they had no qualms with this *mythical* army, and seeing how our alliance hasn't been made official yet, they're not sending their men to fight and risk upsetting this *mythical* army."

Genesis wrinkled his nose. "They said mythical twice?"

Elyot nodded. "It seems the Damrian Republic doesn't believe our claim of demons."

The Damrian Republic, a counsel of seventy-five members making the decisions for its people. Rin needed to thank her father for making her study politics all those years ago.

"They believe it enough to cower in their state walls," Genesis muttered. "They're waiting to see how this pans out before making a decision of who to side with. Melde too."

Rin still couldn't believe it, even after Zarus suggested it. Could a human society ally with Eretimis? Was it possible to be that blind to his brutality? Or perhaps, blinded by greed of power...

Rin swallowed. The Dark Tyrant's depthless eyes swelled in her memory. She looked to Elyot, biting the inside of her cheek. "We could ask the Resurrection."

Elyot's expression fell. He was no easier to convince than Gillan, but with their backs pinned against the wall by thirty thousand demons...

Rin spoke before the commander could comment. "I know what the Resurrection has done. But when this city goes up against the Dark Tyrant, it won't only be us struggling. It will be the Resurrection, it will be the citizens who were too stubborn to listen a month ago and leave. Red will run in the streets, and then it will be impossible to tell whose side it belongs to. An alliance will show Damrok and Melde how grave the situation is. If joining together could help us withstand the demons long enough for more help to arrive, isn't it worth considering?"

The honored, beloved commander of Nokomic stared wordlessly at her for a long moment. Rin never learned what drove him to start the New Light, but she had heard rumors it was terrible. The Resurrection was the sole place he directed his rage afterward.

This wasn't a war against humans; this was a new enemy intent on killing them all.

"You've sought peace for over a decade. Here's your best chance for it; don't let pride be Xandra's end." The words fled Rin's tongue before she thought to stop them.

Finally, Elyot Iver opened his mouth.

***

"Erin Nowell, I could kiss you."

Rin sat beside Genesis on the edge of her bed. Hours had passed since Elyot agreed to send a letter to the Resurrection heads, and she still couldn't believe she convinced him. She had nearly broken her arm sparring with Tatsuo that afternoon, her head lost in the wonder.

"It's likely we won't get any support from them," she said. Her stare lingered on nothing in particular. "Even on the slight chance the leaders agree, the demons are only two days away. That's barely enough time to organize their men."

"So?"

"*So?*" she repeated. "We're right back to where we started, *Your Highness.*"

The prince laid on the bed, crossing his arms behind his head. "That's not the point, *Alentye.* You convinced the leader of the New

Light to offer an alliance with the very group he's working to destroy. Madness as it might be to ask, the act might save our skins. Neither I nor Zarus could convince him. But you did." One of his eyes gleamed open. "You're something extraordinary, Rin."

Rin couldn't help the heat from her face. She looked at the smile on his lips.

"I..." The words evaded her tongue, lingering just out of reach. She unraveled against that damn smile. Her hands dug into the blanket below. "Gen, I..."

Slowly, the prince sat upward, his gaze ensnared on her eyes, then on the edge of her lip. He drew close, so close the warmth of his breath caressed her cheeks. She sucked in a breath.

"I wasn't lying..." his voice brushed her ear, stirring the butterflies in her stomach. His lips slid fragments away from her cheek until they hovered a breath from her own.

Rin leaned in, closing the gap to a hair's breadth. She flicked her gaze to his eyes, back to his lips. A moment unending, they waited. Looking further into one another than ever before. Her hand slid toward him.

"Rin," he whispered, and it took everything she had not to fall in.

"Yes?" She pulled her eyes back to his, radiant and beautiful as the promise of light.

"Can I kiss you?"

Her heart hammered. That question. Her magic swirled inward, cresting against itself as she dug her fingers into the blanket. So close. He was so close and she wanted him closer.

Yes, you may.

You better.

Took you long enough to ask, Your Highness.

Yes. His head tilted to fit against her, the strands of his dark hair tickling her cheek. *Yes.* Rin parted her lips. *Yes.*

"No."

The word was an anchor, weighing down so hard she winced against it. Genesis's eyes tore open. No disappointment, no shock, but his gaze hardened. Slowly he pulled away, turning to the wall they sat facing.

Her heart raged against the distance between them. Her magic crashed against her mind. She wanted it, more than anything she wanted him and wanted to be more than this with him. But...

"Gen..." she breathed, unable to look him in the eye. "You mean more to me than controlling my magic, more than saving this city..."

Rin closed her eyes against the tears creasing them. When they reopened, his glassy stare focused on the ground.

"You don't have to explain yourself," he said gently. He glanced in her direction, looking right through her as he forced his lips into a smile.

She bit down on the tremble of her voice. "It's not that I don't want this. I want..." the words slipped her grasp, only reeled back with a sharp pain in her throat. "I don't know what I want. There's so much going on right now."

Her tears streamed, cupping her chin and trickling onto her blouse. "Between this invasion, Eretimis, the gods—I'm so confused and I don't know what is going to happen next. I—" She couldn't hold back the crack of her voice. "I can't do this right now."

Silence overtook her bedroom—silence that left her empty.

Genesis sat motionless. She watched his chest rise and fall in deep breaths. The clock on the mantle ticked until an eternity passed, waiting. One more breath and the prince slowly rose to his feet. She opened her mouth, tried to reach for him, but her body didn't obey. Silently, Rin watched from the corner of her eye as Genesis walked to the door.

"Genesis," she cried. He already had one foot out the door. She forced herself to look at him. "I'm sorry."

The prince convinced another weak smile onto his lips, pushing the pain from his expression.

"There's nothing to be sorry about." He walked out the door.

Chapter Sixty-Six

"It doesn't make sense, Tatsuo," Zarus grumbled into the mug at his lips. "No demon would confuse the living for dead." The ale was bitter against his tongue, but it was comforting in the cold draft of the tavern.

The tavern had brimmed with nightlife only a handful of days before, but now sat barren of warmth amid the invasion evacuations. No candles danced on the chandelier; no fire blazed in the hearth. The owner of the establishment fled the city at the beginning of the week, leaving an empty bar sitting behind a fragile lock.

After a long day of finalizing strategies, Zarus gladly accepted Tatsuo's invitation to the no-longer-locked tavern. The two had spent the better part of an hour chatting before Zarus shared his thoughts on Aiden Iver's story, something he had kept to himself after telling Rin and Genesis.

"Maybe if the demon had drunk as much as you have, he would." Tatsuo retorted, pouring himself another mug behind the bar.

Zarus glared at the *narikaah* across from him. "You think I'm overreacting."

Tatsuo offered a dry glance. "You'd take the crown of overreacting, Zarus," he said, swallowing his glass in one go then wiping his mouth. "These humans are preparing for a war against myths."

"What's your point?" Zarus scoffed.

"*My point,*" the dragon enunciated, his tone dripping with exasperation, "is how should a human who learned demons were real a month ago know anything more than what they've been told. If Aiden said the demons thought he was dead, then he must have believed they thought he was dead."

Zarus pinched the bridge of his nose. He couldn't tell if the throbbing in his head was from the ale or the sleepless nights.

"Shouldn't they expect more?" He wiped the exhaustion from his face. "Humans don't need to personally meet us to tremble at the name. It doesn't make sense that Aiden was left alive. Hunters don't make those kinds of mistakes."

"Maybe their final strike didn't kill him like they thought it would. You saw the bandages around his neck."

"You can still hear a beating heart even if its bleeding out," Zarus grumbled.

It was Tatsuo's turn to sigh. He leaned his elbows onto the bar and looked Zarus directly in the eye.

"Look, Zarus, you're overworked and stressed, but so is everyone else. Aiden has spent his entire life helping his father reunite this kingdom; there's no motivation in burning it. Instead of accusing him of treason, see his life for the blessing that it is. We would have been struck on our blind side if he didn't return to announce the invasion was only days away. And the more you let your paranoia fester in this made-up problem, the more you're working yourself up about nothing. We have a war to fight. Stop making enemies out of allies."

Shock widened Zarus's eyes. He stared at Tatsuo for a moment, unsure of what to say. He had spent his entire life distrusting his allies. It was very likely he developed a bad habit over the years. Yet he still couldn't ignore the swell of dread in his gut. Something didn't line up with Aiden's report, or even Elyot and Adrian's run-ins; Eretimis's armies were leaving traces. None of these humans understood the brutality of Eretimis's loyalists. Leaving a witness alive wasn't a mistake the Tyrant allowed.

But that's not Aiden's fault.

Dropping his stare to the counter, Zarus rubbed his eyes with the palms of his hands. "I suppose you might be right."

Tatsuo's reptilian eyes rolled to the moon and back. "Duh. Now go tell that to Genesis. You two not speaking to each other at a time like this is the stupidest thing that's happened since I walked away from you and Rin in the Lennaels. No wonder you've both been in piss pour moods lately."

A reply was sharp on Zarus's tongue, but it faltered in his throat. He fell silent, eventually catching a furrowed brow from the *narikaah*.

"What?" Tatsuo asked.

Zarus searched for the words. "I'm sorry," he spoke softly, bringing his stare to Tatsuo's. He shook his head and found the words he had been thinking for half a year.

"I apologize for what I said in the Lennaels. I told myself I was protecting you, but I was just trying to limit the lives I needed to protect. It was selfish. And it wasn't true; you never needed to be protected. I envy your strength, and the humans are lucky to have you in their ranks." He weighed his next thought. "Your parents would be proud."

Tatsuo's eyes didn't widen, nor did his expression tighten. He stood straight behind the counter and briefly watched Zarus before speaking.

"Thank you," he grinned. "Besides, I'm glad I came to my senses and ignored you. Not only did I find Rin, but..." his smile softened, and his stare fell to the empty mug in front of him. "I have a family again. I was blinded by revenge for so long, but now I have more to offer the world than blood lust. It's what my parents sought when they escaped Eroz to begin with."

The wind outside blew hard against the thin windows. Zarus carefully asked, "You're no longer interested in revenge?"

Tatsuo's stare sobered. He drew in a level breath. "What answer are you looking for?"

A sullen silence roamed the desolate tavern. It seemed the wind blew louder. Zarus shifted in his seat, knowing he stepped one foot too far. "I didn't mean to—"

"I don't know what I feel toward Errogan anymore," Tatsuo interrupted, staring at nothing in particular. He tapped his sharp nails on the polished counter like a tune was stuck in his head. "He followed the order to kill my parents. He nearly killed all of us six months ago. I should hate him, but what will damning him accomplish?" He trailed off in thought before exhaling. "I pity him."

Zarus shook his head. "Why?"

The dragon tilted his head from side to side. "It sounds like he's stuck from what you've said. Eretimis has a way of getting into people's heads, manipulating their pain to do his bidding. It happened to you, and it happened to myself." Tatsuo's gaze eventually landed back on Zarus. He shrugged. "Maybe you can be the one to get him unstuck. I'll take up my complaints then."

A draft found its way through the gaps under the door.

"It's pointless," Zarus said, rising from the bar stool. "Errogan believes he has no choice of his own."

Tatsuo considered this as he walked out from behind the bar. "People like you and I can help others realize they always have a choice. Some are just more stubborn than the rest." Tatsuo offered a wry grin.

The two of them walked across the creaky floor until they stood at the door. Once the life of the street, the establishment was now comparable to the ruins of a temple. He watched the dark street for a moment. People gathered here and there, candles lit in the windows. It was all he could do to glower at the foolishness of humanity. Tatsuo's sigh paused his step.

"I didn't understand why Rin allowed him to live for the longest time," the dragon said quietly, and Zarus wasn't sure if it was meant to be heard or not. "It took me until we rescued you to realize she saw something no one else did. Errogan is fighting against Eretimis just like the rest of us."

Zarus stalled in the doorway. The windy night stirred a cool air, but the sky was speckled with stars. Human ale or not, he hadn't had a drink in centuries, and his head swayed in the moonlight.

"I envy your strength, Tatsuo. War wouldn't ravage our worlds so often if more people had hearts like yours."

Laughter erupted from his side, and Tatsuo's arm patted him on the shoulder with enough force to stumble his step. "Keep talking like that and everyone will realize how much of a softy you actually are." He chuckled as he helped Zarus walk back to the Iver Estate.

Chapter Sixty-Seven

"Everything's moving slow in this district," Rin muttered in the pale moonlight.

Zarus watched her glance over the edge of the roof, her foot a little too close to the gutter.

"Take a step back before I have to scrape you off the road," he sighed.

She glared, this century's obscene gesture fluttering off her hand. Zarus focused on the street below.

"Evacuation warnings went out weeks ago," Zarus sighed, taking a step closer to the drop off. "These are the people who ignored them because they're too worried about their belongings to save their lives."

"But Elyot turned it into an order this morning," Rin sighed, pacing back and forth. "So why are they trudging their feet?"

The burly man sitting behind Zarus rustled. "Because they don't want to leave," Adrian Nowell commented. Zarus cast a half glance toward the forest-eyed Nokomai.

"But why?" Rin pressed. "Don't they understand how dangerous it is to be here?"

Zarus loosed a sigh, feeling his temper as stretched as the New Light's capabilities. When Genesis asked Rin and him to help with the evacuations, he knew that the prince had truly become desperate.

He fully intended to say no. If Rin hadn't agreed for the both of them before he could answer, he wouldn't be wasting his time. The argument with her wasn't worth the headache.

He glanced back to the slow progress. "They're figuring out how much they can carry." Rin traced his stare. Carts and carriages cluttered the road, men and women dressed in the finest of clothes rushing out of their mansions with chests and cases.

Rin fidgeted with the sash tied to her belt. "They need to be out by sunrise... the demons could be here at any moment. Why won't they just—"

The girl couldn't finish her thought before the world erupted.

The ground trembled, the buildings rocked back and forth, and Rin very nearly tumbled off the roof. Her father lunged forward and pulled her back to safety while panic spread like the plague below.

Horses bucked, taking off without their owners to guide them. Screams, shouts. Zarus's heart thundered with the madness. Before he lost himself in the ice creeping along his spine, he forced the breath in his lungs out. Calm settled in his mind.

"What on Armiria was that?" Rin heaved.

"A quake in the earth?" Adrian asked, helping his daughter to her feet.

The stench of burning wood roamed into Zarus's nose. He hoisted himself onto a chimney behind, searching the cityscape until his eyes settled on a cloud of obsidian smoke spiraling into the distant western sky. As if on cue, a New Light sentinel pulled himself onto the roof.

The watchman gasped as he directed Zarus from the base of the chimney. "Sir, demons have been spotted slaughtering Nokomai in the western stretch of the city!"

Zarus jumped down and walked to the edge of the roof facing the billowing smoke. "*How* in all the realms of Ashnagz did a group of demons sneak into the city?"

Rin's pale face swallowed a dry breath. "Better question is how an entire army snuck up on the city without being noticed."

Adrian followed suit. "It's Zelenia all over again."

Panic shook the watchman's head. "I haven't the slightest idea where they came from, they just started—"

Zarus didn't care to hear excuses. "Take over the evacuation. Make sure the people get out of the city and head to safety with the others." His voice fell low.

Xandra would fall in fire. He should have known... What other visions had the gods sent to warn him six months ago? He didn't take his eyes off the orange flames staining the horizon. A knot clenched in his chest. Rin placed a hand on his forearm, a flare of magic lighting her palm.

"Sir?" The watchman hesitated.

Zarus sucked in one last breath, casting a glance over his shoulder. "What?"

"What if these people still won't leave, sir?" The sentinel glanced to the street below. Panic raged, yet people still ran into their houses for more belongings.

Ice crept along Zarus's fingers. "Don't give them anything more to take."

"How do I do that?"

"Burn the houses."

***

Rin ran faster down the road; against the fleeing crowds and toward the raging fires. The breath in her lungs stung like pins and needles. All because Zarus decided to jump off the roof and take off without a word. A rush of urgency consumed her. She nearly forgot to hug her father goodbye when she told him to go find Ma and any healers they could muster.

Rin sprinted to catch up to the mania coursing through the streets of Xandra on her own.

The air grew hotter with each step. It wasn't until she turned the corner and nearly rammed into a frenzied group of bystanders that she understood.

Her lungs spasmed against the smoke and debris dust. Shops, taverns, inns, homes. The street laid in ruin of what it used to be. Rin ripped the sash from her belt and tied it around her mouth and nose. She couldn't keep track of the corpses. Smashed under debris, torn apart piece by piece. So many bodies littered the crumbled cobblestone.

Bile scraped her throat. It was too familiar.

"Get out of here!" Rin shouted through the nausea. The gawking bystanders jumped at her call. "Head south and get out of the city—"

Another explosion ignited at the end of the street. The force threw Rin back with a thud on the stone. Her ears rang, her skin stung with scrapes and bruises. She crawled to her feet in a daze. When her vision cleared, she was met with a wolf and god-touched eyes.

"F-Feyne?"

The shifter's eyes were set ablaze in the fire light. He glanced at her for a split second before a blur of grey skin erupted from the burning debris. Feyne caught the snarling beast in his mouth.

The creature scraped and snapped its yellow teeth at Feyne's neck, but the shifter held the lean monster in place long enough for an arrow to find its skull. The lone creature fell limp, and only when the final leg twitched did Feyne let it hit the ground. Its murky eyes faded brown.

Nausea swelled in Rin's stomach. Black blood pooled from the beast's head at her feet.

"*Alentye*," Scarlette said in a low voice, "we're with you." Rin glanced at the bow in her grasp. The scholar held herself stiffly.

"Where did you come from?" Rin whispered.

Scarlette drew another arrow from the quiver on her back as she turned her attention to the surrounding madness. "We were monitoring the evacuation."

The scholar's eyes narrowed, searching until she shot an arrow clean through the smoke. A moment later, the husk of another beast crashed to the ground across the street with an arrow through its head.

Rin watched the creature lying still. The same beasts that attacked her outside the temple. She waited for the creatures to draw energy from one another and heal, but they remained on the ground. Someone screamed down the road.

Another beast sprinted out of the burning bakery behind. A light that dulled the raging fires consumed the two-legged beast. The monster hissed, shielding its eyes with its arms. Rin burned its soul until there was nothing but ash left.

Rin panted. "What happened?"

"I smelled something," Feyne said grimly as he sniffed the air. She hadn't even noticed he shifted back, wearing a cloak to cover his bareness. "Not human. Scar and I investigated, and found Nikolai Druvisk talking to someone..."

The most infamous of the Resurrection leaders, the head of the Assassin Guild.

Scarlette pointed to her eyes. "He was talking to a demon disguised as a human."

"Disguised?" Rin repeated. "How is that possible?"

"Magic," Scarlette answered.

"Druvisk noticed our attention and disappeared into the crowd," Feyne watched the barren street for survivors, finding none. "His friend ran to the sewer... The explosion went off seconds later."

Rin's chest hollowed. Tatsuo... he was supposed to be securing the sewers.

Deep breaths, Rin. Calm down. Calm down calm down calm down.

In and out she forced the air, until the magic in her head no longer thrashed.

"How did demons get inside the city? We had the entire place guarded under lock and key for the whole month. It doesn't make sense!"

"Perhaps you should check your locks."

The voice behind turned Rin's gut to liquid. She spun around and drew her scimitar in the same breath. The silver sword showed bright at Errogan's hip, perched high atop the debris.

"I should have known you'd be the first to strike," Rin spat. Her magic boiled. "You couldn't resist a drop of blood to save your life."

She waited for the taunts from the arrogant prick who drank her suffering like wine. The demon who slaughtered all of Base and strung Scarlette a fae hair's breadth away from death. Yet Errogan seemed estranged from the chaos, his expression grim.

The demon barely opened his mouth before Feyne tackled him as a bare *ghren*.

Feyne dragged Errogan down from the ledge of crumbled bricks and into the veil of smoke. Scarlette ran after, an arrow strung in her bow. Rin followed, but when she passed through the ashen curtain, she found Feyne on top of the demon, bashing his face with his fists over and over and over. Skin bruised and split, blood welled. Errogan landed awkwardly on the rubble beneath him, stunning him.

Over and over Feyne beat down on the White-Cloaked Reaper, and over and over Errogan's eyes rolled back.

Rin shouted for Feyne, but she couldn't hear her own voice over the inferno. Not even Scarlette's voice struck, but the woman didn't move once she saw who was on top.

Rin bit down on her tongue hard enough to well blood. Errogan... he *deserved* to die. Just as he had on that day in the desert when she held a blade to his throat. She had lowered that blade. Something in the way he looked at her. And here, through the blood and bruises, she saw it again.

He never budged, never flinched to kick the shifter away. He welcomed the pain, welcomed the blood. Zarus claimed the only reason he was a free male was because Errogan helped him, that something inside this demon rebelled against Eretimis. Yet here he was, leading the strike on Xandra.

Rin sucked in a deep breath.

Light sparked the ruined street, like lightning veining through the storms. No pain, no heat, but brighter than the flames roaring around. Bright enough that Feyne was blinded. He yowled, tumbling back as he rubbed his eyes. Scarlette knelt to his side, removing the cloak on her shoulders and draping it over the naked *ghren*. Her bow still held an arrow.

Slowly, the demon on the ground stirred. He dragged his hand over his face. A bitter cackle escaped his throat, a splash of crimson spraying from his lips in the same breath. "Six months did you well, Wulfan."

"I wouldn't test him if I were you. It's a surprise you're still speaking after that."

Zarus's voice echoed through the ruins before he stepped through the berth of smoke.

A weak smirk crossed Errogan's swelling face. "I'm inclined to ask how long you've been standing there, but have a feeling I won't like the answer."

Zarus stalked across the street and met Rin's side. She glanced back to Feyne and Scarlette, and found nothing but rage pooling in the shifter's eyes.

"Give me one reason not to tear you apart," Feyne growled.

Errogan couldn't even muster a smile, only a sigh of a laugh. "Is this the part where I cower and retreat?" The demon mused as he sat upright, an eerie humor to his tone. Rin tried not to shutter when that crystal stare pierced into her.

"No," Zarus said flatly, taking a step between her and the demon on the ground, "this is when you tell us what's going on."

"You're going to have to be more specific than that," Errogan huffed, gesturing to the burning city.

An arrow pierced Errogan's shoulder. His face contorted as he plucked it out, but Scarlette released another into the dirt inches from the demon's head as he stood. "Where's the invasion?"

The realization rattled Rin's bones. The chaos had been contained to only a few blocks. Two explosions, not even spanning the entire neighborhood. She looked behind to where the beast had fallen dead at Scarlette's arrow. The street was quiet outside.

"We would've received word that your army was on our doorstep," Rin breathed. "You're not putting up any fight..."

Errogan looked as if he planned to speak, but an unearthly shriek from behind interrupted him.

Rin's skin crawled. A silhouette loomed behind the ember smog, lurking closer until a beast stood behind Errogan. Swaying from side to side, balancing on two legs, Rin watched the creature silently examine everyone present. Greyed, bleak eyes scanned over her, the snout of a bat rapidly inhaling. Its bare, clawed feet stuck out of the unpolished armor covering its grey body.

"*H-hoomaan*," the beast heaved, no better than a rusted croak. "*Hoomaaan*," it said again, pointing a crooked finger in her direction.

Rin stared into its empty eyes, her spine chilling. "What?" she forced herself to ask.

"*H-h-hoomaann*," the beast mindlessly panted. It's head jerked in all directions, its short nose huffing. It tried to take a step forward, but Errogan held his hand up and stopped the beast.

"Eretimis was right," Errogan shrugged, intrigue cutting through his somber demeanor. "His Mighty's finest trackers are never incorrect. Congratulations, Nowell, you're officially the holder of unimaginable divine power."

"Trackers?" Rin repeated, looking the beast up and down.

"Best trackers in the mortal realm," Errogan nodded over his shoulder to the creature. "Made by Eretimis's very magic."

Zarus shifted beside her, but kept his thoughts to himself. After a short moment, he directed Feyne instead. "The New Light already set out to combat the *trackers* attacking the civilians when I left them at the explosion site. The fires are contained to this street, everyone able already evacuated. There's no further threat on Xandra; Eretimis got what he sought here."

Feyne's glare shifted to Zarus. "And what was that?"

"He wanted to make sure I held the Infinite Key," Rin muttered, looking at Errogan's bloody face. He wasn't smirking, nor was he advancing.

"Where is the rest of the invasion?" Scarlette demanded, bow still raised at the demon.

Errogan caught the scholar's expression, and knew there was no bluff in her aim. He gestured to the creature looming like a ghost.

"The zylk are the invasion on Xandra. They're drawn to sources of great power, and they found one." He settled on Rin. She didn't tremble, but his solemnity frightened her.

"Eretimis only wanted to verify that I had the Key?" Rin retorted. "Then why send these *zylk* to begin with? Why destroy the city!" She waved to the flames outside of the brick walls, however it was in the violent movement that the beast screeched. It writhed behind Errogan like a rabid dog.

"*Hoo-hoomann,*" the creature stammered, stumbling toward her so raggedly, its grotesque feet tripped on a piece of debris. The creature's head landed on the edge of a fallen stone. "*Hoo...*" it cried, but the whimper died. Black blood leaked from its temple.

Rin's heart hammered. A beast. This creature was a beast made for violence. Yet the beast whimpered on the ground, squirming as the blood pooled. Its murky eyes confused.

"Why isn't it healing?" she asked frantically. "They used to be able to heal off of each other."

She desperately looked to Errogan, but rather than ruthlessness, a shadow fell over his crystal gaze. The yelping beast on the ground grabbed at its grey scalp with ghastly fingers.

Errogan carefully moved to the beast. His step was soft, as if not to scare the thing. He placed a careful hand over the monster's bleeding head.

"Hush," he whispered. The creature relaxed once it looked at Errogan. Before anyone could react, the demon summoned a mass of brewing shadows into his hand and gently placed the magic over the creature's heart. The festering magic soaked into the beast like water.

"Errogan, wait!" Rin cried.

She threw herself forward, falling to her knees on the other side of the creature. Taking its cold, veiny hand in her own, she searched for a pulse, but the shadows seeped into its chest. The whimpers ceased.

A hollow silence coursed through the ruined building.

Rin dragged her glassy eyes to the demon in front of her.

"I could have saved it!" She delved for the depth of her magic and rose to her feet, yet Errogan never tore his sober stare away from the dead creature.

"They can't heal each other when they're too far apart," he said quietly. "They can't be healed using our magic. Eretimis made them disposable."

The desolation in his words settled the storm of Rin's wrath. She watched the demon with winded, confused breaths.

"Their service won't be forgotten," The Moonlit Bastard whispered.

A cold breeze pushed through the smoke, unnatural and working against the wind. She cast a glance at Zarus. Frost crept along the floor; he fought off the fire.

Silent footsteps crackled the ice. Zarus met her side, examining the body below. She had described the beasts she encountered in the city to him before, but they weren't like this. Even Feyne neared and sniffed at the body. After the sullen silence reigned, Zarus spoke.

"What has Eretimis done?"

"That's not a demon," Scarlette said warily. "Its aura is muddled and grey, like it was melted together."

Errogan drew his attention to the enemies surrounding him. "We call them zylk."

Scarlette couldn't help the scoff escaping her throat. "You don't expect me to believe that, do you?" Errogan did not flinch.

Rin closed her eyes, taking a deep breath. "Why a zylk?"

Errogan's forlorn stare looked at no one when he spoke. "The term describes beings made without the gods' consent. They were all ordered to be exterminated after the Divine War, but Eretimis doesn't follow rules. He deduced that combining the different races would reveal untapped strengths."

Rin and Zarus shared an uneasy glance. She licked her lips, craving the moisture that fled her tongue.

"These creatures are Eretimis's experiments... they're people?" She looked down to the zylk's grey skin. Suddenly, she recalled the internal struggle of the four-legged beasts she fought the day of the temple. Their murky eyes had faded to that of a mindful being.

Errogan finally rose to his feet. No one attempted to stop him. No one could tear their thoughts away from the creature lifeless on the ground.

Dazed, Rin looked to the white-haired demon on the other side of the zylk. He walked away from them.

"Eretimis created them with the purpose of hunting down the Infinite Key. That's why I was sent here: lead them to you and see if you truly did possess its power. But they're also an army."

Rin's stomach churned. The zylk a few months ago attacked everyone but her. She swallowed hard on the thought. "You set the city on fire to find me?"

Errogan halted, glancing over his shoulder. He didn't wish to be here at all, it was clear as day.

"I didn't start the fires." His focus trailed to Zarus, something hesitating to get off his lips. "This is your last chance, Z. Run away while you can. Go live freely like you always wanted."

Zarus was silent, no hint at what laid behind his glower. "Why did you come?"

Errogan's head cocked as if he didn't understand, but his lips straightened. He looked to Rin, then Feyne, then Scarlette before inhaling deep. "To warn you. All of you."

Feyne's derision verged on a growl. "Your master will have your head for this."

The White-Cloaked Reaper met the shifter's hate long and hard. "Eretimis is after the Infinite Key. It's the sole reason he invaded Armiria two thousand years ago, and it's the driving force of his plan." He looked at the fallen zylk one last time. "He'll do worse than this until he attains it—when he attains it."

Rin's shoulders slacked. What was Eretimis planning? She glanced at Zarus, who looked like he was piecing together the same puzzle. Feyne and Scarlette too.

Errogan turned toward the wall of flames. He was all but one step away from disappearing into them before a female voice shouted his name.

"General Errogan!"

Rin startled, reaching for her scimitar as the female jumped down from the roof of a fallen building. Her jet black hair cascaded like spilling ink. She landed behind Errogan, the axe strapped to her back clinking against the armor on her shoulders.

"Word just came in from our Emperor."

"I don't care, Nessriq—"

The girl's dark eyes narrowed, her nose wrinkling in a sneer. "Croft fell in a day."

Chapter Sixty-Eight

C roft had fallen. *Croft.*

Zarus's stomach churned. Eretimis didn't invade Xandra, he invaded Croft. The city where the civilians of Xandra were told to seek refuge. Where thousands of Nokomai had gathered at his and Genesis's direction.

Fallen.

Elief told him Eretimis was going to Xandra. Elief wouldn't have—unless she would. Unless she was just another spy Eretimis used to get to him... It would be fitting for a demon lurking in his ranks. But Elief...?

Zarus dragged his stare up from the charred floor. A flicker of pain bit at the corners of his vision, but he bit back. Nessriq watched him curiously.

"Eretimis is in Croft?" Rin uttered.

Nessriq cast a cool glance the girl's way. Her voice was a drop of rain amid a monsoon.

"Has been since the crack of dawn this morning. Only the early risers had time to warn everyone, and even then..." her eyes trailed elsewhere, "it was only moments before our Dark Emperor leveled a fifth of the mangy city to the ground." A sweet, bitter smirk pulled her lips.

"That's her," Scarlette said behind him. "That's the demon Nikolai Druvisk spoke with."

The female smiled at the scholar. "Nessriq Wythorn."

Zarus glanced at Rin, her rounded eyes flooding with horror. The shifter's visceral growl spoke for itself. Ultimately, Zarus settled on Errogan.

His heart pounded. "*How.*" Zarus didn't ask, only demanded.

Errogan stared at him for a long moment. The smoke raged, but it thinned. The fires were dying.

"Like I said," Errogan spoke without a hint of inflection, "I was sent to see if she contained the Infinite Key."

"You came as a diversion!" Rin barked through her teeth. Ire drove her step. "You marched an army of zylk right up to Xandra's doorstep. You made our scouts think *demons* were coming for the city!"

These humans are preparing for war against myths. Tatsuo's words echoed in Zarus's head until it made sense.

"Humans wouldn't tell the difference between a zylk and a demon," he muttered. He cursed himself for not having thought of it. "He was drawing our attention and resources to Xandra so no one would notice him marching on Croft. When did he switch his target?"

Errogan drew the conversation to his own end. "The Dark Tyrant is efficient." His words were hollow, and he directed a knowing glance at Zarus before he turned to walk away.

He still warned us. He's covering himself, Zarus realized, watching Nessriq from the corner of his eye.

"Where are you running away to this time!" Feyne called.

"Croft," Errogan said without looking back, "I have nothing left to achieve here."

Nessriq's narrowed eyes shifted to her general.

"Aren't we going to stop him?" Rin's voice was desperate. She didn't understand, none of them saw it: Errogan just delivered a message he could have been executed for.

"No," Zarus said. He watched Errogan's next step into the thin smoke. "Our help is needed elsewhere. The zylk are still terrorizing the civilians," he could hear the screams miles away. "These two will run back to Eretimis and inform him of the Infinite Key. Their work here is done."

A brisk breeze cut through the ruined building they stood in.

"Not all of us conspire against Eretimis Havilurce, Lowwenth," Nessriq spat.

Errogan cut her an indignant glare. "You have no orders to attack, Wythorn. This world is still under my command."

Nessriq scoffed. "You will burn in the coldest Flames for this, Errogan."

Before he could respond, the female rushed toward Zarus. Faster than his reflex. Nimbler than the arrow Scarlette shot. Zarus conducted a shield of ice and a course of shadow to meet Nessriq's assault. She wouldn't break through, and didn't try.

Nessriq reached for the axe strapped to her back and cut deep into the sturdy ice separating them. She held strong to the lodged weapon and swung herself around his defense right to the source of a fizzling light.

Zarus's mind betrayed him: suddenly he stood on the cliffside above Mortality's Edge again.

He gathered a force of shadows, but Nessriq was too fast.

Effortlessly, the female dislodged the axe and unsheathed a dagger from her boot. She sliced all the way up Rin's abdomen.

Crimson sprayed the ground. She didn't scream; Rin only looked down at her own blood before Nessriq grabbed her around the waist and leapt into the blinding smoke.

Zarus's shadows surged into the smog, but when the smoke cleared, only Rin's scimitar reflected the dim light.

Ice tore through the world. Feyne and Scarlette jumped out of its way, but Errogan merely summoned a wall of shadow to block the frost. Zarus tackled the demon through it.

His hands wrapped around Errogan's throat.

"*Where. Is. She.*"

His nails dug into the demon's skin. Errogan drew his hands to his neck, gasping. Zarus slammed his head on the ground.

"*Where did Nessriq take her?*"

"I-" Errogan coughed. The focus in his eyes swirled like the clouds on high. His face red as the blood on Zarus's hands. "I don't—"

"*Liar!*" Zarus snarled.

"I don't know—"

The cold *thud* against the back of Zarus's head sent the world tumbling.

His eyes rolled, his body fell limp. Groaning, he picked himself off the ground next to where Errogan had scraped to his knees and gasped. Zarus stared at nothing in particular, his head catching up with the world around. He glanced at the scholar standing over him with a red brick in her hand. His vision flared, blinding him as he tried to get up. Swaying, Zarus pulled his thoughts together.

"If he dies, we have no way of tracking Rin," Scarlette said gravely.

Zarus glanced down. Errogan was still on the ground, but cast Zarus a coy smile.

"You should let go of your temper more often, Z," he croaked with a semblance of mirth. "It would save you a lot of hardships."

Zarus refrained from reaching for the back of his head. "You lied to me," he snapped. "Where did Nessriq take Rin?"

Errogan looked Zarus deep in the eye. "You really must have forgotten our time together." He shook his head, finally finding the strength to stand. "If I planned to steal Rin Nowell, I would have done it myself and mocked you for your uselessness," he said matter of fact, patting off the ash from his pants.

That... sounded exactly like Errogan.

Zarus sucked in a cooling breath. "Fine, you didn't plan on capturing her, but your second clearly did," he glanced at the wall behind him, or what was left of it. Ice and dark mist simmered in the air around the gaping hole, a line of Rin's blood staining the floor.

"My orders were to find out if Rin possessed what Eretimis hoped she did," Errogan explained, a bit more annoyed than Zarus cared for. "Never said anything about taking her to him. Frankly, that's far more effort than I'd get credit for anyway."

Errogan shook his head, white strands catching the faint breeze from the hole in the wall. "Nessriq must be looking to please her *emperor*. It's what the recruits from Eroz have taken to calling him."

"So who *is* Nessriq?" Zarus pressed.

"The general of Eretimis's armies in Hraesah. She was promoted about a year ago. He sent for her to join us on Armiria some months ago. She's on this mission to help, but..."

"But he doesn't trust you after I escaped the fortress." Zarus inhaled deep.

"Not at all." Anyone could have led the zylk to trick the human scouts, but Eretimis needed to test Errogan's loyalty. Yet Errogan still warned them.

Another scream snatched Zarus's attention. Closer than before. The zylk were moving.

"Where would she head?" he pressed. "Flames, if Eretimis taught her to use portals, she could be—"

"He didn't." Errogan's certainty weighed as steel in his eyes. The demon thought for a moment. "She's heading back to Eretimis to deliver her prize. I don't know which path she would take. Druvisk told us about your defense plans for the invasion, but the explosives the Resurrection packed into sewers are planned to detonate at the bottom of the hour. She'll be on the roofs most likely."

"I'm sorry, *explosives*?" Scarlette blurted. Zarus heard her heart speed up. "Did you even plan on mentioning it?"

"Not unless you asked," Errogan shrugged. "In fact, it will only make things more difficult for me if I freely gave away vital information that would affect the Dark Emperor's plans to overtake Nokomic. The only way I would even think about telling you *anything* is if you beat the information out of me..." The demon yawned. "Or, since you already beat the Flames out of me, you could just ask."

Feyne let out a sigh heated enough to melt steel. "*Where are the explosives planted?*"

A smirk crept onto Errogan's lips. "Along the southern sewers. We heard that was your escape route if things got nasty."

"How'd Druvisk hear that?" Feyne asked.

"Lock and key, Wuflan, lock and key. But I can tell you Eretimis promised the Resurrection Xandra if they could wrangle full control of it tonight. They bargained."

Zarus's heart sank. The Resurrection used Elyot's plea as leverage...

Scarlette shook her head. "Why should we trust you? After all you've done, why should we believe a damn word you say?"

Vexation ran thick on Errogan's face, but he was quiet. A moment where his expression softened. "Bjarkh Grevik is heading east. He's going to search for the shifters."

A name to shock the scholar and shifter. But neither were fools; they pulled their attention back to the matter at hand immediately.

Feyne glared daggers at Errogan, but direness took over. He spoke to Scarlette as he moved to the exit of the building.

"Head south and warn everyone you can to flee through the eastern roads. Elyot should be in that area preparing for the ground assault. Watch out for the Resurrection, they're sure to be lurking nearby. And for the love of Yath Ha, make sure you're out of there before the bottom of the hour."

Scarlette was fast on his heels, replacing an arrow into her quiver and wrapping her bow around her shoulder. "And you?"

The wolf stretched his shoulders. "I'm going to find Fire-for-Brains and get rid of as many of those explosives as we can." He offered her a daring grin, but Scarlette returned no such thing. She looked at the shifter like she was savoring the image for an eternity, until finally she wrapped her arms around him.

"You better come back," Scarlette whispered into Feyne's ear. "You're mad if you think death would get you away from me."

Feyne smiled. "I'd never dream of it."

Errogan wasn't keen on privacy. "Remember," he called out. "Make sure to check your locks. You never know who has a key."

A flash of light illuminated the roofless structure. Feyne's presence drew further and further away as his cloak dropped to the ground.

"And you," Scarlette called, drawing Zarus's attention. She leaned down as much as her chest would allow and gathered the cloak. "Get her back." Her stare promised a worse fate than death if he didn't.

Zarus nodded, his gut clenching at the scent of Rin's blood lingering in the air. Scarlette offered him one last nod before she sprinted out the hole in the wall.

"Isn't that heartwarming," Errogan muttered.

Zarus walked to Rin's fallen blade, sliding it into the belt at his hip. Nessriq was probably halfway across the city. "You're coming with me."

"The Flames I am," Errogan scoffed. "I just said that I wasn't going to make things any more difficult for myself. Eretimis would have my head if I helped you."

Zarus cast a cold glance to the whining demon. "Eretimis is going to crucify you when Nessriq reveals that you warned us. But Errogan, read my lips when I tell you this," his voice fell from anything but ice, "I will tear you apart limb from limb if you don't help me find Rin. And things will get worse than they ever were for you if you crawl back to Eretimis like that."

Zarus raised his chin, awaiting the demon's answer.

Errogan sighed, but he finally nodded his head. "*Fine*. I will help you track Nessriq. But," he emphasized, "I'm not going with you. I have no plans to engage in a fight."

"Scared to fight the whelp general?" Zarus taunted.

"As if, deserter" Errogan growled, following Zarus through the gap in the wall. "I'll be hanging by the rope faster than you could ever extort another favor out of me again if I'm caught doing this."

"You'll be hanging by the rope if I don't catch her." A quick death was high hope for this kind of treachery. Zarus found his eyes settled on the silver hilt of the blade at Errogan's hip.

Errogan quickly traced his stare. "You should take it," the demon said suddenly. His hands untied the blade from his belt. Zarus stared at the sword Errogan offered. It started to wear, the shine less radiant. It wasn't too long ago he nearly got killed over the weapon.

Zarus gently pushed the blade back. "No. You'll need it more than me."

The White-Cloaked Reaper stared. Errogan held the scabbard tight in his hand.

"How do you hope to track this female down without accompanying me?" Zarus asked.

"Easy," Errogan offered, "I don't. They'll do it for me." In a long sway of his arm, he gestured to the open street around them. Among the flames and smoke, Zarus sensed a hoard of silhouettes.

The army of zylk assembled in a mass of grey skin and lifeless eyes. Sniffing, twitching. Their stretched skin pulled against each movement, all searching for one thing: Rin.

Zarus stared in disbelief, trying to figure out how so many creatures snuck into the city so quickly, but a shriek shattered his thought. One creature tilted its head to the sky.

"Is this why you're loyal to him?" Zarus asked. He looked at his old friend, the demon who looked nearly identical to him and held so many secrets. The horde of beasts groaned louder. "Eretimis has created life without Divine consent for longer than you admit..."

"Light finally graces the fortress, you know." Errogan mused as he watched the zylk's attention perk. Desolation laced his smile. "She cut through the darkness smothering the Northern Wastes. No amount of magic will cover the sun again either."

Suddenly, Errogan unsheathed the silver sword's twin dagger from his belt and placed it in Zarus's hand. "Try and keep up with them, Z."

The zylk lifted their heads, catching wind of the same scent.

Before Zarus could so much as open his mouth, the hoard sprinted westward.

Chapter Sixty-Nine

Nausea splintered Rin's head, trailing all the way down her spine and clenching in her stomach. When she finally pried her eyes open, the open sky stared down at her and the tiles of a roof cut into her back. Rin gritted her teeth and prayed to the gods for strength. She fought against fear and looked at her torso.

All she could do was stare.

From navel to sternum, she bled. For as jagged as the flesh appeared, the wound wasn't a death sentence. She hadn't bled out yet. Rin calmed herself enough to think, and that's when she heard the cries below. She only assumed the zylk lurked not far behind.

The numbness of her body blinded her reach, and she couldn't tell whether she was elbow deep in the ocean of her mind or drowning in the waves. Rin squeezed her eyes closed and summoned a burning light into her palms. Her hands pressed on the gaping wound. A scream scraped her throat when she touched the exposed tissue. She sobbed as her light cauterized the wound. The blood stopped, and the sickness toying at her stomach won.

Sweat and blood and vomit drenched her clothes, her body ached to the bone, but Rin put everything she had into flipping herself onto her knees.

"You have me in your grasp," Rin groaned, although it sounded like a yelp when she pulled herself to her feet. "Months of dedication finally paid off."

The demon lurking on the edge of the roof glanced over her armored shoulder. "I've only hunted you for a week now, human."

"You, Eretimis, the rest of his loyalists. You all operate under the same mind."

Nessriq's head quirked. "What objective would that mind have?"

"Lunacy."

Nessriq's amusement pulled the lines of her slender face. She examined Rin's chest.

"You have more will than they made out, Light Bringer. Half of me expected you to bleed out," she spoke in a voice that almost sounded welcoming. Almost. "But then again, not just anyone can stun an entire army without lifting a finger. I was surprised when his Mightiness called me to this land."

"Nokomic?"

"Armiria," the female corrected. "I'm shocked to see you lot so... civilized."

Rin bit the inside of her cheek. Talking to this female was like swatting away a wasp.

She sucked in a cool breath, trying not to lurch at the stretch of her chest. Fighting was no use. She needed to buy herself time.

"What are you waiting for, Nessriq of Eroz?" Rin bit down on herself, wrapping her arm around her torso. She miserably approached the demon, burning her energy and focus.

The female spoke levelly. "I take you to Armiria's Emperor. He decides your fate, Key Wielder."

Light Bringer. Key Wielder. Rin scoffed at the titles.

She swallowed a dry breath. "And if I fight?" Nessriq's unflinching stare didn't have to fall to the wound she inflicted for Rin to know it was a foolish question.

The demon's voice fell. "Then I slice your chest again and make sure you don't move a muscle until we arrive. And perhaps I'll even carve out—"

The burst of red light was so sudden, Nessriq couldn't catch herself before she cried out.

"My tongue? Gods, you lot all use the same threats," Rin ground out.

The single step she took forward nearly buckled her legs, but she advanced toward the demon as she reached into the cresting waves of her magic and allowed the force to wrap around herself.

"I hate to break it to you, *Nessriq of Eroz*, but I'm in no condition to travel. I'll probably die before you ever cross the River of Zelenia."

No wave or wall or spark lit up the world, no object forged of her magic to wield against this demon. Rin had nothing left. She couldn't focus through the sheer *agony* tearing into her very being. This was all she had: a beacon of the hellish red light, towering toward the heavens. There wasn't an inch of Xandra that wasn't cast into the crimson hue.

A cloud blurred Rin's vision, swaying her balance until she didn't know where she stood. The muscles in her chest stretched, and a harrowing cry escaped her throat. Her grip on the tower of light slipped as her wound ripped open.

Blinded by tears, Rin stumbled toward the edge of the roof. The red light faded as she fell. But someone grabbed her.

Rin dangled midair, suspended by her arm. The warmth of blood soaked her shirt.

She thrashed, but the person holding her would not let go. Her chest ripped open, her shoulder pulled on the socket.

"Hang on!"

Rin wasn't sure when she was pulled back onto the roof, nor when she bit her tongue hard enough to draw blood. Her body wouldn't take anymore.

When she opened her eyes, the fiery hair of Tatsuo Kurosawa caught the night's breeze. Dread choked his countenance.

"What took you so long?" she breathed.

She saw the answer on his face; bleeding and smothered in soot and ash. His tunic; once pale green, now singed and burned at the edges. A burst vein dyed the white of his eye crimson, offsetting the yellow-green of his iris. He looked like he was caught in an explosion.

Rin opened her mouth, but Tatsuo shook his head. "I'm okay," he assured. "We got caught in some of the debris."

She thought he had died. Rin settled the twist of her gut and bit down on another yelp when she tried and failed to sit up.

Tatsuo's eyes narrowed. He examined the gash where her torn shirt allowed and cast her a grim glance. Rin nodded, prompting him to get it done as quickly as possible. Tatsuo wiped away as much of the blood as he could. In and out she breathed, but she couldn't do anything to prepare for the scorching touch.

Rin cried, slamming her fist on the rooftop until she could breathe again. The skin around her chest burned red and raw, but the wound was closed. Tatsuo did a better job of cauterizing it.

"Feyne joined Elyot to fight off the swarm of creatures raiding the city after we dealt with the explosives. He told me a demon snatched you away." Tatsuo scooped his arm behind her back and helped her upright. "Then I saw that flash and knew it was you... I expected Errogan's second to hang around a little bit longer. You must have torn her to pieces if she ran away that quickly."

Ran away...

Rin scanned the roof. She had left Nessriq burning in the light. The green clay of the roof tiles faded white where her magic had towered, but nothing out of place. Not taking the risk, she sent a wave of light cresting from her body. Ebbing shortly after it started, the brush of magic faltered against something on the other side of a chimney.

"You won't gain anything by cowering— " Rin called, but nothing more than a breath lay between her and the axe that swung down. Tatsuo pulled them both out of the way before she could jump.

"Such rudeness, human," Nessriq mused, heaving the blade from the tile.

With the same neck-breaking speed, Nessriq charged forward, but Rin unleashed another spiral of light aimed for the demon's heart. Nessriq redirected her step. Her axe chopped down, metal clashing on metal.

Tatsuo arched backward, using both hands to bar his spear against the attack. "Don't any of you demons know how to attack outside of the shadows?" he growled, throwing the axe to the side. He leaned onto the staff of his spear and kicked the female back.

Nessriq gathered her balance effortlessly. "Don't any of you half-breeds know how to submit to your greater part?" She rested the blunt of her blade onto her shoulder. "It's like you think your filthy dragon blood gives you the right to rebel."

Rin glared at the demon, and in doing so caught a glimpse of the dark veil covering her eyes. Shadows stretched across Nessriq's face and neck as well; any exposed skin was covered in the imperceivable magic. Yet she hadn't summoned a lick of magic herself yet.

Tatsuo snapped. "*You arrogant leech!*"

Blue and red flames erupted from the *narikaah's* hands, conducted along his spear. The blade was inches from Nessriq's eye when the demon shifted backward, the pierce only slicing the edge of her pointed ear. She raised the axe while Tatsuo raised his spear toward the heavens.

A wall of flames erupted from the sky, falling over the female's head. Rin's face burned against the explosion. Magic was her only shield against the scorch.

Within the roaring flames, Rin saw movement. Twirling round and round, faster than any axe that large should have been moved, the demon broke the flames pushing down on her. Nessriq strode out of the inferno. The axe spinning above her head was a blur. Tatsuo's knuckles went white as he strangled the grip on his spear.

Nessriq called across the clearing. "I have no doubt you would have killed someone... lesser. But I'm not so much like the others. I don't suffer the same weaknesses—"

A lance of light ripped through the air. Nessriq jumped out of its path, hissing as her hand grazed the white flames behind. Rin's magic shattered on the ground amid the dying flames, but Nessriq lurched over her bubbling skin.

Nessriq didn't attempt to heal it, just as she hadn't summoned magic to block the flame or light. Rin didn't care to learn why. Her magic sat waiting.

It looked like lightning, but no thunder rumbled the earth. Above in the skies, hundreds of magic bolts suspended above Nessriq. Rin rained the lethal array onto the female. Yet when Nessriq tried to escape the assault, Tatsuo set the ground ablaze. A cry ruptured. Rin's magic struck, but a blur of midnight rushed past her. Rin stood face to face with the demon.

A magic bolt pierced deep into Nessriq's shoulder, but the layer of shadow magic around her body dimmed the bolt until it disappeared. A flare of light erupted between them, one that not even the shadow veil could blot out. Stumbling, the demon was blinded.

Rin swallowed against the writhing of her wound and shifted to the side. She cleared a path between Nessriq and the light-footed *narikaah* charging from behind. Tatsuo sliced his spear into her waist. The demon's axe clattered on the tiles below. Nessriq Wythorn fell to her knees, both hands pressed against the exposed tissue on her side.

Crimson beaded down the corners of her lips. "That was a sly move, Light Bringer." A bitter laugh spat red onto the rooftop. "You'll tarnish your reputation if you keep using tricks like that."

"I don't give a damn about reputations," Rin retorted.

"Dangerous words for a dangerous girl."

Rin regarded the demon from a safe distance. "You're not like the others. You think before you act."

Nessriq smiled through the welling red. "A rogue amid the single mind?"

"A black sheep in the flock."

Nessriq smirked as the roof shook and the terror in the street cut into cold nothing. A heartbeat passed before the first zylk sprung onto the roof's edge. An entire pack of four-legged beasts followed. Their nostrils flared as the wind picked up, and all six of the godless beasts locked their sights on the Infinite Key.

Rin's gut twisted when one beast charged. Its ghastly claws scraped the roof tiles to splinters. She summoned her magic a moment too late. The zylk's gaping jaw opened to snatch her, but a splatter of crimson sprayed across her face.

Tatsuo bellowed against the teeth sinking into his forearm, throwing the zylk over the edge of the roof. He jumped in front of her without hesitation.

The *narikaah* shifted his guard, materializing his spear as the next beast lunged open-mouthed. The zylk swallowed the blade until it was skewered all the way through.

"*Get out of here, Rin,*" Tatsuo called out, daring a glance at her as another form leapt. "*Run and—*"

Two more zylk flanked his sides, a third assaulting head-on.

"Tatsuo!" Rin gritted her teeth. A thrum of magic tingled the tips of her fingers. She pushed her battered body up—

Rin yelped louder than the beasts as a hand grabbed the back of her head, yanking her off the ground.

"I don't think so, Light Bringer," Nessriq hissed through heavy breaths. She raised her axe in the same moment Rin burst a ball of light in the demon's face. Nessriq hissed, but her axe's hilt slammed sharp into Rin's spine.

Burning ice shot from the bottom of Rin's back all the way up to her head. Screaming, she called forth a flurry of magic to burn the demon away, but not an ounce of light answered.

The *narikaah* evaded the frontal attack, throwing himself forward below the beast and igniting a blast of fire where the first and second zylk collided. He couldn't outmaneuver the third's slash of claws. Three fresh gashes bled down Tatsuo's shoulder blade, staining his green tunic black in the dull moonlight.

Rin grabbed and grabbed, but found none of the magic that stirred only moments before. As if the entire ocean evaporated. Her eyes rolled back, and when her vision slowly returned, she only then registered the half built brick chimney she had been slumped against. Rin bared her teeth against the throb of her spine. She looked for Nessriq, the zylk, but her heart fell once she saw Tatsuo across the roof.

Caught between two snarling jaws, the zylk anchored him on his knees by his arms. Blood poured from the claw marks slashed across his face, caking his fiery hair to his temples. Nessriq strode to Tatsuo despite the blood leaking from her side.

"You've gotten too used to wielding your magic, human. It's become a crutch." Nessriq cast a sharp glance at Rin over her shoulder. "All you do is fiddle with it. You haven't yet learned its full potential."

"What would a Hollowed know about magic?" Tatsuo spat at the demon's boots, trying to free his arms, yet the zylk bit harder. His teeth clenched, beading blood down his face.

Nessriq considered him impassively. "Assumptions are dangerous, *narikaah*, I wouldn't recommend jumping to them in your condition."

Tatsuo snorted, flashing a deathly smile back at the demon. "You haven't a drop of magic in that dense head of yours. It's not hard to tell. I'm surprised Eretimis ever let a Hollowed enter his ranks. Then again, even the bastard needs fodder to motivate the rest of his subjects."

The dragon clenched his jaw, breathing flames out his lungs and through his lips. Yet Nessriq bade the fire no mind as she stuck her hand through it and grabbed Tatsuo by the neck. The flames sputtered out. Her flesh boiled nearly to the bone, yet she barely flinched.

"Fodder you say?" Nessriq repeated.

Horrified, Rin tried to move, but whatever Nessriq had done... she was stuck. Paralyzed. She could move her arms, but a piece of her was blocked. Her magic was nowhere to be found. An anxious sweat broke out on her temples.

Nessriq released Tatsuo's throat, holding his fiery gaze by a phantom chain as she circled him. "You better learn to respect your superiors, Kurosawa. You wouldn't want to make the same mistake as your parents, would you?"

The dragon seethed. "You scum know nothing of those Eretimis labels as enemies!"

Tatsuo's fists balled until his talons carved into his palms. Rin watched a flame spark around them, but Nessriq slammed the hilt of her axe into his spine too. The flame vanished. The veins in his forehead pulled taut, the chords of his neck stretched as the zylk held him upright. Tatsuo's bellow rumbled Rin's chest.

"Scum?" Nessriq mused, her hand drawing out a monstrous dagger from inside her boot. Slowly, she leaned down and held the tip over his thigh. "I know all about you, Tatsuo, I know all about your parents and their crimes against our people. Hiromitsu Kurosawa, the *narikaah* master bladesmith, crafting his weapons for our sovereign council, sworn to defend Hraesah and all that might stand against it."

"All that might *threaten* it," Tatsuo growled. His arms tensed, the magic tried to ignite, but the zylk shredded his arms. He bled out.

Nessriq sneered. "A worthy ally, until he betrayed his people and fled his home, dragging so many others down in his lies. I know all about Nariko Kurosawa as well, the ancient fire dragon who held the secrets of bridging worlds. She used her knowledge to smuggle deserters out of Eroz. But you? You haven't taken the time to learn about our people, about me."

"You are *not* my people."

Nessriq's smile was soft yet harsh. "Demon blood runs in your veins. That's enough to cleanse the filth of the dragons. What you know of Eroz is a fable of lies woven by your parents. They slandered Eretimis and his greatness, blinding you from the truth that he was born to lead us. It's time you learned about us, Tatsuo, starting with me. You think you can insult a general of Hraesah without heeding the consequence?" Something wicked twisted in her smile.

Rin stirred, the paralysis of her body a silent taunt.

"Your parents spoiled you rotten," Nessriq crowed.

Tatsuo's eyes pained as she plunged the dagger into his thigh, but he never screamed. Deep, dark blood welled, pooling to the ground with the impatience of a river. Nessriq twirled the blade. Tatsuo flashed his teeth at the demon, but he did not yield. Slowly, she pulled the knife out.

Rin bit down as though her spine would shatter at the slightest movement. Her magic disappeared, no longer an option. She heaved herself forward.

Panting, seething, Tatsuo leered at the demon, pulling his arms into himself as much as he could, but the zylk didn't budge. The wrath of Ashnagz's Flames burned in his eyes.

"I commend your strength, Kurosawa, some of my demons wouldn't even keep silent against that. But I'm not here so you can make a point. I'm here to teach you a lesson."

Inches below the bleeding hole in his leg, the demon pressed the dagger down again. Tatsuo's face contorted, but never loosed the cry burning his throat. Not even when Nessriq twisted the weapon. However, she released the dagger when a brick smacked into the back of her skull right after.

Nessriq's rolling eyes whipped to the human she left unattended.

Rin's breath danced out of reach, her arm trembled after throwing the brick. Still stuck on the ground, but she held Nessriq's damning stare.

Nessriq stood. Her step was steady, no daze in her eyes, just deadly calm in her voice. As if pain had no hold on her.

"You're nothing without your magic, Rin Nowell." The demon didn't inflict her rage on Rin; there was no rage to inflict. Nessriq Wythorn operated on calculation. "My kind relies on it too heavily as well. Take magic away from them, and it's as good as tying back their arm and leg. They look down on me for lacking such abilities, but they never saw it the way I did."

Rin couldn't send out another beacon and didn't have a weapon to her name. She needed time. "As a weakness?"

"Precisely." Nessriq didn't even look her way as she paced behind the *narikaah*. "One I learned to expose." Gently, she traced her gloved finger down Tatsuo's back, stopping only at the curve of his spine before striking it with the blunt of her axe once more.

Tatsuo's voice betrayed him. His cry reverberated throughout Rin's bones.

"Just the right knock to the spine," the demon said as she circled the *narikaah*, "and all that festering magic stutters."

His arms tensed, every ounce of strength he possessed failed him. Tatsuo's body fell slack as sweat lined his brow.

Nessriq twirled the axe. "You're the first human it's ever worked on, Rin."

Tatsuo ground his teeth, clenching his fists against the jaws sinking into his arms. "Save it for someone who gives a damn."

The demon turned to face her prisoner, graceful as a snake stalking a field mouse. "I think it's fair you know just who stands before you, and it's fair you know what power I possess."

Rin seethed, forcing herself onto her knees. She needed to get to Tatsuo, needed to find a way around the blockade of her magic. She propped a foot beneath herself.

Nessriq tapped her finger against her leg. "I'm feeling generous today, traitor." A wicked smirk seized her expression, and with it, she turned to Tatsuo. "Beg for your life, and I might let you live."

Tatsuo spat blood on the demon's face.

Rin's heart hammered through her chest. She searched for the ocean of her magic and forced her legs to carry forward.
Your power is not of their kind, child.

Nessriq wiped her cheek with her thumb. "You spit on the generosity of your general? All for the hope of saving the Light Bringer? Don't worry about her, Tatsuo, she's coming with me. But you? You don't have to die, you could choose to live honorably for once in your life."

Bile stung the back of Rin's throat. *This isn't how it was supposed to happen!*

Do not bind yourself to their rules.

Nessriq hummed. "I'll make it even easier for you, Tatsuo. I'll take you with me *alive* to Croft. I'll give you the chance to plead forgiveness for your crimes, but only if you renounce your dragon blood and pledge yourself to the Dark Emperor right now."

Tatsuo roared, his fangs flashing. "My ancestors will greet me in Lyhrëon before I ever plague my family name with your *emperor*!" Smoke trailed from the blood on his arms. A wave of heat pushed out of him. The zylk screeched, finally letting go as the dragon's blood melted their mouths.

Tatsuo Kurosawa lunged for the demon towering over him. They collided in a clash of armor and steel.

Tatsuo wrestled her down, pinning her and bathing his hands in white flames as he beat against the General of Hraesah. Yet Nessriq wore the armor of shadows, and Tatsuo's blood gathered in pools.

His face sickly, his strikes slowed until they missed Nessriq's jaw and hit the roof beside her. Nessriq abused the opening and pushed him off with her legs then jumped to her feet. Tatsuo tumbled flat to the ground, unable to find his balance with so little blood in his veins and magic expended.

Nessriq lifted her axe, the polished head shadowing Tatsuo's face from the moonlight. Rin threw herself forward. Magic be damned, she would tear Nessriq apart with her hands. She would not lose—

The zylk rammed into Rin's blindside, its melted jaw sizzling as it used the other beast to heal itself. She hit the ground, something in her spine snapping. Dazed, she looked at Tatsuo on the ground.

No.

Rin cried as the axe cleaved. The warmth of blood sprayed her face.

Chapter Seventy

Iron assaulted Zarus's nose when he reached the end of the street. He drowned in the stench before he ever reached the building they fought atop. Blood and ash and fear smothered him, yet he pulled himself onto the roof.

The axe cleaved down, Rin screamed, Tatsuo stared death in the face, and just moments before the blade struck, a blur wedged itself between Nessriq and Tatsuo.

Zarus stood in horror, shock. Tatsuo Kurosawa's head would have rolled across the roof tiles if Errogan hadn't rammed himself against Nessriq's axe just before the blade cut down.

Errogan came back. Errogan *saved* Tatsuo. Zarus couldn't fathom it. Did he use a portal? While the fragment of a smile tugged his lip, it halted. Blood dripped off Nessriq's axe head.

His heart dropped.

The female lifted her weapon again. Zarus's magic raged with winter's wrath; howling winds and burning ice whirled, aiming for the demon and her zylk. The zylk towering over Rin yelped, tumbling to the ground with a rod of ice piercing through its side. Ice consumed Nessriq Wythorn, frozen solid where she stood, axe raised above her head.

Zarus dove to Tatsuo's side. His breath staggered. The gorge spanning the young dragon's neck revealed jagged bone and sinew, but mostly blood. Dark oozing blood that welled too deep.

Breaths too heavy, Tatsuo spasmed on the ground. The only person able to mend him... Zarus glanced at Rin. Tears streamed down her face, but she didn't move.

No.

Errogan pressed his hands over Tatsuo's bleeding neck.

Zarus knelt beside Tatsuo, gently grabbing his hand. The dragon's nails dug into his skin. Panic laced his eyes. Zarus swallowed. That gash. What could he say—

The demon beside him shifted. "You fought well, dragon," Errogan said in a hush. Zarus knew that tone. That hopeless tone. "You bring glory to your kin."

Gasping wet breaths, Tatsuo looked Errogan hard in the eye. No mockery. He lifted a trembling hand and clasped it onto Errogan's forearm.

Zarus's throat pulled. The memory of a healing spell dabbled on his lips, but Tatsuo squeezed his hand and stopped him. The *narikaah* parted his lips, revealing a mouth flooded with crimson.

"Ki-kind'l th- fl-ame." Tatsuo drowned on the words.

Kindle the flame. What flame?

Zarus gritted his teeth. The burning in his throat was too much. "I am honored to call you my friend, Tatsuo Kurosawa." He tightened his grip on the dragon's hand. "*Honored.*"

A sad smile tugged at Tatsuo's bleeding lips before his stare trailed off to nothing. The trembling stilled.

Zarus looked at Errogan. The Moonlit Bastard's stare was grim, unmoving from the lifeless *narikaah* below them. Errogan came back.

While Zarus was slowed by the zylk horde, Errogan risked Eretimis's terror and returned. Yet they were both too late.

There wasn't a thought in Zarus's mind. His chest hollowed. He was too late.

Looking at his friend's corpse was like ingesting poison. He glanced at Rin. Her eyes unblinking, her body motionless. She stared at the *narikaah,* alive, but not an inch of her moved. Unaware of the world other than the corpse. Zarus's very soul paralyzed. Slowly, he dragged his stare to the frozen female.

Zarus's lips pulled back. His fists clenched at his sides, but before he shattered the demon into a million pieces, a zylk rushed onto the roof and rammed into Nessriq Wythorn.

***

Rin stared into Tatsuo's chartreuse eyes, stared at the slitted pupils within. Empty and hollow and lifeless.

She assumed the zylk was killed by Tatsuo's fire. She didn't see it rush from her side, tackling her a heartbeat before she rammed into Nessriq Wythorn. She was going to save him... Her heart burned, her chest cried, that *crack* pulsating along her spine.

Tatsuo Kurosawa's blood splattered her face.

***

Nessriq's frozen form hit the rooftop, but rather than shatter, the ice sizzled where the zylk hit her. She thawed, and the beast died whimpering at her feet, all of the dark magic inside saving its mistress.

She stood, regarding Tatsuo with disappointment. "The older generations blemish us. This one could have been so much more if his parents hadn't poisoned his mind."

A calmness seized hold of Zarus, not a tremble in his hands.

The beat of a heart. That was all it took for Zarus to lunge.

***

Rin's body sprawled in the crimson pool. She felt nothing, not her magic, not the beast hovering over her. Not even when something pierced its torso, spraying oily blood all over her face. The hum of conversation murmured in the back of her head. She swam in the damp void of nothing after that snap along her spine.

***

Nessriq's axe flashed in the moonlight. Errogan tackled Zarus before it struck him. The female shifted her assault, forcing both males to retreat faster than they could gather their footing.

"I knew it was a matter of time before you betrayed us, Errogan," Nessriq laughed.

Zarus gritted his teeth, ice and darkness blending into a shield just before her axe cut his skull in two. Ice fractured and shadow fizzled, but the barrier held.

Nessriq pulled the blade free, resting it atop her shoulder. "The emperor will have a field day when I deliver all three of you to his feet."

Errogan met Zarus's side and unsheathed the silver sword. His eyes raged, but he didn't look at Nessriq. The dead zylk sprawled across the roof held his gaze. Some fizzled as they tried to heal, others didn't. Rin still hadn't moved.

Clenching his jaw, Zarus spoke from the corner of his lips. "Weakness?" Frost enveloped his hands.

"Never trained with her," Errogan spat his regret.

Zarus cursed. Falling into a frenzied rage would not kill Nessriq, but channeling it to find a weakness could work.

Frost spread across the roof. Liquid shadows stirred at his side.

***

Silence molested Rin's ears. Yet something stirred. A whisper. A murmur. It wasn't in her head. It wasn't in her ears. The voice rumbled through her soul, her blood, her heart. Flickering like a candle caught in a draft. She tried to stir on the ground, tried to look past the red drowning her.

Who-who a-re you?

A cry, a call. Rin couldn't tell.

The paralysis leaked into her focus, wrung her free of her spirit. She hung from her body by a thread, and the more she struggled, the more it frayed. Rin forced her eyes to blink. It was a flash, but when her lids closed, she could have sworn she saw a grand hall bathing in sunlight. Another blink. Gone.

A curious pang drummed in her heart. She shifted her eyes to her torso, then to the roof. Beside her laid a skewered zylk, skin fizzling closed as it whimpered. She forced herself to look past Tatsuo, where she found a like-wraith dodging the swing of Nessriq's blade. And moonlit hair beside them.

Rin opened her mouth, but nothing emerged. She closed her exhausted eyes, and suddenly saw it again.

The light of the grand hall not only blinded, but it warmed. She could turn, she could move, but only within the realm behind closed eyes. Ivory pillars towered out of reach, into the open rays of sunlight. Lush ivy sprouting blue and white flowers wrapped the beams. The floor was a sparkling mirror—no, an ornate pond. So still, so clear, it reflected the pink, orange, and purple of the twilight sky. Not a ripple disturbed the peace, yet power thrummed from it. Much like the mirror Zarus kept in Hilyan's Peak. Four statues surrounded her, wrapped in garbs and carved in fine detail. More than lifelike. The kaetha, and the double-faced Yath Ha.

Rin marveled at the courtyard, but didn't understand why she set her eyes on the realm of Lyhrëon. She, a broken mortal from the outskirts of a broken kingdom, unable to stop that axe from chopping down. Perhaps she was dead too.

Do not limit yourself, Alentye.

A whisper of wind caressed the back of her head. A call from an old friend, the tug of a memory. It wasn't Yath Ha's ethereal voice that spoke. Soft, but deep.

It is not your time to see these shores.

She looked back and forth, searching for whoever spoke into her soul. Her only company were the statues. Or, perhaps...

Rin squinted against the falling sun. Only one figure was made of stone, the one with two faces. The other three... her tongue dried.

The statue of Lhaerem the Knowing suddenly looked at her. Still as stone, but there was no stone on his body, only flesh, bone, and flowing white and blue robes over dark skin. His fair hair didn't catch the wind, yet his blue eyes looked at her with gentle care. Rin searched, but words cowered. Lhaerem watched her, waiting. She opened her mouth. Nothing came out.

She knows not of what you speak, Lhaerem, nor is there time to explain.

Fierce and strong. Mynil watched her with vigilant grey eyes. Red hair hung over the shoulder of her green garbs in loose braids, free waves curling around the kaeth's rosy face.

The Attendants. Rin was in the presence of the Attendants. If that were true... She glanced over her shoulder. The two-faced statue hadn't moved.

They are not here right now, girl.

Divine or not, standing in the Court of Lyhrëon or not, Rin couldn't help the chill from her mind. The Lord of Ashnagz spoke peacefully, yet his voice thundered. Slowly, she looked into his gaze. Stoic was Vulyn's expression. His violet eyes seemed to look through her to the statue of Yath Ha behind.

"They're everywhere at once, are they not?" Her voice, it was just as distant as the Divine's. Like talking through water. It was Lhaerem that spoke.

They are, Alentye, but while they can see us now, they have not the time to participate. They are frenzied writing for our fate.

If both of the Creators needed their combined focus, Rin supposed she shouldn't be too disappointed. She was talking to the Attendants, after all.

"You're right before me, why do you sound so far away?" She looked about the courtyard. The depthless skies of twilight seemed to bend toward her and the still water below their feet. Not even the voice of Vulyn disturbed it.

This is the stretch of our power right now. The Dark One keeps us out of your realm. We could only bring a part of you here.

***

Nessriq did not possess a lick of magic. No darkness, no elements, no psychic. A Hollowed. Zarus finally understood why she hadn't used a portal to flee. Yet it became apparent why she had been promoted to general.

Zarus kept his breath even despite the sweat lining his forehead. For the fifth time, Nessriq parried his strike, throwing him back and keeping as a wall between him and Rin. She evaded his phantom weapons, deflected them with the axe she twirled around. Even when the ice under her feet snagged her balance, she knew how to shatter it while avoiding Errogan's sword. She barely reacted to her wounds, acting like pain bore no weight. Blood flowed from the curve of Zarus's neck thanks to one of her daggers. He managed to slice her abdomen with his shadows, but alone she was faster than him and Errogan together.

Zarus rammed his shoulder into Nessriq's chest, sending her stumbling back as she parried the slash of Errogan's sword with the axe. When Zarus advanced to Rin's side, Nessriq caught his foot with the head of her axe. He climbed to his feet as fast as he fell.

"I expected more from you," Nessriq taunted, but pressed a firm hand into her chest.

Shadows seeped through Errogan's fingers. The magic boiled on the ground, but with the raise of her brow, two zylk leapt for Errogan's throat. Zarus shifted to cover the male's back, but a beast of his own pounced in the way.

Nessriq flicked a smile at Zarus.

"Zarus Lowwenth, the Shadow of Evenfall, the demon raised by humans and saved from their barbaric wrath by our Dark Liege. You've leveled cities and massacred armies with the blink of an eye. A gust of fell wind walking through the halls of the northern fortress, barely seen except by a select few eyes. Some say you were the bastard child of the night's deepest shadows and the void's icy grasp. Others say you crawled straight out of Ashnagz and not even Vulyn himself could keep you tethered."

Zarus *tsked*. His shadows crept into the ground, spiraling up beneath Nessriq's feet. Despite her thick armor, she jumped off the magic with ease, but shifted right into Errogan's swell of shadows behind. The wave would have killed her if the zylk guarding Zarus hadn't rammed her out of the way and fallen into the magic instead.

Errogan tried to run to the struggling creature, but Nessriq's axe split through the air before his head.

"Nothing attracts the poets like power." She spoke to distract. "But here you are, and you've barely made it an arm's reach past me. All those legends, built up just to support some half-wit playing at a god."

A trail of ice bridged the gap between Zarus and Nessriq. Frozen stalagmites rose from the trail, tearing through everything in its path until it reached her.

Nessriq watched the oncoming magic and adjusted her momentum upward as it sprang forth beneath her. Before her feet touched the ground, she dropped her axe and pulled out two throwing knives.

Zarus solidified the shadows in his hand and slashed the first knife to the side, but the second landed. Blood welled, the blade grazing his shoulder as she advanced. The axe heaved off the ground and chopped for his abdomen.

Zarus deflected the axe with a burst of ice, and with it a smog of darkness smothered the rooftop.

A grunt sounded from behind, and Errogan slammed into his back a moment later. Zarus glanced over his shoulder. Blood leaked from the demon's brow, but no zylk advanced through the smog.

"She'll use those beasts as shields until we fall from exhaustion," Zarus huffed.

Errogan's eyes hardened. The blood of the zylk riled his temper like nothing else.

"Plan?" The words echoed an age long lost.

Zarus shifted to the swaying mist. "Cover Rin."

Errogan barely nodded his head before Zarus lunged through the darkness. His movement was silent as a ghost, but their voices couldn't hide from another demon.

The axe blade cleaved before his step. Rolling out of its way, the sheeted ice cracked beneath Zarus's weight. On cue, the mist shifted before him.

Nessriq erupted through the darkness. He grounded his feet, catching her weight and tossing her the other way. Nessriq skidded, balancing keenly despite the awkward weapon in her hand.

"You're not easily riled, do you know that?" she asked.

Zarus kept a tight leash on his stirring magic. He moved in and swung at her head with a phantom blade. A general wasn't this passive. Not Eretimis's generals. What was her angle?

She sneered, catching his strike with her axe. "You haven't killed me yet." She caught glimpse of the sweat beading down his brow. "Growing a bit worn?"

Zarus dismissed the shadow blade in his hand, letting Nessriq fall a step closer before gathering the magic again. The edge of the phantom dagger pierced her skin, and it was only then that Zarus finally saw the magic protecting her.

A cocoon acting as armor. He'd recognize Eretimis's shadows anywhere. Nessriq quickly retaliated with the slice of her dagger in his side, but couldn't help the shock from her eyes when Zarus pulled her and the knife closer.

His words were ice. *"Just shut up."*

Zarus suddenly threw Nessriq off of him, letting her roll to the edge of the roof. It happened so fast, she never noticed the storm clouds drawing in until the wintrous gusts tore through the mist and revealed the maelstrom above. His magic raged against the grasp of the natural element, but he held tight until the dark mist cleared and he saw Errogan a breath away from Rin.

The maelstrom of ice rained down.

***

Rin's brow creased. *"Eretimis? He's keeping you out of our world?"*

Vulyn's scoff answered.

Yes, Eretimis. The name that will tear down the worlds. Followed once and followed again. The mortals flock to his bidding, and we are left tethered to our realm as a result. Their arrogance is enough to drown the life from your worlds—

Enough, Vulyn.

Lhaerem's chide silenced the Lord of Death.

Followed once, and followed again. Rin shook her head. *"I don't understand what you're saying."* Ice. So much ice. Her thoughts stiffened in its grasp. She barely heard Lhaerem.

It is not time to discuss such events. You are needed elsewhere.

A cry escaped her throat. She grabbed at her head, at the frost prying deeper and deeper. This was not the touch of a kaeth. This harsh cold was familiar. Like the echo of the abyss, so far that it barely brushed her ears.

Rin suddenly heard Zarus's call across the void. Urgency seized her curiosity of the Attendants. *"What do I need to do?"*

***

The lethal ice hit the female. Nessriq shielded her head with her arms, teetering on the edge of the roof, but the magic slamming into her body didn't cut through the shadows protecting her. Despite the ice forcing her backward, the female lunged. Zarus braced himself, but she rushed right past him.

Zarus barely turned in time to see Nessriq raise her axe over Errogan and Rin. Yet instead of chopping the blade down, Nessriq rammed the handle into Errogan's midback.

Errogan's crystal eyes writhed. He fell to his knees beside Rin with little more than a grunt.

"Errogan!" Zarus screamed, running to his friend, but Nessriq intercepted him.

Moonlight flashed on the axe's blade.

***

"What do I need to do? My spine is broken; how can I fix that?"

Rin's vision blurred. The entirety of the counsel faded momentarily, her body burning from the cold. Whatever power held her there wore thin. Her mind pulled from two sides without slack. Mynil's voice was further now.

Reach beyond the walls you placed on yourself, Alentye. Learn from your other half and do not bind yourself to their rules.

"The only walls around me are the ones Yath Ha placed when they brought me into this world!" Rin pleaded.

Vulyn's scoff echoed.

How long will you ignore it, girl? The power that separates you from the world, the power that bridges our realms. Not one, but this is now two wars he has waged on us. You were equipped with half of the means to drag Eretimis Havilurce to retribution. You cannot wait for someone to enact your destiny for you. Stand by your other half and bring peace to the mortal realm.

Rin gritted her teeth against the Divine's scorn. Her thoughts jumped between realms. *"You're placing the impossible upon my shoulders."*

It seemed Vulyn had voiced all his thoughts, for only Lhaerem spoke.

You alone can determine what lies along the line of impossible.

Lyhrëon blurred again.

Easy for a deity to say. She closed her eyes, preparing for the last breeze of the divine paradise, when suddenly someone grabbed her hand. Rin's eyes shot open. She still stood in Lyhrëon, Mynil before her.

Mynil pressed Rin's hand to her chest; no breath, no beat of heart, but life thrummed through the deity. The call of the wild. Rin's breath hitched as the divine power tugged on her. Mynil's words were urgent.

You have placed your magic into a mold, Erin. As long as you keep it there, it will not grow as it should. Reshape your power to your own accord. You have done it once before, all you need is to break down the walls you closed yourself into.

Rin parted her lips, but the presence pressed down on her shoulders. Mynil's hands faded, as did the kaetha behind. She blinked, and suddenly her stare refocused on the mortal realm.

Frost grew on Rin's body. Steel clashed.

Chapter Seventy-One

A flash. A spark. Rin didn't flinch at the blinding magic that erupted when her eyes opened. She grasped the tether of power hiding behind the walls of her perception and pulled. The barriers turned to rubble in her wake. Rin delved into the abysmal bank of magic.

A shell of light formed over her spine and the wound on her chest. She sucked in her first living breath and climbed to her feet.

The axe lifted in the air, the merciless handle aimed for the curve of Zarus's back.

Rin's magic flowed with her, welling in her mind and pulsing until it thrummed through her entire body. Not a separate entity, but it *was* her. An orchestra waiting to be conducted. The sudden flash startled Nessriq, allowing Zarus to grab the axe's handle and redirect the demon's momentum away.

Zarus looked through the blinding light. They shared a knowing glance. Tatsuo's blood still drowned the roof. The dragon's spear lay fallen in the pools.

"Nessriq Wythorn," Rin called; calm yet so thunderous, her voice didn't entirely feel like her own.

The general caught her balance and looked at Rin through veiled shock. "What blessing have I been granted to be directed by such holy power, Light Bearer?"

Rin struggled to keep her voice steady. "Beg for mercy."

Nessriq guarded herself from Zarus's advance, but didn't notice the blast of shadows from behind. She stumbled, forced forward into Rin's path. Nessriq's eyes beheld the *narikaah's* spear in her hands too late. Rin looked the demon in the eye as she thrust the spear into Nessriq's gut.

Rin's magic conducted through the spear. She could see nothing, but her magic burned through layer upon layer of life. Every coursing wave crested in to gather more power.

Slowly, the light faded from the streets of Xandra. Her arms gave out, and Rin leaned her weight onto the base of Tatsuo's spear to keep herself from crashing.

Before she ever swayed, a pair of arms caught her shoulders. Zarus stood at her side until the luminescence of her power was no more. A glimmer under his jacket caught her eyes, the shimmer of a red ruby. She opened her mouth to speak until she heard movement.

"*How,*" Rin bit down.

Nessriq stood across from her, the other side of the roof stripped of color. Not a fleck of her skin was singed. The demon kicked at the zylk corpse that had leapt in her way and taken the heat of the blow. The stiff husk was burned to the core with nothing left to heal, but that didn't explain why Nessriq remained unscathed. Rin's jaw clenched. She cursed the shadow-veil covering the female.

"She's protected," Rin said to Zarus. *Flames, how far does Eretimis's power stretch?*

Zarus nodded. "What's a scrap of shadow but a curtain to tear down."

A chill ensnared Rin's spine. She glanced at him. Frosted rage rampaged in his red eyes. Something white in her peripheral stirred, and it was only then that Rin saw Errogan prostrate on the ground. The demon that haunted her for months writhed much the same she had after Nessriq tried to block her magic.

When did he...

"They're rather useful, you know." Nessriq spoke with such ease, she pulled Rin's attention slowly. "All you need to know is how to attract them, and you have an entire army of shields waiting to take the hit. I would watch yourself, human, your blood is in high demand."

A paralyzing howl pierced the vacant street below. She saw the first zylk whip around the edge of the road, slamming into a building with its barreling speed. Then came the next. And the next. Until an entire horde of zylk swarmed the road. All after her. Her heart ran rampant.

An army. She was to fight an army. Two against one hundred, two hundred? Who could say. And Nessriq Wythorn planned to hide behind all of them if it meant her own survival.

"They listen to one another," Errogan suddenly coughed from the ground. He dragged himself toward her and Zarus. "Like a hive—they communicate. We can guide, but nothing more."

Rin watched the demon with wary eyes. He hadn't attacked before and willingly told them what Eretimis was after... Zarus claimed Errogan wanted out, but blood covered his hands, his chest. Rin knew it was Tatsuo's blood.

"Zarus?" Rin glanced up to the demon's unfairly calm face. He paused his calculations of survival and looked at her.

The zylk were halfway down the street, the world rattling as their claws scraped the cobblestone.

"I just want you to know," she took a deep breath, drawing out the scimitar tucked into his belt, "someone else has probably done something far stupider and survived."

Zarus's brow furrowed, but Rin ran.

Some hundreds verses two. Scimitar in one hand, spear in the other, Rin lunged for the general, but before they crashed, she sliced the curved blade and spear head deep into her own arms. Blood flowed anew, and she swooped below Nessriq's confused guard and locked the general in an embrace from behind.

Stuck and covered in Rin's blood, Nessriq prepared for an attack from Zarus. However, the first zylk scaled the roof and sprinted at them.

***

Doomed to meet the Divine that damned them with this fate.

Zarus had assumed Errogan dismissed the zylk horde he sent after Rin, but it was only a matter of time before found the key on their own. He prepared himself for the first attacks, but instead stared dumbfounded at the human charging forward, slicing her arms and bleeding like a stuck pig.

Erratic, foolish...

Genius. Rin Nowell, you're a genius!

Zarus watched the zylk file onto the roof. The beacon of blood soaking Nessriq lit their path.

When Rin slid behind the general, Zarus didn't need any other clues. The female was stuck between a zylk and Rin's sudden burst of light. His magic surged in response. By the time the first three beasts slammed into the wide-eyed general, huffing and shrieking as they pinned the demon to the ground, Rin let go and sprinted out of the way. Zarus struck true.

Crimson shadow and ice melded together in a flurry of whipping winds around the demon and her shields. Nessriq drowned in the phantom storm, all the while the world struck like a match.

A wall of light erupted along the edge of the roof, and even the sizzle of the power didn't silence the snarling of the zylk that ran into Rin's magic.

His ice cut into Nessriq's armor, her clothes, and the shell of shadow protecting her body. Yet the bonds of Eretimis's magic ran strong. Even from Croft, the Tyrant's magic refused to yield. Blood should have poured, flesh should have been torn, but not an ounce of pain rang in the female's eyes. He couldn't crack through her defense, but perhaps he could pull it away.

A surge of radiance shone through the night besides him. The same radiance that shattered forth the moment Rin awoke from her trance. The wounds healed on her arms, leaving scab nor scar. Yet the light walling the zylk out fizzled.

"That barrier won't keep them out forever," he yelled to Rin as he condensed the storm closer around Nessriq and the zylk battling within. Lupine cries shuttered through the ice and shadow.

"She'll try and block your magic with a blow to the spine." Rin called back. Her voice fell, as did her eyes to where Errogan crawled against a chimney behind.

"Rip away Eretimis's shadows when there's an opening." Something of a growl scraped up her throat. "I'll handle the rest."

Before he could respond, Rin sprinted for the cloud of shadow and frost.

Ice seized his blood, forced him after her. "That cloud will shred you to pieces!" Zarus barked, but Rin ran.

A shell of pale blue magic surrounded her body, cutting through his storm without a hiss of struggle as she barreled through. She was not torn to ribbons, but her magic ran wild alongside his own.

Zarus stared, but only for a moment. He ran through his storm, cutting a path through the magic so as not to be sliced to the bone.

Rin lunged for Nessriq, the scimitar in her hand aiming for the demon's throat. Nessriq had finished slicing through the last of the zylk, and met Rin's strike with the silver bracers on her forearms.

Zarus ran through the black blood of the beasts and whipped a tether of darkness at Nessriq. Rin thrusted Tatsuo's spear in the same motion. The general dropped to a squat below the tendril and spear.

There wasn't a finer opening. Zarus bit down on his focus and stretched the reach of his power to the demon general. Aimlessly his magic clawed at the shadows protecting her, not able to grip a single edge of the fine-tuned magic. By the time Nessriq sprung up, he abandoned the effort, dodging the dagger she aimed for his chest.

"I don't need to knock the magic out of you," Nessriq seethed, "I'll rip your spine out myself!"

Zarus evaded another advance, grabbing the demon's arm and kicking her foot out beneath her.

Nessriq hit the ground head-first. The focus in her eyes dazed, but not long enough. Zarus reached a hand towards the demon's face, hoping to tear that shadow-veil away, but she wrapped her legs around his arm and flipped him onto his back.

He hissed at the impact. Nessriq towered above him suddenly. This Hollowed who had forced her way through ranks and ranks of magic-users and trampled them through wit and strength alone; relentless.

Nessriq knew he was up to something, but didn't voice a retort before Rin threw herself at the general. Both human and demon tumbled across the rooftop before skidding to a graceless stop.

Nessriq groaned to her feet, holding firm on her shoulder, but Rin stayed on the ground.

Zarus clenched his teeth. He knew what he needed to do to end the fight.

Zarus rushed forward. Rin laid on the other side of Nessriq, and he directed himself for the human. Nessriq matched his speed. The blunt of her dagger slammed into the curve of his spine.

Nothing compared to the roar that erupted from Zarus's throat; not the wailing of the winds, nor the fizzling of the light still protecting the rooftop. It was like being ripped out of his body while Ashnagz's Flames consumed him.

Zarus reached for the demon, grabbing only her forearm before he crashed to his knees. The shadow storm calmed until the misty darkness and crystalline shards sat still in the air before disappearing.

His magic had been drained before, but this was not the same. The power that raged for centuries on end was blocked from grasp, but he heard it. All he could do was hold tight to his fists as the demon general sneered down at him.

Nessriq spat out a laugh, ripping her arm out of his grasp, and holding his shoulder to keep him from doubling over.

"I suppose I don't know you," she hissed in his ear. "The demon of legend I've heard so much about wouldn't have fallen. You're just like the rest of them."

He looked deep into her rich brown eyes, so deep that he saw himself within. His breaths were broken glass in his throat. Nessriq rose to a full stand, and Zarus doubled over.

She could have warned me it would hurt that bad...

Suddenly, the world lit up. He couldn't reach the magic to veil his eyes right then. But then again, neither could Nessriq.

***

The storm of shadows disappeared. Rin put everything she had into that blast of light. Nessriq screamed.

Her dark skin waned, her inky hair singed; there wasn't an inch of Nessriq's body or clothing that wasn't burned by the light, and Rin only released the magic when she saw the demon's eyes swell as red as the blood splashed on her face.

Blinded and seared, Nessriq howled, slashing outward for what she could not see. Rin was out of her reach, but not the spear's.

A bellow scraped her throat, and Rin forced the spear into the female's heart.

Red flowed like a spring, the demon's armor cutting like paper against the white dragon scale on the tip of the spear. Nessriq's veil of shadows vanished, and she only then noticed.

Gasping, the clever general found Zarus's body and looked at the dark aura grasped in his hand. Nessriq stumbled forward, catching hold on the spear. The gap between them closed, and the demon's breath warmed Rin's face.

Rin growled in a low voice. "I don't need magic to kill you."

Nessriq returned the gesture. "I should be so honored."

Rin yanked the spear free from the general's chest.

Nessriq swayed on her feet. "*What* are you two?" the demon gasped, that gleam in her eye growing duller and duller by the second. She shook. Was it fear?

"He told me I could take you. He said you were *mortal*. He told me you weren't strong enough! You shouldn't be standing—*how are you moving?*" The demon grew hysteric, her eyes flashing between her and Zarus faster than she could keep up with.

"Ask the gods yourself," Zarus hissed. He barely scraped to his knees.

Despite the blood flowing, despite the tremble of her words, Nessriq gathered herself and loosed a cool smile. "Why don't we ask together?"

The demon became a blur. Nessriq threw herself with nothing other than her bare hands to claim Zarus's life. He was in no condition to fight her off.

Rin snatched the battle axe in an instant. The axe severed flesh and bone. Nessriq's scream wasn't that of a mighty general who crafted her way to the top, but a defeated demon whose leg was chopped off at the knee. Her rancid blood poured over the green roof tiles. She thrashed, grabbing the stump of her leg with no means for relief.

"*Maggoty human!*" Nessriq seethed through her tears. "*You haven't the spine to raise that axe again—*"

Rin did just that. The general's face contorted. Yet before Rin swung the axe into the demon's neck, Zarus slammed the pommel of his silver dagger into the demon's skull. The general fell limp. Rin grit her teeth and stepped forward. The sight of Tatsuo's blood blazed in her mind, still warm on her skin.

She screamed and swung the axe, but Zarus caught the handle before it killed Nessriq Wythorn.

Rin raised the axe again and again, but Zarus stopped the weapon. He called her name, but Rin ignored it. Until finally, her skin blistered over the wooden handle. Her muscles burned. The wall of light protecting the roof raged. The world slowly returned to her senses, and Rin met Zarus's stare.

She swung the axe behind her head one last time. "Let me finish this," she pleaded. "Please."

***

Zarus tried to keep his eyes clear, but tears welled. He longed to step aside and let Rin do it, but he stayed between her and the demon who killed Tatsuo.

She begged him once more, but he shook his head with more pain than he could contain. Slowly, the axe slid out of Rin's hands and clattered on the roof. She fell into him and sobbed.

Zarus lowered as her knees gave, heaving a heavy breath to fight the cry in his throat. "She can give us information," he finally said in a low, broken tone. Rin squeezed him tighter. "Then she can die."

A warm breeze gusted through the air between them, the hum of magic hissed from the roof's edge.

Zarus glanced at the wall Rin upheld, but hissed at the sudden pierce in his eye. Eretimis's magic... he glanced at the shadows swarming to return to its host in his hand.

"Pull the wall down." Errogan's voice croaked. Rin whipped around to the demon limping away from the lifeless zylk. Burned and blanched, he looked no better than Zarus himself probably did.

"So we'll all be killed?" Rin's words were sharper than a knife. Errogan flinched at her tone. A gesture that staggered her anger.

The White-Cloaked Reaper's stared at the dead zylk. He sighed. "I'll direct them back to the fortress, out of the city. Flames, just stop burning them!"

"Rin," Zarus forced himself to say. She shifted her wary eyes to him, and the only effort he could put forth was a nod. Rin looked uncertain, but eventually drew in a heavy breath.

The wall of fizzling magic ebbed, fading until darkness seized the city. Zarus was left temporarily blinded. When his eyes adjusted, the zylk did not approach.

Rin's scoff tore through the sudden silence. "Why didn't you send them away to begin with if you really wanted to help?"

Errogan sighed again, sheathing the silver sword as the zylk swarmed northward. "I told you, I can only guide them. You drew them here with the Key, and Nessriq held them."

Soothed by no means, the answer quelled Rin's anger enough to keep her from yelling at Errogan. Zarus was actually surprised. Though, not too surprised when she walked away from them both.

Zarus shook his head. "You sent them after Rin so I could find her. You said you were leaving. Why did you come back?"

Errogan thought for a moment. "Eretimis uses the zylk as fodder." His crystal eyes dropped, the muscles in his jaw clenching. "Disposable..." He lifted his hardened stare. "Godless or not, they're still alive."

"Errogan..." Zarus's voice was a whisper. *Is that truly what you think you are?*

His old friend looked away. "And now I have to take them back north. Give me that." Errogan pointed to the shadows fighting to be free in Zarus's hand, but held up a hand to silence Zarus's refusal. "It's too dangerous to be left here. I can take it as proof of Nessriq's defeat. I... I *have* to return, Zarus." His bright eyes shifted from him to the northern horizon. "There's no choice for me."

Zarus was sick of the notion. But the sting of his eyes at that moment made him understand. He mirrored Errogan's grim expression. Tentatively, Zarus handed over the swarming magic.

The demon took a single step before Zarus caught his arm.

"I will figure this out," Zarus promised. "Come back to me, and I will figure out how to free us both."

The edge of Errogan's lip tugged, though not enough to be called a grin. "We'll see if there's anything left to free."

They shared one final gaze before the horde of zylk cried distantly. Errogan slipped out of his grasp and disappeared off the roof. Godless, without purpose of their own. How many souls did Eretimis twist and break before he raised his army of the innocent damned?

Zarus stared northward until the blood on the rooftop rippled. Behind, Rin knelt in the pools. He swallowed one last breath before falling at her side as she hugged the lifeless body of Tatsuo Kurosawa.

Her sobs shook the night.

The thrum of her magic brushed Zarus's skin, but Tatsuo's skin never warmed. His neck never healed.

Chapter Seventy-Two

"It is with a heavy heart that we stand here today. It is with the heaviest grief that we do not celebrate a victory, but instead mourn the lives of those valiant souls who sacrificed themselves."

The murky clouds blotted out the afternoon sun. The air was far too cold for late spring.

"None shall be forgotten, no names lost to the tides of time. History was made in a single night; history to be written down and taught, history that has branded us and our children and their children for generations to come."

Rin watched Elyot Iver address the crowd of mourners. He stood on the platform of the temple steps adorned with ceremonial ivy and golden sconces. His face was stone, his voice no better. Genesis stood at his side, holding a torch in silence. As far as Rin could see while tucked to the side of the lower steps, the crowds garbed in black and grey filled the square, standing shoulder to shoulder from the farthest street edge to the overflowing steps of the temple. Shoulder to shoulder, Rin and Zarus stood amid strangers after failing to find her family.

"These valiant souls will not be laid to rest in vain. Our draconic brethren will not be burned by funeral pyre only to be lost to memory.

We will not allow our brothers and sisters to fall to the hand of war without a word!"

Slowly, a murmur of fervor stirred the crowd. Rin watched from her position before the platform as the trance of heartache thinned. Yet she only saw the wooden structure doused in oil on the temple steps.

"I stand here before the living—the *surviving*—before those who defended their city against an enemy so legendary, it hid in our bed stories until a month ago. We will not leave the survivors of Croft to claw for life! We will not stand by while they are slaughtered and dragged to the frozen north! I stand here before the hope of our realm that defeated this force, the hope that will defeat them again!"

Someone bellowed amid the masses, heavy and passionate. Another followed. It echoed in their hearts, it echoed in Rin's heart. Elyot shouted it over the growing hum of bereavement and vengeance.

Rin couldn't help the weak scoff welling in her throat. "There's no hope to find here. He out of everyone knows that."

Elyot Iver stirred enough morale to rile the crowd, but his voice strained, his expression pulled.

After days of ghostly silence, Zarus spoke. "Do you not think he knows that?"

He hadn't looked to her, eyes stuck on the pyre. A response bubbled on Rin's tongue, but the gaze of crimson eyes stifled her urge to snap back.

"The man just buried his son, Rin, and he still stands before the people looking to him for answers. That is not something to mock."

It was true. Zarus's suspicions of Aiden Iver were wrong. The man had been slain in battle the night of the attack—his face ripped clean off by the zylk as he defended a magic user. No ploys, no faking deaths.

Aiden had died defending the city he loved, the people he loved, and yet his father stood on a damned platform at his funeral.

Her eyes narrowed. She couldn't help it. "Are we supposed to feed into these lies?"

The demon studied her. "You can't discern truth from lie when blinded by fresh grief."

"So what are we supposed to do? Move on?" The words hissed through her teeth. "I can't pretend like this is pointing toward something better!"

"No one's asking you to."

Zarus's tone didn't shift; he didn't shout. Rin raged against his calmness. She balled her fists deep in the depths of her pockets. "Then what are you asking of me?"

"To live." Zarus redirected his attention to the memorial service where Elyot was listing off the names of the dead.

The names were a whisper against Zarus's voice. "Every breath," *Danrial Zettalichk*— "every word off your tongue," *Anartha Rivellun*— "every beat of your heart," *Kaenyth Brettan*— "is proof that there's still such thing as hope. Whether its against Eretimis or the voice in the back of your head telling you to give up. You are living, breathing proof of hope. So just keep living, Rin, and you'll find it again."

Rin's eyes stung with tears. She supposed if he could speak such words, there might be something of truth to them. She fell silent, listening to Elyot's voice.

"Lastly, a name that forged our trust and friendship with another species, Tatsuo Kurosawa. May his name live on forever in our praises, and the Guiding Hands of Vulyn bring him eternal peace."

Elyot lifted the burning sconce from the post beside him. The leader of the New Light glanced into the crowd, through the hundreds of faces watching his every breath, only to fall heavy onto her.

Rin bit down on the sob. She tightened her fists around the urge to scream and rage at the heavens and hells. Someday. Someday she would find the truth to Zarus's words, but it was not as Elyot lowered the torch and lit the *narikaah's* body ablaze.

***

Dusk arrived, and Rin watched as Tatsuo's flame burned out. She went home that night and drowned herself in the numbness of sleep. Even when she woke, she didn't stir until evening the next day when she was needed.

It was Elyot's idea. He waited until after the funeral, but demanded the users who came to defend the city be recognized. Freia and her band had saved thousands of lives from the zylk. They had stayed when countless people told them to leave and threatened their lives. One older gentleman caster even hunted down the zylk that ripped Aiden's face off.

Elyot was eternally grateful, but Rin saw the shame in his demeanor. He had left the users to fend for themselves for so long, he was determined to set things right.

Iver organized a ceremony of recognition, and Genesis helped. They called the band of users in front of Xandra, called any who were willing to stand tall before hundreds of eyes, and thanked their strength and bravery.

Her mother—bearing her true name once more—had been chosen as their representative. Cissrey stood nearest to Elyot, next to Freia. Cautious, yet each user finally held some ounce of pride.

Genesis revealed plans for a new school for magic in Xandra, where users could learn to master their craft and live peacefully. He told Cissrey the job of headmaster was hers, if she would have it. Rin was pleasantly surprised when her mother accepted. Just as the users and Genesis began to file off the platform, Elyot halted the prince.

"I cannot run this kingdom alone," the aged commander admitted. He turned toward the crowd of Nokomai. "This kingdom has grown and shaped in ways beyond our expectations, and it will continue to do so until it reaches what glory it once possessed. I know what we need to reach that glory, and that is the leadership of our true King."

Despite everything, Rin cracked a smile. The wide-eyed king found her through the masses. She nodded at him, and mouthing the word *yes* as if he needed a clue. Genesis shifted his stare to the citizens of Xandra awaiting his answer. Finally, he spoke.

"It would be my honor to pick up where my father and uncle left off."

Elyot smiled. "I'm glad you said that."

He summoned Gillan from the crowd. The stoic woman walked onto the platform missing half of her left arm. A gift from the zylk. She carried a long object covered under a black cloth and held it in offering to the commander.

"I hope this inspires you to bear us a little while longer, Your Majesty."

Elyot pulled back the cloth, revealing an ornate sword with a gold handle. Rin couldn't see very well from where she stood, but it looked finely crafted, decorated with jewels and engravings. Emotion surge in Genesis's eyes.

Elyot Iver smiled at the King, his voice tender. "General Albus's sword."

Genesis reached for his father's blade. He managed a wavering smile.

Scarlette was the first to shatter the silence, followed by Feyne, her father, and even Zarus clapped. Then the New Light members erupted with a cheer until the crowd shared their excitement. Rin made sure to help.

Croft would not be left for dead. Nokomic would not perish. However, the Dark Tyrant openly walked Armiria. The world flipped upside-down, even if they all had yet to feel the consequences.

Chapter Seventy-Three

Rin scratched the back of her head. "I'll be... here. I'll be there. I'll be a bit everywhere."

"That's not exactly an answer," Scarlette groaned.

Rin pursed her lips, but a surge of magic arose in response. With all the commotion of the last few weeks—cleaning up debris, search and rescues, planning and strategizing—her magic was still the most frenzied force she'd met. No longer raging, but it coursed round and round in her soul waiting to be directed. She had yet to get used to it, especially at such a late hour.

She sucked in a deep breath, rubbing her temples before looking at Zarus across the dining table. They had only just sat down to eat before retiring. "What do you think?"

He closed his eyes, inhaling deep. "We'll be here to straighten up the city, but we need to search for a way to reach Eroz without Eretimis noticing. That could take us anywhere."

Rin resumed her attention on Scarlette standing under the doorway. A shrug wiggled from Rin's shoulders. "Forward any information you find to Ma, I guess. I'll be back eventually to pick it up."

Cissrey Nowell would be in Xandra for some time, seeing as she was now the headmaster of the magic school and sent out word to every user across the kingdom. Adrian Nowell, her faithful companion and recently hired teacher, would also remain at her side. While her father didn't know the first thing about magic, no one else was more qualified to dissect the tedious texts.

Scarlette nodded. "Sounds good. However, I hope you're not expecting any urgent news from the east. If it has to travel across the sea *and* wait for you to find your mom..."

Rin's fingers warily tapped on the table. "How can you be sure the messages won't be intercepted?"

Scarlette shifted her weight from foot to foot. She never seemed to stop moving once she recovered. "Feyne grew up on the other side of the sea. He says he still has allies. We'll find who we can trust and make sure the information gets to you safely."

Rin rubbed her temples, soothing the magic. Her stare fell into focus, only then noticing Scarlette had taken a seat beside her.

"Feyne and I will be okay. This isn't his first time crossing the sea, and I'm more than strong enough to watch both our backs now."

A truth; after Rin embraced the new spans of her magic, Scarlette's infection cleared right away. Her mother worked hard to regrow as much of the girl's muscle as possible.

"Where are you going to start once you get to shore?" Zarus asked.

"We're looking to dock farther south, then head north to Ghandarah. Hopefully there will be rumors regarding the shifters' whereabouts."

Rin trekked through the mental maps she tried to memorize, trailing all the way along the eastern continent's coastline until she found the city port at the edge of a desert. "Why not go straight to Ghandarah?"

"The demon colonies on the continent make large cities dangerous," the scholar explained. "Showing up on the city's doorstep by
ship is riskier than walking in with the crowds."

"I guess running around the desert all those years is going to pay
off," Rin mused.

Scarlette groaned. "I'm not sure I share your enthusiasm, Alentye.
If I get bored along the way, I can always scare the souls that cross
paths with me by telling them all the little details that make them up,"
Scarlette said, waggling her eyebrows above god-touched eyes.

Rin chuckled. "I think that's abuse of power."

"Perhaps, but perhaps it will teach all those who cross me to heed
my every command." She added a haughty laugh at the end. At that,
Feyne suddenly rounded the corner into the dining room.

"Make sure you don't scare all the shifters before we have an alliance, love," the wolf sighed, leaning down to kiss Scarlette on the
forehead.

An alliance to stand against Eretimis. Scarlette and Feyne would
head east to convince the elusive shifters and human cities to stand
against the Tyrant. Genesis and Elyot would write a lot of letters and
visit a lot of people. Every allegiance Elyot had made over the last
eleven years, every relationship and trust developed—they would call
on every thing. Rin doubted Eretimis was complacent with only the
Resurrection under his wing. He would reach out to the kingdoms of
the west, luring them with promises of prosperity.

"Are you sure you'll be alright on your own?" Rin asked. "There's
a lot to do for just two people across the sea. We could probably—"

Zarus shot her a sharp look over the candles on the table. Right.
Time was a resource, and they had yet to find a path to their destination.

Scarlette smiled again. "We'll be alright, Rin. Promise. Two people is better anyway; faster travel, easier to keep a low profile."

"Beside," Feyne added, "the fae are a world away, and Vi hasn't been back around to help us gain their favor. You have a lot on your plate."

She and Zarus were set for Milganos to convince the fae to join their cause—an endeavor that chilled her blood. However, the endeavor proved difficult since they were stuck on Armiria.

A chill traced down Rin's spine. She propped her chin onto her hand, looking to Zarus.

Something brewed in his head that had been there ever since the night Tatsuo died; ever since she relayed what the kaetha had told her. Rin supposed she wouldn't know what unless she asked or pried. Neither of which she felt like doing.

"How long did it take you to master that skill?" Zarus held an intense stare on Scarlette's eyes.

Scarlette looked surprised at the demon. "It took no time to memorize the technique, about six months to finally get it to work, and I've been perfecting the skill ever since."

He leaned into the table. "Six months and you could read anyone's aura?"

"Yes—er, well, the first layer of it. It takes longer to dig deeper, more practice."

Zarus paused for a moment, chest barely rising with each breath. "The first layer is what species they are?"

Scarlette nodded, but quickly, her expression lifted.

"I think it would be in our best interest to teach more humans how to use that power," Zarus thought aloud. "Telling friend from foe might come in handy."

"I'd reckon it would take even less time since they have me as their teacher and not a dusty old scroll," Scarlette added. "Might even be an incentive to those who stand with us."

An army with god-touched eyes. An army capable of stopping the enemy from sneaking into a city and setting off enough explosives to spark an invasion. Scarlette's eyes were the only reason they knew the Resurrection was working with Eretimis, the only reason they knew Nessriq was a demon right off the bat. Being that prepared, that ready... something of excitement stirred Rin's mood.

"My father," Rin stated. "Teach it to my father and ask him to help you teach the others. He'll be able to help while you're away."

Scarlette's eyes brimmed with excitement. She never missed a chance to work with the older scholar. "I'll make a plan tonight and talk to him in the morning! I'll know how to go about this before we leave."

Scarlette Draelin shot to her feet. She headed for the dark hall, audibly muttering to herself along the way.

Feyne sighed, rubbing his eyes. "You couldn't have waited until morning to suggest that, Lowwenth? She was all set to finally go to sleep, but nooo. You had to add another idea to her agenda." He glared sleepy daggers, and Rin nearly laughed at Zarus's confusion.

"He's joking," Rin explained, but her smile faltered as she looked at Feyne. "Right?"

The wolf's expression lightened, but the yearn for sleep didn't. "Only somewhat. It's a battle every night to convince her to sleep. Have a good night, you two. Make sure to get the rest I won't be receiving any time soon." He shot Zarus another sharp eye, but the jest was clear as night. At least to Rin it was. Zarus on the other hand looked as confused as a pup lost in the streets.

The shifter waved a silent goodbye, but Rin was on his heel before he passed the door.

"I'll walk with you," she announced. "My room is on the way."

Rin strode out of the dining room before he could say a thing. Feyne fell in step with her.

"Everything alright with you two?" he asked once they were up the stairs.

"All's well. I want to get to bed before anyone else stops me."

"You suck at lying," Feyne said, throwing a wrench in her thoughts. "You did half a year ago, and you do twice as much now."

Rin opened her mouth to bite at the shifter, but she was met with a wry grin. In fact, it left her sinking in on herself.

"What's on your mind?" he asked.

What isn't. Rin sucked in a hardy breath.

"I can't," she began, piecing her thoughts together. "I can't keep quiet for too long. I can't sit still. It's like I'm falling inside my mind and I can't come back out and—" Her head pounded. Before she could go any further, the shifter placed a hand on her shoulder.

"I understand, Rin," he offered. "Zarus isn't the best person to take your mind off things."

What an understatement. She sighed. "I can't sit in sullen silence alone right now. Not yet."

A moment passed. Then two. Two more than she'd have preferred, but she couldn't blame the wolf. It was a lot to dump in a matter of seconds.

"Rin," he said carefully.

She looked at him, though his focus had fallen to the floor.

"When I lost Scarlette last year, I didn't want to go on. I wanted to give up, but you were determined to help me. You kept encouraging me to heal, even when I fought against you. You and Tatsuo are the only reason I didn't lose myself..."

He scratched the back of his head. "I've been trying to find the words for months now, but nothing seems right. Pain isn't an excuse to take advantage of kindness or lash out at those trying to help. I'm sorry. You're not alone right now. I promise that I'll do better. Even if it's a continent away. I'll convince the shifters to join us, make things right."

Rin's mouth gaped. "Feyne," she bit down on her tightening throat. "Thank you."

The wolf returned a smile, allowing what hovered between them for months to dissolve.

The shifter nodded. Before he sought out his frenzied scholar, Rin wished him goodnight and good luck. She turned around in hopes of finding her bed, but ran face first into a king when she rounded the corner.

Genesis grimaced, taking a sharp step backward. "Would you watch where you're going, Nowell? Vulyn's Pits, you'd think you'd get the sense when my royal presence is in front of you by now." Clad head to toe in his day clothes, he still had his father's sword strapped to his belt—still looked like he hadn't slept in ages too. Thank the gods he finally shaved though. He must have just gotten home.

Instead of retorting, Rin held a silent finger up to her lips then gestured at the door they stood before. Genesis followed her stare, realized it was Gillan's room, then promptly paled at the memory of the last time they accidentally woke the woman up by talking outside her door. He probably still had a bruise from the vase she threw at his back

"I suggest we finish this conversation in my room," Rin whispered. Genesis nodded, following close until they filed into her quarters at the end of the hall.

Rin chuckled, casting a small globe of light on the ceiling. "Why, may I ask, are you up creeping around the halls at this hour?" She flopped onto her bed.

"I was on a quest to seek out the rumored Light Bringer. I only wish that she would bring some sliver of joy to my life and let me speak with her."

"You're too humble, Your Majesty," she jeered, whipping a pillow at his face.

Pushing his disheveled hair out of his eyes, the King went on. "Scarlette was looking for you earlier. She told me to give this to one of the Two Chosen when I saw you." Reaching into his overcoat, Genesis walked to the bed and dropped a book beside her. "And since it slipped my mind when I was talking to Zarus a few minutes ago, here you go."

Rin sighed, forcing herself to sit up. Old, like any other book Scarlette shoved her way. Pressed between the pages rested a piece of paper reading, '*This might be of interest to you god-chosen bunch.*' Scarlette's handwriting.

Of course the scholar didn't mention it when she happened to find Rin in the dining room. For the same reason Genesis hadn't mentioned it to Zarus. Everyone had so much on their mind. Rin looked at the prince as he sat down in the armchair near the hearth.

Puzzlement creased her brow. "Did she say what it was about?"

"She was already walking down the hall when she handed it to me."

Rin placed the book on her nightstand. "Well, thank you my loyal messenger. I can always count on you." She stretched her arms and closed her eyes. "But I am completely spent and want nothing more than to pass out right now. I'll see you in the morning?" The warmth and comfort of her bed called to her. Rin cracked an eye open, but was met with the King's frown.

A hollow pang rang through her chest. "I'm not seeing you in the morning, am I?"

Genesis opened his mouth, but the words lodged in his throat. "I'm leaving at dawn."

Rin swallowed her disappointment. Even Genesis had agreed it wasn't the time for them to be together, not after the attack on the city. He needed to rebuild a kingdom, she needed to carry out the gods' unspoken work. That didn't make it any easier.

She kept her voice steady. "When will you be back?"

"I don't know." He shook his head, slumping against the chair. "The Resurrection slipped out of Xandra without a trace, but we have no idea if they went to Croft, the fortress, or if they're hiding somewhere else. Elyot and I are leading searches in the villages nearby. From there, we'll work our way out." A heavy sigh hissed through his nose.

"Nessriq still hasn't woken up, so we can't interrogate her for answers, but we can't wait. The mercenary we captured told us Bjarkh Grevik sought out Nikolai Druvisk, and they came to a deal. They have no idea what's waiting for them in Eretimis's welcome. They have no idea of the things they're about to go through. How many more of them will turn into one of the zylk?"

Rin's gaze fell to the floorboards. Genesis was the first of those experiments, and after seventy years, Eretimis perfected his craft. What horrors awaited those foolish humans?

She pushed the thought far away. "So this is goodbye?"

Sadness sank into Genesis's eyes. The King of Nokomic nodded.

Part of Rin wanted to make some witty retort, casting him off with a farewell to leave them both laughing. Truth be told? Her heart lay empty.

She stood from the bed and walked across the room. The King stood from his chair. Tears streamed down his cheeks. Rin threw her arms around him, resting her head against his neck. She wanted nothing more than to remain in his warmth.

They stood in silence, their sobs relentless. She didn't want to stir, not when she knew this moment would end and he would leave. Softly, his fingers brushed against hers. She uncurled her hand to hold his, but a weight dropped in it instead.

"What's this?" She looked at the copper piece in her palm.

"Coin for your thought." He gently wrapped her fingers around the coin and smiled. Genesis hugged tighter, his voice lulling her tears. "Nothing will ever keep me from you, Rin Nowell. If you need me, call and I'll be there. I promise I will always be there."

One day. One day they could find peace, but that day had not yet come.

Chapter Seventy-Four

Part of Zarus wanted to say more. The King sought him out, the King apologized immediately, the King asked for his forgiveness. Zarus didn't know what to do. Genesis hadn't even been the one out of line. Zarus forgave him, and apologized for his claims of Aiden's betrayal, and less than appropriate comment. Yet despite being on good grounds with his friend once more, Zarus couldn't get the bitter taste out of his mouth.

He had been wrong about Aiden. What if he had gone straight to Elyot like he wanted? He could have single-handedly ruined all trust built between him and the humans, possibly between Genesis and the New Light. Up in flames, and the ashes would have stained his hands for the rest of his life. If Tatsuo hadn't talked sense into him...

Zarus closed his eyes, inhaling the darkness suffocating the sleeping house. He walked the halls in silence, allowing the nighttime ambience to mingle with his senses. He needed to talk to Rin. Hopefully he caught her before she fell asleep or ran away from him again. To his relief, light showed beneath the crack under her door. A shadow paced back and forth.

He knocked three times, and the shadow halted. Even through the door, Rin's magic pulled at him, the wisps brushing his mind. So much stronger than he had ever known it. And so different—so akin to his own. He knew she felt the tug too. He got the message. Zarus turned on his heels, but the doorknob clicked.

"You can come in."

He glanced over his shoulder, squinting against the light. It no longer blinded him as it once did, but it wasn't pleasant to look at in a dark hall.

"I don't wish to disturb you."

"It disturbed the Flames out of you when you took me in last year." He heard the jest, but it didn't carry to Rin's face.

She still wore her day clothes, boots and all. He nodded at the girl. Her face glowed like a star, not a shadow cast onto her body. How far could that light reach? A beacon to guide or a warning to repel, he couldn't figure out which.

"Don't your neighbors ever complain?"

He walked into the door, softly closing it behind. He glanced around the quarters, the fading scent of Genesis Masquarem lingering around the armchair. It suddenly dawned that this maybe wasn't the time to talk. He knew the King was leaving in the morning. He must have said his farewell to Rin already. Zarus was about to suggest that they wait to talk, but once he looked up, his thought was lost to the wind.

It wasn't only Rin that brightened the corridor. All around the room, glimmering light sprawled. In spheres and rods and flowing cascades. Tendrils and wings and mist and frays. White and yellow, warm and cold. He blinked twice at the rippling waves of blue and green and red illuminance.

There wasn't an inch of the room the light didn't touch. He stood in awe. All at once, that light slung back from whence it came. A wave of energy pushed past him and landed in Rin, catching his hair and clothes in its course. As controlled as the moon's tide. All light faded, save the orb floating at the ceiling.

Rin stared evenly at him. "They don't complain after the zylk."

Zarus's expression pulled taut. Unease settled in his gut; one he couldn't decipher. So he didn't try. "Speaking with the Divine channeled your power well."

"Working without the limits I set on myself cleared way for new paths," she shrugged. "I finally understand what you meant when you told me not to follow the rules others set down. I don't know why, but I'm not the same as other humans. I can do so much more than them."

Yet there wasn't a hint of joy in her face. How often had he known the same weight pulling her beneath the guilt? Zarus swallowed the breath stuck in his throat and stopped looking at her like he was trying to solve a puzzle.

"Look," he began, his stare falling to the gold stitches in the rug, "We both want answers from the gods. We both want to watch Eretimis fall to his knees and force him to pay for everything he's robbed. But Rin..." He closed his eyes on the hate frosting his blood. "Don't make yourself miserable."

Her brow furrowed. "I don't understand what you mean."

Of course she didn't. He wouldn't either.

Zarus sighed, rubbing the top of his head as he tried to make sense of his thoughts. "Don't come to Eroz with me."

Not the right way. Definitely not the right way. A frown the length of Nokomic's boarder pulled her expression. "You don't want me to go?"

Zarus winced at the sadness in her voice. "No, I do want you to go."

Sadness dropped to irritation. Rin's hands propped on her hips. "Then why shouldn't I go?"

A groan rumbled his chest. Zarus fell back into the armchair, rubbing the frustration out of his temples. "You *can* come with me, but you don't have to."

Her hands fell back to her sides. "Oh," she mumbled, vexation easing. "Well I know that."

She waved off the issue with a hand, walking across the quarters and sitting on the edge of her bed. "Did you come all this way only to tell me that?" The girl began sliding off her boots.

Zarus couldn't massage the headache away. He gave up hope, leaning his elbow on the chair and propping his head. "I thought you would like to know."

Rin cast him an uncertain glance as she threw her shoes beneath the bed. "Can I ask why?"

He released the tension from his mind, feeling his magic stir with it. "With everything that's been going on, I didn't want you to feel like you have to come with me. You could aid Genesis, or Feyne and Scarlette, or even stay here with your parents."

Rin finished fighting her boots away, and gazed at him with inquisitive thoughts. Her fingers tapped along the bedpost. Until finally, she clicked her tongue.

"I appreciate the offer, but do you really think that you're getting rid of me that easily?"

Zarus blinked. "I, uh... no?"

A smile broke through Rin's melancholy. "We have too many things to figure out, too big a task convincing the fae. I'm not letting you have all the fun."

Zarus stared. "That's your idea of fun?"

A chuckle escaped her hold. "You and I are in this together, like it or not. The Two Chosen, whatever that means. How are we supposed to train together if you ditch me in this world?"

Rin stared at him, her warm, joyful smile peeking through.

He couldn't help himself. Against all the questions he still had, against the image of Tatsuo dying on the rooftop, the barreling ignorance he had been tossed into regarding the gods and this girl, Zarus grinned.

"In this together," he repeated.

Rin tipped her head upward, eyes veiled shut. "I'm not leaving you to help Errogan on your own either."

Zarus heard the steel lingering at the edge of her tone. "Still don't trust him?"

Rin cast him a humorless glare. "I trust your word that he tried to save Tatsuo. I trust your word that he wants to leave Eretimis. I don't trust him to make the right choice."

Zarus lowered his chin. The demon was the only reason Tatsuo's head didn't roll off the roof. He helped defeat the female held in their very dungeons. What other right choice was there?

Sharing blood, godless beings, copies of the original. Zarus could piece together what Errogan always left unsaid—why he was forced to return to the Tyrant time and time again. He didn't know how, but Zarus was certain Eretimis's dark magic kept Errogan in check. And he intended to do whatever was necessary to free his friend from the Tyrant.

Rin blew out a sigh. "You said it yourself, there are demons feigning loyalty to the Tyrant on Armiria and Eroz both. They're afraid. If we can convince them to turn on Eretimis... we might be able to stop him. That plan might start with Errogan."

Zarus watched the girl for a long moment. She didn't trust Errogan, she didn't like him. He wouldn't doubt if Rin blamed Errogan for the death of Tatsuo. But Rin Nowell would help him save the demon that almost killed her. Zarus suspected she'd never stop surprising him.

"I think we have a journey to plan, Erin Nowell," he smiled. Rin reached down and threw her boot at his head. Luckily, he was warned she preferred her nickname and caught it. "Although, not having a path to Eroz hinders our progress."

Where in the world would they begin their search? Despite the attempt, Zarus hadn't been able to open a portal since the crypt. The seals holding the worlds apart were too strong—and he was positive the only reason he managed it last time was because the gods helped. Only Eretimis and a select few loyalists knew how to break the seals between Armiria and Eroz. Zarus didn't even know where to start.

"We could beat it out of Nessriq." Rin's words were cold as steel.

"We might have to," Zarus admitted. He steepled his hands to his lips. The female had been out cold since their battle, thrown into the deepest cell in Xandra's prison and put under constant watch. "But if she doesn't wake up, we need another plan."

Rin's expression strained suddenly. "Didn't Tat—" It was like watching her chew glass. The name lodged in her throat. Her stare dropped. "He said his parents came a different way, one unknown to Eretimis. That's how they were able to sneak into Armiria."

Zarus recalled the *narikaah*'s tale. "It could be possible... That still leaves us without a clue of how to find it."

They both fell silent. It would take a miracle, and Zarus had spent all his luck recently. He loosed a sigh.

"We'll meet tomorrow and ask around. Maybe Scarlette knows a legend or two about it." Slowly, he rose to his feet, biting down on the twinge of his eye. His grip around the dark magic hadn't been solid ever since the attack.

Rin noticed, but watched silently. Her hands clenched at her sides. So many unanswered questions. His head ached.

Without another word, Zarus walked himself to the door as Rin blurted out. "Before I forget!"

Zarus glanced over his shoulder, the very act sending splinters through his iris.

Rin ran behind him, carrying a book in hand. "Scarlette said this might help us, but it's all in another language and I'm too tired to look through it." The bags under her eyes were as dark as his.

Zarus took the book from Rin's hand. The peeling leather frayed under his touch. Flipping the heavy cover to the first page, he sighed.

The ink bled with age. Smudged characters and faded lines. As he held the text closer, the stale aroma of libraries filled his nostrils. He deciphered a few strokes of ink.

Written in a distant Caenlin dialect, Zarus read aloud, "*Hidden Treasures: A Personal Research of Forgotten Riches.*" The book was old—archaic. How it had upheld all those years, he was curious. How Scarlette managed to dig it up? Curiouser. The name of the author had worn too thin to read, so he flipped the book open where the scholar tagged a note. After reading the first few lines, Zarus's heart skipped.

"What's it say?" Rin pried.

"It's—" Zarus paused, rereading the page. Could it *really* have been that easy? He stared in disbelief. He didn't know whether to praise the gods or curse them for showing off.

"It's a guide for traveling among worlds... *Three* different worlds."

Epilogue

Hidden Treasures: A Personal Research of Forgotten Riches

For so long, humanity thought it was alone, that all our myths and legends were simply that. We were never so wrong.

I have spoken of the shifters mostly in these pages, since they are the most welcoming to our kind, but I long to meet them all. I know they are out there, the beings called demons and fae and dragons. So elusive to our human eyes, but I can feel them.

The chief of the shifter tribe I visited warned me against them, saying that those kinds only stirred trouble on Armiria. If that is the case, where do they not stir trouble? The ghran *said nothing more on the matter when I asked, warning me to stay away from them. That unfolded so many new questions. Answers I have spent the better part of my life searching for. And here, at the long reaches of my years, I have gathered as much research as I can regarding the distant worlds Eroz and Lathaelon. Yet despite digging up all the worlds' secrets—despite unlocking the hidden paths to travel there—I am afraid I have become much too old to partake on that journey.*

Research is not conducted for one lone soul. It is for the generations after me to utilize. I have broken up this small portion of research into sections, hoping someone in years to come will find this book and use it to visit the wonders that elude our grasp.

Gates

Gateways were the most mainstream technique. It is a portal that opens in one location and exits in another. I believe the skill was inspired by the magic of a black mage if I am honest, and it was invented by humans (who would have thought!).

There are two uses for gateways: traveling among the three different worlds, and using the portal to travel in the same world. The technique is simple, needing only two things: the official seal for the world in which you would like to travel, and magic. Magic is what makes the simple rather unsimple. If you are not a magic user, myself included, then skip this technique because it would be equivalent to entering an archery contest with naught but an ill-tempered hen as your tool. It is a futile approach. But if you are gifted with such abilities, I bid you read on.

First you would perform your choice of meditative methods to collect your magic. When you are ready, extend the index and middle finger on your dominant hand. Focus your magic into these fingers, and use them to draw out your desired destination's world seal in the air (it is the same technique for world-jumping and same-world travel). The seal should appear as you draw. Your fingers are the pen, your magic the ink. So draw carefully, else you might open a faulty gateway. After completion, the seal should light up, and a gateway should open in its place. If it does not, perhaps meditate your magic once more, or ask yourself if you are truly a magic user. Be sure to investigate the stability of your gate. If it is hissing, sputtering, or looks at all like it will snap shut, I would not advise using it.

Below I have drawn Armiria's and Eroz's emblems from an age long passed. Though it pains me to say, it seems all knowledge of Lathaelon's emblem has been forgotten, along with most knowledge of the third world ever since it withdrew from the Worlds Alliance before the Crimson War. I fear that the fabled Untouchables will forever be only that.

Once your gateway is open and thrumming with magic, it is ready to enter. I do not know what it feels like to enter a gateway, nor do I know what to warn. Enter at your own risk, and be prepared for anything. It is rumored that the gates operate by ripping two holes in reality. You step in one and out the other, leaving the in-between unknown. I have heard ghastly tales about the in-between. If you see something stir in the split, best to retreat...

However, I can warn that world-connecting gateways, while easy to open, are near impossible to direct. When you open a gateway to another world, it will act like the aforementioned ill-tempered hen and create a link to wherever it pleases. This could mean opening to the middle of a desert, the bottom of an ocean, or—though the probability is incredibly low—exactly where you want to go. Always make sure to look at the gateway before you step through, else you cannot blame me for your own foolishness. And cursing a deceased scholar while being crushed at the bottom of an ocean seems like such a sour thing to do in one's last moments.

There is one last thing to be said about gateways, one I think is fair to note, or possibly warn. When you open these portals, you are not only creating a gate to another place, but you are also using the same possible magic as countless others. If you open a gateway leading to Eroz, and another user on the same world opens a gateway to Eroz while yours is still hovering in the air, you will both be aware of it. All gateways leading to the same world are connected, and it might even be possible that you mistakenly walk through each other's and end up on the other side of the same world. I suggest keeping it in mind if you attempt to use gateways for travel.

Lastly, as I am poor at planning and the ink has already dried, I heard there is a trick to direct gateways to specific places only when using them for same-world travel, but the likelihood of it working is less than effective. I do not know how, but I would highly recommend looking into it if you are tired of taking months on end to travel across the world.

This concludes my research of gateways.

Armiria's Emblem

Eroz's Emblem

Paths

Here we have the non-magic approach to travel. Only magic users are allowed through gates, but anyone can travel a path.

Paths are like bridges linking worlds together. You only need to know where to find them. But for all my time and energy spent searching hour upon day upon year upon lifetime, I was only ever able to uncover one pathway.

This pathway is something the Worlds Alliance crafted to bridge all three worlds together. You could use this path to travel to Armiria, Eroz, and Lathaelon (until they left the Alliance and used their skilled magic to cut themselves off from the other two worlds—saddening, truly.)

I had to dig deep in the archives at Arwyrn, but I found it described as a grand hall, equivalent to one of the palaces in Lyhrëon. The open ceiling showcases the untampered cosmos. The floors look like a kaleidoscope agleam with the spectrum of light. Arches span the doors leading to a multitude of destinations, towering hundreds of feet high and wide, darker than the Pits of Ashnagz. And it is large, so large that it could fit a brigade of two thousand men and their supplies. But that would be its downfall. This large bridge takes time to cross, and if you do not know which way you mean to go, you could get lost in it for some time—however, I have yet to learn if the laws of time rule the same in this space between worlds. The original architects took precautions to ensure no one would walk off the edge of this platform in the stars—to keep us in, or beings lurking beyond out? You could walk your entire life trying to reach the edge of this bridge, but you would look back to find you've only walked a step.

While safer than gateways, this bridge is crafted with spells. Countless spells, in fact. And it was with countless spells that the bridge was hidden after the Alliance fell. Once able to walk right up to it, now you have to know the password, or pass-symbol. To get this pathway to open once more, all you must do is draw the Worlds' Alliance symbol (as shown below) onto the door that closed the path. Whether you're a user or not, the spells cast onto the bridge will work its own magic, and the pathway will open.

The bridge links multiple entrances to various places. The towering arches could take you to Milganos, or Hraesah, or Weslyc, or the eastern continent. You cannot open it anywhere in the worlds, but it offers more direct, assured options than gateways.

Let it be noted, after the Alliance ended and tensions were high between races, the ends of these bridges were heavily guarded. Though there is no written record of attempted trespassers, the punishment for crossing without permission was death. For humans, for demons, for fae, for shifters, and for dragons, however, I do not think anyone could do much about a dragon. They did not take much part in the Crimson War anyway.

For humans, as knowledge of the other races fell to legend, this ancient pathway was forgotten. The shifters seem to have no recollection of it either. I cannot say the same for the residents of Eroz, however. So enter at your own risk, and Yath Ha be with you.

As for where it opens, I have only found one entrance in Armiria. It resides on a small isle in the middle of a lake, about a week's hike from Sheng Ní in the east. To the unknowing mind, it appears as a slab of stone, tangled with ivy and moss. But my mind was knowing, and my mind recognized it immediately. Or so I like to say. In reality, it took me two weeks of scouring the area to narrow it down to this specific stone, and then another four days of debating whether or not this was it. But the tell tale hum of ancient times that echoed in my veins told me it was.

I nearly opened the pathway right there, but caution begged me not to. Not without preparation. Well, preparation grew me old, and now I do not possess the strength for a boat across the seas again. Though more paths have been told of, my life is too short to find them all.

This concludes my research of pathways.

World Alliance Symbol

Somewhere In Between

Somewhere in between gateways and pathways lie what I have never actually seen with my own two eyes. The Mirror of Grekur.

I found little of the Mirror of Grekur, but I discovered this piece of art was crafted by the master smith demons of Grekur. It was the easiest form of travel, for the magic-fluent demons, at least.

The mirror's reflection is lined with magic, and can be used to jump from world to world. It was last accounted for by the people of Aelius before the mighty empire fell to ruin. Since then, it has been lost to time.

The mirror is not quite a gateway, but not exactly a pathway either. It is something in between. It allows the being using it to open a portal to anywhere they want in the worlds. A specific location, unlike gates, constantly opening and closing again, unlike paths. Once you step through, the mirror will also step through, *and arrive on the other world with you so you are not stranded.*

Hypothetically, it is rather easy to initiate. The mirror acts as a sponge that absorbs magic from its surroundings, then uses that power to create the portal. This could be from the world's natural power, or a user could give the mirror their own. After you pour in your magic, picture where you want to go in your mind's eye. You need not draw any symbols, but you must have before been to the location you are seeking. Your memories of the location direct it where to open. However, if you have not been to the location you wish to travel, and you attempt to use this something-in-between, you will find yourself in a closed cage with the ill-tempered hen again I am afraid. Only this time, the hen is back with vengeance.

Say, if you wanted to go visit Eroz on your holiday, but you have never stepped foot in Eroz and tried to use the Mirror of Grekur, you might very well step foot into Lathaelon. It is near impossible to predict where the mirror will open if not properly directed. Furthermore, all you need are sensory details to guide the magic. Who is to say an exceptionally detailed description of a location would not do the trick, or a masterful painting? As long as you have a clear scene in your head, I bet it would work just as well.

This concludes my research of something-in-between.

The means to travel the worlds is out there, friends. All we need to do is search.

Acknowledgements

This book would not have been possible without the constant love and support of my family and friends. Thank you Ethan, for allowing me to pitch new ideas to you late at night, and loving me every step of the way. Thank you mom and dad for teaching me to carry on through the hard times; Rachel and Xaikar for your encouragement; and Grandma for your zealous marketing tactics. Lisa and Brian, thank you for encouraging me to publish the sequel sooner.

This book would unintelligible without the savvy eyes and mind of Rebecca Weil-Hoskins.

I am blessed to have such a wonderful team backing me, and thank God for the ability to share my creative endeavors with the world. My readers make this possible, so thank you for giving my indie books a try!